RICHARDS BROTHERS

1-3

Annie Seaton

The Trouble with Paradise

Marry in Haste

Outback Sunrise

Annie Seaton

This book is a work of fiction. Names, characters, places, and incidents are the product of the author's imagination or are used fictitiously. Any resemblance to actual events, locales, or persons, living or dead, is coincidental.

Originally published as:
 Holiday Affair
Italian Affair
Outback Affair
Copyright © 2012 by Annie Seaton, revised and expanded May 2019.

Richards Brothers Boxed Set © 2024
ISBN 9781923048256

The Trouble with Paradise

Annie Seaton

Richards Brothers: 1

Dedication

To Ian, my wonderful husband of many years...you are always there for me.

Chapter One

Melissa McIntyre sat on the side of the timber sailing ship as it rounded the point into Butterfly Bay on the north side of Hook Island in the Whitsunday Islands. Reaching down for her camera, Lissy smiled as she caught her reflection in the smoky black glass of the hatch window beside her. Emerald green eyes surrounded by a tangle of sun-streaked auburn curls twinkled back at her. The days spent basking in the warmth around the pool at Hamilton Island over the last week had deepened her tan and she had almost forgotten it was winter back home on the New England tablelands.

"No more prim and proper Dr McIntyre." She smiled to herself. Looking down at her raggedy denim shorts and the bare tanned feet resting on her rucksack, she grinned as she imagined the reaction of her history colleagues at the university if they could see the elegant Dr McIntyre in backpacker mode.

Strands of hair were pushed across her face by the breeze, and she lifted her hand to brush them away; she didn't want to miss one second of this amazing view.

Sails snapped sharply as the wind caught them and the crew scurried to tighten the ropes, calling to each other as they worked to bring the sails down as the beautiful old timber schooner eased into the bay for its overnight anchorage.

The musical tone of backpackers chatting in different languages provided a cheerful end to the first day of her sailing adventure. The vessel was crowded with young people from many countries, and everywhere she looked they seemed to be in couples. An unfamiliar pang of loneliness tried to settle in her chest, but she pushed it away.

Lifting her camera, Melissa stood and positioned herself to capture the best view of the sunset. When she went back to work, she'd put the photo on her computer desktop and remember this beautiful place when the winter weather got her down.

She blinked as a rugged face filled the viewfinder, blocking her view of the sky, and one brilliant blue eye winked as a member of the crew peered cheekily into her camera from afar. She leaned back and took a quick distant shot of the guy up the mast, and then turned to snap a series of images of the sun setting over the water as flashes of pink, silver-tipped clouds suffused the sky, and the golden orb slipped towards the horizon. Lowering the camera, she waited as the sailor climbed down the mast towards her. He swung down on the lower ropes, his deep voice serenading her with a bawdy sea shanty. She laughed and finished off the last two lines of the song with him.

"What shall we do with a drunken sailor? Put him in bed with the captain's daughter?" He stopped beside the deck esky and held up a can of beer and a small bottle of wine.

"Wine or beer?"

"Wine, please," she said with a shy smile. She'd barely spoken to anyone all day; just the usual greetings as the passengers boarded the boat and found their own place to sit. Melissa liked her own company and had been happy keeping to herself. The sailor closed the lid of the esky and sat on the step beside her.

"Cheers. I'm Nick." He handed her a small plastic wine cup and she waited while he unscrewed the bottle, and then poured it in. He put the empty wine bottle in the bin beside them and lifted the plastic water bottle as he tilted his head to the side with a questioning look. "A toast to the sunset?"

She nodded and smiled at him as she lifted her glass. "Just water for you?" she asked.

"Yes, I'm on duty for another hour, but then the fun begins," he said and flashed her a cheeky smile. "But now, a toast to a beautiful lady."

Melissa caught her breath as deep blue eyes locked with hers. Her hand shook as he captured her fingers and she squeezed the plastic cup with her other hand. He was almost too good-looking. A bright blue bandana held back a thatch of shaggy sun-bleached hair. She held his gaze as he touched his water bottle against her wine. Dr McIntyre would have blushed, but Melissa McIntyre took it in her stride. It wasn't every day that a man as gorgeous as he was, sang to you and offered you a toast. She took it in the holiday spirit, which she was sure he'd intended, although he did hold her gaze a little longer than a casual look called for.

"Thanks, and cheers. I'm Lissy."

"Backpacking?" He sat comfortably next to her, his muscled legs stretched out on the timber deck, his shoulder resting casually against hers.

She looked up at him and felt a strange unfamiliar urge to pull loose the bandana and run her fingers through his shaggy hair.

Where on earth had that come from?

"Sort of," she finally replied, and her voice was husky.

Nick turned to her, revealing laugh lines around his deep blue eyes and sexy mouth. He was a fair bit older than she had first thought.

"Just a bit of a trip around North Queensland. How about you?" She was not going to give away too much. She wasn't ready yet to slip back into her real world of boring history professor. She had found comfort in being her Gramps's *Lissy* in the ten days since she'd scattered his ashes on Blackrock Beach and then flown to the tropics for a restful holiday.

"Same. Just crewing on the boat for a friend for a few weeks," he replied. "Speaking of which, I'd better go and help with the anchor. We're almost to the island." He tipped his head back, swigging the rest of his water. He grasped the rope to swing himself to the upper deck, the muscles in his arms bunching. Giving her a broad wink, he grinned cheekily at her.

"Save a dance for me tonight, Angel Face." Nick headed to the bow of the vessel with a swagger that would have done a pirate proud, chatting and joking with the other passengers as he went. It was almost a primitive sexuality that surrounded him, dangerous to any woman. He was one of the best-looking men she had ever seen, and an unfamiliar warmth ran through her. Reluctantly, she dragged her eyes away from the breadth of his tanned back and tautly muscled legs as a voice interrupted her thoughts.

"Half your luck. You've been chosen for the night."

Lissy turned to see a blonde girl in the charter company's uniform looking at her with a bemused expression. "Excuse me?"

"You're obviously the chosen one for tonight."

Unease unfurled in her chest. "What do you mean?"

"Nick had the same bet with the crew last trip. He picks his conquest for the party on the way into the bay. The woman he chooses to share a drink with before we moor, is the chosen one, and the crew bet on it either way, depending on their impression of the girl. I overheard the boys laughing about it last trip."

Lissy cursed herself for her naiveté.

"Thanks for the warning, but they'll lose their money. I'm not interested."

"Your call, but he is a good catch if you can pin him down." The girl shrugged as she gathered up the empty cups and made her way towards the galley. "No one has been able to, so far."

Lissy mouthed a very rude word under her breath.

The hide and confidence of the man, how dare he think she looked like an easy target?

No matter how good-looking he is.

Then again, look at yourself, Lissy McIntyre. Swigging wine on a backpacker's yacht in tattered shorts and with tangled hair, is not a look the usually staid Dr Melissa McIntyre, of the elegant French roll and navy-blue suits, should be comfortable with.

Melissa gritted her teeth, curling her fists by her sides.

Even so, it didn't matter how she looked—did he really think she was that easy? History was not going to repeat itself. One absent backpacker father was quite enough for this family.

This guy needs to be taught a lesson.

Her throat ached. Unshed tears stung her eyes as the emotion of the last week caught up with her. The cancellation of her mother's flight from Denmark had left her alone at the memorial service, except for Gramps's fishing mates. As she had looked across the water to the rising sun, she'd whispered the words Gramps had penned for her to read while scattering his ashes to the chilly easterly wind.

"Let the ocean soothe your sorrow. I am now with you always; in the sea, the sands, and the wind." She breathed in deeply as she looked out at the sapphire blue of the Pacific Ocean, letting the serene blue of the water soothe her grief.

The anchor clattered to the sandy bottom of the bay, interrupting her sad thoughts. Brushing the tears away with the back of her hand, she waited for an opportunity to make her move. It wasn't long before Nick turned and walked back towards her, and she caught his eye, blowing him a kiss.

He smiled wickedly at her. "Looking forward to that dance." She watched him swagger to the side of the boat to lower the dinghy, with more than a touch of arrogance in his bearing.

"Me too." She smiled as she stood and bent over in front of him to pick up her rucksack, making sure he got a good view of her legs. Out of the corner of her eye, she watched as two crewmembers gave each other a high five. The anger built in her chest and she gritted her teeth as they helped Nick with the ropes holding the rubber dinghy high on the side of the yacht, joking and laughing.

Picking up her rucksack, she made her way to the group waiting to climb down the rope ladder to the dinghy for the short trip across to the island. Standing next to two Italian girls, she grimaced. They whispered and giggled, pointing at Nick expertly steering the dinghy through the coral heads in the bay. He dropped the first group on the island and turned back to those waiting on the boat. He stood aft, one hand on the tiller, the other shading his eyes from the setting sun, his muscled legs braced against the small waves hitting the boat. Nick looked up to catch her eye, and a slow, sexy grin spread over his face.

She swallowed.

No man had the right to be so sexy.

Melissa was the last to climb down the rope ladder and as she prepared to step across to the dinghy; a rogue wave pushed it away from the side of the old schooner.

"Quick, jump!" yelled Nick. She threw her rucksack into the dinghy and jumped, landing awkwardly on her backside.

"Are you hurt?" Nick put out his hand to help pull her up, his eyes full of concern.

"Only my pride," she said. He took her hand and a tingle of warmth shot up her arm. Her fingers felt weak in his grasp and she fought the urge to snatch her hand away as he looked down at her sprawled half on the floor, and across the seat at the side of the dinghy.

The Italian girls giggled, clapping their hands with delight and pretending to swoon as Nick pulled her up into his arms. He held her firmly against him, the hair-roughened warmth of his chest brushing against her bare shoulders.

"Thank you, she said breathlessly, as she fought the mirth building in her chest.

"No injuries from the fall?" he asked softly. Melissa shook her head and removed her hand from his grip. She sat down on the soft side of the dinghy and Nick steered through the coral to the island where the rest of the crew were setting up camp.

Two hours later, Lissy sat watching the sparks that whirled in the breeze as Nick added more driftwood to the fire. The crew had given them a feast of fresh fish, salad, and tropical fruits. Replete, both tourists and crew settled on sand still warm from the sun. The campfire provided a soft flickering light and one of the backpackers gently strummed his guitar. Melissa gazed into the fire, remembering the days at Blackrock Beach when she and Gramps had fried fresh fish over a driftwood fire on the beach. For the first time in a week, she moved past the grief and found joy in the memory.

"He must have been good." Goose bumps raised on her arms as she felt the warmth of Nick's breath on her neck.

She moved away slightly. "Excuse me?"

"There's only one thing that will put that look on a woman's face," he whispered in her ear.

"Oh yes, he was." She grabbed her rucksack and used it as a pillow. She looked up at the brilliant stars dotting the black sky. "The very best." Gramps had been the only stability she had ever known. If Nick thought she was talking about a previous lover, so be it, since he deserved everything he was about to get.

He held her eyes and then dropped his gaze to linger on her body stretched on the sand. She held her breath as he slowly looked down from her shoulders to her breasts and then back up to capture her gaze. Lissy shivered, imagining the tips of his fingers caressing her skin. The music increased in tempo, and a couple of the girls began to dance on the beach. He leaned down to her, his breath tickling her neck as he whispered in her ear.

"Come on. Dance with me?" She shivered again, and goose bumps ran down her arm despite the warmth of his body pressing into her side.

He pulled her up and Lissy's eyes held his as he held her close. Wrapping her arms around his neck, she moulded herself to the hard planes of his body and they moved in time with the slow music. Their bare feet slipped through the soft white sand as they danced slowly around the fire, the crackling of the flames and muted guitar music surrounding them. He gently pushed towards her and her lips found their way to his neck, her mouth opening slightly as she inhaled, his musky scent teasing her nostrils.

Closing her eyes, she sighed softly. His hard chest pressed against the softness of her breasts, and she forgot why she was dancing so closely with a stranger. She pretended Nick was someone who cared about her. As he guided her around the fire in time to the soft music, his hand caressed her back. The pressure of his hand increased as he guided them towards the shadows at the edge of the clearing. The first fluttering of panic began in her chest. With every step she became more aware of the proximity and warmth of his body and the temptation she faced. He dropped his lips to her neck and gently sucked on her skin. An explosion of feeling raced from her neck to her stomach. She pulled back gently and looked up at him, giving herself some space between them. She breathed rapidly, her lips slightly parted as Nick looked down at her.

"I admire a woman who knows what she wants." His voice hinted at all sorts of pleasures.

"Mmm … very tempting." She regretted the words as soon as they were out of her mouth.

Get yourself out of this before it's too late.

Standing on her toes, she moved her hands from his neck to his shoulders and put her face close to his.

"What a shame all the tents are so close," she breathed into his ear. "No privacy here, and I do show my 'appreciation' rather loudly."

She pursed her lips, fighting to keep a straight face. She tried to hold back her laughter, imagining herself as a femme fatale, a passionate woman of the world, and a lusty participant in the bedroom. Nothing could be further from the truth—especially the last few years when she'd buried herself in her studies and research.

She quickly lowered her head to hide the laughter in her eyes and Nick pulled her close, whispering in her ear.

"It's okay, babe. I'll take care of you." She looked up at him, tears of laughter threatening to spill over. She swallowed the giggle bubbling in her throat and it came out in a snort. He looked at her with a slight frown, and she reached up as though she was going to kiss him.

"Sorry, mate, you've lost your bet tonight." Pushing him away, Melissa strolled across to the group around the fire and sat down next to the Italian girls. After tying her sarong tightly around her breasts, she clenched her hands to still the shaking of her fingers.

Yes, a real femme fatale.

Chapter Two

Nick had first noticed her standing apart from the group of noisy backpackers at the marina that morning. Boarding the vessel alone, she had kept to herself all day. Deep in thought as the old schooner sailed across the Whitsunday Passage to Hook Island, he'd noticed her brush away tears a couple of times. He had also taken several long appreciative looks at her sunbathing on the front deck from his vantage point high up the mast as he rigged the sails. After watching her all day, he was not surprised to feel that jolt of heat run through his body when he'd caught her as she'd fallen. She had a tilted nose with a light sprinkling of freckles and full red lips. Red-gold hair fell in a tangle of curls to brush her delicate bare shoulders. She was older than most of the backpackers on the charter but had a maturity and a beauty that made him look again…and again. It would have been an enjoyable way to end his last trip on the boat.

No commitment, no strings attached; just the way he liked it.

Now, Nick was angry at his stupidity in getting himself entangled in this situation on his last day on the boat. It was because of that stupid bet. He'd lost control of the situation because he was so attracted to Lissy. On the other trips this week, he'd simply shared a few flirtatious kisses with the chosen girls to win the bet with the crew. It had been a stupid thing to do, and he wasn't proud of himself.

When he'd looked down at Lissy, he had been lost in her sad, dark eyes. As he shifted his eyes to her soft mouth, her lips had beckoned him. He had only to dip his head slightly and he could have covered her mouth with his own, savouring the tempting sweetness of those luscious lips.

He shook his head in frustration.

What the hell is wrong with me? I'm getting soft.

It was time to get back to work and finish the blasted report or the funding would dry up. The recent calls from his family indicated it was time to go home and be the dutiful son and brother for a while. The emails from his mother hinted at upcoming changes in the family, and how much they missed him. The pull of Italian blood was strong. As much as he hated to admit it, he loved his time back in Armidale on the family farm. *La mia famiglia ...* the close bond that held his brothers and sisters together no matter where they were in the world was fostered by their mother.

"Penny for your thoughts?" He jumped as a hand touched his arm.

The first woman who had really attracted him for a long time stood in front of him, backlit by the flickering firelight. Smarting from the unflattering image of himself as a Lothario who would make money from a demeaning bet, he knew it was time to make amends.

"You really don't want to know what I'm thinking. Boring thoughts about work," he said. He walked over to the camp fridge, grabbed two beers, and held one out to her. "Peace offering?"

After a pause, she reached for the beer. "Why not?"

They sipped their beers in silence as they walked back to the group sitting around the fire. They sat on the soft sand and Lissy looked over at him and spread her hands. "Can you really call this work?"

He laughed and decided it was not the right time to tell her all about himself, now that she seemed to have forgiven him for his crass behaviour. He would give it a while and then admit that there was more to him than just a drifter in the Islands.

##

The whoosh of waves breaking on the crushed coral beach woke Lissy early the next morning. Rolling onto her stomach, she opened the flap of the one-man tent and propped her chin on her hand, enjoying the view of the old sailing ship silhouetted by the rising sun. She saw tanned muscular legs through her tent flap and sighed at the sight of Nick heading for the water, clad only in a pair of black swimming trunks. Closing her tent flap, she rolled on to her back, crossing her arms on her chest. Even though she knew what Nick had been playing at, she still found him incredibly attractive … and kind. His apology last night had shown there was more to him

After breakfast, the crew packed up the campsite in preparation for the sail back to Hamilton Island. Lissy and some of the other backpackers climbed to the lookout on the peak of the island. As they reached the top of the path, she caught her breath and moved across to the lookout, taking in the beauty of the view down to Hamilton Island. Patches of brilliant white sand edged the blue waters, backed by verdant green hills on each island.

"Are you coming, Lissy?" Bella, one of the Italian girls, called. "We sail at eleven."

"I'll catch up with you." She glanced at her watch. She stood there for a long time after the others started the trek to the beach. This short holiday had helped her cope with her grief after Gramps's funeral, and she was feeling ready to go back to work. Deep in thought, she jumped as a deep voice intruded in the silence.

"It's the best view in the Whitsunday Islands." Nick stood at her shoulder. "Did you know the islands were first recorded by Captain Cook on Whit Sunday in 1770, and that's how they got their name?" He was standing so close to her she could feel the heat coming from his body as he pointed to the islands spread below them like emeralds on the blue water.

"Not far north from here, Cook ran aground and had to repair his ship, the *Endeavour*." His breath on the side of her face sent goose bumps down her neck. Her serenity disappeared instantly; he was trying his luck again.

Well, two can play this game. My mother might have been a sucker for the first good-looking man that came along, but I won't follow in her footsteps.

"How fascinating. I don't know much history at all," she said, settling into her role. Professor Andrews would be horrified to hear those words from his Pacific history lecturer.

"I'm a little bit scared to walk down the track alone. I heard things rustling in the bush before." She widened her eyes, deciding not to bat her eyelashes as that might be a bit of overkill.

"Nothing to be scared of," he replied, holding out his hand to her. She reached out and held it and an instant electricity seemed to ignite between them. Nick put his warm hands on her bare shoulders, pulling her in close. Her heart thudded and her knees trembled.

"I feel safe now," she said breathlessly, even though safe was far from what she felt. She hoped the combination of her demure expression and the huskiness of her voice would have the desired reaction. She kept her eyes lowered as his hand slid down her arm and he lifted her hand to his mouth. He moved his lips gently across her palm.

"Come on, the dinghy's waiting to take the last group back." He kept hold of her hand as he led her down the track through the coastal she-oak trees. When they were on the beach, hundreds of black butterflies fluttered from the bush at the eastern end of the bay.

"Spectacular, isn't it? That's why they call it Butterfly Bay." He looked down at her and reached across to push a strand of hair from her eyes. "Delicate creatures, a lot like you." She pushed his hand away. She was done playing games.

"You're not going to give up, are you, Nick? What's the time frame on the bet? I told you last night. You've done your money. You chose the wrong girl." She picked up her backpack and stalked across to the waiting dinghy.

***

Nick's body suffused with heat. Fighting to keep his temper, he struggled to maintain an impassive expression. Lissy glared at him from the edge of the water. Nick Richards, who rarely backed away from a challenge, was intimidated by this slip of a woman. He had avoided this sort of situation for years, since Olivia had dumped him for a richer prospect. Heartbroken, he had sworn a pretty face would never suck him in again, and he had enjoyed his playboy "love'em and leave'em" lifestyle of the last ten years. This stupid bet hadn't given him the opportunity to lay down his usual ground rules, and one thing he hated was dishonesty. Now, he was having a strong and genuine attraction thrown back in his face. Strolling over to the dinghy, he picked up the last of the camping gear and turned to face Lissy, hurt driving his words.

"You are an extremely beautiful young woman, Lissy. All bets aside, flaunting yourself to all and sundry gives an impression of availability, whether you mean to or not. I believe there is a word for women who tease and don't deliver the goods." As he headed for the dinghy he looked over his shoulder and drawled, "So sweetheart, take care or you may find yourself in trouble one day."

Chapter Three

Lissy strode along the road from the marina at Hamilton Island down to her beachfront cabin still fuming from Nick's parting shot. She sat with the Italian girls on the front deck listening to their chatter and laughing with them as they tried to converse in two languages. When the vessel moored, she bid a cheery farewell to Bella and Anna, disembarking without a backward glance. The only time she had been near Nick was during the morning briefing by the crew, and he'd ignored her—which suited her fine. His stinging comment would not leave her. She regretted the two days on the backpacker charter. She should have saved her money and stayed in the luxury cabin at the resort. She couldn't believe how rude he'd been. Working in an international playground where people are relaxed and receptive to romance had distorted his view of the way normal people behaved. He'd started the whole mess with his demeaning bet.

Unlocking the door to her cabin, she angrily threw her backpack into the corner. She was upset with herself because even after his nasty comment, she was still aware of the attraction between them. She had encouraged him a little bit more than necessary. Her T-shirt and shorts followed the backpack into the corner, and she pushed open the door to the luxurious marble bathroom.

A long soak in the hot tub with lots of bubbles would wash the salt out of her hair and clear her mind. She planned on dressing up and relaxing with a glass of wine and dinner in the resort restaurant. Lissy would enjoy the last night of her holiday, before the prospect of going back to the cold winter of the tablelands, and being Dr Melissa McIntyre at work, resurfaced. Standing in front of the mirror, water filling the large spa bath, she touched her lips, imagining Nick's lips on hers. She could dream—she would never see him again and could file him away as a fantasy.

The bath wasn't the total escape she had hoped for. As the fragrant oils soaked into her skin and the steamy heat lathered her face with moisture, Nick drifted in and out of her thoughts. Damn the man for being so sexy! She sank down in the water and closed her eyes, but images of him climbing the mast, his long, tanned legs lightly covered with blond hair, and standing bare-chested as he steered the little dinghy, flicked through her mind in an erotic slideshow.

Sitting up, Lissy pulled the plug, dismayed at the direction of her thoughts. She climbed out of the bath, dried off and wrapped herself in a soft white towelling robe, and stepped onto the sunny deck to dry her hair. She pulled up the chair on the front deck that overlooked the tropical gardens at the back of the resort. The front door of the neighbouring cabin opened and caught her attention. A red-faced cleaning maid hurried down the pathway in front of the cabins, pulling her cleaning trolley along behind her.

"Apologies, *monsieur*, I will send someone down with fresh towels for you immediately. I am so sorry that your room was not ready."

"Not a problem," drawled a familiar voice. "I'll borrow one from my friend next door." Lissy looked over to see the subject of her erotic daydream standing there wearing nothing but a wicked grin and a small towel strategically placed across his hips.

"Got a spare towel, sweetheart?" Glaring at him, she draped her spare towel over the low wall between their decks before storming inside and slamming the door behind her.

She closed her eyes as Nick's laughter drifted through the open window. The sooner she was on a plane home, the better. Cold weather and work, with no Nick to bother her, was quickly becoming very appealing.

***

Nick strolled into the restaurant an hour later and spotted Lissy sitting alone at a table by the window overlooking the bay. Her chin rested in her hand as she gazed out over the water. With a quiet word to the *maitre d'*, he walked over to her table and sat opposite her.

"You know I'm beginning to think you're following me." Lissy turned and glared at him, but he reached over and took her hand, ignoring the instant tug of attraction as he looked into her eyes.

"Hey, I want to apologise for the way I spoke to you this morning. I was way out of line." Nick had regretted his harsh words all day, and when he realised Lissy was staying at the resort, he had decided to seek her out and apologise. Finding himself in the cabin next door to her had been an unexpected bonus.

"Let's pretend we've just met and forget the last two days. Good food, good wine, a great view, and great company. I owe you a drink for lending me a towel anyway."

To his surprise, Lissy didn't react with the sarcasm he expected.

"Why not? I'm going back to reality tomorrow. I may as well indulge the last night."

He tilted his head to one side. "Indulge?"

"Don't get your hopes up, matey. I'm talking food and wine, nothing else." Her face brightened. "Good company will be a bonus. It's past time that we quit playing games. A civilised meal together, a casual conversation, good memories, and we'll go our separate ways tonight." She held out her hand. "Deal?"

Holding her gaze, he reached over and took her hand. "It's a deal."

Over dinner, Nick talked about his trip around the Pacific over the past few years and Lissy laughed at his stories of thrill-seeking adventures. Parasailing, mountain climbing, volcano viewing, and surfing off isolated islands. If he embellished his adventures a little bit, it was purely for the pleasure of seeing her laugh. He sympathised as she told him about moving from Blackrock Beach to the city and growing up with her mother and first stepfather and then going to boarding school.

"Father?" asked Nick.

"Only Gramps," she said sadly. "My father was an Irish backpacker who married Mum but didn't hang around long enough to meet me. Now she's sampling a variety of nationalities in the husband category. Started off with the Irish boyo, moved on to an Aussie, then an American, and now she lives in Denmark with her fourth husband."

"I can understand why you were a little bit aloof from the backpacker crowd, and that stupid bet made it worse."

"I don't see my mother very often, and when Gramps died a couple of weeks ago, she didn't even make the service." Nick reached out for Lissy's hand across the table as her eyes filled with tears.

"Gramps was the rock in my life and so proud of me. I was hoping to have some good news for him about a promotion in a few weeks, but he died suddenly in his sleep."

He rubbed his thumb across the top of her hand and Lissy seemed unaware of it as she stared into the candle flickering in the centre of the table. He couldn't take his eyes off her face as the love for her grandfather shone from her eyes.

"The last time I visited him, he teased me." She looked up at Nick and the determination in her face surprised him. "He asked me about my plans, and I can still see his faded blue eyes crinkling at me. He didn't believe that I'd commit to my career and he always teased me about ending up with three kids, a house with a white picket fence, and a dog named Rex. And, of course, a husband. Gramps was a great believer in love. But nearly thirty years watching Mum search for it taught me that security is far more important. I'm about to achieve a milestone in my career and I'm well on the way to security."

"What do you do?"

"No, no details," she said. "Let's just be ships that pass in the night. What about you? Family?"

"Yes. Lots of brothers and sisters, all settled down in the country, producing the required grandchildren for my parents. I'm the son with the wanderlust." Looking across at her, he raised his wine glass. "Like you, I'll never settle down. I like my freedom too much."

He clinked her glass across the table. "To a happy life. I hope you find what you're looking for and it brings you happiness."

Her brilliant green eyes lit up and a sweet smile spread slowly across her beautiful face as she clinked her glass against his. A little bit of sadness lingered in her eyes, making him feel even more of a louse for the way he'd treated her. The candlelight formed an aureole of light around her auburn curls and she looked back at him, her eyes full of trust. Eyes that could suck a man right in. It was time to get out of here.

Now. Before he did something he'd regret.

"Right," he said briskly, reaching for the bill folder. "My treat. Apology for the last two days?"

"Thanks for listening tonight. You've been sweet." Lissy placed her hand on top of his.

They walked along the path to their cabins, the sweet smell of frangipani blooms wafting over them. Looking up at the white flowers, Lissy stumbled on a thick root at the edge of the path. Nick reached across and placed his arm casually around her shoulders to guide her. Reaching around, he grabbed and twirled a long curl around his finger. He looked down at her and warmth filled his chest. His hand cupped her shoulder and then he gently skimmed his fingertips down her bare arm. She leaned into him with a long, drawn-out sigh and he pulled her close. He sensed her crying silently before he felt the tears through his shirt and he held her as she cried. His gut clenched as he realised his crass behaviour had added to her troubles the past couple of days. "I'm really sorry, for upsetting you so much." She drew back, looking up at him through her tears. He cupped her jaw, lifting her tear-streaked face so that she was looking directly at him.

"Don't be silly, I came up here to have a break after Gramps died. No need for an apology. I played the game too. A couple of wines has made me emotional. I'm sorry."

He took her hand, squeezed it and held it as they walked back towards the cabins.

When they reached her cabin, Lissy unlocked the door and

turned to Nick.

"Thank you for paying for dinner."

He leaned down to kiss her cheek and bid her goodnight. She looked deep into his eyes and the grief and loneliness on her face turned to naked longing. A powerful desire rocked through him as she reached up and brushed a light kiss along his lips.

Nick wanted her with an intensity that he'd never felt before. For a moment, he stilled, aware of her closeness, her touch, and the soft breath of her gentle kiss. He held her gaze until his mouth covered hers. She slid her hands under his silk shirt and sighed into his mouth as she caressed his warm, bare skin. With a groan, he deepened the kiss and his mouth roamed her face and throat as his hands tangled in her luxurious hair. She reached behind her back with one hand, opened the door, and pulled him into her cabin. Her body was quivering, and her lips were warm, heat seeping into him, warming a cold place deep within that had been chilled for too long. Struggling against the need to rush and realising that she needed gentleness, he moved her slowly across the room until the back of her legs pressed against the bed.

"Okay?" he murmured against her mouth. She answered by reaching up and pulling his shirt above his head and then moving down to the buttons on his jeans.

God, am I insane? What am I doing?

***

For a brief moment, Lissy's fingers paused in their journey downward. She must be crazy because she didn't want to stop what she'd started. She reached around and splayed her fingers on the bare skin under his shirt, resting her cheek against his broad chest. Both hands were now under his shirt and his bare skin was warm beneath her fingers.

"Lissy?" he asked softly.

"Shh."

"Are you sure?"

In answer, she slid her hands back around to his chest and one hand skimmed over smooth warm skin. Lissy pressed her face against his chest, feeling the beat of his heart against her cheek. "I can't think of a nicer way to end my holiday."

Nick took her hands in his and gathered her into his arms. His fingers played with her long curls as he held her close. For the first time in a long time, she felt safe and happy. But he was right—she needed to be sure about this. Closing her eyes, she came to an easy decision. Despite her doubts, she wanted him. She needed to feel his skin against hers. She wanted him, of that she had no doubt. Reaching up with one hand, she brushed his face with trembling fingers as his eyes glinted in the moonlight.

"Has anyone ever told you how beautiful you are," he said quietly.

Her own need was mirrored in those deep blue eyes. She lifted her face and touched her lips to his. Nick's hold tightened, but she moved away and sat on the side of the bed.

Waiting. Needing. Wanting.

His strong body was silhouetted by the bright moonlight streaming through the window, and Lissy shivered with anticipation as he moved closer. His breath whispered along her neck as he unbuttoned the small pearl buttons on her silk dress.

"Sweet perfection," he murmured against her lips. He lifted his head and smiled at her, the sexy laugh lines crinkling around his eyes. Lissy caught her breath.

"You're really sure about this?" he asked.

"I'm sure." The room darkened as his head lowered to hers, blotting out the moonlight streaming through the window.

Chapter Four

The faint light of dawn helped Nick search for his clothes that were scattered around the room. Lissy murmured in her sleep. He moved to the side of the bed and stood quietly looking down at her. A tangle of red-gold curls spread across the white lace pillowcase and her face was perfectly serene. If he was to catch his flight, he had to hurry, and he was torn between reaching down and kissing those inviting lips one more time or leaving quietly.

Love and leave 'em mate, time to move on.

But his conscience pricked him, and he looked for a pen to leave her a brief note.

What do I say? Thanks for the sex, it was great. Have a good life?

Running his hand through his hair, he glanced down at his watch and realised if he didn't hurry he would miss his flight. He took one last look at the beautiful woman curled in the king-size bed and moved quietly to the door. Locking it behind him, he stepped out into the early morning.

The resort was already waking for the day and gardeners were sweeping fallen blooms from the paths. Nick said a brief good morning to a worker who was trimming the tree between their cabins.

In his own room, he had a quick shower and threw his casual clothes into his backpack, grimacing as he pulled out trousers and a long-sleeved shirt. He was not looking forward to leaving the tropics. Tossing his bag over his shoulder, he let himself out of his room with one last regretful look at Lissy's cabin, half-hoping she would be standing at the door, so he could say good-bye.

Half an hour later, Nick had checked into the airport on Hamilton Island and was waiting for his flight to board. He pulled his mobile from his pocket and dialled, shaking his head in amusement as the cheery voice of his brother answered, even though it was only six a.m.

"Hey, bro," Nick greeted his older brother.

"What's wrong?"

Nick smiled. Tomas was the staid one of the three brothers and he took life very seriously.

"Something must be wrong. One, you never call, and two, it's hours before you usually get up."

"Nothing's wrong. I just called to say I'm thinking about delaying my trip home until Sunday night."

Where the hell did that come from? he wondered.

"Well, Nick, you can't," said his brother. "There's a big barbeque to welcome you home on Saturday and Mama would have your guts for garters if you didn't show." Tomas sighed down the phone. "There's a woman involved, isn't there."

His big brother knew him well.

Nick laughed bitterly. "Yep, bro. You know me, can't all be perfect like you. Always a woman. Forget it, I'll be there. I can't upset Mama."

"It's been two years this time. The whole family is coming to dinner and Mama has been cooking all week. Don't let her down."

"Okay, I'll see you Saturday. Tell Mama I'm picking my bike up in Brisbane and I'll be there about six."

Tomas cleared his throat. "With a friend."

"A friend, hey? What sort of friend?"

"You'll meet her on the weekend. Be careful on that highway. I'll see you Saturday. *Ciao.*"

"Looking forward to it, bro. *Ciao.*" Nick shook his head. Tomas was organised and lived his life by a strict routine; they couldn't be any more different. Sometimes it was hard to believe they came from the same family and the news that he had met someone was no surprise. Tomas always said he would marry at thirty-five. He only had a few months to go.

Nick grinned and shook his head. It would be good to be back home.

The call came for his flight to Brisbane, and he picked up his backpack and headed for the gate.

***

Lissy opened her eyes as sunlight streamed in through the graceful foliage of the tree outside her window, tracing a delicate pattern across the white sheets. Stretching luxuriously, she lay on her back, watching the red blooms of the poinciana tree sway in the soft morning breeze. If she was inclined to believe that the night's events had been a fantasy she had conjured up while lying in her bath, the aches and soreness she felt attested to the experience of the night. She remembered the pleasure they had shared; it was the first time she had ever truly let herself go, not hiding behind her cool facade. The whole night took on a dreamy quality and she'd fallen into a deep sleep after Nick had reached over and kissed her a lingering goodnight in the early hours.

She lay there, wondering how she would feel when she saw him this morning. Even though it had been a night of passion, she still had to put it behind her. She would pack her bags ready to catch her flight, have a civilised breakfast with him, and wish him well as he set off on his next adventure.

Pulling her wet hair into a loose roll after a quick shower, she applied light makeup, smiling as she saw the traces of pink marks on her neck, where Nick's rough stubble had grazed her. Warmth shot through her—she needed to see him this morning to keep her feelings in perspective.

You can do this; you're a mature woman of the world. Enjoy his company over breakfast, kiss him good-bye, and then go catch your plane.

Stepping out on to the veranda, she looked across to see if there was any sign of life from Nick's cabin. There was a flurry of activity as two cleaning maids dumped sheets and towels into the trolley, pulling a vacuum cleaner through the front door. Lissy walked down the path and she realised she didn't even know his last name. A cold feeling settled in the pit of her stomach.

"Has my friend checked out already?" she asked.

"Yes, he was our first checkout this morning. Gone before sun-up."

She paused, fighting the tightness in her throat as tears threatened to fall. "I'll be out in a couple of minutes. I'm heading for the airport myself."

The girl gave her a wave and lifted fresh towels from the trolley. "Thanks. Have a safe trip."

Gathering her suitcase and backpack, Lissy glanced at her watch, trying to ignore the hurt of Nick leaving without so much as a good-bye. She had shed enough tears over the past two weeks. By the end of today, she would be home and this interlude would be behind her. The genes had really kicked in big time. *Mum would be proud of me. Hah!*

It was just as well he had gone. He was probably running, because he thought she would be the clingy type that wouldn't let go. Nothing could be further from the truth.

She took one last lingering look at the bed and the rumpled sheets before locking the door. Walking through the tropical garden to reception, she took care not to trip over the tree root that had led to her downfall last night. She made her way to the main building, the wheels of her suitcase disturbing the quiet of the garden.

A good lesson in life, Lissy. A warning that it's easy to go with the lust of the moment and get let down every time. Never again. Just think of Mum. We have Declan, and Greg, and Lincoln and Lars...and then whoever Mum marries next!

"Okay, look on the bright side," her positive side reminded her. "When I am old and grey in my rocking chair, watching my grandchildren play around my feet, I will look back with fond memories and dream about the kind pirate who stole my heart for one night. A bit like the old lady in Titanic."

"Bollocks," chipped in her negative side. "I have to have children, before the grandchildren come along." She thought back to her last conversation with Gramps. After he had teased her about the white picket fence and the dog named Rex, he had put his gnarled hands on each side of her face.

"Sweetheart, believe in love. It's out there waiting for you."

"Gramps," she argued, "I don't believe in romantic love and happily ever after."

Gramps had always said, "Wait and see, my darling. Love makes a fool of plans. Wait for your destiny and promise me you won't settle for less." He had constantly teased her about her weekly outing with Tom, one of her work colleagues, a quiet friend for whom she held a steady affection. Gramps had probed her feelings for him and warned her not to settle down for the sake of security.

But there was no fear of that. It was a platonic friendship, and one she intended keeping that way.

##

The trip home was exhausting–Melissa had to change flights in Brisbane on her way to Armidale. It was dark by the time the taxi dropped her off in front of her semi-detached cottage on the outskirts of town, and she went straight to bed. Rising early the next morning, she shivered as her feet touched the cold floor. Determined to put the events of the last two weeks behind her and get back into her normal routine, she prepared for her morning run. Pulling on a tracksuit and sneakers, she did some stretches before stepping outside. She gasped as her breath misted in the frosty air and pulled a beanie over her head before setting off.

Mrs McGovern, her neighbour and landlady, was also up early and working in her front garden in the frosty morning.

"Hey, Mrs Mac, you'll get frostbite on your fingers!" she called out. I'll pick up Luney and Sylvester on the way back."

Mrs Mac gave her a wave as Melissa broke into a light jog on the footpath. Breathing in the chilly air, her cheeks tingled from the cold. Autumn leaves crunched underfoot as she picked up the pace and did her circuit across town around the back of the university. She was surprised to see two cars and a large black motorcycle parked outside the history building, even though it was the weekend. Two men came out of the building. One of them gave her a quick wave and she waved back, realising it was Professor Andrews.

That must be the new professor with him.

As she jogged around the corner, the motorcycle roared past her and she glanced up, nearly tripping over. The bike rider reminded her of Nick. She tried to push thoughts of him from her mind as she picked up the pace. If every man was going to remind her of him, she had no chance. She had to get over it!

She blocked her holiday from her mind, trying to concentrate on her preparations for her return to work on Monday. By the time she'd completed her circuit, she was warm and had shed her beanie and sweatshirt. Opening the gate to Mrs Mac's cottage garden, she bent as she caught her breath. The old lady came out of the front door, a birdcage in one hand and a fluffy white cat tucked under her other arm.

"I hope Luney behaved this time. No breakages?" The cat was company for Melissa and kept her entertained with his antics every night as he ran around the apartment. Sylvester, the budgie, chirped as she picked up his cage.

"No worse than usual. Still a mad cat but settling down a bit. She is well named." Mrs Mac was used to the pets, often minding them for Melissa when she'd travelled down to the coast to visit Gramps.

"By the way, your new neighbour is moving in on the weekend. It's all been organised by the university. I believe he's a new professor."

"Yes," Lissy nodded. "I heard before I went away there is a new professor coming to finish his doctorate and do some lecturing with our faculty. I'm looking forward to meeting him. Let me know if there's anything I can do to help you get the cottage ready. I have the whole weekend free."

Mrs Mac had split the old bluestone cottage into two rentals.

Lissy loved living in the front half of the old home and helped look after the rambling cottage garden, and often helped out with renovations and odd jobs around both properties.

"I haven't forgotten you want the front fence whitewashed. I've set tomorrow aside for that. Thanks again for minding these two. I'll see you later."

She hurried up the front steps; her phone was ringing. She let herself in the door as she juggled the cat and the birdcage. Putting them down gently in front of the fire, she picked up the phone.

"Melissa McIntyre speaking."

"Hi, darling, just checking you're home safely. How was your trip?" Her mother's voice was bright and happy.

How was the trip? Well, Mum, I learned that foolish behaviour is genetic, and I fell for the first good-looking male who came along. Spent the night with him and moved on. However, I have more sense than you did, and we used protection, so there won't be any lonely children growing up with only one parent.

"Great, thanks, Mum. Got a good tan and I'm relaxed and ready to go back to work."

They chatted for a while and she was surprised to hear her mother and Lars were planning a visit back to Australia in the spring.

"We've timed it with your university session break, so we can spend some time together at the coast. I have to wrap up some of Gramps' business and get his house sorted."

"It will be great to see you both." She wondered whether Lars would still be on the scene then and if she would even get to meet her latest stepfather. As soon as she ended the call, the phone rang again, and Luney jumped up and started to run around the room.

"Hello." She chuckled as she answered the phone, watching her crazy cat run around the furniture. The budgie chirped in encouragement.

"Hello, Melissa, it's Tom. Welcome home. I'm calling to confirm our date for tonight." Tom Richards was so predictable. He was nice looking, well-mannered, and a stickler for doing the right thing. But his structured life and predictability appealed to her and she always enjoyed their Friday night outing. You couldn't call it a date; they just enjoyed the same movies and food.

"Yes, looking forward to it. It's good to be home and back to normal." There was no way she would share her holiday stories with him this time.

Tom hesitated and cleared his throat.

"Melissa, I was wondering if it would greatly inconvenience you if we changed our routine this week."

They usually dined at Ivy Cottage, a restaurant on the river, and had met there at seven o'clock each Friday night for the past six months, often followed by a movie, apart from the occasions Tom was away on business trips or Melissa was down the coast visiting Gramps.

"There's a family dinner at my parents' home tonight that I must attend, as my brother is coming, and we have all been summoned to the family home." He sounded nervous. "Not that I don't want to go, of course I do, but I was looking forward to our dinner and seeing you. I missed you while you were away."

She was surprised. Tom didn't usually touch on anything personal, and it was most unusual for them to have a conversation like that. She hadn't even known that his family lived in town.

"I would love for you to come with me. It would be a great opportunity to meet my family, while we are all together. It doesn't happen often. I'll pick you up at your place, if that suits you?"

Lissy hesitated. The emotional rollercoaster of the past few weeks had left her feeling fragile, and although it would be nice to meet Tom's family and see him in his comfort zone, she didn't want him to think there was anything more in their relationship. She'd make sure he knew that, so she made a quick decision and spoke before she could change her mind.

"Okay, I'll look forward to it. Is it formal or casual?"

He laughed. "Very casual. I will apologise for my family in

advance. Er ... Melissa, there is also something I would like to discuss with you before we get there, so I'll come over about five?"

She felt a rush of affection for Tom. He had shown more emotion in this short conversation than he had in the six months she'd known him. He had been a steady friend as she eased into her new position at the university, and although he was always businesslike and fostered that image with his dress and attention to his personal appearance, she enjoyed his company.

She began to look forward to the evening and sang along with the radio as she went hunting through her wardrobe for something suitably casual to wear. She felt happier than she had since Gramps's death. Sylvester chirped along with her and Luney gave them both a disdainful look as she stretched out on the sunny windowsill washing herself. Lissy laid out a light wool suit in forest green, with her ankle-length boots, before settling down to reading through her notes for work on Monday morning. She wanted to be up-to-date and well prepared for the new professor; he would have some input into her promotion.

She had worked hard at her research to become the youngest lecturer in the history faculty at the small, rural university. Word was out that she was being seriously considered in the current round for a promotion to senior lecturer and it would be an achievement to get that promotion at her age.

A whole new life was about to open up for her.

Chapter Five

Tom arrived at Melissa's front door at precisely five o'clock. Her hair was confined in an elegant French roll and pearl studs in her ears finished off the sedate look. Nice and understated for meeting Tom's family, and casual holidaymaker Lissy's beach clothes were packed away until the next trip to the coast. She ignored the ripple that tingled through her when she thought of the holiday.

No! Back to sedate Melissa, all ready for work.

She ushered Tom in from the cold and was surprised when he pulled a large bunch of roses from behind his back. Reaching over, he kissed her on both cheeks and handed her the flowers. Feeling surprised and a little bit off balance, she hugged the roses to her chest. Tom had never kissed her cheek before, let alone bought her flowers. They even went Dutch at their weekly dinners.

"Thank you, Tom. How thoughtful of you."

"Welcome home. I really missed you." His voice was happy. "You look wonderful. Great tan. Did you have a good break?"

Lissy hadn't told any of her colleagues about her grandfather's death. As in all aspects of her life she kept herself private and professional at the university. She nodded, smiled and attempted to regain her composure. She wasn't sure about this newly confident and casual Tom. "I'll get a vase from the kitchen. Would you like a drink? I have some white wine in the fridge."

"A small one, please."

Luney jumped down from the chair and wrapped herself around Tom's ankles. Tom picked up the cat and moved across to the fire as Lissy went to the kitchen. Returning with a tray holding a bottle of wine and two glasses, she was pleased to see him sitting on the long settee in front of the fire, stroking Luney. She sat down next to them and placed the tray on the low table between the settee and the fire. Tom poured the wine and held his glass up to hers.

"Cheers," he said. A fleeting image of a tall, tanned sailor flitted through her mind as she looked back at him. Similar eyes, similar cheekbones.

God, she was seeing Nick everywhere in her imagination. Last night, the guy on a toilet paper ad on the television had even looked like him.

Tom fidgeted in his seat and straightened his already perfectly straight tie. Luney jumped across to Lissy's lap when he cleared his throat.

"Is everything all right?" she asked. "Everything's fine at work?"

"Yes." Tom turned and sat up even straighter. "I have something to ask you and I don't know how to go about it."

She tilted her head to the side and smiled at him, he was worked up about something.

"We are really great friends and I know how you feel about love and marriage." He paused and cleared his throat. "I have always had a life plan and I would like to get married and have a family. I intend to do that before I am thirty-five ... get married, that is. What I am trying to find out, Melissa, is if you would be interested in considering my proposition."

"Proposition?" A giggle rose in her throat and she fought it back. She mustn't have heard him right.

"I suppose you could call it a proposal in a way. I don't really mean a proposal, but just suggesting that maybe you give it some thought."

"Give what some thought?" Melissa screwed her nose up as she stared at him.

"Maybe that you get to think of me in the light of a future life partner. Come and meet my family tonight and then we will discuss it again next Friday night."

Melissa was speechless. But poor Tom looked really anxious.

Reaching over, she took both of his hands. "Hey, I'm so flattered that you'd consider me as your partner, but this is not us. You know that."

He sighed and eventually agreed. "I know."

"What's happened to bring this on, Tom?"

"Something happened, and I got thinking. Maybe you can learn to love me. And then if and when it comes time for me to turn this proposition into a real proposal, perhaps on bended knee, you will have had time to think about it. I've always thought romantic love was overrated. If you're wise you choose your marriage partner sensibly."

"You know what my grandfather used to say?"

He shook his head.

"Wait for your destiny, and don't settle for less." Gramps had actually made her promise that she would, but there was no need for Tom to know that. "And okay, so you said something happened?"

A glum expression crossed his face as he nodded. "Jill's back."

"Your old girlfriend?"

He nodded again.

"And this has led to this conversation how?"

This time it was an out-of-character shrug. "I guess I got thinking about how she dumped me and how I was going to reach my life plan by thirty-five."

This time Melissa let the laugh bubble out. "Oh, Tom, you are so precious. But you know we're just friends. Tell me honestly, have you ever had one romantic thought about me?"

His lips tilted in a smile. "No. We're good mates."

"Good, let's leave it there and finish our wine and forget about your 'proposition'." His shoulders relaxed and she realised how nervous he'd been. She reached over and gently kissed his cheek.

"Now let's go so I can meet your family." As she stood up, she had a worrying thought. "You haven't mentioned your proposition to them, have you?"

"No, they know you're my friend from the university."

Tom had a luxury car, an imported British saloon in a silver grey, which suited him, and Lissy loved the feel of the leather upholstery against her legs. They drove a short distance out of town past beautiful old houses, crossed the river; and then he turned through an ornate set of gates, opening to a long drive lined by huge trees. It was a massive double-storey home, and iron lace edged an upstairs veranda that wrapped around the whole house. She counted five chimneys.

"This is absolutely beautiful," she said. "It must be one of the original settler homesteads."

Tom nodded. "It's almost as old as Saumarez Homestead on the Uralla road. This one was built in 1900 by my father's grandparents and it's been in our family for over a hundred years."

After he parked his car in a carport adjoining the side of the main house, he reached over and took Lissy's hand. "Now, don't be nervous. Dom coming home today has brought the whole family together for the first time for ages."

Melissa patted her hair into place and took a deep breath. She could do a lot worse than Tom, if she was honest, and God knows, after the last week, she was even more convinced of the dangers of physical attraction, and how unwary romantics could be easily ensnared.

A marriage based on common sense and friendship mightn't be such a bad idea.

She shook her head as Gramps's voice circled in her thoughts. She took another deep breath, squared her shoulders, and followed Tom into the fray to meet his family.

He ushered Melissa across a wide veranda at the back of the house that was cluttered with shoes, garden tools, potted plants, and bags of potting mix. He opened a heavy timber door leading into a warm kitchen that was suffused with the golden light of the setting sun. The aroma of baking bread and garlic surrounded them, as did a cacophony of noise. Pausing in the doorway, Melissa watched Tom push past a pair of arguing children, slap the back of a young man talking into a mobile phone, and then plant a noisy kiss on the cheek of the elegant woman standing by the stove.

"Mama, *deliziosa* ... what are we eating tonight?" Tom leaned forward to lift the lid and peer into the bubbling pot on the stove.

Melissa hadn't known that Tom's background was Italian, and she'd never heard him speak the language before. His voice was full of life as he spoke.

"Tomas, where are your manners?" she said, slapping his hand away. "Who is this lovely young woman you bring to my kitchen?" Mrs Richards was a tall woman, with a tumble of black curls held back loosely with a checked ribbon. She came across to Melissa, wiping her hands on her bright red apron.

"You are Melissa. I am so happy to finally meet you. Please, call me Tessa. Tomas has been very remiss in not bringing you over before; we have heard all about you and your good influence on him."

"Yes, you've gotten him away from his desk and his numbers," interjected the young man as he put his mobile in his pocket.

"Alex, don't be rude!"

"Yes, Mama." He grinned widely at Tom and Melissa. "Welcome. You do you know you're too beautiful for my ugly old brother? Why don't you run away with me instead?"

"I'm not running away with anyone." Melissa smiled and took Tessa's outstretched hands. "It was very kind of you to invite me tonight, since I know it's a special family dinner. I feel welcome already."

Tessa broke into a wide smile. "Tonight, our second son, Dominic will be home from his work in the Cook Islands, and we are all together for the first time in three years. It is a very special night. Now, Tomas, take Melissa into the living room. Your sisters are in there."

Tom ushered her into a beautiful room that seemed to be full of children and was as noisy as the kitchen. Lissy felt overwhelmed by the noise and the number of adults and children sprawled on lounges and on the floor in front of the crackling open fire. Tom spread his arms in a wide gesture and said proudly, "*la mia famiglia* – my family."

She experienced a surge of true affection for Tom. He was so obviously a part of this boisterous and loving family. Tom, in his family setting, was very different from the polite and shy accountant she dined with on Friday nights. She smothered a smile as Alex followed them into the room.

"Come on you old stuffed shirt, you don't have to impress anyone here," he said as he undid Tom's tie and flung it on the table.

"Enough, enough! Your manners, Alessandro." Tessa picked up the tie and handed it back to Tom. "Take the children outside and run off some of your energy, so we can introduce Melissa in peace."

"Yes, Mama," said Alex, with a twinkle in his eye. "Come on kids, a quick game of cricket before Uncle Dom arrives. First one outside gets to bat." He winked at Lissy as he ran out to the veranda followed by half a dozen children of various ages and sizes.

Even after Alex led the children outside through the French doors, the room stayed noisy. Lissy was fascinated and looked around the elegant but welcoming room. A cricket game was blaring from the huge television on the far wall as three men loudly criticised the failure of a fieldsman to take a catch. Two beautiful babies with big blue eyes were yelling as they climbed over their respective mothers' legs.

"Quiet, please. Girls, this is Melissa." Tom had to raise his voice over the din in the room. "My three little sisters, Sophie, Allie, and Lucy."

Lissy greeted them as Tom moved on to introduce their assorted husbands and the two babies still in the room, and Alex's fiancée, Emily. In the middle of the introductions, a huge golden retriever came bounding through the room chased by two small boys, almost knocking Lissy from her feet. She fell into the chair behind her as Sophie, Tom's oldest sister, chastised the boys.

"Be careful!" She turned to Lissy and laughed. "Welcome to our madhouse!"

"Thanks," said Lissy, settling into the chair and following the different conversations with interest. She was immediately included as though she was a part of the family and felt welcome and comfortable even though she was in a room full of strangers. She recalled Gramps's comments. *Maybe I have found my destiny. Maybe Tom was under my nose the whole time and I didn't appreciate him.* She looked across at Tom watching the cricket game with his brother-in-law, trying to imagine herself in an embrace with him. As hard as she tried, Nick kept pushing into her thoughts and she shook herself in annoyance.

"Is everything all right?" Tom leaned towards her, a look of concern on his face.

"I'm sorry?" She realised she had spoken her thoughts aloud and Tom was sitting next to her on the lounge. She felt her cheeks grow rosy and reached for her glass of water on the table, as excited cries drifted in from the back garden.

"Yes, I'm fine," she said.

"Uncle Dom's here!" The throaty roar of a motorcycle coming up the driveway drowned out the excited squeals of the children.

"Thanks!" Lissy found herself with two babies unceremoniously dropped on her knees as the three sisters jumped up and ran out through the French doors to the driveway.

Tessa ran through the living room like a young girl, her black curls tumbling from the ribbon. Tom reached over and took one of the babies from her lap.

"Sorry, I did try to warn you about this mad lot, but they are in even finer form tonight with Dom coming home. Once Mama assures herself that he is really home and in one piece, things will settle down and we'll probably have a relatively civilised meal." There was a flurry of noise and movement as the children ran back inside, chattering with excitement, followed closely by the adults.

"Uncle Dom, did you bring us any presents? Any shrunken heads?"

Lissy looked at Tom and laughed. "Shrunken heads?"

"It's a common occurrence. I don't know if I mentioned to you that Dom is the new professor in the history faculty. He's been doing research in the South Pacific for the last two years and has come home to write up his thesis and do some lecturing in the undergraduate Pacific history course. He's always sending gruesome bits and pieces to our nephews and they love it."

"He's going to be in our faculty." Lissy looked up at him, surprised. "Mrs Mac, my landlady, was talking about him this morning. He's moving into the other flat in the cottage. I didn't realise he was your brother."

"Mama won't be happy about that. I think she hoped he would stay at home for a while, although I can understand why he wants his own place. The noise level here tonight is normal and there wouldn't be much chance of getting his thesis written."

Lissy stood up and shifted the baby to her hip, and small chubby hands reached out and grabbed a handful of her hair. Tom placed one hand gently on her neck as he untangled the baby's hand from the bunch of curls he had pulled from her clip. His body blocked her view of the newcomer and her heart almost stopped as she heard a familiar deep voice.

"Tomas, a girlfriend and a baby? About time!" Tom turned around laughing as he grabbed his brother in a huge hug with lots of affectionate backslapping. "Girlfriend maybe, but this is Sophie's third-born, you idiot."

Lissy turned in shock and her head spun as she looked up into familiar blue eyes. Dom's attention shifted to her, and the tight smile on his face sent a chill shivering down her spine as she struggled to keep a firm hold on the baby and fight the dizziness blurring her vision.

She felt her heart thump and then race.

My God! How wonderful, and bizarre, to see Nick again, even though he looked surprised, even angry. She opened her mouth to say hello but was interrupted by Tom.

"Dom, this is Melissa McIntyre, a friend of mine from the university. Melissa just told me that you'll be working in her faculty."

Nick reached over and took Lissy's free hand in his as she carefully juggled the baby on her hip. "What a coincidence," he drawled. "Delighted to meet you, *Melissa*."

She turned and handed the baby back to Sophie as Tessa came over and clapped her hands, inviting everyone to make their way out to dinner. The room began to clear as the family followed Nick outside and she took the opportunity to dash to the bathroom.

Wide-eyed, she raised trembling fingers to her cheeks as she looked into the mirror and saw the pallor beneath her tan. She pinched her cheeks before running cold water over her wrists.

What was the probability of Nick—*Nick* from her holiday fling—being the new professor in her history faculty at the university? And the brother of her friend who had come up with a stupid proposition tonight? And her new neighbour? The coincidences were staggering at best.

She groaned and fought to pull herself together. How typical. It proved to her once again that you didn't trust physical attraction under the moonlight. Not only was Nic a liar—his name was Dom, he'd even lied about his name—he was going to be her new boss! And on top of that, he would be the one with the final say in her promotion.

You can kiss that good-bye, Dr McIntyre.

##

Gas heaters lined the wall to ward off the New England chill and Melissa moved to the dark end of the table, away from the heat. Sitting down, she watched Nick hugging his mother at the other end of the table.

I know how good those arms feel. Closing her eyes, she remembered him holding her close. Had that really happened only two nights ago?

She was hot, despite the chill in the air, and her heart was still pumping hard and fast. Reaching for the carafe of water, she poured herself a glass, the ice cubes tinkling as her hands shook. She was so angry at his lack of acknowledgement that they'd already met in the islands, she felt as though sparks should be jumping from her. He had made her a liar too, with his omission, and she hadn't had time to query it.

"Are you okay? I hope my family hasn't overwhelmed you?" Tom frowned and leaned close as he sat next to her. Nick was watching from the other end of the table and she deliberately put her hand up to touch Tom's face.

Stuff Nick. Let him think what he wants.

"It's absolutely wonderful. Being an only child, I've never been part of such a big family celebration before."

Tom seemed surprised at her touching his face but he put his hand over hers. "You're welcome to visit whenever you want. I didn't realise you have no family around."

Melissa looked down the table. Nick's expression was cold and aloof as he met her gaze. She was going to have to cut ties with this family to save her sanity. Her feelings in chaos, she longed for the evening to be over, so she could escape.

"What do you specialise in at the university, Melissa?" Nick had moved down the table and had taken a chair in between two of his sisters, across from her and Tom.

"Pacific history," she said. She put her head down and fiddled with her hair clip.

"Interesting. You don't look like a girl who would know anything about history. Glorious hair, by the way. I hope my brother has told you how ravishing you look this evening. What a fabulous suntan." His eyes blatantly ran over her, completely different to the gentle way he had looked at her only a couple of nights before. She froze, frightened she would lose her temper and make a rude comment, but Tessa rescued her.

"Stop teasing. You and Alex are incorrigible. No wonder poor Tom rarely brings anyone home. Behave while I retrieve your father from the study. He's so immersed in his new book, that he hasn't even heard you arrive."

Nick leaned back and gave his mother another kiss on the cheek as she walked past.

"It's okay, Mama. Melissa and I will get to know each other at the university. I'm sure she'll get used to me." Lissy looked across at him and saw his eyes glittering with a promise of things to come.

##

It seemed the night went on forever. She met Professor Richards senior, who had been firmly ensconced in his study through all the excitement of Nick arriving, and had sat bemused as a procession of aunts, uncles, cousins and neighbours dropped in to greet Nick. Word had spread that the Pacific adventurer was home. She met so many people, her head spun and the effort of keeping calm and friendly was making her feel ill. All night she was conscious of Nick's simmering mood. She had learned to read him so well in such a short time. She sat quietly, and only spoke when someone included her in a conversation. Not only had he left her that final morning on Hamilton Island without so much as a good-bye or see you later, the coward had slipped out in the darkness.

And lied about his name, so she couldn't find him.
Talk about wham, bam, thank you ma'am.

And the lying sailor was actually a university professor. And one she was going to have to work with.

Lissy sat there alternating between feeling hot and cold and considered Nick's deception. Her jaw ached from clenching her teeth. Her mood must have been obvious because Tom offered to drive her home.

"No, call me a taxi. Enjoy the rest of the night and catch up with your brother." She said her good-byes to the family after he reluctantly agreed and called the local taxi company.

"It was wonderful to finally meet you. I do hope Tomas brings you again soon," said Tessa, enfolding Lissy in a warm embrace. Tom's sisters all gave her hugs as she made her way through the living room, where children of various ages were asleep on cushions on the floor. Nick followed Tom and Lissy out to the front veranda, as Alex yelled out to Tom.

"When's the wedding, big brother? You're almost thirty-five."

Tessa glared at Alex and turned to Lissy. "Once again, I apologise for my sons, they have no manners. They take after their father."

Professor Richards gravely shook her hand and Lissy was sure he didn't even know who she was in the procession of visitors who had been through the house that evening. With a great sense of relief, she saw the lights of the taxi as it pulled up in the driveway. She gave Tom a brief hug and a light kiss on the cheek.

"I'll give you a call next week about Friday night," he said.

Nick appeared behind them.

"Goodnight, Melissa," he said, emphasizing the second half of her name. "I'll see you on Monday at work. I'm really looking forward to getting to know you better."

"Me too, I can't wait to hear about your adventures in the Pacific, *Dominic*," she said, emphasizing the Nic in his name. Tom opened the door of the taxi and she slid across the seat, her hands over her eyes.

Why the hell didn't we just laugh and say we had already met? What a fine mess I'm in, so much for destiny. Not only do I have to put up with him at work, he's going to be living on the other side of my cottage. Wait until he finds out about that coincidence!

That was about the only thing that made her smile. She knew he wasn't going to like that.

***

Nick stood silently on the stairs watching the taillights of the taxi disappear down the driveway. Tom walked up the stairs towards his brother, his movements precise and considered, like everything else he did.

"Well?"

"Well, what?" replied Nick, knowing his brother wanted him to say how great Melissa was.

"What did you think of Melissa?"

Nick tried to think of a suitable reply as they went back to the veranda.

"Great. Very pretty." He turned and thumped Tom on the back. "Come on, mate, enough of women tonight. You know me...love 'em and leave 'em." He reached into the refrigerator and threw his older brother a can of beer. "You and I have a lot of catching up to do."

He was cranky with himself because he'd been so attracted to Lissy on the island, and then he'd slept with her. He felt bad because he'd scarpered out of her room before she woke up the next morning because the response he'd had to her was something way out of his experience.

It had scared him, and like a fool he'd thought it was easier to make himself scarce. Serious relationships weren't for him, and he didn't know what he was going to say to her.

Maybe he was being old fashioned. Maybe it had been just casual sex to her.

And what the hell was she doing up there, sleeping with him if she was Tom's girlfriend? He'd had a lucky escape, and somehow, he was going to have to warn Tom.

Women. They were all the same.

Not to be trusted. Ever. With the exception of his mother and sisters, of course.

Tom caught the beer and leaned against the railing.

"Tell me about your latest trip. Did you get your research finished ... are you happy to be back at the university? You don't look very impressed."

"You know me," replied Nick. "I prefer to be on the Islands, but I have to spend some time at the university or the funding for my projects would dry up." He turned and looked out into the darkness and shivered as the late night breeze picked up. "I don't know how you cope, going to the same boring office, day in, day out."

Tom sighed and made an admission that startled Nick. "You know, if I'm honest? I was starting to get a bit bored with it but having

Melissa as a friend has livened up my life."

Nick grunted.

"I asked her to consider a future with me when I picked her up tonight. But—"

"She's not your type." Nick knew his voice was short. Tom had always needed his approval, even though Nick was younger than him. Well, this time, for his own good, he'd have to do without it. He pushed himself away from the railing and tried to ignore the lump that seemed to have settled in his throat. "I've had enough to drink. I'm going to bed."

"Night, bro." Tom reached over and enveloped him in a bear hug. "It's great to have you home, even if it will only be for a short while."

Nick kept the smile on his face even though he wanted to drag his hands down his face in frustration.

Sleep eluded him for a long time. What were the odds of Lissy being on his staff, two thousand miles from the playground of the Whitsunday Islands, and with her eyes firmly set on Tom? She had thought Nick was a drifter, and to top it all off, he'd slept with her. He had to forget that night. There was nowhere for it to go. He would work with her and get the project finished and return to the Islands as quickly as he could.

Chapter Six

Lissy hoped to fall into oblivion the moment her head touched the pillow, but the events of the night kept her tossing and turning into the early hours. Waking late, she got up in a very sour mood. Her eyes were scratchy from lack of sleep. Sipping her coffee in the kitchen, she watched Luney run around and knock over the pile of kindling next to the old combustion stove. The mad cat's antics added to her bad mood and she banished the cat to the laundry room.

She decided to work off her mood by getting an early start on whitewashing the cottage fence. Changing into her oldest shorts and sweatshirt, she tied her curls back with a bandana and then collected the painting gear from the laundry cupboard.

"Sorry, Luney, it's not your fault I'm so grumpy this morning." Melissa stepped out into the old cottage garden, which was bursting with the bronze and gold of late autumn, the leaves crunching underfoot as she walked across to the fence. Kneeling down on the footpath outside the garden fence, she opened the bucket of whitewash and began to paint the old timber. The rhythmic motion of the brush going up and down the palings did nothing to soothe her mood as she simmered over the events of the previous evening.

Thoughts of revenge flitted through her mind as she pictured a variety of punishments suitable for Nick. By the time she was halfway along the front panel of the fence, he had walked the gangplank, been clapped in irons, tied to the mast, and marooned on one of his tropical islands. Yes, marooning sounded good, preferably on an isolated island a long way from her.

The roar of a motorcycle thundering up the quiet street interrupted her fantasy. Putting the brush in the paint tin, she turned around and stood, hands on her hips, as Nick turned into the driveway and cut the engine. He swaggered over to her, his eyes snapping with anger.

"Good morning, *Melissa*." Throwing the helmet aside, he bent down so that his eyes were level with hers. "Or is Lissy back this morning in the sexy shorts? Who will I be living with? Lissy or Melissa?"

"You won't be living with either!" She stepped away from him. There was a loud clatter as she backed into the paint, knocking the bucket over and white paint splattered up the backs of her legs.

"Now look what you've done!" Bending down, she set the bucket upright, looking around for something to wipe the paint from her legs. Swearing to herself, she pulled the bandana from her hair and her curls cascaded around her face as she scrubbed furiously at her legs.

Nic stood back, looking her up and down, a tight smile on his face.

"Well, we definitely have Lissy back. Fascinating how you move so easily from one to the other."

"You are full of it, Dominic." She threw the paint-soaked bandana to the ground and picked up the paintbrush. "What happened to Nic, the sailor?"

He ignored her question. "Demure Melissa, what a lovely wife she would have made for Tom. I bet he hasn't met the free and easy Lissy," he said.

"How dare you pass judgment on me. What about you, *Dominic*? Just thrill seeking around the Pacific for a few years, professor? Having a few bets and picking up any gullible female for a bit of fun and sneaking out before they could find out the truth? Or is that just a line you use to make you more attractive to anyone who doesn't fall for the 'angel face' line straight up?" She stepped towards him, emphasizing each word with the paintbrush. Dollops of white paint flicked on to his face and black T-shirt. He grabbed her wrist and held the brush above her head.

"I don't want my brother hurt by a cheating girlfriend again."

Nick's voice was getting louder. "The elegant suit and fancy hairdo may suck him in, but I know a hypocrite from a hundred yards away. Trust me, I've had lots of experience."

"Oh, I'm sure," she said between gritted teeth, as she tried to ignore the crazy little flutters that were travelling up her arm from where he held her.

Hurried footsteps and a concerned voice stopped them both in their tracks.

"Is everything okay?" Mrs Mac stood on her front porch. She looked taken aback as if she sensed the tension in the air. "I was just going out when I heard your voices."

Lissy carefully removed the paintbrush from Nick's hands and turned to Mrs Mac. "Oh, it's okay, Professor Richards came to collect his key and I accidentally flicked him with paint. He was helping me with the brush. It was so nice of him."

Mrs Mac didn't look convinced that the man clad in black leathers and a T-shirt towering over Lissy could be a professor. Nick stepped forward with his hand outstretched, giving the older woman the benefit of his devastating smile.

"Mrs Mac, I'm delighted to meet you." He held her little wrinkled hands between his, and Melissa rolled her eyes. "Please call me Nick. I signed all the paperwork at the university yesterday and I believe I'm supposed to collect the key here."

Lissy watched Nick put on the charm and saw its immediate impact on their elderly landlady as she fell under his spell. He saw her expression and responded with a brilliant grin, and, despite her anger, she felt the inevitable tug to her heartstrings.

"It's okay, I've still got the spare keys inside. I'll show the professor through his side of the cottage," Melissa said. Looking a lot happier, Mrs Mac bid them farewell and headed towards her little car. Melissa's shoulders slumped in defeat. "You had better come inside and get cleaned up, and then I'll show you your half of the cottage."

Nick looked at her closely and she knew that the tension of the past few days was visible in the dark shadows under her eyes. Sighing, she turned, and he followed her up the steps into the laundry. Handing him a washcloth to clean the paint from his face, she went into the kitchen to collect his keys.

She reached over for the keys on the hook and turned, bumping into a rock-hard chest. She stepped back, but he took a step closer and warm hands gripped her shoulders.

"We have a problem here, Lissy. Simple fact ... I want you out of the picture with my brother." He paused, and she could hear the frustration in his voice.

"So how is that a problem?" His eyes were holding hers intently and she found it hard to look away."

"Because if I'm honest, I don't want you out of the picture ... my picture. Despite common sense and logic, you fascinate me. Can you explain that to me?"

Her heart began to pound. "No, I can't," she said with a sad weariness.

He pulled her closer. "Let me show you." His head tilted down towards her and she watched as his lips parted, and quite suddenly, Lissy felt anger take over her whole body. The range of emotions she had experienced since she had first seen Nick swinging down from the mast of the yacht coalesced into pure black rage. She pulled away and shoved him.

"You know nothing, *nothing* about me! How dare you stand there and tell me I'm not good enough for your brother. And then tell me you want me! You've got a nerve."

Turning away from him, she lowered her voice. "Go away and leave me alone. Go look at your cottage. Move in, bring in a harem for all I care. I don't care what you do, just leave me alone."

"You confuse me," he replied softly.

"I want you to leave, now." Her voice was firm. "I have work to do."

She walked across and opened the door.

"Lissy, Melissa, I mean. Come with me and show me the cottage." He ran his fingers through his shaggy hair in frustration. "You live here. I've signed the lease. We have to sort this out. Come on, let's pretend this is the first time we've met and you're showing me my new rental. I won't touch you again."

But how much did she want him to?

She stood, without answering for a short time, then squared her shoulders and answered him. "I'll show you around only if you promise not to have any contact with me once you move in, apart from work."

"Fine," he said carefully, moving around her to go out to the veranda. As he walked past the laundry window, a lazy paw swiped out at him, lightly scratching his forearm.

Melissa reached over and gave the white cat a quick rub on the head. "Nick, meet Luney, she'll keep you on the straight and narrow."

***

The entrance to the other side of the cottage was at the far end of the front veranda. Nick followed Lissy as she unlocked the door; they entered an airy room bathed in sunshine. An open fireplace bore testimony to the cold New England evenings.

"You'll have to set up a firewood delivery. I can give you the phone number," she said. Even her damn voice was attractive.

"Thank you," he said, moving into the next room.

"It's a mirror image of my side." Lissy moved quickly through the rooms. "Two bedrooms. I use one for a study, a separate dining room and the small bathroom and laundry."

She went through the cottage showing him the basics. As she turned to go back toward the living room Lissy stumbled over a loose piece of carpet. Nick put out his hand and caught her before she could fall. His elbow brushed the softness of her breast and his arm automatically went around her waist. He groaned and pulled her into a close embrace. His face was almost level with hers and he could see the deep green flecks in her eyes. He ran his hands through her wild curls and remembered the pleasure of her hair on his body that one night they'd spent together.

Nick's heart was thumping hard. Despite knowing that he should not touch her, his heart was telling him a different story. Looking down into her eyes, he saw a small smile playing around her lips as she touched the flecks of white paint on his chin. He lowered his mouth to hers and closed his eyes revelling in the sensation of her soft lips opening under his.

He pulled her closer, oblivious to anything as she whimpered with pleasure and then realisation kicked in for him. He had never lost control like this before. Lissy stiffened in his arms and it was like a trigger back to reality for him. He pulled away from her. He had never felt like this before and it unsettled him.

Years ago, Olivia had thrown his love back at him as though he had not meant anything to her. Even then, he'd never lost control like this.

Damn her! He had not fallen for a woman since then, and he was not about to start now.

"You are really clever, aren't you?" he said. "You know what you want, and you go for it, don't you?"

Her open palm hit his cheek with a crack that moved his head sideways and left his cheek stinging.

"You sanctimonious bastard!" She threw the house keys at him and stalked from the room, slamming the door behind her. He watched her go, his blood still pounding from kissing her.

Chapter Seven

Melissa spent a lonely weekend ignoring the flurry of activity, the removalist truck and assorted vehicles that pulled into the driveway. A couple of times someone knocked on her door, but she turned up her music and ignored the knocking. An occasional glance from her window confirmed that most of the Richards family had arrived to help Nick at some point over the two days. Late on Sunday afternoon, Luney meowed incessantly at the door until Lissy let her out.

"Traitor," she murmured when Luney ran to Nick as he carried boxes across the back garden.

She worked hard at regaining her equilibrium on Sunday, keeping herself busy cleaning out cupboards and avoiding her new neighbour. Each time his face appeared in her mind—as it did most of the day—she deliberately blocked him from her thoughts. By the time darkness fell, she had calmed down and as the night chill slipped in, she split some kindling on the veranda. As soon as she had a fire going, she indulged in a hot bubble bath and put on her flannel Mickey Mouse pyjamas.

"Okay, time for work," she muttered as she opened her briefcase and read over the research notes she had left unfinished before going to Gramps's funeral. Even though she was aware of an occasional noise through the wall, she managed to concentrate on her research for a couple of hours and kept thoughts of Nick and his close proximity at bay. When her eyelids began to droop, and she couldn't hold back the yawn any longer, she packed her notes up ready for her return to work in the morning. Looking around for Luney, she realised the cat was still outside. She went to the door to let her inside but there was no sign of the cat.

Don't tell me another female has fallen for the irresistible professor, she thought with disgust. Pulling on her boots and grabbing a thick coat off the laundry hook, she went out to the veranda, softly calling to the missing feline.

Damn cat, she thought as she moved across the lawn, the frost crunching under her boots. Standing by the fence, she stood still and continued to call Luney. A sliver of light appeared on the back veranda; Nick's back door opened and the light shining from inside the cottage silhouetted his tall figure.

She eased back into the shadows near the fence. The old swing seat on the veranda creaked as Nick settled into it. The chill wind blowing from the west sent a flurry of dry leaves skittering across the path near the gate. If she stayed outside much longer, she would freeze. A white streak of movement near the fence alerted her to Luney's whereabouts and the mad cat sat down at her feet, meowing loudly. Knowing that Nick would see her as she crossed the lawn to go back in, she gathered the folds of her coat with as much dignity as she could muster and strode out across the grass, calling the cat to follow her up the back steps.

Nick was sitting legs outstretched, arms akimbo, looking relaxed. He reached out and grabbed her hand as she attempted to slip past him.

"Lissy, we need to talk."

"What about?" Her words were clipped, and she pulled away from him, trying to escape the warmth of the fingers grasping hers.

"Living here together, working together, setting some ground rules."

"I don't need any rules. Living here was fine until you rode into town on your noisy motorbike." She glared at him.

"You can't stay bunkered down in your half of the cottage forever. This is the first time you've been outside all weekend."

"Been spying on me, have you? You keep to your side, I'll keep to mine. I'm sure we'll pass occasionally in the corridors at the university, but that's it. You think I'm smart? Well, I am. Smart enough to keep out of your way."

She knew her voice was angry, but she was. Angry, that was. Angry that he thought so poorly of her.

It took two to tango.

Nick stood and let her hand go, burying his own hands in his coat pockets. She backed away from him and turned towards her door.

"Lissy—"

"No, don't you dare call me that. You want rules. Well, the first rule is you call me Melissa or Dr McIntyre. Second one, you keep your distance from me. Third, you keep your hands off me."

She bent down and picked up Luney, who was winding around her legs. Pushing past Nick on the narrow veranda, she walked to her back door. He made no move to stop her and she didn't look at him as she closed the door firmly behind her.

***

Melissa had slept like the dead for the first time in a week and woke in a panic when she realised she was going to be late on her first day back at work. Getting dressed as quickly as she could and skipping her morning coffee, she ran to her car and drove across town to the university.

Grabbing a coffee from the cafe, she was greeted by two colleagues from her faculty.

After a chat about her holiday, she said to her friend, Jenny. "I'm thinking of taking some leave."

"More leave? You just got back, Melissa." Jenny knew her well enough to know when something was bothering her. "Is everything okay? Why do you need more leave?"

"Anyway," chimed in Clare. "The head of faculty has cancelled all leave applications until the current budget period is over. That's three months away. Besides, who wants to leave now? You should see the new professor. Everyone's been running around this morning trying to get a glimpse of him. Talk about a hunk. Roared up the drive on a big black motorcycle. Drop dead gorgeous ... looks like he just stepped out of a *Pirates of the Caribbean* movie."

Melissa pulled a face as Jenny hurried them along. "Come on, gals, we have to be in the conference room in five minutes for a faculty meeting."

She hurried to her office, juggling her handbag, briefcase, laptop and coffee before she placed them on the floor next to the door. Her hands shook as she pinned up a couple of curls that had come loose. Using the mirror behind the door of her office, she reapplied her lipstick before picking up her laptop and coffee and heading for the conference room.

Most of the faculty were already seated at the round conference table and several of her colleagues greeted her as she hurried past. She found a vacant seat at the far end of the table just as Professor Andrews, the head of the history faculty, entered the room, accompanied by the new associate professor.

She took a deep breath, determined to remain calm and professional as Clare kicked her under the table.

"See what I mean," she whispered. "Johnny Depp look-alike." Lissy scowled at her.

"You're incorrigible. Besides, Johnny Depp has dark hair and a moustache in the pirate movies!"

As Professor Andrews called for quiet, Lissy sat back and caught Nick looking down the table directly at her. His hair *was* darker, as the sun-bleached thatch had been trimmed to a neat short back and sides since she had last seen him. The relaxed and easy-going buccaneer had disappeared and in his place was the clean-shaven academic clad in a three-piece suit and tie. She glared at him down the length of the table, and he raised a sardonic brow.

"I would like to welcome you all to this morning's meeting and thank you for interrupting your busy schedules," intoned the deep voice of Professor Andrews. "This morning, Professor Dominic Richards joins our history faculty and we'd like to extend a warm welcome to him. I will introduce him to you individually at the morning tea after the meeting. I'm sure you'll all make him very welcome." He continued with the faculty arrangements for the rest of semester and his monotonous voice fell into the background as Lissy mulled over the situation she found herself in at home, and at work.

I should be able to avoid him for most of the time. I'll do my research in the library, and hopefully, he'll take the vacant office on the next level. I won't go near the Richards' farm, and if there are any faculty social activities, I'll go down to the coast for the weekend and I'll—

"Dr McIntyre?" she felt another kick to her leg under the table from Clare.

"Dr McIntyre!" repeated the head of faculty.

"Yes, Professor Andrews?"

"As I was saying, I would like you to meet with myself and Professor Richards after morning tea, to organise the project."

"The project?"

"Yes, Dr McIntyre, the project." Professor Andrews looked annoyed. "I just finished explaining that the major thrust of our research for the next semester will be related to Professor Richard's Pacific study, and you will be his primary research assistant. We will meet in my office after tea to finalise the arrangements."

"Yes, Professor Andrews." Lissy groaned inwardly and looked down at the table. Clare and Jenny were looking at her with envy. The meeting ended and as the staff moved to the table at the back of the room to the morning tea table, she made for the door.

"Not so fast, Dr McIntyre." Nick appeared in front of her.

Conscious of the curious looks coming her way, she paused before greeting him politely for the benefit of the staff within earshot. Her words of welcome were aided by the self-control she was exerting. "Welcome to the university, Professor Richards." He took her arm and drew her into the corner. A frisson of warmth lingered where his fingers lightly held her elbow and her heart started to race as she fought the urge to shake his hand off her arm.

"Thank you, Dr McIntyre. Now, how do you want to play this?" he asked quietly when they were out of earshot. "Will we say we have already met? I don't want you to be embarrassed."

"I am not embarrassed, Professor. I believe we met at your parents' house on Friday evening and then you moved into the cottage next door to me on the weekend if my memory serves me correctly."

"Look, Lissy, even though we had a rocky start, we still have to work together and socialise—not to mention—live in the same house."

"A rocky start, that's an interesting way to put it." She folded her arms and glared at him, despite the curious looks of her colleagues. "Hmm, let me see. Lying to me, a sexist bet, taking advantage of an innocent tourist. Yep, you could call that a rocky start."

Frustrated, he ran his hand through what was left of his hair. Looking up at him, she was amused to see that there were a couple of stray flecks of white paint remaining in the stubble.

"Look, I'm trying to be the adult here," he said. "We need to sort this out and quickly."

She couldn't help herself as she pointed to his hair. "Been painting, Professor?"

"A run in with a little harridan's paint brush over the weekend." She stared at him and the amusement on his face surprised her. A warm feeling tugged at her tummy.

"Okay, let's call a truce," she said. "I need another coffee. We can talk over that."

They moved across the room to the morning tea table, acting like two colleagues getting to know each other. Nick poured her a cup of coffee in one of the elegant cups provided by the caterers, and Lissy's hand trembled as she held the cup and saucer. Jenny and Clare wandered over and introduced themselves to Nick. Lissy ignored the jealous feeling that ran through her.

Professor Andrews' voice boomed out. "Okay folks, back to work. Lots of planning to be done, and there are students waiting for the ten o'clock lecturers." A couple of academic staff scurried out to their lecture halls as the professor glanced pointedly at his watch.

"Dr McIntyre, Professor Richards, give me five minutes and come up to my office please," he said.

Lissy made a quick escape as Clare and Jenny kept Nick talking. She entered her office, closed the door, and leaned against it, her eyes closed and heart thudding.

What on earth am I going to do?

Chapter Eight

Taking a deep breath, Lissy turned and looked into the mirror on the back of her door. Even her hair had come loose from its tight French roll, with a couple of curly wisps falling over her flushed cheeks. Her green eyes glittered with emotion. Her legs were shaking and felt as though they wouldn't hold her up.

One look at him and my body goes into meltdown. I will not let him make me feel like this.

With trembling hands, she pinned her hair back and applied fresh lipstick as the memory of their night together filled her thoughts. She swallowed back the tears as she rummaged in her handbag for a rarely-used compact, and then patted a little bit of natural beige powder onto her flushed cheeks. She drank a big glass of water from the cooler in the corner of her office and a semblance of control returned. Picking up her laptop, she headed upstairs to the faculty administration offices.

Nancy, Professor Andrews' secretary, ushered her in, with a huge smile.

"Lovely tan, Melissa. Did you have a nice break?"

After a brief conversation, she entered the large office and joined Professor Andrews and Nick at a low coffee table in the corner.

"Professor Richards has carried out extensive research in the Pacific over the past two years, and we're proud to be associated with his final research paper. Dr McIntyre, I want you to put your work aside for the rest of the semester and assist the professor with the final research and writing of the report. Your previous research will lead into his perfectly. I anticipate that the paper will acknowledge you as a co-author and that will look magnificent on your curriculum vitae. As you know, there is another associate professorship coming up later this year and you would be well-placed to apply, as co-author of a report of this importance."

Nick sat quietly as Professor Andrews outlined the project to Lissy. He was polite and considerate and showed a keen interest in her previous research, asking several pertinent questions. After they had covered all of the items that the professor raised, she stood to leave.

"Thank you, Professor Andrews, that is a wonderful offer and I will give it serious thought," she said. It was a golden opportunity to advance her academic career. To be an associate professor by thirty would be amazing.

"Dr McIntyre, you have misunderstood. It is a *fait accompli*," replied Professor Andrews. "One of our new research assistants took over your project while you were on holiday. I have placed Professor Richards in the office next to yours and I expect you to start work together immediately. I am sorry if that inconveniences you." He looked over his glasses at her, not looking the least bit sorry, more confused at her reluctance to take this opportunity.

"I have also cancelled all leave for the rest of the semester as we are under funding pressure to get all of our research papers finalised by then."

Lissy looked at Nick, who was sitting there quietly and turned to Professor Andrews.

"I would be delighted to work with Professor Richards, sir. I am sure we will forge a productive partnership."

Professor Andrews indicated he had another meeting to attend and as they left his office, Nick turned to her.

"Can I see you in your office, Dr McIntyre?"

"Certainly, give me ten minutes," she said, her face expressionless, as they entered the corridor together.

***

A short time later, Nick tapped lightly on Lissy's office door, unsure of the welcome he would receive. The damn woman confused him no end. Seeing her at his family home, cosy with Tom, had given him a tight knot in his stomach.

He'd felt her sadness so strongly when they had dinner on Hamilton Island, and even though she seemed to regret their night together, he had no regrets. He'd felt like an utter louse leaving her all rosy and sweetly asleep, but the strong attraction he felt to her had frightened him and he decided he wasn't going to risk his heart again. If he'd known he was going to see her again maybe he would have stayed.

Maybe he would have run a mile.

He ran his hand through his hair, still not used to the short haircut his mother had given him last night. He had gone to the farm on his motorcycle after Lissy had closed the door on him, hoping the ride would clear his head.

"Dominic, you look like a pirate." Tessa tapped his head with the clippers. "You need to look like a professor." He'd enjoyed sitting in front of the fire as his mother cut his hair and caught him up on all the family news.

"What about Tomas, Mama? Is this a serious romance?" he asked casually. Tessa laughed.

"No, I don't think so. Remember Tomas's life plan says marriage at thirty-five and we have a couple of years to go before that. Although, I wouldn't mind. Melissa seems like a very lovely girl."

"Yeah, his list making." Nick chuckled.

"Remember the list on his bedroom wall when he was ten," said Tessa laughing.

"Seven o'clock, wake up, seven fifteen eat breakfast, seven thirty, brush my teeth," they chanted together. Tessa paused, holding the clippers aloft, looking thoughtful.

"I watched Melissa the other night and she looked sad. She was far away in her thoughts a lot of the time during dinner."

Nick bit his tongue; he didn't want any inkling of his relationship with Lissy to get to his brother. Tom had gone out with Olivia before she moved on to Nick, eventually dumping him after all and marrying a rich grazier. Obviously neither of the Richards brothers had measured up financially in those days.

He came back to the present as Lissy called him to come in. He opened the door to the office and walked inside. She sat straight-backed behind her desk and he took a moment to look around her office, noticing a couple of photos on the wall. Beach scenes with two elderly men in the foreground, in front of old fishing boats.

"Take a seat," she said primly. Before he sat, he wandered over and looked closely at the photos.

"Your grandfather and his boat?" he asked gently. He looked at her and was surprised to see the traces of tears on her cheeks. Her lipstick was gone, and she had a tight expression on her face. She nodded and pointed to the chair.

"Where shall we start, Professor? I am not at all familiar with your research."

So that's the way it was going to be. Straight to business.

Her hands were clasped tightly on the desk and he saw the effort she was making to keep her emotions hidden. He sat in the chair opposite her and leaned forward, resting his elbows on his knees as he dropped his head in his hands. Shaking his head, he asked, "How are we going to do this? What a mess."

"What do you mean? A mess?" she asked.

"Well, to be honest, you don't like me ... and I don't trust you, so how are we going to work together?"

Lissy stood up so suddenly her chair tipped over behind her and hit the floor with a crash. She strode around her desk.

"You don't trust me," she said with a strange look on her face. He looked up at her.

"Did you say, you don't trust me?" she repeated, her voice getting louder. She pushed his shoulders and he had to balance to stop the chair from tipping back.

"Let me tell you something, Mr High and Mighty Professor, Mr Spoiled and Idolised Big Brother, Mr Just Drifting around the Pacific Liar! You're the one who can't be trusted. I am sick of your 'holier than thou' attitude. You want to lay all the ground rules? Well, now I'll tell you how we'll work together. You will show me some respect, you will develop some integrity, and you will not tell me what to do with my life. Is that clear?"

He looked up at her, eyes flashing and that wonderful hair, falling from that ridiculous clip. He reached up and pulled the clip from her hair, studying her as her eyes widened. She backed away from him until she was against the door. He stood up and walked over to her, watching the wary expression on her face.

The anger died.

Aggression slid into desire.

His stance changed, and he broke eye contact to lean forward and slide his lips down her bare neck. His lips paused just below her ear and he felt her shiver.

She turned her head and he found her lips. He was not touching her with any other part of his body; his palms were braced against the door above her head. In her heels, she was almost as tall as he was, and he only had to dip his head slightly to taste her sweet lips.

Soft and willing lips opened beneath his; she closed her eyes as she gave in to him. His tongue danced with hers, and then he moved his lips to feather soft kisses across her cheeks and slide down her neck once more. He felt her trembling. He paused and placed his forehead against hers.

"Oh, God. I'm like a fourteen-year old boy around you."

"How about we go somewhere public and lay down some ground rules for work and home?" Her voice was husky.

"One more kiss," he said pulling her into him. He could not believe the effect she had on him. The hard part was, despite his inability to resist her, he knew that he couldn't trust her. He was sure she was playing head games with both he and Tom.

He pulled out of the kiss with a groan, ran his hand through his cropped hair and looked at her, feeling disgusted with his behaviour.

"Cafeteria, five minutes." He walked out and pulled the door shut firmly behind him.

Chapter Nine

It took fifteen minutes before Melissa was composed enough to go to the food court. She stood at the door of the cafeteria. Nick was sitting reading the paper, with a mug of coffee in front of him. The cafeteria was crowded and noisy and that was just how she liked it for this meeting. She went to the counter, ordered her coffee and moved across to join him at the table.

"Thank you for meeting with me, Dr McIntyre." His voice was calm, without a trace of emotion, and she nodded in return.

"What I would like to do is discuss our research and how we are going to work together. We are both mature adults and professionals and know that we have some personal issues. However, you'll agree that we must work around this to get the research report completed. You're aiming for your associate professorial promotion and I want to finish my thesis. This research is critical for both of us. Do you agree?"

She nodded. This formal Nick was easier to deal with than the man who'd just kissed her senseless in her office. Her face heated, and she swallowed, focusing on what he was saying.

"What I propose is that once we're finished at the end of semester, I'll return to the Pacific and continue my studies in the field, and we will not have to spend any more time together."

She looked at him, trying to imagine not seeing him.

"Well?" he asked. "Do you have an opinion on that?"

She certainly did. The thought of not seeing him again tore at her heartstrings, but there was no way she was going to share that with him.

"That sounds like a good plan, Professor. I also think that a lot of our collaboration can be done by email, and we shouldn't need to meet more than once a week to discuss our progress in person. Do you agree with that?"

He nodded. She drained her coffee cup, stood up, and left him to his paper and coffee.

Melissa returned to her office and decided to leave early and work from home. After she cleared her mail, emailed some files to herself and set her laptop to auto reply, she walked past Jenny's office and put her hand in the door.

"Hey, Jen. I have decided to take a half day of time in lieu, to get myself organised. I'm going to be snowed under with the new project and I need some personal time."

Jen looked at her with concern.

"Are you feeling okay? You're very flushed."

"Just a head cold coming on, back in the air conditioning always does it. I'll see you in the morning."

She took the long route home and pulled up at the lookout on the edge of town. She stood at the brass compass plate that pointed in all directions to many locations and traced her finger over the arrow that pointed east and said Coffs Harbour, 118 miles. Looking east, she saw paddocks of brown grass burned by the early frosts of winter, dotted with sheep, very different to the verdant green of the coast and even further away from the sapphire vista of the Islands that were embedded in her heart.

Not only did the pictures of the boat and islands flash through her head, but a tanned sailor with a bandana around his head, singing a silly song to her filled her thoughts. The same sailor who had taken her to places she had never been before, in an unforgettable night of passion. She stood looking towards the east for a long time. If only Gramps was still alive. She had some big life decisions to make. A solitary tear spilled over her cheek and she brushed it away. Looking around, she saw that she was alone.

Okay, girl, let it all out, and then apply some analytical methods to this problem. She put her hand down on her arms and let the tears fall.

She blew her nose, climbed back into her car, and turned the car towards home, putting in her favourite mix CD, sang along, and felt much better when she turned into the driveway. Mrs Mac was in her garden as usual, and she looked up with a worried expression on her face. She took one look at Lissy's red eyes and stood with her hands on her ample hips. She wagged her finger at her as she opened the car door.

"I knew something was wrong when that man turned up on Saturday. Then you were bunkered down in your cottage all weekend. Come on, we're going to have some lunch and a nice cup of tea, and you can tell me all about it."

Taking Melissa's hand, she led her across the driveway, through her wild cottage garden and up the steps into a warm welcoming kitchen. Soup bubbled on the old combustion stove and the smell of baking bread made her mouth water.

"Mrs Mac, you're a sweetheart," she said, pulling out a kitchen chair and sitting at the pine table in the middle of the kitchen. Her elderly landlady bustled around and made a pot of tea, covering it with a knitted tea cosy with pink tassels hanging down the sides.

She poured a cup, and handed Melissa a piece of warm bread, dripping with butter. "Soup's nearly ready."

"I'll have to go for an extra-long walk now!" Melissa said with a chuckle.

"Now," said Mrs Mac. "What were all these tears about?"

She took a sip of her tea and thought about how much to tell Mrs Mac. She had to be careful. Armidale was a small city and the Richards family were well known. She also had to think of Nick's reputation, as well as her own. On the other hand, she knew she could trust Mrs Mac. She was a kind friend who had supported her since she had moved into town two years ago, not knowing a soul. Mrs Mac sat down at the table and reached across for her hands and rubbed her fingers.

"It's okay, you don't have to tell me. I know it has to do with that man. Never trust a man on a motorbike. They were always my undoing when I was young!" Mrs Mac winked and giggled.

She smiled. "Mrs Mac, you are naughty. I know you're just saying that to make me feel better." Taking a deep breath, she outlined her dilemma in simple terms.

"I have some important decisions to make and I decided to come home and apply some of my research methodology to the problem, without interruption. I really miss Gramps. He was always my sounding board." Mrs Mac raised an eyebrow at Melissa, indicating that she understood what she really wanted was to get away from the professor for some thinking time.

"Gramps told me to follow my destiny before he died. He didn't approve of my thoughts on love and marriage."

"What do you mean?"

"Well, Mum's been married four times, and she always falls in love and says that she has found the 'one.' I was lucky when she married Greg McIntyre, because he provided such a stable background for me through my teens. But Greg was too busy working and Mum got bored, and she met Lincoln at one of her courses and divorced Greg."

She paused and took a sip of her tea.

"I stayed on at boarding school and Greg paid for me to finish my schooling and helped me with my university costs. I lost touch with him when he remarried, but I've kept his name because he was the only father I ever really had."

"So your Mum is with Lincoln now?" Mrs Mac asked.

Lissy gave a rueful sigh.

"No. Now Mum is with Lars. The new 'the one' and I'm waiting to see how long that lasts. Although Gramps reckoned he was the one this time. So you can see why I don't believe in romantic love."

Mrs Mac shook her head. "You mustn't let your mother's experiences taint your view on life and love."

"That's what Gramps always said. Now I have a lovely friend who said he was thinking about proposing to me. I like him very much, and I trust that he wouldn't let me down. I think maybe we *could* have a good life together."

She reached for another piece of bread and paused as she lathered it with butter.

"Then there's the motorbike professor—my new neighbour. We

have this explosive effect on each other; however, I don't like the man. He's untrustworthy and he has no integrity. Now I have to work with him and try to fight my attraction for him, and to top it all off, I live next door to him."

Mrs Mac shook her head. "Oh dear. You can't do an empirical analysis of this one. I would be like your Gramps and tell you not to rush into a convenient relationship just because you don't think you believe in love. You're the only one who can truly know what's best for you." A little smile played around her mouth. "But, I am the landlady and I can evict any tenant. Especially if he is hassling my *favourite* tenant."

"Oh no, Mrs Mac, you can't do that, I wouldn't expect that. I'm going to think about what Tom said…'

"Tom? Not Tom Richards who picked you up the other night? But isn't he Nick's brother. They're a lovely family … and then there was Olivia. Oh, dear girl. You poor thing. You do have some serious decisions to make, don't you?"

Melissa gently pulled her hands from Mrs Mac's tight grip and stood. The old lady bustled over to the stove, served out another bowl of soup and insisted she take it home.

"I'm a big girl now and there's an associate professorship that I really want, no matter who I have to work with. Thanks for the soup, and don't worry about me. I'll be better in no time."

And I will, she thought as she walked slowly back to her flat.

Even though she couldn't help listening for the sound of a motorbike coming up the road.

Chapter Ten

Lissy was pleased with the composure and professionalism she maintained for the rest of the week. She survived three meetings with Nick in the first week they worked together. As she became absorbed in his research, she realised there were many similarities in the viewpoints they had been exploring. In his office one day late in the week, she said, "Nick, the parallels in our research documents are remarkable. My research from the primary sources, and your first-hand research and the oral histories you've recorded in the Cook Islands, indicate almost the same pattern of Polynesian migration."

"The only place our research differs is the date of the first migration to New Zealand. The Cook Islanders are convinced that the great Maori migrations to New Zealand began from Rarotonga possibly as early as the fifth century AD. Current thought is that the starting point was Ngatangiia on the eastern side of Rarotonga. There's a gap in the fringing reef at the widest part of the island's lagoon."

Nick looked across at her. "I'm going to have to make one more trip out to record the last hereditary chief before I can finalise my report. I'd like you to come with me."

Lissy raised her head and looked directly at him, her heart thudding slow and heavy.

"Come with you?"

He put his hands up. "No hidden agenda, I promise. I'd like you to see the research happening firsthand. It'll help you write the report. I would invite whoever was working with me on the same trip, even if it wasn't you. We're professionals and we can be cool about this, can't we?"

She continued to look at him as thoughts raced through her head. She looked back down at her work. "I'd look forward to that, Professor.

I haven't done much work in the field lately."

She thought about how far they'd come this week. A common interest in the research had made them put their personal differences aside. What Nick didn't know, and never would if she had anything to do with it, was how difficult the week had been for her. How did a woman ignore a man, who could make her respond with a look, an accidental brushing of hands, or even the sound of his voice at the end of the telephone? She was even a shaking mess when she saw an email pop up from him!

The phone on Nick's desk rang and after greeting the caller briefly, he held the phone out to her.

"It's Tomas, for you," he said tersely. She raised her eyebrows, surprised at his curt tone.

"Hello, Tom," she said guardedly. Nick sat there and watched her as she spoke to his brother, his arms folded across his chest. She turned her back to him.

"Yes, I'm fine, thank you." She paused, listening to Tom. "Yes, we've been busy, it's a very tight time frame until the report is due."

She glanced over her shoulder at Nick; he was staring at her with his lips set in a straight line. She ignored him and focused on the call.

"Lunch, tomorrow, that would be great. See you at 12:30. Bye."

Gently placing the telephone on the desk in its cradle, she turned to Nick and put her hands on her hips. "What exactly is the matter with you now, Professor Richards?"

He continued to look at her without saying a word. He stood slowly and walked over to the desk and took her elbows in his hands, keeping a distance between them. It was the first time he had deliberately touched her in a week and she felt her heart rate escalate as a warm tingling shot up her arms. Pulling away from his grip, she tossed her head angrily, and the usual recalcitrant curls fell out of her clip. He reached up and tucked the stray curl behind her ear, and a shiver ran down her back as Nick's fingers brushed her neck.

"If I asked you reasonably and seriously not to see my brother, what would you say?"

"I would ask why." She turned her face away from him and closed her eyes, shutting him out before he could see past her expression of indifference. All she really wanted was to reach out and touch him. Turning back to him, she looked up into a granite-like visage.

She was wearing flat pumps today and had to lean back a little to see his eyes. As she stepped away, he reached for her again and pulled her close. Lowering his head, he moved his face so close to hers she could feel his breath on her skin.

"My brother's an easy target," he said. "He was hurt badly by his last girlfriend, and he's always had this life plan mapped out. We all tease him about it, but I know he's serious about being married and settled by thirty-five. Somehow, you've gotten into his good graces and I think he's starting to look at you with a view to marriage. I want to warn you, before he springs it on you. You need to stop leading him on, before it's too late."

Once again, Lissy could feel the slow burn of anger that Nick always seemed to light in her, starting in the pit of her stomach and working its way up to heat her cheeks. She pulled her arms from his and stepped away from him.

"And what if I was to tell you that it's too late, we've already discussed it, and I'm seriously considering it?"

His face darkened. He spoke slowly and enunciated each word clearly, locking his gaze with hers and holding her elbows firmly in a tight grip.

"I would tell you that I would stop it in any way I could... whatever it took."

"Whatever it took?" Her voice was ice-cold. "That sounds like a threat. I'm sick to death of your attitude. You treat me as though I'm a total gold-digger, with no morals and certainly no feelings. Obviously, in your mind, I'm not good enough for the hallowed Richards family." She took a deep breath and poked a finger into his chest.

"Let me remind you, *you* slept with *me* on the Islands too."

She turned away from him in disgust, letting her breath out slowly. "I've done enough work with you today. I think I'll be sick if I have to spend another moment listening to your holiness. What's it like to be perfect, Nick?"

She picked up her laptop and strode to the door. "I'm going to work in my office. I have enough to work on until next week. Please don't bother me unless it's urgent."

She opened the door and turned to him. "And if it *is* urgent, email me."

She made it back to her office before she lost her temper completely. She flicked the lock on her office door and, with shaking hands, put her little kettle on and made herself a cup of tea.

It's an improvement on the tears anyway.

She was trying to figure out why their holiday relationship had made him so bitter. She recalled the evening they'd had in the restaurant on the island, and the rapport that had developed between them. Although neither of them had been honest about their backgrounds, it had still been an enjoyable evening that had culminated in the most unforgettable night of her life.

Admit it. You would love to be with him again.

She almost dropped her teacup as she realised what had just gone through her mind.

You are falling for the man. Just like your mother, a sucker for looks and charm... although he has been a bit light in the charm department lately.

She put her teacup on the saucer, walked over to the window and looked down at the sweeping lawns of the university. It was lunchtime, and everywhere she looked, there were couples entwined on the grass and walking hand-in-hand.

*****

Nick was angry at himself. He already regretted showing his hand to Lissy and asking that she not see Tom anymore. He walked into his office and shut the door firmly, pulling his tie off and throwing it onto the desk.

He sat in his swivel chair and placed his feet on the deeply varnished desk. He hated these stints at the university and the complication of this one in particular, with Lissy's involvement doing his head in. He was much more comfortable out in the Islands in shorts and bare feet, heading out for a surf when the day's work was done.

Even my demeanour changes when I'm in this work situation. If only Tom hadn't called when I was there, I wouldn't have even brought it up.

Shaking his head, he reached over and booted up his laptop, ready to start work and hoping to get it done sooner so he could get the hell away from the university.

And a beautiful red-haired woman who had bewitched him.

Chapter Eleven

The next day Melissa met Tom for lunch. He greeted her in the foyer, reached over, and kissed her cheek, taking her hand to lead her into the restaurant where there were small intimate tables covered with white linen tablecloths. Gleaming cutlery sat on the table and a black-suited waiter was waiting to seat them.

"I've never been in here before. I usually grab a sandwich at the student union," she said looking around, taken aback by the opulence of the staff restaurant.

He smiled at her. "This is where all the high-powered decisions and finances of the university take place. Business lunches with a very good wine list. Would you like wine with your lunch?"

"No, thank you, I have a lot of work to finish this afternoon. I'd fall asleep at my desk," she said laughing.

"How are you finding working with Nick? He can be a hard taskmaster."

Melissa held back all the words that came to mind, and none were as kind as 'hard taskmaster'. She pulled out her most professional response.

"It's extremely challenging, but I'm learning so much. He has wide experience in the field."

Tom reached over and put his hand on hers.

Lissy looked down and realised that she had absolutely no reaction to his touch. No matter that he was a nice guy who was being very sweet and showing an interest in a relationship with her. She felt more reaction when she turned the hot water tap on, she thought sadly.

"You look tired." Tom looked concerned. "I hope you haven't been losing sleep over what I said the other night. I still think it's not a bad idea."

She looked across the table at him. His white shirt and subtle tie complemented his dark blue suit. His hair was immaculate and his grooming impeccable.

"We're friends, Tom. Let's keep it that way," she said gently.

As she spoke, Nick's strong face intruded on her thoughts, and she pushed him out of her mind. The fact that he had asked her to stop seeing his brother wasn't the reason she was refusing to consider Tom's 'proposition'.

His face fell. "I knew you were going to say that. While I am thinking of it, I will have to cancel Friday night this week. A small family occasion has come up."

She nodded at him.

"Not a problem. I've been invited to Clare's thirtieth birthday dinner on Friday night, so that works out well."

He looked relieved and passed her the menu. "However, my mother did ask me to invite you to a barbeque on Saturday afternoon at the farm, if you're free."

Well, that would be one way to annoy Nick, she thought.

"That would be great," she said. "I'm free on Saturday. Is there anything I can bring?"

"No, just yourself. I'll pick you up at about one."

After they finished lunch, Tom insisted on walking her back to her office, even though he was located at the other side of the university in the main administration building. As they walked along the corridor of the history faculty, they heard laughter coming from the staff room. An attractive blonde woman came out of the room, saying over her shoulder, "Professor Richards, you're incorrigible."

Tom rolled his eyes. "Looks like my brother is up to his old tricks with the ladies," he groaned.

Nick was at the door when they passed and looked pointedly at Tom holding Melissa's arm.

Lissy shivered at the angry look he directed at her as she walked past him.

***

Oddly enough, as the days passed, Nick helped Lissy in her resolve to have as little to do with him as possible. He flew to Sydney twice for meetings and had one overnight visit to Brisbane. He rarely entered her office and only attended a couple of the faculty meetings. He was charming and polite and might as well have been a chance acquaintance. She managed to sit at the other end of the conference table and focus on her laptop on the occasions that he spoke to the faculty.

Contact between them was mostly by email. Nick would send her an area of research that he required her to verify, and she would email the results of her inquiries back to him. As the week drew to a close and he wasn't required for lectures, he worked from home and she didn't even see him at the university.

But it wasn't as easy as she had anticipated to push Nick from her thoughts. She could hear every move he made in the cottage next door and there were times when her resolve was threatened. She heard his shower running, she knew when he had the television on, and she could hear his telephone ring. She felt as though they were living in the same house. She dreamed about him regularly and woke aching, unfulfilled.

Jenny had offered to pick Lissy up at her place and drive her to Ivy Cottage for Clare's birthday party, and Lissy gladly accepted the offer. She was looking forward to going out to the restaurant with the girls, having a few drinks and forgetting about Nick Richards for one night.

"Wow, look at you! I nearly didn't recognise you. You should wear your hair down more often. You look fantastic!" Jenny said when she laid eyes on Lissy.

She had settled on a brightly patterned skirt that brushed her ankles and a figure-hugging red body suit with a deep-scooped neck. The shell necklace Gramps had given her for her last birthday highlighted a hint of cleavage. She put some mousse in her hair and scrunched her curls, and heavy dangling earrings completed the gypsy look.

"The only downside of being pregnant," Jenny said with a sigh, "is I can't have a drink with the girls tonight."

When they entered Ivy Cottage, they heard a scream of delight as Clare spotted them in the foyer. She came running over with a glass of champagne sloshing in her hand.

"Well, looks like the party has started," said Jenny, leaning over and giving Clare a birthday kiss, narrowly avoiding champagne spilling down her back as Clare returned the hug one-armed.

"Happy Birthday, Clare." Lissy gave her friend a hug before they made their way over to a table, where about twenty of Clare's friends were already seated. Clare made Lissy and Jenny stand up at the end of the table while she introduced them to the other girls. There were a dozen of her friends from school, and others up from Sydney. Clare sounded as though she had already downed a few birthday drinks.

"Ladies, ladies, listen up. These—" she paused and put an arm around Melissa and Jenny, "—are my two very best work friends in the whole, wide world. This is Jenny, and this is Lissy." A chorus of greetings came from the group as Lissy and Jenny sat on the last two vacant chairs.

Lissy looked around the restaurant and was pleased to see only a couple of other tables with customers who were almost finished with their meals. She had a feeling this was going to be a loud and noisy party, quite different from the usually formal Friday night atmosphere at Ivy Cottage. A loud pop signalled the opening of the next bottle of champagne and she took a sip from the glass that was handed to her.

"Happy birthday, Clare," the girls said in a toast, holding up their glasses.

Melissa sat at the side of the table against the wall, and the girl on her left started up a conversation. Within five minutes, she had heard all about the girl's job, her family, and her two broken relationships and how horrible all men were. She didn't get a chance to get a word in and smiled gratefully when Jenny interrupted and rescued her. The waitress came out with menus and the table quietened as the girls discussed what they were going to order.

All of a sudden, Clare hissed across the table at Jenny and Lissy. "Sssh, sssh. Girls, girls, quick." She was gesturing madly at the door behind them and her whisper was loud enough to be heard by all of the diners in the room.

"It's Johnny Depp," she whispered urgently, pretending to swoon.

Melissa's stomach took a dive to her toes. Refusing to turn around, she waited until the group walked past the table of girls and were seated in the opposite corner of the room. Looking up slowly, she met Nick's sardonic gaze and to her absolute horror, she realised that Nick, Tom, and two very attractive women were seated at the table. From a distance, she heard Clare's voice.

"Earth to Melissa, earth to Melissa." She looked up and saw the waitress standing next to her, pen poised waiting to take her order.

"Oh, sorry." She grabbed the menu in front of her and read out the first thing she saw.

"I'll have the chicken, please."

"Salad and chips, or vegetables?" asked the waitress.

"Ah...salad, please." Her hands were shaking, her heart thudding. She picked up her champagne and drained the glass in one gulp.

Not only was Nick flaunting his next conquest in public, but dependable, honest Tom had a woman with him as well.

"Lissy, are you feeling okay? You're really flushed," said Jenny.

She pulled herself together and plastered a smile on her face. "No, I'm fine. I just need another drink." Grabbing the champagne bottle out of the ice bucket, she filled her glass and tipped her head back and drained the glass in one go.

Clare burst out laughing. "Go, Melissa! This is going to be a great party."

The noise level in the restaurant increased as three more tables filled with customers. Luckily for Melissa, the lights were dim, the girls' table was in a corner, and she could avoid looking at the group of four across the room. On the odd occasion that she glanced over there, Nick was watching her with a tight expression on his face.

Damn him, she thought, and threw back another glass of champagne.

Their group got louder and more raucous as the drinks flowed. Melissa was not used to being out with a group of women determined to let their hair down. Her social life during university had been limited because she had studied hard, determined to succeed.

After a couple more drinks, she stood and announced loudly to the group that she was going to the ladies room and invited all of them to join her. Clare elbowed Jen and said with a giggle, "You'd better go with her, Jen, and make sure she comes back."

As they passed the Richards' table on their way to the restroom, Lissy was pleased to see the shock on Tom's face when he looked up and saw her sashaying past. She waggled her fingers at them.

"Hi, Tom. Hi, Nicky. Hi, lucky ladies with Tom and Nicky" A giggly champagne--fuelled hiccough escaped her lips and Jenny dragged her into the rest room.

"Melissa!" exclaimed Jenny. "The professor is a hunk. Tell me all...you called him by his first name. Have you been out with him or do you just know him from work?"

"Nuh, juss from work", slurred Lissy. "He's a nightmare to work with, very full of himself...not very nice at all."

"What about Tom? Are you still going out with him?"

"Nuh," said Melissa "Thought he was different, but they are tarred with the same hairbrush."

Jenny burst out laughing. "Oh, you are so funny with a few drinks under your belt. You mean brush, not hairbrush!"

She tried to be serious for a minute and had to hang on tightly to the basin to keep her balance. She squinted into the mirror and frowned; her curls were out of control.

"Woo...a bit giddy," she announced. "And I'm hungry."

Jenny pulled a chair over and sat her down in front of the mirror. "Okay, let's fix you up a bit." She stood behind Lissy and tried to tame her curls down with her hand. "Speaking of hairbrushes, did you bring yours, hon?"

Lissy fumbled in her bag and tipped it out onto the bench. The contents of the bag rolled around and fell over the edge, just as the two glamorous women who were with Tom and Nick entered the restroom. She dived to the floor to catch lipstick, brushes, keys, and coins as they hit the floor.

"Oh, hello," she said looking up from where she was crouched on the tiles. "Your legs match the rest of you."

The two women laughed and moved into the cubicles.

"Come on," Jenny said. "Our meals will be there soon."

She helped Lissy pick up the contents of her bag, straighten her hair and lipstick, and they headed back into the restaurant after visiting the cubicle.

"Oh, no you don't," said Jenny as Lissy spotted the two empty chairs at the Richards' table and dragged Jenny over. She plonked herself down next to Tom, whose eyes were like saucers.

Nick sat back and folded his arms, looking at them with interest.

"Hi, boys. I would like you to meet my very best friend, Jenny. It's her birthday and she would love a birthday kiss." Another hiccough escaped her red-painted lips and she giggled.

"Hap...happy birthday, Jenny. Nice to meet you," said Tom.

Nick continued to sit and look without speaking, but Melissa caught his eye. She leaned over and said, "Nicky darling, why do you look like the cat that got the cream?"

He shrugged. "I wasn't aware that I did."

Melissa leaned closer; she was sure there was a hint of a smile on those gorgeous lips.

"No." She shook her head and muttered. "Not gorgeous. Not at all"

"Thank you, Tom, but it's actually Clare's birthday," Jenny said.

"Come on, Lissy, our meals will be there. See you later."

She grabbed Melissa and pulled her to her feet.

"Come on, we'll leave this pair to their floozies," Melissa said.

Jenny looked mortified and whispered behind her hand to Nick and Tom.

"Sorry, guys. Melissa's had a bit too much champagne."

Jenny dragged her across the restaurant to their table and sat her down next to Clare so that her back was to the Richards' table. She had a whispered conversation with Clare who turned to Lissy and started up a conversation with her.

"So, tell us about your holiday."

Melissa's laugh was shrill, and heads turned at some of the tables close by.

"Ooh..." she giggled. "I had the best time. I went on a yacht and I met a gorgeous man and we..." She was sober enough to think before she continued. "And we became very, very good friends. She paused for a moment. "But now I am home in the cold weather and back at work and the man is horrible."

She stopped and put her head down as the table wavered in front of her. Their meals arrived and she decided she had better eat something. Picking up her knife and fork, she tried to concentrate on her meal, which seemed to be moving from left to right. As she speared a chip, it shot over the table.

Jen leaned over and laughed. "Let me be mum. I'll cut it up for you."

"Nuh. It's easier if I have champagne for dinner." She picked up her glass and swallowed the rest of her drink on one hit.

After a couple of hours of laughter, conversation, and several more bottles of champagne, Clare decided it was time to go dancing. The other girls had drunk champagne all night and Lissy's out-of-character behaviour didn't stand out too much.

"Who's up for the nightclub?" asked Clare, as they stood in the foyer paying the bill.

The Seven Brothers dance club was around the corner on the next street. Jenny looked tired. "No, but thanks. I think I'm done," she said, as she patted her baby bulge. "Lissy, do you want a ride home now or will you catch a taxi?"

There was movement behind them; Nick was standing in the foyer next to them.

"It's okay, Jenny. I'll take Melissa home. We live close to each other," he said.

Lissy looked up at him and giggled.

"But, Nick, that's not in the rules anywhere, is it? And I want to go dancing."

He shrugged. "I can wait."

"But what about your guests?" Jenny asked.

"Not a problem. Tom will drive the girls back to the farm."

Lissy was faintly aware that there was something bothering her but couldn't put her finger on it. She looked up at him, squinting, trying to figure it out.

"Okay, come on. Nick, you're welcome to come dancing with us," Clare said.

Nick followed them down the steps. As soon as the fresh air hit her, Lissy's head started to swim and her knees buckled.

"Woo..." she said, clutching for the railing.

Strong arms reached beneath her legs as Nick swept her up. The girls were halfway along the street and turned to see if she was all right.

"It's okay, ladies. Melissa has decided she wants to go home now." Nick reassured them. She squinted again, looking up at him, trying to figure out who he was and what he was doing, but it was all too hard.

"Night, girls," she muttered putting her head on the lovely warm, soft shoulder that was beneath her head. She recognised the familiar smell of spicy aftershave and snuggled in closer. She was vaguely aware of being bundled into a cold car and having her skirt tucked in around her.

She slipped into the realms of a very drunken sleep.

Chapter Twelve

The screeching birds outside the window woke Melissa at dawn. Opening one eye, she tried to ignore the little hammers that were tapping in her head. Her mouth was so dry it felt as though her tongue was sticking to its roof. Looking around, she recognised her room and squinted, trying to figure out why it was facing the wrong way—the window was in the wrong place and the door was facing east. The colours were right, but her furniture was gone. It was like a parallel universe. The bed moved, and she reached out her hand to stop the head spin and pulled her hand back as she unexpectedly encountered a warm, bare chest.

She opened her other eye and grimaced as the bright morning sun streaming in the window bathed the tanned body next to her in sunlight. Nick was flat on his back, a sheet covering him from the waist down. She closed her eyes, hoping it was a hallucination caused by her hangover. Opening her eyes again, she looked down at herself and groaned–she was wearing an unfamiliar shirt and her underwear. Sexy, red lace underwear that she had put on under her gypsy skirt last night. She groaned again and tried to sit up but fell back to the pillow as the room began to spin. The bed shook as Nick's deep laugh made her head ache even more.

"What are you doing in my bed?" she croaked. Her voice sounded like dry sandpaper rasping on a board.

"No, what are you doing in my bed?" Awareness dawned as she looked around.

"Oh, God," she groaned, "what have you done?"

She sat up, clutching the shirt across her breasts and tried to swing her legs over the side of the bed. His shoulders shook with laughter. She could not hold her head, keep her balance and clutch his shirt together at the same time.

"Lissy," he laughed. "I haven't done anything. You did it all by yourself."

She managed to sit up and leaned back against the pillows, both hands over her eyes.

"How did I get home?"

"I carried you."

"What, from the restaurant?"

"No, to my car. Unfortunately, you were sick on the way home and when you couldn't find your key, it was easier to bring you in here, rather than wake Mrs Mac up for the spare key."

She moaned again through her hands, unsure if it was the distress of finding herself in his bed, or the hangover causing it. "Let me die, now."

"Would you like a cup of tea, Lissy?" He'd managed to contain his laughter, but now he was grinning down at her. She felt so ill, she couldn't even appreciate the bare chest in her vision. The way she was feeling, she didn't think she'd ever appreciate anything again.

"Yes, please, and aspirin," she said, rolling over, pulling the sheet up over her head, and promptly went back to sleep.

##

Melissa woke up the second time to an empty cottage, and a cold cup of tea on the bedside table. She sat up and gulped down the aspirin Nick had left her. Lying back down, she thought about the night before, and dread washed over her as she remembered some of the evening.

A family function indeed. She thought about the two stunning women who had been with Nick and Tom last night. With black cascading curls down their backs and dressed in elegant clothes, they both could have been models. Something Nick had said last night tugged at her memory, but she couldn't hold on to the thought as her head spun.

As the thoughts ran through her aching head, she put both hands over her face and groaned.

Nature called, and she swung her legs over the side of the bed. At least Nick had had the decency to leave her alone in his bed. When she stood, the room spun; she squinted at the bedside clock and was shocked to see it was after noon. She stumbled into Nick's bathroom and tripped over her skirt and top on the floor. She almost passed out with embarrassment. There was no way she could ever look him in the eye again.

Let alone work with the man.

But you have to, reminded her ambitious side, *if you want that associate professorship.*

She looked into the mirror in his bathroom and sighed. Her mascara had run down one cheek, surrounded by the worst case of bed hair she had ever seen. The other cheek was a map of pillow wrinkles and she hoped Nick hadn't looked too closely when he had left her the tea and the aspirin. Scrubbing her face and loosely tying back her hair, Melissa repaired the damage as best she could. Gathering her clothes from the floor, she turned her nose up at the smell of vomit. The next problem was finding her keys and getting into her side of the cottage without being seen. She sat down on the bed and pulled her cell phone out of her bag. At least that was still there. She dialled Mrs Mac's number. It was going to be difficult explaining why she needed the spare key. The phone rang, but there wasn't an answer. She felt relieved; no explanations needed as to why she was semi-naked in Nick's cottage without her key.

She had no idea where Nick had gone or how long he would be. She had to get out of here, and into her own flat before he got back. Looking around, she spotted her shoes underneath the table. Gathering her clothes, shoes and bag under one arm, she crept over to the door.

If I go around the back, I can get into the laundry window.

Lissy looked down to make sure she was decent, and decided that the long, white shirt covered enough. Opening the front door, she stepped out and peered around the corner. Nick's car was in the driveway, but there was no sign of him. She pulled the front door shut behind her and then groaned; she shouldn't have, in case she couldn't get in her window. She tiptoed around the veranda, keeping an eye out for neighbours, but there was not a soul in sight. The veranda tiles were cold under her bare feet and she walked around the corner towards her back door. As she crept around to the back of the house, she was horrified to hear another car pull up in the driveway. Doors slammed, and she looked around in vain, knowing there was nowhere to hide on her porch. Footsteps crunched on the gravel around the side of the house, and she prayed for the ground to open up as not only Nick, but Tom, walked around to the back steps.

"Melissa, I er...I'm here to pick you up for the barbeque," Tom said.

She looked angrily from one to the other. Nick held up a shopping bag. "I was walking back from the shops, and Tom stopped and picked me up. Chips and coke... good hangover food." He had a smug grin on his face.

Tom looked from one to the other in confusion, and then his face changed as he realised she was wearing Nick's shirt and not a lot under it.

"Lissy?" He turned to his brother, confusion written all over his face. "Nick?"

Melissa snapped back. "It isn't what it looks like. Anyway, who were those women *you* were out with last night?"

"They were family," Nick said. "Mama asked Tom and me to take two cousins visiting from Italy out for dinner since she and Dad had a function to attend. Isabella and Talia were most amused that some little hussy thought we were their boyfriends."

She looked at him open-mouthed. "You set this whole thing up, didn't you?"

"Set what up?" Tom asked again, stepping forward.

"Help me get into my cottage please," she said stonily. "Nick can explain it all to you later. The laundry window should be open. If you push it right up, you should be able to climb in, Nick, and open the door for me."

She sat down on the chair at her back door and folded her arms. Tom looked at her with a strange look on his face but didn't speak. Nick handed her the bag of groceries as he strolled past. He pushed up the laundry window with some difficulty and climbed through the small space. Tom still looked as though he was in shock. She obviously wasn't in contention for wife of the future anymore. *Good.* At least Tom could forget about his stupid idea.

"Am I right in thinking that you're not coming out to the farm for lunch?" asked Tom.

She responded by crossing her arms tightly and trying to look dignified—as dignified as one could look in a man's shirt, with bed hair and bare feet.

"No, thank you, Tom. I will not be coming to lunch. Please thank your mother though."

"Right then," he said, pulling himself together. "I'll call you later." He looked so confused, for a moment she felt sorry for him, but she was feeling too sick and frustrated to explain everything to him.

Nick can do it later.

Tom disappeared down the stairs and his car started up and went down the driveway.

Her back door opened, and Nick came out and stood in front of her. He held out his hand to help her up. Ignoring it, she leaned down and picked up her clothes and shoes from the floor, leaving the bag of groceries behind. She stood up and walked into her cottage.

"Thank you for bringing me home safely last night and thank you for the bed and the aspirin." She turned to close the door but looked down as a large booted foot stopped it from closing.

***

"Wait. You and I have some talking to do." Nick pushed his way past her, groceries in hand and the door behind him. He went over to the table and pulled out a chair and sat down, leaning back in the chair, his

90

boots crossed casually in front of him. He looked settled in for a long chat.

Melissa dropped her clothes and shoes and groaned with her hands over her face. "Why has my life turned upside down since I met you.?" She looked down at him, shaking her head, and then put a hand to her forehead.

"Headache, still?" Nick pushed the chair back and rose to his feet, her distress tugging at him. He had deliberately taken their cousins to Ivy Cottage last night, knowing that Lissy would be at the birthday party. It had been the talk of the faculty staff room the whole week. He had hoped that she would see Tom with the girls and think the worst. His plan had worked, but he couldn't understand why he felt so bad about it this morning. He shouldn't care about her being upset.

The sight of Lissy in his shirt, legs barely covered by the shirttail, hands over her face, was the last straw. He'd watched her sleep in the early hours this morning, before she had woken up the first time, and the feelings that had settled in his chest were unfamiliar. He couldn't resist her. He was going crazy thinking about her.

Reaching out, he held her shoulders gently.

"What do you think you're doing?" she asked, but there was a tremor in her voice. He took her hands in his and raised one to his mouth, running his lips over the inside of her palm, as he looked down into her eyes. She closed her eyes and swayed, and he reached out and caught her before she fell.

"You're going to be the death of me. God help me, this is all I think about."

He slipped his hands up beneath her shirt, brushing his fingers against her warm skin. She leaned into him, as he placed his hands on her back. He rested his head on top of hers and took comfort from the warmth of her body leaning into his.

"I need a shower and I need to brush my teeth."

Her vulnerability brought that unfamiliar feeling back. Nick lifted her and carried her into the bathroom. Lowering her gently onto the tiled floor, he turned on the shower taps and hot steam billowed out of the shower recess. She rested her forehead against his shoulder. "Thank you. I'll be fine now."

"I'll wait in the bedroom." Nick closed the bathroom door and sat on the bed. He stared at the door, wishing he had stayed in there with her, but it wasn't the right thing to do.

For more than one reason. Not just because she was hung over. His response to Lissy confused him, and he didn't think rationally when he was around her. He sat there brooding for a few minutes, and then looked up when the door opened. Her cheeks had colour in them again, and she had a towel wrapped around her.

"Can you pass my robe please?" Her voice was soft as she stood in the bathroom doorway, one hand against her forehead. Nick stared at her as the unfamiliar feeling intensified. What he wanted most was to make her smile again. Emotion clogged his throat. All of a sudden he wasn't sure whether he could survive this.

"Where is it?" He stood and cleared his throat.

"On the hook on the back of the door."

Walking over to the door, he reached up and lifted the white towelling robe from the hook. The next time she emerged from the bathroom, the robe wrapped tightly around her, her damp hair was combed and pulled back into a clip. Her eyes were shadowed and again, her vulnerability hit him like a sixer.

For the life of him he couldn't help himself.

He moved across to place a gentle kiss on the dark shadows under her eyes. "Late nights don't agree with you," he said softly.

"It's you who doesn't agree with me," she murmured as she leaned into him. "Nick?"

"Yes?" He feathered another kiss across her cheek.

"Why did you set me up last night?"

Nick stepped back and shook his head. "I think you need to get some sleep now. We'll talk about it when you're feeling more human. In fact, we need to talk about a few things."

Chapter Thirteen

Lissy slept the afternoon away and woke after the sun had set. She stretched, and for a moment, she smiled and thought how good she felt, considering the amount she had drunk the night before. The memory of the afternoon slammed into her. She rolled over and groaned, pulling the pillow over her head. She lay there quietly and became aware of the noises coming from the other side of the cottage. Nick was still home and obviously hadn't gone to the barbeque at the farm. She groaned as she thought of the mistake she had made assuming Nick's cousins were their dates, and when she remembered the look on Tom's face that afternoon, she wondered if she would ever be able to face him again.

I need to talk to Nick and find out exactly what he was trying to achieve last night. If I'm going to do it, I'm going to do it now.

She climbed out of bed, had a quick shower to warm up, dressed in tights and a jumper, and ran a brush through her unruly curls. She brushed her teeth, humming to herself. This sexual tension with Nick had finally come to a head, and they would have to sort something out. It didn't have to be a lifelong relationship; maybe they could just see each other for a while, enjoy each other's company and move on. She opened the door to the veranda and Luney shot between her legs, meowing for her dinner.

"Oh, Luney, I'm so sorry. I forgot all about you. You must be starving." She tipped out some food into the dish, closed the door and walked outside. Tapping lightly on Nick's door, she stood, waiting for him to open the door. It seemed to take forever. She heard him moving around the room and knocked a second time. Finally, the door opened, and he looked down at her. His face was impassive, and her stomach dropped.

"You'd better come in."

Oh my God, here we go again. He's so bloody moody. She followed him into his living room.

"Sit down. Would you like a cup of tea, or a drink...?" A ghost of a smile crossed his lips.

"A cup of tea is fine," she said. She sat down at the dining table; he went into the kitchen and filled the kettle. He stayed in the kitchen until it boiled, and she heard him clinking about with the teacups. He placed a neatly set tray with tea, milk and sugar on the table in front of her. Sitting down opposite her, he poured her tea silently. She began to feel anxious, the easy mood that had been there this afternoon had gone. Her confidence was fast disappearing.

Nick sat back and looked at her. "What can I do for you?"

She dug deep for a strength that she did not feel. "I came in to thank you for bringing me home last night and looking after me, and to let you know I'm fully recovered now. I'm going into work tomorrow to catch up, so I won't be around if you're looking for me."

She was babbling, her hands were tingling, her heart thudding and her stomach churning with the rejection she could sense from him, but she was determined not to let him see how upset she was. She drained her tea, smiled brightly at him, and lied.

"Poor Luney is waiting for her tea, so I'll catch you later in the week." Standing, she held her hand out to him. "Friends?"

He slowly took her hand and looked up at her.

"Yes, friends," he replied.

With a smile fixed on her face, her jaw aching from holding it there, she walked to the door and let herself out with a wave over her shoulder.

"See you Monday, maybe."

She just made it to her door and let herself into her side of the house, before she bent double, the intensity of his rejection hitting her like a physical blow. She sat in her soft lounge chair, arms wrapped around her stomach, and rocked backward and forward.

She wasn't good enough for him.

The hurt went too deep. Luney jumped on the chair, sensing her distress and rubbed Lissy's cheek. She reached down to the floor, pulling the blanket that had fallen up over her and the cat and closed her eyes, willing sleep to take her into oblivion.

She spent the rest of the weekend hiding in her cottage. She was as quiet as a mouse, so Nick would think she had gone out. She could not cope with any questions from Mrs Mac and she certainly didn't want to see Nick.

Skulking around in my own home, like a prisoner.

The phone rang late on Sunday night. She had pulled on her fluffy flannel pyjamas and sheepskin boots for comfort, and was sitting in front of the fire trying to read some notes in preparation for the following day at work. The delay before the beeps indicated an international call, and shortly after the tone, she heard her mother's voice.

"Hey, darling, just ringing to touch base. I haven't had an email from you for a few days."

"Sorry, Mum, I've been busy at work, and then I went out with the girls on Friday night and I've spent most of the weekend recovering."

"A big night?" Her mother's voice was playful.

"Yes, most out of character as you know, but a very big night for me. Never again. I still feel tired...I drank way too much champagne."

"Lissy...?"

Here we go, thought Lissy, *the end of Lars. I've been waiting for it.*

She propped her chin in her hand and waited for the news. "Yes, Mum?"

"Lars and I will be arriving in two weeks, a little bit earlier than we planned." Lissy sat up, surprised by the news.

"I know you're busy at work, but would you be able to get away to meet us at the coast?"

"Absolutely. I wouldn't miss it for the world. I'm so looking forward to finally meeting Lars. I can't get leave but I could come down on the Friday night and stay for the weekend. How long are you staying?"

"How about we meet you at Gramps's place and then come back to Armidale with you, so we can have some time with you after you finish work? If you have room for us, I can cook, and Lars can keep the fire going. He's very good at that." Her mother laughed. "And I don't just mean a wood fire. He's a wonderful man. I can't wait for you to meet him."

"That sounds great. It'll be so good to see you. I'm going down to the coast next weekend, so I'll get some supplies in and air out Gramps's cottage."

Her mother hung up after extracting a promise from Lissy to take care of herself and not go drinking again.

##

By Monday morning, Lissy had shed the hangover and accepted that any chance of a relationship with Nick was not going to happen. She puttered around, getting ready for work. The cottage sparkled, the ironing was done for the week, and she'd cooked dinners ahead and placed them in the freezer.

Still feeling embarrassed, she hoped Nick had not sensed the real reason that she'd gone knocking on his door on Saturday afternoon. She tried to hold on to her anger, but she felt quite sad.

He's impossible to understand.

She groaned as she remembered the look on Tom's face when he had seen her come out of Nick's door, obviously fresh from Nick's bed. She was determined to phone him from her office on Monday and explain that it wasn't what it looked like, not that she owed Tom anything, but they had been friends, and Nick was his brother.

She stood in front of the mirror, putting on her makeup and pinning up her hair.

I hate the way Nick makes me feel.

No, you don't, said the truthful part of her heart. *He makes you feel alive and you love it.*

She paused, mascara wand halfway to the wide eyes staring back at her from the mirror.

Where the hell did that come from?

She was not going to listen to her heart. After the weekend, she realised that she needed to get out of this mess. In a way, she was grateful to him for his clear rejection. Better now than later, when she'd gotten used to having him around. God knows, she had seen the effect of that on her mother over the years.

Lissy finished applying her makeup, all trace of hangovers, tiredness and tears camouflaged. Nodding at her calm reflection, she moved to her bedroom and chose her red suit and highest heels for confidence and headed off to work.

***

"Woohoo, here's Dr McIntyre, life and soul of the party." Lissy was greeted by giggles from her work colleagues as she walked tough the main office. She'd forgotten about Clare and Jenny, as she had worried all weekend about Nick and Tom.

"Don't know about life and soul, but the headache was a beauty," she said laughing with them, not letting any hint of her true feelings slip.

I could win an Oscar, she thought to herself. It was like being two different people—the happy carefree woman chatting to her friends, with a sad and tightly curled up emotional wreck hidden deep inside.

"Did Professor Richards get you home safely?" Jenny asked.

"Yes, he was very nice. Got me home safely," she said, lying. "I slept most of the weekend away. Nothing like a good night out with the girls to clear the cobwebs."

"Are these yours, Melissa? They found them in the ladies room." Clare held up a set of keys.

"Yes, what a relief," said Lissy. "I was worried they'd been stolen."

"How did you get in on Friday night?" asked Jenny.

"Um, through the window." The vision of Nick climbing through the window, with Tom looking like his world had come to an end as she stood there in Nick's shirt, popped into her head.

"Anyway, girls, I have a ton of work today, so I'll catch you later," she said as she turned towards her office. She entered the room and shut the door firmly, preparing to bunker down. The morning passed uneventfully and there was no sign of Nick.

She called Tom as soon as she sat at her desk. He answered his telephone across the other side of the campus in his usual calm and polite manner.

"Tom, it's Melissa."

"Good morning, Melissa." Tom's voice was guarded.

"I owe you an apology. I was very rude to you and your cousins Friday night."

Tom accepted her apology and said he'd made her excuses at Saturday's lunch. He cleared his throat as she said good-bye to him.

"Err...just one more thing, Melissa."

She held the telephone to her ear, looking out at the clear winter sky through her window, wondering what was coming.

"Yes?"

"Melissa, I think it would be best if we don't have dinner this Friday evening." He said quietly. "I'm not sure what's happening with you and Nick..."

"Nick and I, we're not an item."

He sounded sceptical. "Be warned, while I love Nick dearly as my brother, I am aware he can be hard on women. He has never forgotten how badly Olivia, and then Rebecca, hurt him."

"Tom, I have to go now." She didn't want to hear about Nick's love life.

"Just be careful with Nick, Melissa. He knew you were going to be at Ivy Cottage on Friday night and he insisted we go there. We'd planned on staying at home. He's up to something. I know Nick well and I'd hate to see you get hurt."

She put the phone down carefully, determined not to let thoughts of any scheme of Nick's interfere with her hard-won calm or her work. Booting up her computer, she tried to immerse herself in her work and forget about Nick Richards.

Lissy spent the week in her office, typing up her research and annotating her web references. She survived on cups of coffee and didn't leave her office during the day for the whole week except for the faculty meeting on Thursday. To her great relief, Nick was at a teleconference in another room and the meeting finished before she could attend. She also managed to stagger her work hours, leaving and arriving so that she didn't see Mrs Mac or Nick. She was feeling so brittle she thought she would snap if anyone tried to have a conversation with her. Sleepless nights and dreams of Nick in her bed contributed to her edginess.

Chapter Fourteen

The week dragged, and it was with a great sense of relief that Lissy turned eastward out of Armidale after work on Friday afternoon. She was headed for Gramps's house on the coast, where she would meet up with Mum and Lars next weekend. When she deposited Luney and Sylvester with her neighbour, Mrs Mac's brow furrowed.

"I've hardly seen you this week. You've been working too hard," she said. "And you look tired...*and* you've lost weight. Are you eating enough?"

"It's okay, Mrs Mac, work is really busy. That's why I'm taking a break down at the coast this weekend. Catch a bit of sun and warm up." She reached over and hugged her friend. "You really are a sweetie to help with this pair." She handed over the cage, but Mrs Mac persisted.

"Is that professor still giving you a hard time? I've hardly seen him around either."

"Just at work," said Lissy. "We have a deadline looming." Mrs Mac still looked sceptical as Lissy backed out of the driveway.

She always enjoyed the drive from Armidale down to the coast. The road wound past the green pastures of the huge cattle properties on the fertile plateau for the first hundred miles, before it meandered through the quaint village of Dorrigo, perched on the edge of the escarpment. A flashing sign at the top of the mountain road advised the roadway would be closed for repair at night from Friday evening through to Sunday.

The drive down from the top of the mountain to the coast through the World Heritage rainforest always made Lissy nervous as the narrow, winding road passed two waterfalls that often crossed the roadway in heavy rain. Crews were constantly repairing the road as the mountain was unstable and there were frequent rock falls. Although the scenery was breathtaking, she breathed a sigh of relief as she reached the bottom of the mountain and turned on to the flat land of the Bellinger River valley.

An hour later, she turned into the driveway of Gramps's fishing cottage behind the dunes of Blackrock Beach. The afternoon light had faded, and the headlights lit the front of the old cottage. The grass was long, and newspapers littered the front porch. Removing the key from under the big rock in the unkempt garden, Lissy squealed when a sticky spider web clung to her face as she crossed the porch. Her footsteps echoed on the wooden floorboards of the front hall and she swallowed a sob, her throat aching, when she saw Gramps's raincoat hanging on the hook inside the front door. The house was silent and cold, and she looked at the mess scattered throughout the small space. Piles of newspapers covered the table and chairs, and boxes of old fishing gear lined the bench along the wall.

Next weekend, when Mum is here…this weekend is to recharge my emotional batteries, not cry over Gramps's belongings. It was late, and she was tired, so after a quick sandwich and a wash, she went to bed in her old room. The gentle lull of the waves breaking on the sand lulled her off to the deepest sleep she'd had all week.

The screeching of the rainbow lorikeets woke her the next morning. Lying in bed, Lissy—she always felt like Lissy, not Melissa, when she was at Gramps's place—watched the birds hang upside down in the huge bottlebrush tree outside her window as they ate the honey from the red flowers. Their squawking contrasted with the muted roar of the ocean coming over the dunes. Stretching, she stepped out of bed feeling more at ease than she had for weeks. This was her true home, and the familiar sights, smells and sounds soothed her.

She pulled on a pair of shorts and a T-shirt, appreciating the warmth of the coast. Even though it was winter, the warmth from the ocean kept the temperature mild all year. Putting some money in her back pocket for breakfast at the cafe on her way home, she headed off for a walk along the beach. Lissy waved at a few familiar faces as she walked to the boat ramp. Recognizing Harvey's battered four-wheel drive and rusted trailer, she realised he was still out fishing for the morning. Crossing the esplanade, she headed up the hill and walked onto the veranda of the coffee shop on the headland overlooking the beach. She would sit with a coffee and paper and wait for the fishing boats to come in.

"Hey, Kevin," she said greeting the owner of the coffee shop.

"Hi, Lissy, long time since we've seen you. How's life up on the tablelands?"

"Pretty good, thanks. How's business?"

"Tourists have been steady and fishing's good. Have you caught up with old Harve yet?"

Shaking her head, Lissy ordered her coffee and gazed out over the ocean. She saw a couple of fishing boats in the southern bay and she tried to concentrate on them rather than the thoughts that were crowding her head. She had blocked them all week and had concentrated on her research. She would love to share this view with Nick. With her chin propped on her hand, she gazed out over the ocean, wondering how it would feel if he were here sharing breakfast with her.

Pushing that thought from her mind, she realised she needed to sort out the situation in her head—and heart—before she went back up the mountain to her life in Armidale. She was so sorry that Tom had got caught up in the middle of her affairs with Nick, but it couldn't be helped. He clearly knew something was going on. She sighed as she tried to analyse her feelings for Nick.

For the life of her, she could not read him. One minute, she was sure that he cared for her and showed how kind and thoughtful he could be. The next moment, he was cold as ice and treated her with contempt. She compared the happy-go-lucky guy of the islands with the cold and unreachable professor at the university. Unless he was in her bed, everything was different.

The wind blew softly from the ocean and Lissy pushed a strand of wayward curls back and sipped her coffee. Since last weekend, she had been trying to fight her strong attraction to him. She would be sensible and apply logic to the situation. A relationship with him would never succeed, even if he did want her.

The attraction was purely physical. As soon as he left her bed, he lost interest in her. It had happened twice, no matter what he said. Each time they slept together, he'd walked out and left her.

So, time to move on and ignore the attraction ... or just take what he offers and enjoy the sex.

She paid for her coffee and headed back to the beach. Harvey's boat was coming in through the break. When he spotted Lissy waiting on the sand he sent one of his crew up to get the boat trailer and unload the fish boxes. Arms outstretched and a huge grin on his weathered face, Harvey held her tightly for a fishy-smelling hug. His hands held her face and looked closely at her, and he gently flicked his finger on her cheek.

"What are these black circles under your eyes, girl?"

"Big drive down after work last night," she said, grinning back at him.

"Hmm." He stared at her with a frown. "After we've finished here, give me time to get the boat cleaned down, and come back for a coffee. This afternoon we'll have time for a good chat."

As she turned to walk back home, a black motorcycle roared up the hill from the beach and her heart jumped in anticipation, even as she shook her head at her foolish hope. She sauntered back along the sand track to Gramps's cottage, and even though the water would be chilly, she decided to have a swim while she waited for Harvey to get his boat home. Putting on her bikini, she found a clean beach towel and headed back through the dunes to the beach and ran into the waves. The cold water was exhilarating, and she floated on her back, letting the waves wash over her, clearing her mind and gazing at the cloudless sky. Goose bumps eventually sent her from the water and she headed up the beach towards the dunes, away from the north-easterly breeze that was starting to tip the waves with white caps out in the bay.

Flopping onto the towel, Lissy lay on her stomach, with her head on the soft white sand. Her eyes slowly closed. She dozed, drifting in and out of a light sleep, lulled by the sound of the surf and the happy shrieks of children splashing in the waves. The gulls swooped and squawked above the dunes, and the sun warmed her bare skin. Contentment stole over her like a soft blanket as her mind cleared for the first time in days.

Footsteps squeaking in the sand woke her a short time later, and she lay there, eyes closed, enjoying the kiss of the sun on her shoulders. The steps paused, and she slowly opened her eyes to see a pair of tanned, male legs in front of her.

With a groan, she rolled over and sat up, knowing without looking up just who those legs belonged to and understanding that those few minutes of peace had come to an end. Nick walked closer and sat down on the edge of her towel. She reached for her T-shirt and pulled it over her head to cover her bikini.

Hunching her knees up against her chest, she snapped at him.

"What are you doing here?"

"I asked Mrs Mac where you were when I couldn't get hold of you this morning." He put his hand on her arm as she attempted to push herself to her feet.

Lissy stood looking down at him and watching warily as he played with handfuls of sand, funnelling it through his fingers as though he didn't have a care in the world. He repeated the action three times without either of them speaking a word until she couldn't stand it any longer. She kneeled down next to him on the towel, her eyes level with his as he played with the sand. She put her hands on his shoulders and felt the instant jolt of heat through her fingertips as she gripped him tightly.

"Nick," she said, enunciating each word clearly as though she was speaking to a child. "You didn't come here to build sandcastles.

What are you doing here?"

His hand stilled, and he lifted his eyes to meet hers.

"The simple truth? I had to come. I couldn't stay away from you."

He reached for her and tried to pull her into his arms. Her body trembled as a sudden strength surged through her. She pushed him, and he fell back on her towel as she stood and ran through the dunes, leaving him lying on the sand. The passion she'd experienced with him was already unforgettable and had touched her in ways she had never felt before. If she allowed him to touch her again, she didn't think she would have the strength to face his next rejection.

Much easier to stop him now. She was panting by the time she reached the cottage and she slammed the door shut behind her. Standing at the sink, gripping the edge of the bench, she looked out the window at the big black motorcycle parked in the driveway. Her heartbeat slowly returned to normal as she caught her breath. She reached for the kettle and stood wearily waiting for him to follow her, as she knew he would.

***

Nick waited on the beach for a couple of minutes before he followed her. It was important that he say the right thing to her and not come across as an adolescent with raging hormones. The look on her face had unsettled him; he didn't want to hurt her again.

Because he knew he had.

He walked up the track through the dunes and pushed open the squeaky screen door and entered the old fishing cottage. Waiting beside the door and watching her warily as she stood at an old stone sink, he waited for her to invite him in. He looked at her white knuckles and felt a pang of regret for the distress he always seemed to cause her.

Lissy looked at him for what seemed an eternity before silently pointing to a chair at the old wooden table. As she made a pot of tea, he noticed the tense set of her shoulders and nodded his thanks when she put a tea-stained mug in front of him.

105

After pouring her tea, she wrapped her hands around her mug before moving across to the other side of the room and sitting on a chair under the window. Her face was flushed and her eyes wide as she sat, with her long, bare legs tucked underneath her; he could see the control she was exerting over her emotions.

She sipped her tea and looked at him over the rim of the mug. "I don't trust you, but I'm going to be honest. I can't think straight when you touch me. You leave me so confused. One minute you want to sleep with me, the next minute you're not talking to me. I won't play these mind games any more. We either have a sexual relationship with mutual honesty or you leave me alone." Her voice was hard. "Stop turning hot and cold and confusing the hell out of me." Placing her mug carefully on the kitchen bench, she stood and put her hands on her hips. "Now tell me, why are you here?"

***

"I was worried about you." Nick stared at her. "I wanted to check you were okay." The guilt was like a brick in his chest and it was overtaking him; the more she seemed to shrink into herself, the worse he felt.

I have to get this sorted out, he thought. *If we just go out for a while, have some great sex and then move on, all this emotional crap will go away.*

"Hah! You didn't come near me all week and then you drive a hundred and fifty kilometres because you're worried about me. Give me a break," she said.

"I deliberately left you alone all week, and then I went to see you. I couldn't find you and Mrs Mac told me you were down here."

He chuckled ruefully. "But I got poked in the chest by that big umbrella of hers several times while she sternly told me how much I had upset you."

She put her tea on the windowsill and looked outside for a long moment. The sun was dropping behind the trees and the late afternoon sunlight darkened the room, making it difficult to see his expression.

"Why...why? I came to you last Saturday and you threw my feelings back in my face."

"I was ashamed of my behaviour all week. I was scared you would take it as a commitment if I responded to you."

"Did I ask you for commitment?" she asked, her voice frosty. "Me. This is me. Remember, I don't do *commitment*, Nick. You know how I feel about that. I don't believe in the sort of physical attraction we seem to have for each other ending up in any long-lasting relationship."

"I know," he replied. "But I didn't trust you. I thought I could avoid hurting you, but I think I did the opposite." He watched as she wrapped her arms around her chest and appeared to go into self-preservation mode.

"Not at all. I barely gave you a thought. I was busy all week with the research. It's not long till we go the Cook Islands and I have a heap of writing up to do. I will admit I was a little embarrassed about my behaviour at the restaurant, so I kept a bit of a low profile at the university."

Nick knew she was not being honest with him and it amazed him how well he could read her, but he didn't want to push his luck and upset her even more. She turned away from him and looked out the window, her arms still crossed in front of her. There was also no way he was going to let her know that all he wanted to do was come over and hold her. Not sex, just comfort.

"Well," he said. "Now that I know you're okay, I'll head home."

She looked at him, frustration in her eyes.

"You can't...the mountain is closed tonight. Didn't you see the signs at the top? It's closing at night for road work over the weekend from six p.m. and you won't make it there in time."

He had noticed that on the way down and hadn't given it any thought. All he had been concerned about was making sure she was all right.

"Oh damn ... I forgot."

"You can sleep here and go back up in the morning, if you like."

"That would be great." He stood up slowly and walked over to her, pleased that she'd invited him to stay so readily.

"In the sleepout."

"Of course."

Lissy stared at him as he reached out and tucked a stray curl behind her ear.

He held her gaze and electricity sparked between them.

"Pretty potent combination we make. Let's hope it carries over to our work."

"We can only hope," she said softly.

Nick's eyes dropped to her soft pink lips and he groaned.

It was hard to say who made the first move; he reached for her at the same time she stepped into his arms. He lowered his head as her lips rose to meet his. Her mouth opened to welcome him, and she put her hands into his short hair and pulled him closer. The wind blew the shutter on the kitchen window closed with a loud *bang* and Nick was only vaguely aware of the noise. His hand slid under her shirt and she groaned into his mouth as his fingers caressed the warm silken skin of her back. Her legs wound around his hips as he lifted her onto the bench and kept kissing her until he thought he would expire from lack of breath.

God help me, she is like fire in my blood.

He couldn't keep his hands off her, and a smile tugged at his lips as he realized the feeling was reciprocated, no matter how snarky she had sounded on the beach.

"Not here," she gasped.

"Where's your bedroom?" He lifted her from the bench and followed the direction she pointed in. Kicking open the door with his foot, he carried her into her bedroom and placed her on the bed. "Tell me to stop if this isn't what you want too. And I'll leave."

Lissy's lips met his and he knew what her answer was.

A long time later, she pulled the blanket up over them as the chilly late afternoon breeze blew in through the open window. She turned her back to him as he cradled her to him.

"Lissy—" he whispered, as he nuzzled his lips on her warm skin.

"No words," she replied sleepily. "That's what causes all the trouble between us. Just sleep for a while and then we'll go out and eat." As she drifted off to sleep with a little happy sigh, he stayed beside her and held her soft, warm body close. He had some serious thinking to do.

***

The fragile peace between them didn't last long, and Lissy wasn't surprised. She woke first and had a quick shower before calling Harvey to explain she had an unexpected visitor and she would catch up with him in the morning.

As they ate dinner at the Chinese restaurant in the small coastal town near Blackrock Beach, they skirted around the topic of their relationship and avoided contact of any kind. It was awkward, the way they carefully avoided even brushing fingers as they shared the menu.

Lissy couldn't stand it. The longer they sat there, the more she could see Nick withdraw into himself and her chest tightened, and her appetite fled. The waitress brought their coffee; she looked across at him.

"Well, Nick, this is fun."

He looked up at her.

"It's going to happen again, isn't it?" She tried for a matter-of-fact tone in her voice. "A quick roll in the hay, scratch your itch for the week and off you go again. You have your aloof face back on again."

He put his head in his hands. "What we have frightens me. I don't mean to be aloof."

"Nick, what we have is sex. S...E...X..." Her face heated as the couple sitting at the table next to them paid more attention to her words than to their meal. She lowered her voice. "What upsets me most is the fact that you promise me each time that it won't happen again. You're so predictable and I'm over it."

There was little conversation during the time it took to finish their meals, and as she climbed on the back of the bike and put the spare helmet on, she reluctantly held on to his waist as they took the short trip back to the cottage. Once back, they walked from the driveway to the cottage.

"There's a bed made up on the pull-out couch in the sleep-out. I'm going for a walk."

She turned and walked down the track to the dunes. The full moon hung fat and golden above the horizon, reflecting silver moonlight off the big swells out towards the horizon.

She sat and watched it rise high in the sky, her knees pulled up under her chin. It was almost midnight before she made her way back to the cottage, but she was not surprised to see Nick sitting in the chair on the front porch. Desire had fled as she sat watching the water. The hurt went too deep and she wasn't prepared to trust him. She slowly walked up the steps and stood by him. He reached up and pulled her hair from its ponytail, so that her curls fanned down her back. He buried his head in her curls and put his arms around her.

"I'm sorry I can't promise you anything. I hate hurting you." His voice shook. "I can't stay away from you. You're all I think about. I can't sleep, and my research has come to a standstill."

This was a very different Nick from the confident, sometimes arrogant professor she had worked with for the past few weeks. She leaned her forehead against his.

"I don't want you to promise me anything, Nick. I don't believe in it. I hope when I settle down with someone, it will be based on mutual liking and respect. I don't trust this fire between us. It'll burn itself out."

"Exactly. That's what happened with both Olivia and Rebecca."

He lifted his hand and twirled a curl around his finger, holding her face close to his. "Your hair is magnificent. I love touching it." He put his arms around her and tried to pull her close, but Lissy pushed him away gently, determined not to let him hurt her a second time in one day.

"You're on the pull-out. I'm going to bed. Good night, Nick."

He looked at her, reached over, and ran his finger down her face. "Good night, Lissy. Sleep well."

She tossed and turned all night.

##

Nick looked at her quizzically the next morning as he straddled his motorcycle ready to make the trip up the mountain. "You're different down here, Lissy. You're in your element...you're like you were in the Whitsundays."

She smiled. "I have the best of both worlds. A great career and it's close enough that I can come home regularly." Nick was staring at her with a strange look on his face.

"You really are happy here, aren't you?"

"Yes, if it makes sense. It's my place. I love being near the water. It gives me peace. I always bolted back here, when I was unhappy at the university. Even though it was an eight-hour train trip, Gramps and the ocean were always waiting for me. It was one of the only certainties in my life."

He reached out and cupped his hand on her cheek. The simple touch set her legs trembling and left her with a need for something she knew he couldn't give to her. The tenderness of his touch and the caring look on his face almost undid her. She turned away from him, so he wouldn't see the longing, which she knew was plainly written across her face.

"Be careful," she said, her voice shaking. "That mountain road is treacherous."

Oh my God. I sound like a wife.

As he roared down the driveway, she gave him a short wave and turned back to the empty cottage. Stripping his bed, she stood for a long time with his pillow against her face, breathing in his distinctive aftershave that lingered on the pillow.

***

An hour later, Lissy walked along the beach to Harvey's shack. The wind had come up and her curls blew into disarray around her face. The temperature dropped as the morning sun disappeared behind the clouds and she rubbed her arms to keep warm. She felt cold both inside and out. She knew Harvey would be in from fishing since the southerly wind had come through, so she was not surprised to see his car and boat parked in the yard at the back of his shack. She helped him unload the fishing gear from his boat and wash it down. After the fish was packed in ice ready for the markets, they sat down for a chat over a pot of tea.

"Okay, young lady, now tell me what you've been up to, and tell me about your biker friend."

Harvey frowned at her across the chipped red laminate table, his bushy eyebrows almost joining. Lissy briefly told him of the events of the past few weeks since she had last seen him at Gramps's service. She sighed, her hands wrapped around the mug.

"There's a bit of an attraction there," she said. "But we're both fighting it for various reasons."

He lifted her chin, with his wrinkled hand and looked into her eyes. "Is he right for you, Lissy?"

"I honestly don't know," she said. "You know how I used to say to Gramps that when the time came I'd choose someone based on sense and security?" She looked at him over the rim of her cup. "I don't know if I think that any more. Even a short relationship would be better than nothing." She spoke more to herself than the old fisherman who was looking at her with concern on his face.

"You know what to do then," he said. "I'll only say one thing to you." He gripped her hands tightly. "It's the same advice that your Gramps always gave you. Follow your heart."

##

Lissy had one more thing to do before she packed up and returned to Armidale. She picked up the phone and dialled her friend from school, the local hairdresser.

"Hi, Kerry. It's Lissy."

"Hey, Lis. Are you home? We haven't seen you for ages."

"Yes, just home for the weekend, but I'm heading up the mountain this afternoon. I have a big favour to ask. Can you fit me in for a haircut this afternoon, before I go back to Armidale?"

***

Lissy drove into the garden of the cottage and quietly unpacked the car. She was relieved to see that Nick's lights were off and the bike wasn't in the carport. She shivered as the cold wind brushed her bare neck. She felt liberated, but strange, without the weight of her curls.

"Not the best hairstyle for Armidale in the winter." Kerry had tried to persuade her to change her mind, but when Lissy had convinced her that it was what she really wanted, she had done a great job. Kerry stood back with the mirror and admired her work. She had cut it short all over.

"Lissy, it makes those green eyes of yours look huge and all the sun gold bits are gone." Lissy looked down at the curls on the floor surrounding her feet and then up to the mirror.

"I love it, Kerry!"

I am a new woman with a firmed resolve.

She gave her friend a hug and promised to catch up for coffee the next time she was home. She didn't leave the coast until mid-afternoon and it was late when she unlocked the cottage, turned the lights on and lit the fire. She hurried over to Mrs Mac's to pick up Luney and Sylvester.

Mrs Mac opened the door. "Great timing. I've just cooked some soup for you to take home." She put her hand up over her mouth as Lissy walked in and she saw the short red curls, barely covering her neck.

"Oh, my goodness, young lady, what have you done? Your beautiful hair..."

"A very sudden and knee-jerk decision." She reached her hands up and fluffed the short curls. "Long story—" and she gave her landlady a huge grin, "—but I love it. It feels wonderful."

##

Lissy was eating her soup and laughing at Luney's attempts to get her attention when the telephone rang. Picking it up, she automatically went to hold her hair back behind her ears and laughed when it was not there.

"Melissa McIntyre," she said. There was a slight pause before she heard Tom's voice.

"Hello, Melissa. It's Tom."

She frowned, surprised to hear from him again and her voice was anxious.

"Hello. Is everything all right?" Her first thought was that Nick had not got home safely on that motorcycle.

"Yes, yes. Everything's fine. I have an invitation for you." Tom sounded a little embarrassed.

"Yes?" she replied, her voice guarded.

"Melissa, this is difficult. I know you're angry with Nick and me."

"No," she replied. "I'm not angry."

"Well, Mama is having a barbeque next weekend because Nick is going to the Islands and she knows you're going too, and she asked me to call and invite you over."

She paused. *Why not.* "That sounds great. I'd love to come."

"Great."

"And," she said. "It'll give us a chance to catch up."

Lissy went to bed feeling more settled and in control of her life than she had for weeks.

The next morning, she dressed in a suit with a turtleneck sweater underneath; she missed the warmth of her hair. The last thing she wanted was to catch a cold before they left for their research trip to the Cook Islands. She carefully made up her eyes, a little more than usual, and found big dangly earrings.

"Not bad, Dr McIntyre," she said to her reflection in the mirror before she left for work. "Looking confident."

That was not the reaction she got from Nick later that morning. He dropped by her office to see her about some research before morning tea and the loud roar that came from him when he saw her hair brought Jenny running from the reception desk.

"By God, woman." He looked at her in disbelief. "What have you done?" She and Jenny looked at each other and burst out laughing.

"Getting ready for the tropics, Professor."

He glared at her for a minute and then grunted before disappearing into his office.

Chapter Fifteen

Lissy heard laugher and the buzz of happy conversation as she made her way around the back of the Richards's farmhouse on Sunday afternoon. The barbeque had been a hot topic of conversation in the history faculty; many of the staff had been invited and apparently the Richards were renowned for their hospitality. Since it was a casual affair, she had dressed in jeans and an olive-green cashmere sweater that brought out the deep green of her eyes. Her new trademark dangling earrings complimented her short curls. She'd decided as the week progressed that Nick had done her a favour, and she felt liberated by the freedom the short haircut had given her.

Tessa moved towards her as she walked up the steps, hands outstretched in welcome. "My dear, it is wonderful to see you again. Look how beautiful you are."

Lissy touched her short curls as Tessa gently kissed both cheeks, Italian style.

"Amazing what a good haircut can do."

"Thank you, Tessa. you're the only person who likes it!"

Tessa reached up and touched her face with an elegant hand. "It shows off your beautiful green eyes."

Lissy laughed, a little embarrassed by Tessa's attention. "My hairdresser was almost weeping as she cut it."

"I think it looks spectacular," said Tessa, "and if you're happy then that is all that matters." She looped her arm through Lissy's. "Come and meet my nieces. They are visiting from Italy."

Lissy's cheeks warmed and she looked across the garden, sensing someone watching her. Nick was sitting at the table under a tall tree next to an attractive blonde woman, and raised his glass in a silent toast to her.

Tessa followed her gaze. "Don't worry about Nick. He's been in a bad mood all week and we're ignoring him."

Lissy shrugged her shoulders. She knew what his problem was.

If only I could ignore him so easily, she thought.

"Isabella and Talia, this is Melissa, Tom's friend from the university. She also works with Nick, and I've already apologised for his bad mood." Tessa introduced the two young women standing together in the doorway. The girls giggled and the older of the two said, "*Tessa da zia*, we have already met Melissa." They both smiled at her. "At the restaurant, last weekend."

Lissy laughed with them. "As if I could forget! That was a night to remember. I believe I owe you for finding my keys." The girls spoke perfect English, and as they chatted together, Tom walked around the corner, holding the hand of a small dark-haired young woman.

He looked pleased to see Lissy, came over, and kissed her cheek. "It really is good to see you here." Lissy knew he meant it. He was a great guy and she was sorry she had misjudged him at the restaurant. It looked like it had all blown over and there were no hard feelings. He turned to the young woman by his side.

"Melissa, this is Jill. She just moved back to Armidale and works in the finance department at the university." Jill seemed very shy, and Lissy was pleased to see the coy way that she was watching Tom and that he continued to hold her hand as they stood with the group.

Lissy's neck prickled and she knew without looking that Nick was within her vicinity. She turned and saw him walking over. Before he could reach them, Tessa broke from the group and joined him on the lawn. As the conversation continued around her, Lissy could hear his voice and he sounded angry. She saw him shrug his shoulders and relax as Tessa spoke to him quietly, her hand on his arm. He looked over and saw her watching, and he raised his glass to her again. Tessa gave him a gentle push in the direction of the group gathered on the veranda. Walking over, he stood next to her and said politely, but with no warmth in his voice, "What can I get you to drink, Melissa?"

"White wine, please," she said, smiling brightly at him,

determined not to let him ruin her afternoon. He had tried his best to upset her life and career plans, but she had decided it was time to take control. Once the trip to the Cook Islands was over and the research paper was completed, she was going to reconsider her options. Other universities focused on Pacific history research and she would be well placed for an associate professorship after their current paper was published. Leaving Nick behind would be hard, but she had to do it if she wanted any chance at happiness in her life and career.

Nick returned with a glass of wine for her and as she took it, their fingers brushed, and she was surprised that the arc of electricity that flared between them didn't crackle through the air. Conversation flowed around her, and she was content to observe the social interactions of her friends and colleagues. When Sophie, Ally, and Lucy arrived with their families, she was welcomed as an old friend. As more guests arrived, the barbeque livened up and a game of cricket began in the back garden. Lissy moved to a hammock chair on the veranda, content to sit back quietly and watch the game as conversations drifted around her. The smell of meat and onions cooking on the barbeque wafted across the lawn and guests began to drift to the buffet table.

The evening passed pleasantly. Even though it was meant to be a function to get the faculty together before the trip to the Islands, Nick studiously ignored Lissy after giving her the glass of wine. He remained on the far side of the lawn umpiring the cricket game and she took a perverse pleasure in ignoring him back. Despite the tension with him, she enjoyed spending time with her friends from work and left early to go home and pack for the trip.

***

Determined not to let Nick's attitude ruin her trip to the Cook Islands, Lissy welcomed him professionally as they shared a taxi to the airport on Monday morning. Fog had delayed the flight from Armidale to Sydney and they arrived in Sydney with only minutes to spare. They had to run to catch the bus to the international terminal to catch the flight to Rarotonga.

"Why did you wear such high heels?"

She ran along behind him as they sprinted for the bus.

"Faster," said Nick. He held his hand out and she grabbed it. Lissy was thankful their luggage had been checked straight through and she only had a small bag to hold. They picked up their boarding passes at the Polynesian Airlines counter as the flight was called. There was no time for a coffee or a snack before they were called through customs for their passport check.

They boarded the jet and were preparing for take-off. Nick was polite but distant and focused his attention on the cabin staff delivering the safety instructions. Lissy settled into the window seat and took great care in moving as far away from him as she could, which was difficult in the confined space of the shared double seat.

She looked down at the ocean below with her hands clasped tightly on her lap. She'd always had an irrational fear of flying over water. Nick looked across at her and gave her a reassuring smile when he noticed her white knuckles. It was the first smile he had given her since they'd been at Gramps's cottage. She nodded and turned back to the window. Staring at the water, even though it made her feel light-headed, was better than looking at him.

A light meal was served an hour into the flight and after they finished their coffee, Nick was soon immersed in his laptop. Lissy examined him surreptitiously under lowered lids.

His hair had darkened since he had been away from the Pacific and he had lost his tan. The man sitting beside her bore little resemblance to the swaggering sailor she had first met on the yacht two months ago. He looked the part of an academic now and she sensed that it didn't sit comfortably with him. She recalled one of their first true conversations where his love of outdoor adventure and the ocean had been so obvious, and she knew that most of his time at the university was spent in sedentary activities.

No wonder he has been testy and hard to read, she thought. *Being stuck in an office indoors must be hard for him.* She glanced up and realised that Nick was returning the intense scrutiny she had been giving him.

"Everything okay?" he asked.

"Fine," she said. He nodded and looked down at his work.

Lissy put her head back against the soft padding of the seat and closed her eyes.

No matter how terse or rude he was to her, she could not get over the deep attraction she felt for him. She was going to have to move away when they finished their report. She started to daydream about what life would be like if she could trust her feelings for him and he returned that trust.

She slipped into sleep, lulled by the monotonous hum of the engines. As she slept, her lips turned up into a little smile. She fell into a deeper sleep, her head rolling to the side, landing gently on Nick's shoulder.

***

Nick looked down at the short red gold curls tickling his chin. He had been so angry when he saw Lissy's haircut. Not at her, but at himself, because he knew he was the sole reason she'd cut it off. Because he had been foolish enough to say how much he loved running his fingers through her curls...and showing her.

He'd been fighting his feelings for her for weeks. He looked down at her breathing gently and sighed softly before leaning back and closing his eyes. The turmoil of his emotions over the past few months since he'd seen Lissy sitting on the side of the yacht and he had sung that silly ditty to cheer her up, had thrown him. He couldn't remember feeling this emotional in either of his previous serious relationships. Although, he thought with a grimace, he and Lissy were not in a relationship, as she kept reminding him.

And if she had her way they never would be...

Well, how do you feel about that? he thought.

Not good.

She gave a soft little moan and snuggled deeper into his shirt.

Nick's protective instinct kicked in and he put his arm behind her head and settled her more comfortably into him. She didn't stir. He noticed the dark smudges under her eyes and realised she was losing as much sleep over the situation as he was. He was determined to sort it out this week. Although they would be busy with the final research and writing it up at night, they would still have time to do some serious talking.

I will not touch her all week, he vowed to himself. *We need to step back and get this physical attraction figured out.*

He was ashamed she thought that was all he was in it for.

Chapter Sixteen

Lissy slept until they began their descent into Rarotonga. She stirred, and Nick managed to remove his arm before she woke up.

She looked up at him, her eyes heavy with sleep and her cheeks rosy. "Sorry, I hope I didn't dribble on your shirt."

It had been a long trip and the sun was setting over the ocean as the shuttle pulled up in front of the resort at Avaiki Beach on the western side of Aitutaki. They had travelled by launch from the main island and Lissy felt contentment settle over her as they crossed the water. The majority of their research was on this small island and they had meetings organised in some of the small villages in the centre of the island.

An unspoken truce had sprung up between them, and Nick was polite and responsive to her conversation as the launch ferried them to their final destination.

They were shown to their rooms in the resort by a valet, who advised that their luggage was already there.

"I'll meet you in the bar about seven. Does that work for you?"

She nodded, and the valet showed her to her room. Lissy clapped her hands in delight when she entered her suite. They told her at reception that she had been upgraded because of a double booking. Walking across to the open doors, the front of her room overlooked the lagoon, and she watched in rapture as the sun, a huge golden orb, dropped below the horizon. Stepping out onto her balcony, she was delighted to see her own private lap pool, surrounded by a low fence with a narrow path leading to a private beach.

The balcony and pool were screened by a profusion of tropical colour. Frangipani trees and a myriad of flowering plants that she had never seen before cascaded in a riot of colour down the lattice screen that gave her privacy from the next room. The sweet smell of the blossoms wafted into her room on the light evening breeze.

Stepping back into her room, her eyes widened as she entered the bathroom and saw a huge spa bath set in the floor, with dozens of little candles set into the edge. Two fluffy white robes hung on hooks on the side of the huge clear screen that led into the biggest shower that she had ever seen.

What a waste, she thought with regret. *This is the honeymoon suite!*

Quickly blocking those thoughts, she moved over to her luggage and began to unpack.

I'm not going there. No matter how beautiful it is. We're here to work.

She pulled her laptop from its case and set it up on the desk in the lounge area of the room and checked that the wireless Internet connection was working. Satisfied that she could access her files on the university server if needed, she unpacked her suitcase and had a shower before meeting Nick for dinner.

A pink conch shell on the marble bench in the bathroom overflowed with a variety of bath gels and shampoos. Choosing a black orchid scent, Lissy luxuriated under the steaming shower. Dressing in a pair of loose white pants and pale green top, she put on a minimum of makeup and headed for the bar with a couple of minutes to spare. Steeling herself to meet Nick, she repeated to herself, *we're here to work.*

***

Nick was sitting at the bar waiting for her. He'd already been approached by two attractive women who thought he was alone. Lissy paused at the door and his heart rate kicked up a notch as she walked over to him. The simple colours she wore and the short curls framing her face reminded him of her gentle beauty. She sat on the stool next to him and he looked over at her, his eyes lingering on her face.

"You look very relaxed already," he said.

"Oh, you should see my room. It's fit for a queen! I have a marble spa bath, almost as big as the pool at the indoor sports centre at the university."

He laughed. "That is big, but I'm sure you're exaggerating."

She laughed back at him, and he was pleased to see that they were both playing it the same way.

Friendly, platonic conversation, no touching.

"Well, maybe not quite as big, but you could fit a small family in there."

"Drink?" he asked.

"Yes please, I'm going to have a tropical cocktail, but don't worry, that'll be it for the night. I know we start work in the morning. I'll be up bright and early, ready to go. I'm so looking forward to going into the villages and doing these oral histories."

Nick was touched by her enthusiasm. He had spent so much time in the Islands, it was refreshing to see her excitement about getting in the field and working.

"I was reading some of the tourist literature in my room." Her eyes sparkled up at him as she sipped her cocktail. "Did you know that Aitutakians believe they descended from Ru, the famous seafaring warrior who sailed from Avaiki? Legend has it he arrived at full moon and he was captivated by its reflection in the vast tranquil lagoon and named his landing point *O'otu*–full moon. That's how the beach here got its name."

"We'll have to talk about that one tomorrow," he replied. He was having trouble taking his eyes from her face. "You really love the ocean, don't you? You seem much happier when you are near the water."

"It was my happy childhood with Gramps and running free at Blackrock Beach. My happiest memories are all to do with the ocean." She sipped her drink and he sensed her withdrawal from him. She put her drink down and turned to him, speaking in a brisk, business-like manner.

"Okay, now tell me the plan for tomorrow."

They discussed the sequence of interviews over dinner and Nick was disappointed when Lissy refused his offer of a walk along the beach after dinner.

"Thanks, but I have some work I want to do and some emails to send." He watched as she stood and left the restaurant. Nick finished his drink, signed the bill for dinner and headed out to the beach for a walk.

##

The next morning, they were picked up bright and early by a driver in a brightly-coloured four-wheel drive vehicle to head for Tomara, the first village they were visiting. Nick slid a small tray of bottled water into the back of the vehicle with their laptops.

"Where's the recording equipment?" asked Lissy, surprised to see him traveling so lightly.

"Don't need it," he said. "My laptop has a special external microphone that will record across a room and pick up individual voices in even the noisiest of rooms."

Lissy turned her attention to the road as the driver pulled on to the dirt road. They arrived in the village after a short drive and she smiled as she saw the young children running towards them. The Cook Islanders were an extremely happy people and the driver informed them that the village had been looking forward to the professor's visit.

"*Kia orana*, professor." The chief held both hands out in welcome to Nick.

Nick reached out and grasped the chief's hands, but the old man pulled him in and enveloped him in a back-slapping embrace.

"Come, come." The chief led them across to a rectangular ceremonial building, decorated with ornate carvings. The doorway was low and even Lissy had to lower her head to walk through the intricately carved doorway. They were greeted by the excited voices of a group of women, sitting in a circle in the centre of the room. Waves of brightly coloured fabric covered their legs and spread across the floor of the room as they stitched with fine needles. Lissy walked to the edge of the circle and pointed to the fabric and asked what the women were making.

"*Tivaeva.*" A young woman gestured for her to sit with them. She looked across at Nick and the chief nodded his head vigorously.

"You bring your wife too, professor?" He slapped Nick on the back good-naturedly. "Welcome, Mrs Professor." She opened her mouth to correct him, but Nick glanced across and shook his head almost imperceptibly.

She glared back at him, confused by his direction as the young woman pulled her down to join the circle on the wooden floor. Lissy looked closely and realised the brightly coloured fabrics were patchwork quilts, overlapping each other. One of the older women must have noticed the surprise on her face.

"This is the meeting hall and the *vainetini*. Our group of women from the village meet here in the mornings to do *Tivaevae*. Our islands are famous for the magnificent bed covers we sew; they are very popular with the tourists." She held up the one she was stitching. "They are given to important guests as gifts. This is for you and your professor husband to take home. It is good for fertility." The other women giggled.

Lissy shook her head and stood, moving across to join Nick as the chief invited them both to drink juice from a carved wooden bowl and eat from a platter of fresh fruit. She watched with interest as some of the women began to sing while they stitched.

When they finished eating, Nick leaned across to the chief. "Are you ready for us to set up our equipment and start recording?"

The chief nodded. Nick booted up his laptop and set it up on the low table in the middle of the building, the webcam pointing towards the chief. The chief called over two more old men and nodded at Nick. The men sat cross-legged on the woven mat next to the chief and Nick pushed Lissy gently behind him. He asked the first question and settled in comfortably as the chief spoke for a few minutes without pause.

He described how the women would leave the meeting room at midday and the men would come in and spend the afternoon working on wood carvings, but one of the other men explained it had lost its spiritual and cultural emphasis and was now mainly for the tourists to purchase.

Each time Lissy tried to ask a question, Nick raised his hand and stopped her before she could say a word. The chief nodded and thumped Nick on the back as he let out a deep booming laugh.

Her temper simmered. She sat there for two hours and didn't say a word and couldn't get anywhere near the laptop. Eventually, the women gathered their fabrics, left, and the chief stood indicating that it was time to eat. He pointed out the ablutions block to Nick and invited them to freshen up for the meal.

As soon as he left the building, Lissy stood up and marched over to Nick, who was packing up his laptop.

He turned, his hands raised in front of himself for protection.

"All right, Mr Professor, would you like to tell me what that was all about? You knew before you started that I wouldn't be saying or doing anything. Why did you need a research assistant on this trip? What ulterior motive did you have?" Her voice rose with each question. "I can't trust you, can I?" Lissy pushed him in the chest and took a step back as she saw the anger flare in his face.

"While we are talking trust, let's talk about you! You're the one with the trust issues, Melissa."

She knew with the 'Melissa' that he was really angry.

"It wasn't the chief I was expecting," he said. "The adviser warned me that it depended on which of the four chiefs we saw. He said to me that if we had this one, he would not speak to a woman. That's why I didn't want you to talk and I let him believe you were my wife."

"I didn't do my doctorate to be decoration!" Lissy was trying to stay calm, but her temper was taking over.

"Keep your voice down," he said. "I don't want to blow this before we finish."

"Well, you can stay here and finish," she said pushing to her feet, hands on hips. I'm getting the driver to take me back to the town. I have plenty of work I can do in the historical museum."

"Whatever," he said dismissively. "I don't care what you do. You're too hard to follow."

"Well," Lissy replied. "I don't care what you do either!" She glared at him and picked up her bag and laptop, walking out to the car with as much dignity as she could muster. The driver was sitting under a leafy mango tree, his hat pulled over his eyes. She stood there and cleared her throat to get his attention, but he didn't stir.

"Ahem."

Nick walked to the door of the building and stood and leaned against the carved wood entry, watching her, his expression inscrutable. Lissy stood over the driver and shook his shoulder. "I'm sorry to wake you. I want to go back to the town. Can you drive me please?"

The man scrambled to his feet and opened the car door for her. With a last glare over her shoulder at Nick, she slammed the car door and they headed down the hill back towards the coast. As the vehicle rattled and bounced over the rutted track, her anger threatened to overwhelm her. She had not been so angry for a long time—Nick brought out a temper that she thought she had outgrown many years before. The anger settled like a cold stone in her chest. Nick managed to make her feel absolutely useless. It was not the fact that the chief wouldn't speak to her that upset her; it was the fact that he had known and not mentioned it. He knew she would not have travelled with him if that was the case.

It made her question the entire reason he had wanted her to come to the Islands with him. *Does he have any respect for my work at all?*

She had a quick lunch at the buffet in the dining room, freshened up and grabbed her laptop, heading for the museum. Despite Nick and his games, there was plenty of additional material she could glean from local sources. She could start the research she had planned for later in the week now, and if she finished earlier she would change her flight and leave him here.

She had set up a database with the research that she was

finalizing and had many records that needed updating from primary source material at the local museum. A tall islander with a friendly face greeted her as she knocked on the office door at the back of the building.

"Dr McIntyre, how wonderful to meet you. I have read some of your publications on our Islands and love reading your theories, especially the one about—" He broke off and smiled.

"Oh, I'm being rude, I'm so sorry. My name is James Toki." He reached out and took her hands in his as he introduced himself. "I studied in Sydney and Auckland and came back here to my home. I think you will be pleased with the recent progress we have made on dating the first arrivals and tracking their journeys."

Lissy spent a pleasant afternoon with Jim, as he insisted she call him. It was a refreshing change to be respected for her research and her professional standing. It made her realise Nick considered her from a physical and emotional point of view only. Although, she did concede that perhaps she was being too harsh. He had always shown the utmost respect for her work at the university. She shook her head angrily—she was sick of him messing with her thoughts and emotions.

Glancing down at her watch, she realised she had kept Jim way past the closing time.

"Oh dear," she said. "I've kept you for too long."

"It's been a pleasure," Jim said.

"I have so much more to ask you about the information I collected this afternoon. May I come back tomorrow?"

"How about dinner tonight?" Jim looked down at her. For a brief moment, Lissy worried about Nick's reaction and then cast it aside.

"That would be great."

"Where are you staying? At the resort on the beach?" When she nodded in agreement, Jim reached out and shook her hand. "I will come and join you there if that suits you. About seven?"

"That would be fine. I look forward to it." She couldn't help but be aware of the admiration in his eyes as he bid her good afternoon and closed the museum up. She strolled along the beach back to the resort, satisfied with her afternoon's work.

Lissy went back to her room, stripped down, put on her bikini and did a number of laps in the private pool on her balcony. After drying off with one of the luxurious beach towels, she took a beer out of the fridge in her room and sipped it as she gazed at the magnificent view across the lagoon.

Mmm, I could get used to this.

She picked up her laptop and stretched out on the deckchair next to the pool. She started to read through her notes from the morning, trying to push away the little fingers of guilt that were trailing across her mind. She felt as though she should explain to Nick what she was doing and where she was.

Damn him. Even though he had been the cause of her bad mood, and her leaving the village, she'd had a productive afternoon despite his arrogant attitude. She probably could have found out the information from the museum by email from the university in Armidale.

But I wouldn't be lying here in the warm sun, looking forward to a dinner date with a good-looking guy tonight.

The sun warmed her back as she dozed and thought about Nick and Jim. They were both great-looking guys, so why the attraction to Nick and not to Jim? Tall and dark-skinned, Jim had a killer smile, a keen intelligence, and the same research interests as she did, but she had not felt one jolt of physical attraction to him. On the other hand, she thought angrily, one thought of Nick drifted into her mind and her body turned into a quivering mess.

What is it about the man that causes me so much grief?

Lissy lay in the sun, and the combination of the warmth and the beer lulled her into a light doze.

Chapter Seventeen

After a productive morning interviewing the chief and his sons, Nick finally returned to the hotel. Dropping off his laptop and rucksack in his room, he made his way to Lissy's room. He grimaced as he remembered her anger and the baleful glare she had sent him as the four-wheel drive vehicle had bounced out of the village. Tapping lightly on her door, he waited patiently so he could deliver his apology. He knocked a little louder, but there was still no answer. He listened; all was quiet. Shrugging, he made his way to his room to write up his notes. She must have gone exploring, so he would apologise over dinner.

A couple of hours later, Nick logged off, stretching and rolling his stiff shoulders. He couldn't wait to tell Lissy of the progress he had made today. The information he had written up would speed up the finalization of their research and they would be finished sooner than he had hoped. He would be free to move on and leave Armidale and head back out to the Islands once the research report was written and published.

He frowned to himself as the reality of leaving Armidale and returning to the Islands on a permanent basis filled him with dismay.

That's what I want, isn't it? Yep, get away from all this emotional stuff.

Now it was time to go to the bar and hope Lissy would speak to him, so he could make up for the misunderstanding today.

She was sitting on a stool at the bar, her tinkling laugh drifting across to Nick as he walked in past the pool. A silk dress clung softly to her curves, her lightly tanned shoulders contrasting with the gold hues of her dress. A tall man leaned in close to Lissy, in an intense conversation as she sipped on a cocktail with a little umbrella poking from the side.

"To fortuitous meetings." The words drifted across to Nick standing at the door. Nick walked across the tiled floor to the bar, his eyes on Lissy.

***

Lissy sensed Nick's mood as he approached the bar. She sighed and closed her eyes, waiting for the harsh words. He was so predictable, she could read him like a book and he was spitting fire. She could see it in his eyes and his shoulders.

He walked over to join them and before Lissy could introduce Nick to Jim, they greeted each other by name. A lot of backslapping and banter ensued.

"Jim and I worked together in Auckland a few years back," Nick said, turning to Lissy.

"If you could call it work," Jim said laughing. "It was more party, party, party, if my memory serves me correctly."

She listened politely as they caught up on mutual acquaintances.

Nick looked across at her at her and asked if it was okay by her if Jim joined them for dinner.

"Well, actually—" she started to say.

Jim took pity on Nick and interrupted. "I'd be delighted to, man. I'm sure Lissy is okay with that." Jim turned and winked at her.

It was an enjoyable evening and much discussion took place on their research project, leaving little time for personal discussion. When they bid Jim farewell, Lissy said goodnight to both men and turned to leave.

Nick took her arm.

"Dr McIntyre, there are some things we need to discuss about today's interviews."

Lissy's arm burned where Nick held her. Jim said good-bye to them both, oblivious to any tension, and left, promising to catch up with them before they left the island. Nick continued to hold her arm.

"Will we walk and talk, or will you come to my room?" he

asked.

She pulled her arm from his grasp, turned and said sarcastically, "Oh no, not again. You've already exhausted that line. I won't fall for it twice."

He nodded tersely. "We'll walk."

They stepped from the restaurant onto the sand and Lissy reached down and slipped her high sandals off. Nick put his shoes next to hers and their fingers brushed as they reached across to the grass. She pulled back crossly as though her fingers were burned and felt a degree of satisfaction when she saw the frown on his face.

##

The soft white sand was still warm to their bare feet. They walked past the Polynesian flares that flamed in the soft breeze lighting the path along the beach. The sighing of the waves breaking on the beach filled an uncomfortable silence. The shadows cast by the flames highlighted the gold in Lissy's curls and Nick's stomach clenched with desire. He reached out for her hand and pulled her over to a seat on the edge of the lawn overlooking the moonlit lagoon.

"Sit down...please." He sat beside her and stared out at the water. "I'm sorry about today. I took too much for granted. I'm used to working alone. I didn't think about how much it would upset you. I usually think too much about you and my feelings, but no matter what I do it seems to upset one of us." He reached over and flicked his fingers through her short curls, looking at her trying to read the expression on her face.

"How are we going to get some equilibrium in our relationships, Lis?"

She looked across at him and tentatively reached out and placed her hand on his.

"It's all right. I can understand what happened. I overreacted. It's all about communication."

"Let me communicate with you now," he said, his voice rough. "Let me tell you how I felt when I walked in and saw you laughing it up with Jim. I felt like I had been kicked in the gut." He squeezed her fingers. "I was so jealous. All I could think was, 'Why can't she look at me like that?'"

"It's simple." Her voice was soft, and he had to bend closer to hear what she was saying. She looked back at him, her expression serious. "Physically, we are attracted to each other; however, our minds and emotions are not involved. We have trust issues. We can't be involved because intellectually and sensibly we both know it's not what either of us want out of life."

She looked at him, and her voice shook with emotion. "I don't believe that any relationship between us would last and you don't trust me, anyway, even if I wanted a relationship with you. So, I'm not going to sleep with you anymore because it isn't doing either of us any good. No matter..." Her eyes filled with tears and she reached up to cup his face as she held his gaze. "No matter how much I want to."

The sadness on her face dispelled all desire and calmness descended over him.

"We're a sad pair, aren't we? Wouldn't it be easier to give in and see where it takes us?"

"No way," she said, moving away from him and crossing her arms in front of her soft breasts. "It would give us a lot more grief in the long run."

She stood. "I'm going to bed now. I'll see you in the morning."

He knew she was slipping away from him and maybe, just maybe, it was too late to win her back.

Lissy ran lightly across the sand to the grass, picked up her sandals and disappeared along the path to her room.

***

Lissy tossed and turned all night and came to a decision. When the research report was finished and the publication underway, she was going to look for an associate professorship at another university. It was time to spread her wings anyway. She would look for something in New Zealand or North Queensland where she could continue her research in

Pacific history.

Feeling better now that she had reached a decision, she headed off to the restaurant for breakfast. Half an hour later, sitting at a table that overlooked the lagoon to the west and the garden rooms between the balcony and the sand, she still could not help herself glancing across towards Nick's room, hoping he would join her for breakfast. As she sipped pungent Brazilian coffee and nibbled on a sinfully rich pastry, she tried to focus her mind on the research she had to finish and forget about the man who was causing her so much confusion.

Chapter Eighteen

The week in the Cook Islands had flown by and Nick and Lissy had arrived in Sydney late yesterday afternoon. The call for their connecting flight to Armidale came over the loudspeakers and Nick picked up his bag and turned to Lissy.

"Ready?" He was polite, as she had not spoken to him about anything other than work-related matters since their walk by the lagoon. She had worked on her laptop on the flight from Rarotonga to Sydney, and when the battery power had run out, had pulled out a novel from her bag and remained immersed in that until they landed.

Lissy looked at him. "Oh, I meant to tell you. I'm flying to Coffs Harbour. I'm going home for the weekend."

He felt bereft at the thought of getting on a plane without her by his side after spending the whole week with her. He reached out and put his hand on her shoulder before he headed for the steps down to the tarmac. She flinched.

"Are you okay getting back up the mountain on Sunday? Do you want me to come and get you?" he asked.

"Thank you, but I've already made arrangements to come back up on Sunday night. Have a safe trip. I'll see you Monday in the office." She turned back to her book and he felt summarily dismissed. He walked slowly to the flight attendant at the counter, boarding pass clenched tightly in his hand. It took all of his willpower not to look back at her. His jaw was clenched, and he had a feeling of impending doom in his chest. Something was wrong. It was not in Lissy's nature to be cold and dismissive.

##

Nick rose from the chair in front of the fire and walked over to the windows overlooking the lawn where he'd played cricket and tumbled with his brothers and sisters when they were kids. Tessa walked in with two cups of coffee and broke his reverie. The smell of freshly baked scones enticed him to join her by the fire.

My heart may be breaking, but I still have my appetite. He shook his head angrily. *Where did that come from?*

"Now, tell me about your trip to those beautiful islands. And then I want to know why you are so sad." He reached for a warm pumpkin scone and savoured the taste of the treat drenched in butter.

"Comfort food for me, Mama?"

"Yes," she said. "I do not like to see any of my children unhappy. You have not been your happy-go-lucky self since you came back to the university. You have become *uomo anziano irritabile*." She reached over and placed her hand on his tanned arm.

"It is Melissa who makes you so sad, isn't it?"

He leaned over, ignoring her question and put his head in his hands, impatiently brushing his shaggy hair back from his eyes.

"Time for another haircut, Mama."

"Don't change the subject," she said. "I am not going to let it go. I want to know what is going on."

It was a relief to finally let it all out. "It's Lissy, Mama, not Melissa and not Dr McIntyre. She is driving me crazy. We didn't have the best start."

He told her about their meeting in the Whitsundays, and Tessa indicated she was not surprised that they had met before.

"I knew as soon as I saw the fireworks between the two of you that first night Tom brought her to meet us that you already knew each other. The fireworks almost lit up the veranda, but she looked so sad."

"I feel bad about that. I think Tomas was serious about her," Nick said.

Tessa laughed. "In his life planning maybe, but there was no spark between them. Besides, there is the lovely Jill, and I can see the beginning of a spark there. Tomas is much more reserved than you. You have always shown your emotion, no matter how serious a professor you think you may be."

He looked at her and groaned. "So, the whole family knows?"

"Only your sisters and I have noticed. It has been the subject of some lively discussion between us when we have coffee. There is a bet on when you will get together."

Nick burst out laughing. "Mama, you are incorrigible and you encourage my sisters to be the same. However, the bet won't be won."

Tessa sat on the side of his chair and put one hand on his shoulder.

"Why are you frightened, son?"

Thoughts scattered through his mind as he tried to find the simplest reply that would convince her that he could not have a relationship with Lissy.

"I can't trust my feelings, Mama. I was so let down by Olivia and Rebecca. I can't trust that Lissy won't leave me as well. Besides, even when I've offered my heart to her, she doesn't trust me. She doesn't believe in love, and neither do I."

"Pfffft." Tessa dismissed him, her hands accompanying her words with a very European gesture.

"Listen to me, my son." He looked at her as she took his face between her beautifully manicured hands.

"You were young when Olivia left you, and I never saw you look at her like I see you look at Melissa. You only thought you were hurt by Rebecca. Your pride was hurt both times. Both of those young ladies were astute enough to realise that there was no enduring love to be had with you. But with your Lissy, it is different. The electricity crackles between the pair of you, even when you are on separate sides of the room. Tell me, son, how would you feel if you thought you were never going to see her again?"

He looked at his mother for a long moment without answering and eventually Tessa stood and gathered the cups. As she walked to the kitchen, she said, "Take some time to think about that, Nick."

What his mother was telling him about Lissy was the truth; he knew that in his heart. He walked to the window and gazed out over the green lawn, his heart in turmoil. Lissy hadn't lied to him; she had been true to herself from the beginning. The problems had been caused by his lack of trust, in both himself and in Lissy. He had accused her of manipulation and deceit.

Well done, you idiot.

Sunday night, he thought. I will be waiting for her when she comes home. *We're going to talk about this once and for all...but with absolute trust and honesty.*

He bid his mother farewell and headed for the university to work on his research report, much happier than he had been for weeks.

Chapter Nineteen

Lissy had not told Nick at the airport that she was coming back to Armidale with her mother and Lars on Sunday night. She hadn't even mentioned to him that they were coming from Denmark to visit her. During the short flight from Sydney to Coffs Harbour, she focused on seeing her mother at the airport. She had received an email two days ago letting her know that they had completed the first leg of their trip safely and would arrive in Sydney a day before Lissy flew back from the Cook Islands.

We'll hire a car and drive up to Blackrock, and then we can give you a lift up to Armidale on Sunday night. Lissy, we can't wait to see you. Love, Mum

She was also excited about seeing her mother. It had been almost two years.

Lissy disembarked at Coffs Harbour airport and walked through the avenues of tropical plants lining the entry to the terminal. She saw her mother waving madly through the observation window. Crossing through the automatic doors into the terminal, Lissy saw everyone around them smile as her mother squealed with delight and ran across the waiting area to grab her daughter in a huge hug. Lissy couldn't hold back the tears...and she didn't try to. After many hugs and kisses from her mother, she stepped back. "Look at you, Mum. You look fantastic. Everyone will think you're my sister, not my mother."

Lyn reached over and touched Lissy's short curls. "What's this, where have your beautiful curls gone?"

Lissy grimaced, a fleeting dart of pain overshadowing the reunion with her mother.

"Long story, Mum. I'll tell you over coffee." She looked up at the huge man standing behind Lyn. Lyn turned proudly and pulled him over. "Lis, this is Lars." Lyn looked up at him and Lissy could see the love in her eyes as her mother said simply, "He's the love of my life."

The huge man who towered over her petite mother reminded Lissy of a grizzly bear. He was all brown–brown hair, a thick brown beard, and a brown shirt. Lars reached out and her hands were engulfed in his huge grasp.

"I'm so very pleased to meet you. Your mother has chattered non-stop about you since the day she met me."

Her mother stood and beamed at the pair of them. "Come on," she said, linking her arm with Lissy, "come and get your luggage and then we have a surprise for you."

They retrieved Lissy's bags from the carousel and made their way out to the parking lot.

Instead of heading for the cars parked behind the security fence, Lyn and Lars turned and walked to the fifteen-minute parking bay. Lissy was delighted to see Harvey standing next to his four-wheel drive fishing vehicle. He held his arms open and she ran in for a big hug.

"Harvey offered to drive us up. Lars has found driving on the wrong side of the road rather terrifying."

"She smells a bit fishy, Lis, but the old girl will get us back to Blackrock," said Harvey, laughing. Lars and Lyn climbed into the back and Lissy sat up in the front with Harvey.

She reached back and gave her mother's hand a squeeze. It was so wonderful to see her. She looked over the front seat and was surprised to see Lyn and Lars holding hands like teenagers. She turned back to the front of the car, thoughtful.

He's certainly different from my other stepfathers.

Lyn and Lissy talked into the early hours after stopping at the local Chinese restaurant and having dinner with Harvey on the way home. "Lars is wonderful, Mum." Lissy gave her approval and Lyn visibly relaxed as her face lit up.

"Oh, it's something so special. For the first time in my life, I'm truly in love and I feel loved and cherished. Lars would do anything for me and I adore him. We have some news."

"Mum—" Lissy looked at her mother aghast. "—you're not..."

Lyn giggled like a teenager. "God, no. Way too old for that. Lars has two grown children and I have you. Our family is complete. No, it's even more exciting than that. Harvey and Lars have been talking. Lars has a fishing boat, and he fishes out of Frederickshavn, where we live in the summer. Harvey is looking for a new crewman to help him out, so we're going to spend six months in Denmark and then come over here for the summer each year, and Lars will fish on Harvey's boat."

Lissy's eyes filled with tears and she reached over to hug her mother. "Mum, that is the best news ever." Once the tears started, she couldn't stop them, and she snuggled into her mother's comforting shoulder. Lyn gently patted her short curls.

"I knew something was wrong. Harvey told me you hadn't been happy, and you're too thin. What is it, darling?"

Lissy cried even harder. Her happiness with her mother's news was overlaid by her grief for Nick and the lost relationship that never was. She told her mother all about Nick and how even if he had wanted her, she wouldn't commit to him.

Her mother pushed her gently away and held her gaze. "Did you ever wonder why you can't trust a man enough to have a serious relationship?" She spoke softly. "You have to trust love and it sounds to me as though you are in love."

"I don't understand how you can be so trusting, Mum. Look at your relationships, your marriages. Nothing—" she rubbed angrily at her tear-streaked cheeks, "—nothing ever lasts." She pulled away from Lyn and walked over to the kitchen window, looking out into the darkness.

Lyn walked back over to her daughter and placed her hands on either side of her face. "Lissy. Look at me...tell me what you see. Really look at me."

The tears clogged Lissy's throat and she stifled another sob.

"I see somebody who is happy and very much in love. I see Lars look at you and realise that he is protecting you and—"

"Exactly. I love him, and he loves me. Do you remember what Gramps used to say? Wait for your destiny. It will find you. Well, I didn't wait. I married Declan because I was pregnant with you. What we had together was fun, and I don't regret one minute of it, because it gave me you. Then Greg came along, and I could see the security he could provide for us. When he left me for his secretary, I wasn't surprised. We really didn't have a close relationship. There was no spark. I'm a slow learner and poor Lincoln came in on the rebound. But, darling girl, please believe me now. When love arrives, and sometimes from the most unexpected direction, you will know it. You can't live your life and make decisions based on my experiences. Heed what Gramps used to tell us. He was a wise man and he and your grandmother knew true love for almost fifty years." She walked over to Lissy and turned her around, reaching up to wipe her eyes.

Lissy reached for a tissue, blew her nose loudly and summoned up a watery smile.

"Now...you are a smart young woman, with your career taking off. You think about what you want out of life. Have you been lonely since Gramps died and a bit of attention from your Nick has got you sucked in?"

##

Lissy went to bed and slept dreamlessly. Rising late, she was sitting on the porch with her coffee as Lyn and Lars walked back from the beach, arm in arm. She watched as Lars picked her mother up and kissed her, and they stood together in the sand dunes, watching the ocean. The love between them was obvious and Lissy realised it was the happiest she had ever seen her mother.

It's the best news ever.

They walked through the gate, laughing and greeting Lissy with a good morning kiss.

"My turn to cook up a big Aussie breakfast," said Lissy. "You look hungry, Lars." As she bustled around in the kitchen, Lissy paused and turned to Lyn.

"Mum, I have a big favour to ask."

Lyn looked across at her.

"I'll come back and help you with Gramps's things next weekend. I was hoping that you would give me a lift to Coffs Harbour this afternoon."

Lyn looked at her, a knowing look in her eyes.

"I'm going to hire a car and go back up the mountain to Armidale this afternoon. I've made some big decisions and I have some important things to see to." Lyn looked up at Lars who nodded happily.

"I'll come along and keep your mother company when she drives back from Coffs Harbour after you have gone back up your mountain."

Lissy laughed. "Lars, if only you knew I am climbing more than one mountain!"

Lyn reached over and pulled her into a hug. "I can't wait to meet him."

"We'll see, Mum. We'll just have to wait and see."

***

It was early afternoon by the time they finished breakfast, cleaned up and drove up the winding Pacific Highway to Coffs Harbour. Traffic was heavy as they pulled into the car rental place on the north side of town; the winter school holidays had begun, and a light rain was falling.

"You be careful driving up that mountain, Lis. The road will be slippery."

"It's okay, Mum. I'm used to it." She smiled at Lars. "You be careful driving Lars up tomorrow. He's used to the flatlands of Denmark. It may be a bit scary for him." She hugged them both and waved them off. She went in to collect the keys for the rental car that she had arranged by telephone earlier in the day. Lissy stowed her luggage in the small hatchback and left for Armidale, determined to sort it out with Nick before the day was done. She had accepted she was in love with him and even if he didn't want to hear it, she was going to be honest. The problem for the past few months had been her lack of honesty and trust, and that had gotten them nowhere.

By the time she turned the little car off the coastal highway, it was late afternoon and a storm was brewing in the mountains. She hated driving in that twilight between dusk and dark, and switched her headlights onto high beam. The rain started to pour as she drove slowly through the little town of Bellingen at the base of the mountain. She pulled over to get a coffee. The traffic coming towards her was heavy as school holiday traffic travelled from the Western Plains and the New England tablelands for a warm winter holiday on the coast.

She started up the mountain and the rain eased a little. Relaxing into the drive and reached over to turn the music on. When she took her eyes from the road, a large car crossed to her side of the road, the bright headlights blinding her for a moment. Lissy yanked the steering wheel to the left and sighed with relief as the car passed her safely. She relaxed too soon, and the wheels of her small car slid in the soft mud at the side of the road. Suddenly a steep precipice loomed in front of her. Lissy screamed as the car lurched over the gaping drop and slammed head-on into a large tree on the edge of the cliff.

***

Drip. Drip. Drip.

Lissy opened her eyes, confused, not knowing where she was and why there was water dripping on her face. Her limbs trembled with shock; it was pitch dark. She tried to sit up, but the pressure of the seat belt across her chest held her back. She reached for the interior light and switched it on, but all that did was light the interior of the car. She couldn't see outside or where she was. Her head felt cold; when she touched it, her hand came away covered in blood. Her heartrate picked up and she panicked.

Take a deep breath, calm down.

Lissy reached up and felt for the damp patch in her hair. Feeling a little bit ill, she gingerly explored the wound and realised it was only a

145

small cut. She stretched and tested her arms and legs, and understood it was the bump on her head that had knocked her out. Her head must have hit the side of the small car when it lurched over the mountainside. The seat-belt latch had cut her scalp when she slammed into the side of the car. Reaching for her phone to call for help, she pressed the on button before she remembered there was no service on the mountain. About to throw it aside, she decided to send a text since sometimes they would get through as the service came in and out.

But to whom?

She didn't know Nick's number. She had never needed to call him, working in the same building and living next door to him. She scrolled through the numbers on her phone and Tom's number flashed up. She sent a brief text message.

I'm OK but have had an accident. Gone over the mountain about three kms up. Help please.

Desperately, she prayed the message would go through. She was about to put the phone down when she remembered the flashlight app. Turning off the interior light of the car, she turned on the flashlight and shone it through the window. All she could see was the leaves and tree trunks of the rainforest.

Please God, let me be wedged securely. Reaching for the tissues in her bag, she formed a cotton wad and pressed it against the wound on her head. After a few minutes of pressure, it came away with only a small amount of blood. She leaned back and tried to rest. Her head was thumping, and she was a little worried about a concussion. She couldn't see any lights or hear any other vehicles, so she figured she must be a fair way over the side down in the thick rainforest.

Drip. Drip. Drip.

The smell of fuel wafted through the car as the dripping got louder. Undoing her seat belt and putting her phone in her pocket, Lissy slid over to the door. She opened it carefully, shone her torch out and saw that the front wheels of the car were wedged in a tree. The rear of the car was hanging over a huge black drop. Her choices were to stay in the car with the dripping gasoline or try to get out and clamber down the tree without falling down that huge drop.

She turned the flashlight off to save her battery and put her wallet in the deep front pocket of her jeans. The rest of her luggage didn't matter. She carefully climbed through the open door, gripping the roof of the car as she slid out and shone the flashlight into the tree. A huge branch was butted up against the side of the car and she was able to climb out of the door and put her arms around the branch as she stepped to a horizontal branch a meter down.

I have to get down in case the car catches on fire.

Looking into the dark and feeling the misty rain dripping onto her hair and neck, she gripped the tree trunk and slid down. It seemed she was only a few metres up and it wasn't too difficult making her way down, although her hands and arms were soon scratched by the sharp prickles on the leaves. When her feet landed on the ground at the bottom of the tree, her legs slipped out from under her in the mud and she slid to the bottom of the slope, losing her phone.

I have to stay awake.

She touched the wound and her fingers stayed dry. It had stopped bleeding, although her head was aching. She felt cold mud on her legs and shivered as she thought of the leeches and the snakes that abounded in the rainforest. Hysteria bubbled up in her throat and she fought to swallow it down and remain calm. She had no idea where she was, which way was east or west, or which was the best way to get out of the forest and back up to the road. Listening carefully over the whoosh of the wind in the trees, she heard the river. If she made her way down to the river it would eventually bring her back to the road.

Blocking the thought of snakes and leeches, Lissy headed off in total darkness, walking towards the sound of the running water. She walked for a long time in the dark, slipping and sliding and falling many times until she finally reached the side of the Bellinger River. The water was flowing across the stony riverbed and she reached in with scooped hands and had a big drink of icy cold water. Her legs were too tired to go any farther and the thumping in her head had become unbearable. She was wet and muddy, and the shivering had taken over her arms and legs; Lissy couldn't stop her teeth from chattering. She sat down, leaned against a tree, and tried to fight the sleepiness that was stealing over her.

I must stay awake.

She drifted in and out of sleep. Her heart beat in time with the dripping of the rain that pierced the thick foliage of the trees above the muddy slope next to the river. Fingers of cold touched her legs and she screamed as the first leech pierced the warm flesh of her thigh. Lissy jumped up, her head spinning, and tried to get her bearings. She walked some more and saw headlights in the far distance on the road that snaked along the bottom of the mountain alongside the river.

Chapter Twenty

Nick heard the running footsteps on his veranda seconds before there was a frantic knocking at the door. He opened the door to see Tom about to knock again and Tessa running up the steps behind him. His first thought was that Lissy was in trouble. He had been listening for her arrival all night and was starting to worry.

"Nick, it's Lissy," said Tom.

Nick's mouth was dry, and his heart thudded rapidly as he looked from his brother to Tessa. He knew it was bad.

"There's been an accident." Tessa reached out and took Nick's hands between hers. "How bad is it?" Nick's voice shook, and he cleared his throat. "Tell me ... where is she?"

He grabbed his keys and helmet and strode to the door.

"No. I'll drive. You can't take the bike." Tom grabbed his arm and pulled him away from the door. Tessa walked over and put her arms around him.

"Sit down for a minute and calm down and we'll tell you what happened."

"Mate..." Tom put his hands on Nick's shoulders. "I got a text from Lissy. She's gone over the mountain. She must be okay, Nick. She was able to send me a text."

"How long ago?"

"Four o'clock," said Tom.

"Why the hell didn't you come and get me sooner?" Nick yelled. He stood and pulled away from Tessa.

"My phone was in my briefcase and the text was four hours old before I received it. Calm down. I've called the Bellingen police and they're out looking for her already. It'll take us a good hour and a half to drive down there." After a pause, Tom looked at him intently. "You're in love with Melissa, aren't you?

As the realisation hit Nick, a light came on in his heart.

Of course I am. I love Lissy.

He was in love with her, but he also loved her. "I would feel as though my life was empty if…" He looked up at Tessa, who smiled.

"Exactly," she said. "It is up to you to convince her that it is a love worth fighting for."

"And now it's probably too late," Nick said desperately. "It's all my fault. She was probably upset with me and not concentrating on her driving."

Tom's car was parked out on the road and Tom directed Nick to the passenger seat and opened the back door for their mother. It was the longest trip of Nick's life. Traffic was light, but the winter fog had descended on the Ebor stretch of road and they had to slow to a crawl for about ten miles. Nick sat forward with his head in his hands, not saying a word, and Tessa reached over every so often and rubbed his shoulders.

"Have faith, son. She will be all right."

"She was able to send a text, mate, so she's conscious," Tom said.

"But it's been four hours and you haven't had another one. And the police haven't called," Nick said tersely before he slumped back into silence. Tom reminded him gently that there was no service on this part of the Great Dividing Range. As they approached the little village of Dorrigo, the fog cleared, and they were able to pick up their pace. Tom's phone beeped, and Nick grabbed it as Tom slowed down.

"Keep driving!" Nick yelled as he read the message. "It's from the police. All it says—*Car found. Please call*," and he read out the number for the police station.

"What does that mean? Where is she or have they found her and don't want to tell us by phone?" Nick's voice broke. "Why did I wait so long to tell her how I feel?"

Tessa undid her seat belt and reached over and put both arms around Nick.

"Mama, put your belt on. We don't want another injury tonight," Tom said quietly.

Tessa ignored him and spoke to Nick.

"Dominic, call the number and I will speak to them."

When they came over the edge of the escarpment and onto the road down the mountain, they saw the lights of the coastal towns twinkling in the distance.

"No good," groaned Nick. "Service has dropped out and it doesn't come back till we reach the valley along the river."

"Do you want to turn around and go back to pick up service?" asked Tom.

"No, just get down there." Nick's voice was harsh.

It was twenty minutes before they reached the bottom of the mountain road and came across a police officer in the middle of the road swinging a flashlight to slow them down.

Their headlights reflected off his yellow vest and he flagged them down with the bright light.

Tom pulled over to the side of the road and Nick was out of the car before it had stopped. He ran across to the policeman.

"Where is she? It's my—" he paused, "—my friend."

Tess and Tom came up behind him as the young constable answered. "We don't know. The car is wedged in a tree and there's nobody inside. There was no sign of any passengers. Do you know how many were in the car?"

"Just one," said Nick. He turned away fighting the nausea that clawed at his stomach. He heard Tom talking to the young police officer.

"What's happening?"

"They've sent to Bellingen for some big lights and a couple of officers have clambered down the bank. But so far there's no sign of anyone."

"Mate...brace yourself...they say there was a fair bit of blood in the car as well."

Tessa gave a small cry of distress and grabbed Nick's hand before leading him away from the middle of the road. It had started to rain again, but he was barely aware of the cold rain trickling past his collar.

"It's too late, Mama. I've lost her before I could even tell her how much I love her."

Another police car came slowly up the road towards them. Two officers got out of the car and had a short conversation with the constable who was slowing the traffic down. He pointed to Nick. They came over and explained that the search was not going to start until daylight.

"It's too dangerous in the dark, mate. You would be better off coming down to Bellingen and resting so you can join in at daylight." It took Tom and Tessa a long time to convince Nick that this was the best course of action. After giving the police their phone numbers and extracting a promise that they would be informed of any developments, they left. They drove to the Motor Inn at the east of town and booked one room. Tessa put the kettle on and Nick sat in the lounge. He was quiet, and Tom and Tessa spoke softly in the kitchenette as they made a cup of tea.

Tom opened the minibar fridge and pulled out a small bottle of brandy and tipped the lot into Nick's mug of tea.

"To help you get a bit of sleep, mate."

Nick looked at him in disgust but drank the tea anyway.

Tessa curled up on the lounge next to Nick and held his hand. His fingers played with his mother's hand and he gradually relaxed a little.

Tom stretched out on the bed and they waited for a call.

##

Tom's phone rang as the dawn light began to pierce through the curtains. Nick grabbed for it and listened for a few seconds.

"We're on our way." He brushed his eyes impatiently. "They've found her, and she's just been taken to hospital to be checked over."

"Thank God!" cried Tessa.

"She walked to a farmhouse. I can't believe it. From where the car went over, she walked almost to town. She went knocking on a door as the dairy farmer was heading out to milk. She walked into the barn and the guy got a real shock."

Tom drove them the short distance into town and pulled up outside the little cottage hospital. Tom parked the car, while Nick and Tessa entered the office. There was no one to be seen and Nick paced impatiently.

"Calm down. It's only a little country hospital. The night nurses will be with Melissa and the doctor." Tess pushed him into the chair. As the automatic doors opened for Tom, a nurse came out of a room at the end of the corridor.

"Mr Richards?" she asked.

"Yes," answered Tom and Nick together. She ushered them into the waiting room. "The doctor is with Ms. McIntyre now. Don't be too concerned. She's in pretty good shape. You can see her when the doctor has finished."

"Dr McIntyre," corrected Nick. The nurse looked confused. "Oh, I didn't realise she was a doctor."

"A history doctor," said Nick proudly.

Chapter Twenty-One

The doctor finished checking Lissy over and the nurse stripped her wet clothes off and gave her a quick, warm shower before dressing her in a hospital gown.

"Now hop into bed and I'll bring you a hot cup of tea."

"I have to call my mother first; she'll be worried I didn't call her last night."

"It's okay," said the nurse. "Your fiancé is out in the waiting room. He can come in now that the doctor has given you the all clear. He wanted to do a precautionary head X-ray, but he's sure there's not a problem."

Lissy looked at her in total confusion. *She must be mistaken. There must be someone else in here with a fiancé waiting to see her.*

The nurse had grimaced as she washed Lissy's legs and pulled off a half dozen leeches. There were red marks down to her ankles where even more leeches had fallen off, sated with her blood. "A course of antibiotic to keep the bites from getting infected. All in all, young lady, you are very lucky."

She bustled out of the room and Lissy rolled over, burrowing her face into the soft pillow and closing her eyes. The door opened quietly a few minutes later.

"Just put it down there. I'm going to take a little nap before I drink it," she said in a sleepy voice. The nurse didn't answer, and she drifted off into a light doze, dreaming about what she had planned for Nick. She was standing outside his door, trying to knock, but someone kept holding her hand and wouldn't let it go. She murmured as she drifted in and out of a light doze, frustrated, but the warm grip on her hand got firmer.

Her eyes opened wide as she realised that someone was holding her hand tightly. Looking up, she saw Nick sitting in the chair close to the bed. Her eyes went down to her hand, which was locked in his.

"Good morning," he said softly.

"What are you doing here?" She shook her head slowly in disbelief.

"I'm here because I love you."

Her eyes filled with tears. She began to speak, and he put his fingers against her lips.

"Ssh. I want you to rest. The doctor says they will do an X-ray at eight a.m. when the staff arrives, and if it's clear, which he fully expects, I can take you home."

"Nick?" she asked before she drifted off again. "Would you please call Mum?"

"In Denmark?"

She giggled and went back to sleep.

***

Lissy was given the all clear as the doctor had expected and was discharged at lunchtime. Nick had sorted out the police reports and contacted the car rental company, and all Lissy had to do was sit in the back of Tom's car and enjoy the attention that Nick lavished on her during the two-hour trip. Tessa insisted that they all go back to the farm, and once there, she put Lissy to bed in the guest room. As Lissy sank into the feather soft mattress, she looked up at Tessa.

"I'm so happy. Pinch me and tell me I don't have a head injury." Tessa leaned down and kissed her cheek gently.

"You are not dreaming or concussed. However, you've made my dream come true. The first night I met you, I knew you were destined for this family. Even though it was not with my Tomas. I must go and rouse my husband from his study and tell him all is well." Tessa turned to leave the room and stood in the doorway, her beautiful face alight. "I'm so happy you're here, Lissy. I'm sure we will see you very often."

Tessa left and ushered Nick in, warning him not to excite Lissy. "Even though she's fine, we need to let her rest."

"Mama, I'm not an insensitive boor."

"No, I think you left that at the door of the hospital, my Dominic." She reached over and kissed her son. "She is wonderful. Don't you let her go again."

Nick came in and sat on the side of the bed, looking down at her, happiness all over his face. He took her hand in one of his and smoothed her short curls with the other.

"I'm sorry, I got it cut off, Nick. I did it to upset you."

"I know," he said. "But I like it."

Lissy looked worried.

"It's okay," he said.

"No, it's not that," she said. He leaned forward.

"Are you in pain, should I call the doctor?"

"No, but we do have a problem. I've done something else."

He looked down at her, confusion on his face. "It's all right. After last night, when I thought I had lost you, nothing can be bad. What is it?"

"Well, I applied for a job, an associate professorship...and I got it." He looked so pleased for her, some of her worry lifted.

"That's wonderful."

"It is sort of. But...but it's in Auckland. New Zealand."

Nick laughed. "I know where Auckland is."

His shoulders began to shake and Lissy sat up against the headboard of the bed.

"It's not funny. You'll be here, and I'll be across the Tasman Sea. I can't refuse it now."

"Oh, this is meant to be." Nick stopped laughing, but his lips were still upturned in a huge smile as he spoke. "That will be a great place for me to base myself to begin my next research project. I would much rather be out in the field, back on a boat than working from a university base. I can see myself living on a sailing boat in the marina in Auckland harbour. How would you feel about that?"

He leaned over and put his head on the pillow next to her.

"You're still fragile," he said. "I don't know whether to ask you now."

Lissy looked up at him confused.

"Ask me what?"

"How would you feel about living on a boat in Auckland?"

Her answer was unspoken, and she demonstrated her acceptance to Nick's quiet satisfaction. She wound her arms around his neck and kissed him soundly, despite her fragility.

"I guess that's a yes," he said.

##

Lyn and Lars arrived when she woke from her sleep and Lissy's happiness was complete. By early evening, the word had spread to the family and when Nick escorted her down to the living room, the room was overflowing with the noise of his family and all the children. Lissy looked over and was pleased to see Tom, standing with his arm around Jill, as Alex went over and punched his brother on the arm.

"Looking good for the life plan, Tomas."

"Alessandro. Manners!" Tessa chased her youngest son flicking her apron at him as they ran across the living room, with Alex screaming in mock horror.

She turned to Jill.

"I am sorry, Jill. My sons have no manners, they take after their father." Lissy and Nick looked at each other and burst out laughing. Tom joined in and leaned over to Jill.

"Don't worry, it is always a madhouse. Take me, take my family," She beamed up at him and Lissy whispered to Nick.

"A double wedding?"

"No way," said Nick. "We are going to have *our* special day and it won't be the typical Richards' madhouse." He pulled her close as though he would never let go.

Lissy leaned into him and closed her eyes. All was well with her world.

Epilogue

A light breeze carried the excited voices of children across the sand as the guests assembled on the beach. Three rows of chairs with white satin bows were placed in two semi-circles well back from the water's edge. Four men in formal suits looked decidedly out of place against the backdrop of the ocean and the rocks, peeking out in the low tide. A parade of well-dressed women and men took their seats and the marriage celebrant nodded at the young man who had a CD player mounted on a small table. He fiddled with the speaker and the haunting strains of "Even When I'm Sleeping" drifted across the assembled gathering.

Three ribbon-bedecked cars came slowly down the hill to the beach and the murmur of the group quietened as they stopped in the car park of Blackrock Beach. One of the young men waiting in the car park opened the door of the first bridal vehicle and put his hand out to assist the matron of honour from the car. Mrs Mac stepped out, resplendent in mauve lace and a large hat and gave a huge smile as she waved to those gathered on the beach. She turned and helped out the two little flower girls, one dressed in sky blue and the other in pink. The second car door opened, and Sophie, Ally and Lucy stepped out and the crowd sighed as they completed the colours of the rainbow with their bridal attire.

Necks craned as the door of the final vehicle opened and the females of the bridal party went over to assist the bride.

Lissy stepped from the vehicle and there was a collective ooh as the simple beauty of her wedding dress was displayed. Fresh flowers wound through her short curls and she carried a trailing bouquet of red rosebuds.

The volume of the music swelled as the group stepped on to the beach and an elderly gentleman put his hand out to lead Lissy to her groom.

Lissy smiled up at Harvey and felt the sheen of tears as she missed her Gramps for a fleeting moment. She closed her eyes and felt his presence in the gentle slough of the waves.

As Mrs Mac and the three sisters led her towards the waiting groom and his attendants, she smiled at the guests and as she passed the front row, Tessa and Lyn both reached out and kissed her gently. She smiled to see the tears of joy running down their faces and she looked up at Harvey, determined not to cry. She grinned as she saw the look on his face. She had never seen him clean shaven and hair trimmed before, but it was the look of pride on his face that made her smile. He looked as proud as any grandfather would.

They stepped towards the celebrant and Harvey placed her hand in Nick's. Sophie came over behind her and lifted her veil. Lissy looked up at Nick and was moved by the expression of sheer joy and love on his face.

He mouthed to her. "You are beautiful" as the strains of the music faded, and the ceremony began.

The gulls squawked overhead, and the waves pushed their way onto the sand edged with a froth like a bridal veil as Nick and Lissy made their promises to each other. A cheer went up as the celebrant pronounced them man and wife, and Nick pulled Lissy to him for a long and satisfying kiss.

A breeze light as a baby's breath and as warm as a kiss, teased curls from the flowers in her hair. Children let go of their parents' tight hands and ran down to paddle in the rock pools. Mrs Mac clutched her hat and held on to Harvey with her other hand as Tom looked down at Jill and she blushed when he kissed her lightly on the cheek. Tessa stood and looked at her brood with contentment and leaned over and squeezed her husband's arm.

"All is well with our family, yes?"

He smiled down at her. *"Sì, il mio amore."*

Nick and Lissy were still in each other's arms.

He whispered against her mouth. "Forever, Lissy?"

"Forever, Nick," was the soft reply.

THE END

Marry in Haste

ANNIE SEATON

Richards Brothers: Book 2

Dedication

This book is dedicated to my dear friend, Melissa Lulham, who discovered her own birth grandfather on Lipari Island and inspired Tom and Brianna's story.

Chapter One

The taxi driver tooted his horn and she waved at him to stay. "Five minutes," she called out, her voice shaking. He stepped out of the car and yelled out to her across the rows of headstones.

"Look, love, I don't want to be rude, but if you want to get to the airport in time, we'll have to go now. We're still in morning peak hour and the traffic's heavy."

Brianna Ballantyne's whole life had turned upside down when she'd received the two-page letter from the Italian lawyer three days ago, and her plan to spend twelve months in Australia writing her psychology book flew out the window when she read the typed words she had waited so long to hear.

The letter had led her to her mother's graveside in a small cemetery in Sydney. The grave was unkempt and the long grass brushed against her bare knees. She'd run her fingers over the cold marble and traced the words. Her throat clogged and her eyes pricked with unshed tears.

"Rosa Caranto. b. September 15 1949, Lipari Island – d. March 11 2009, Sydney. A loving daughter."

Her birth mother had died just short of her sixtieth birthday. Brianna had never met her, despite working through an intermediary agency to locate her for more than two years. When they'd notified her they had located her mother, all they would disclose was that she lived in Sydney, Australia. Brianna knew when a person was located they had to give their consent for the applicant to be told their name and to make contact. Her mother had declined, so she had followed the paper trail from Scotland to Australia herself, determined not to give up.

But she had arrived too late. The letter had reached her three days after she'd arrived. It had been forwarded to her Sydney hotel from

Scotland, and now she finally knew her mother's name. Instead of giving her the details to contact her mother, the lawyer informed her of her mother's death and the place she was buried. Closing her eyes, she tried to remember where she'd been in March when her mother had passed, but tears filled her eyes and she couldn't think straight.

Damn it all. If only she'd started looking earlier, she might have made it in time and met her. *Why didn't she want me? When I was born and when I found her?*

She brushed away the tears as they wet her cheeks and gripped the piece of paper that had led her to this small beachside cemetery thousands of miles away from her Scottish home. And not only did it tell her about Rosa's death, but about the inheritance of her mother's cottage in Italy and the bizarre conditions attached to it.

She had to be married to get the cottage.

Well, dammit, if that was what it took to find her birth family, she'd bloody well find someone to marry.

"Rosa." She whispered her mother's name as she traced the letters on the small headstone. "What happened to you? Why didn't you didn't want me? Why do you want me to get married?

The horn of the taxi blared again and the driver revved the engine. Still in a daze, Brianna pulled herself to her feet. Looking around, she spotted a clump of white daisies growing wild at the base of a nearby gum tree. She reached down, picked one and walked back to the grave placing it gently beneath the headstone.

"Good-bye, Rosa . . . Mother," she whispered. "I'll be back, one day."

Climbing into the back seat of the taxi, she composed herself before leaning forward. "An extra twenty dollars if you get me there on time." She slipped the letter into the side of her rucksack and fell back in the seat when the driver hit the gas and they sped off towards Sydney International Airport.

Thanks to the strategic, but wild, driving of her taxi driver, she made the airport in time. She unzipped her money belt and handed him a fifty-dollar note when he pulled her suitcase and laptop bag from the trunk and placed them on the curb.

"Thanks, love. Have a good trip." He nodded at her as a waiting passenger opened the front door of the taxi and climbed in. Brianna hitched the computer bag onto her shoulder and turned to pick up her suitcase.

"Oh, no!" Her rucksack was still on the floor of the back of the taxi. She waved madly as the rear of the taxi disappeared around the corner, but it was too late. Thank God her passport and travel documents were in her money belt. She closed her eyes trying to remember what was in her rucksack and groaned when she remembered the letter from the lawyer. She had slipped it into the side pocket when she got back in the taxi.

Hell. She hadn't taken any notice of his details once she'd read the contents. All she knew was his office was on Lipari Island.

Wheeling her suitcase behind her, she decided there was nothing she could do about it now, without missing her check-in. Squaring her shoulders, she moved to the end of the and vowed to be more careful in future.

Ha! As if.

The queue moved slowly and Brianna tapped her foot impatiently as she waited for her turn. No matter how hard she tried, things never came together for her. Her throat clogged. Maybe if she'd been more organised, she might have found her mother somewhere other than her grave? Never mind, she'd survive without the letter. All she had to do was buy a new toothbrush and some underwear, and remember the name of the lawyer once she arrived on Lipari.

Thank goodness, she'd kept her computer out of the rucksack and hadn't lost her manuscript as well. Which reminded her, she'd forgotten to back it up. First job once she was settled on the plane. That was an easy problem to address. Then all she had to do was find someone who was willing to play the part of a loving fiancé.

She had four days to figure that one out.

If only she had more time, she was sure one of her mates from Scotland would have played the part for a holiday in Italy.

Of course . . . that was it! She would pay someone. Surely she would be able find someone to play a role for a couple of days while she checked out the lawyer and Lipari? And found out about this inheritance and the conditions attached. All she wanted was to find out about her mother and why she'd left her thirty years ago. It wouldn't hurt to play act for a few days.

Four days . . . for someone who usually did things at the last minute that would be plenty of time.

Her phone beeped in her pocket and she pulled it out.

"Oh my God." Heads turned and Brianna grinned back as curious looks were directed her way. For once things were going her way. Phil was flying back in to Sydney from Bali and his flight was on time. He was through customs and she'd get to see him before she turned around and flew back to Europe. Now all she had to do was find the coffee shop where he was waiting after she checked in.

Chapter Two

Long, bare legs flashed past the edge of Tomas Richard's vision and he swivelled around as a high-pitched squeal from their owner interrupted his reading of the *Financial Review*. The tall, dark-haired girl slid to a stop on the polished floor of the concourse next to the coffee shop before flinging herself into the waiting arms of a hippy-looking guy with red dreadlocks hanging over his shoulders. His tattooed arms encircled her and she rained kisses on his cheeks, as she wrapped her legs around the hips of the young man.

Tomas was sitting in one of the coffee shops at Sydney International Airport waiting for his flight to Italy to be called. He watched with amusement as the young man disentangled himself and led his girlfriend across to the coffee shop, one arm slung around her shoulder. They stopped in the queue next to Tom's table, and he turned back to the newspaper. The girl's excited chatter drifted across to him.

"I can't believe you got here in time. Oh, Phil, how lucky was it that our flights were on the same day?" Then she clapped her hand over her mouth. "Oh, shit, wait here." She threw her handbag onto the empty table behind Tom's chair, narrowly missing his head, and ran back across to the lounge area. He watched as she retrieved a laptop case from a vacant chair. He shook his head. She was lucky security hadn't removed it. Hadn't she seen the signs everywhere asking passengers not to leave bags unattended? And now she'd left her handbag on the table next to him.

What a scatterbrain.

She placed the laptop case on the table next to her handbag and her hippy boyfriend looped his arm back around her shoulders as they waited to be served.

"What do you mean 'had' a letter?"

Snatches of their conversation rose and fell in the general noise of the café, and Tom tried to concentrate on his newspaper, until the sound of coins hitting the floor interrupted his reading. He lifted his head. Those long tanned legs filled his vision again, and he appreciated the view of a shapely derriere moulded by close fitting cargo shorts when the girl bent to retrieve the scattered coins. As she twisted around, a sapphire blue stone hanging from a ring in her belly button glinted in the light. Her face was level with Tom's and a pair of chocolate-brown eyes stared at him from beneath raised brows. He grinned at her. Okay, so he'd been caught out checking her out. As he returned her bemused look, he realised she was not as young as he'd first thought, so she should doubly appreciate his admiration.

Closer to his age. She should know better than to leave her bags lying around the whole airport. But a nice figure.

He shrugged and turned back to the newspaper as they crossed to the table behind him and their conversation could be heard over the hiss of the coffee machine.

"Well, I sort of left it in the taxi," she said.

"Sort of?" Her boyfriend sounded exasperated and Tom marvelled at his patience. "Brianna, what aren't you telling me?"

"Well, it was in my rucksack and that's still in the taxi, too. But look, it's all good. Now that you're here, you can contact the company and chase it up for me. Much easier than me trying to do it from Italy. Besides, I'm going to be busy. I've got four days to find a husband."

Bloody hell, talk about a soap opera. Tom had heard enough. He folded his newspaper and tucked it under his arm, picked up his laptop, and headed for the boarding gate where he might find more peace and quiet.

The lounge at gate forty-five was deserted and he smiled to himself. Alex, his younger brother had teased him at the country airport this morning because he'd left for Sydney so early. His siblings all liked to rib him about his attention to detail and ticking all the boxes, but it had paid off—little did they know how well, and he wasn't ready to share that news just yet. Excitement filled him at the thought of life on Lipari Island. He had every intention of relaxing and living life to the full. His days of working in an office were over—careful planning and wise investments had enabled him to do that. He'd only bought the marina to help Aunt Carmen out.

Tom waited for his flight to be called as the early afternoon queue of departing international flights started on the runway. His other brother, Nick, had been the only fly in the ointment when he'd questioned his decision to take off for Italy. Nick had called the shots for too many years. He had married life, and Lissy, to focus on now. His years of wandering the Pacific were over, and if Tom wanted to head to Italy and become the brother with the wanderlust, it was none of Nick's damn business. It had taken him a few months to wrap up his contract at the university and sell his apartment. He didn't want to leave any loose ends behind him. Now Nick and Lissy had been married for eight months, and Alex and Emily were engaged. Tom shook his head; Alex was barely out of university and way too young to think about getting married. But despite both his brothers having partners, Tom was content sitting here alone. Women were trouble.

He did hope his two brothers had chosen wisely. As for him, he'd pulled his office door shut for the last time on Friday afternoon and closed a chapter in his life without a backward glance. For the first time in a long while, he was looking forward to the coming weeks.

Tom folded his newspaper and waited for his flight to be called.

***

The 'now boarding' sign flashed next to the Sydney to Rome flight on the departure board, and Brianna hugged Phil. It had taken ages to calm him down after she had dropped the bit about finding a husband.

"It was great to catch up. I'm sorry I have to go so soon." She blinked back the tears that seemed to be ever present since she'd received the letter from the lawyer.

Phil pushed her back, placed his hands on her shoulders, and bent down to look into her face. "I'm worried about you. Forget this

169

stupid idea, no matter what the letter says. Take some time to find out what it's all about."

"That's what I haven't got. I've only to the end of the week to turn up or the cottage goes to someone else. The blasted letter has followed me around the world." She took a deep breath and tried to make him understand. "This is my last opportunity to find out about my birth mother, Rosa. I have the chance to live where she lived, to talk to people who knew her. I'll do anything it takes to grab that chance with both hands."

"No, they wouldn't care. I haven't even told them I found her or about the inheritance, so please keep it to yourself." She sighed and pulled her braid across her shoulder. "You know what Mum can be like."

"You're too hard on her, Brianna." Phil pulled her close for a brotherly hug and she rested her head on his shoulder. "Even though she doesn't show it, she loves you. She's just a very private person. Anyway, at least you're on leave from work. You can live anywhere and write your book. Promise me you won't do anything stupid."

Brianna smiled back at him. Phil had looked out for her since his parents had adopted her as a baby, and she'd always respected him as a sensible, older brother. She'd never fitted in with the family, her adoptive parents were staid and elderly now, and couldn't understand her desire to travel the world when she had a secure job at home in Scotland. Reaching over, Brianna tugged Phil's long dreadlocks. He had the complexion and hair colouring of a true Scotsman, even though he looked more like a hippy with his wild hair and patterned pants. Their parents accepted Phil travelling the world, so why did she always feel like the outsider in the family?

"I think Dad would be more upset about your hair than me taking off to the wilds of some Italian island. It's okay, chill. Once I see the lawyer, I'll get all the details and I'll email you."

The robotic voice of the announcer came across the system. "Final call for Qantas flight QF46 to Rome. Calling passenger Brianna

Ballantyne. The gate is about to close. Please make your way to the boarding gate immediately."

"Oh, damn . . . how embarrassing." She grabbed her bags and leaned over and kissed Phil's cheek before she headed toward the security corridor. "If you're talking to Mum and Dad, you can tell them you saw me and I'm fine."

Phil gave her a wave and she strode along the corridor. Luckily, the checkpoint queue had cleared.

Jeez, I can't believe I've only been in Australia for five days and now I've got that god-awful twenty-hour flight back to Europe again.

It would have been a shorter flight if she'd gone through Dubai, but she'd pick up a good deal online through Qantas. Two international flights in over a week had severely dented the advance payment she'd received for her book.

She quickly cleared security through to the duty free area and then realised gate forty-five was at the far end of the terminal. "Oh, damn, that's all I need! Miss the flight. Get your skates on, girl," she said to herself running for the gate. Grateful for her flat boots, she sprinted along the concourse and ignored the accelerated walking bays. Arriving at the gate with seconds to spare, she pulled out her boarding pass and hurried down the jet bridge. The cabin services officer smiled and he directed her to the row at the back of the plane, before he turned and pulled the door down. Most of the passengers were already settled into their allocated seats and belted in.

"Excuse me. Oh, sorry." She pushed past the few passengers who remained standing and were loading their luggage into the overhead compartments. Her laptop bumped the seats all the way up the aisle and she apologised, hitching it higher on her shoulder. She cursed softly when she reached her seat at the very back of the plane and opened the hatch above her seat row to find it was already crammed full with bags.

I hate it when that happens. Next time I'll be on time, she promised herself.

She handed her laptop over to one of the cabin staff to stow it in another compartment. Glancing down at her boarding pass, she smiled when she saw she'd been allocated the window seat. No matter how many times she flew, she preferred sitting near the window so she could see the ground approach when the plane landed on *terra firma*.

"Excuse me." She smiled at the man sitting in the middle of the three-seated row. The aisle seat was vacant. "I need to get past."

He ignored her.

"Excuse me." She stood with her hands on her hips as the fasten seatbelt sign came on and the steward gestured for her to be seated. She shrugged her shoulders and pointed to the man who was ignoring her, and then she realised he had earbuds in. She reached out and tapped his shoulder, and when he looked up, she grinned at him. It was the sleaze who'd been checking her out in the coffee shop.

"Sorry," she said pointing to the window. "I'm in the window seat. I need to get through." He closed the laptop and slid his legs to the side so she could get past. Settling into her seat, she reached over and held out her hand.

"I'm Brianna. I hate flying and I talk too much when I'm nervous so I'll apologise in advance."

He ignored her outstretched hand and nodded at her briefly before turning back to the computer screen. She'd had a brief glimpse of deep blue eyes beneath lowered lids set in a tanned face. He was a big man, tall and broad, and he looked uncomfortable in the small airline seat.

He is a bit of a sort though.. Might as well have something decent to look at during the flight, even if he is going to ignore me.

"Pleasure to meet you too, mister. Wake me up when we get to Singapore," she said. But the sarcasm was wasted as the earbuds remained in his ears and his gaze fixed on the screen. With a yawn, she settled into her seat and closed her eyes, but sleep eluded her as she wondered how the hell she was going to find the lawyer, find a fiancé and claim her inheritance.

Four days to find a husband. The mantra echoed through

Brianna's head.

Chapter Three

After the jet reached cruising altitude, the seat belt sign went off. Tom looked across at the woman sleeping beside him. She was sprawled like an adolescent stretched out on a sofa. Her long bare legs finished in short socks and boots, and took up the space in front of his seat. He undid his lap belt and moved one seat across to the vacant seat next to the aisle, so they both had a bit more space.

When she'd shoved past him to the seat, he'd been scrutinised by a piercing gaze, and a shiver had snaked down his spine. He was surprised by the strong Scottish accent. He hadn't noticed that in the airport. He'd pegged her for an Aussie or Italian with her olive skin. Her parting shot about being a pleasure to meet him had him smothering a grin. She might be a scatterbrain, but she was feisty.

And quite beautiful.

Even in repose, her eyes were circled by dark shadows. Soft pink lips were parted as she slept beside him, breathing softly. Her olive skin was unblemished, and dark lashes fanned onto high cheekbones. A long plaited braid lay across her chest, which rose and fell with each breath. He wondered where she was going and why she looked so exhausted. Before she'd fallen asleep, he'd noticed her dab at her eyes a couple of times. He'd shrugged and turned his laptop on.

Not my problem. He had no idea why she was so desperate to find a husband and he didn't want to know. He'd had enough of women to last him a lifetime, although when he looked at Lissy and Nick, he knew they were perfect for each other. God knows he needed a change after the fiasco with Jill. He'd been sucked in by her and she'd played right along, always interested in the plan he'd mapped out for his life.

And too interested in his financial status he'd discovered just in time.

Her parting shot about his boring corporate life when she told him about the husband she'd left behind in Melbourne, had cemented his desire to get away. He'd called Italy and finalised the paperwork with his aunt's lawyer the same day.

He was well aware he held the reputation of being the boring brother, but he preferred to think of himself as sensible. His shrewd and careful approach to playing the stock market through the global financial crisis had paid off, and he'd made a killing, although only his broker knew how successful he'd been. It had given him the opportunity to dump his career and buy the marina. He'd never have to work again if that's what he decided he wanted out of life. He would stay commitment free and that was the way he wanted it.

Closing his eyes, he thought about the next few months. He had to find somewhere to live. He knew how small his aunt's apartment was, and besides, he preferred to live alone. Then he'd sort out the finances of the marina and get a handle on the day-to-day running of the tourist side of things. He'd exchanged several emails with Aunt Carmen's accountant and it looked like he would be able to leave that side of things as they were. Then it was time to start living and experience life beyond the four walls of an office—he was way overdue for a bit of fun. He smiled to himself. By about ten years. Everything a man could ask for in his life—great career, secure finances, and solid investments—had come to him through dedication and hard work. But restlessness had overtaken him over the months since Nick's wedding. What was he missing out on?

He opened up his laptop and tapped away at the keyboard, and began a list. To pass the time, he thought of some ludicrous things that were totally out of character and added them.

Didn't hurt to dream.

"How many guys do you know who wear a suit on a holiday to Europe?" Alex, his youngest brother had teased him at the airport when they saw him off to Sydney.

He'd pushed Alex's hand away as he'd played at straightening Tom's tie. "One of the sons in this family has to dress respectably. However, I'm not going to have a haircut while I'm away, and the suit will go in the cupboard as soon as I unpack."

"I'll believe it when you email me a photo." Alex had laughed.

Now Tom grinned to himself as he typed 'get a tattoo' and then deleted it and typed 'get an earring.' That would send a message to everyone who thought he was a bore. Staid old Tom with an earring and long hair?

Stuff it, he'd do it. After all, who knew him on the island? He grinned as he imagined a whole new persona for himself, focused on having a good time. He looked forward to sending a photo to his brothers. Ten minutes later, a definitive list of ten things he intended to achieve in Italy filled his screen.

"Can I make a suggestion?" A quiet voice close to his ear startled him. He looked across and was taken aback to see his seat neighbour was awake and reading the list on his screen.

"And that would be?"

"Sounds like you're planning a great trip," she said with one eyebrow raised and her head to the side. "Jet ski . . . ride a bike, and—"

"Didn't anyone ever tell you it's rude to read over someone's shoulder?"

A wide grin spread across her face and she nodded. "Yes, but you were so focused on your typing, I was curious. Sounds like a good holiday," she said without a hint of apology.

"Yes, I do plan on having a good holiday," he finally said. "Anyway, what was your suggestion?" It would be too rude to totally ignore her. He'd already done that once and heard her smart-mouthed comment.

"Depends on what sort of motorbike you're going to ride. The Italian Grand Prix is on in Mugello next month. I've heard it's worth seeing if you love your motorbikes, but if you want tickets, you'll need to book them well in advance."

Tom stared at her. "No, I'm not into motorbikes. I'm going to get myself a pushbike."

"Wow, you are a thrill seeker." She put her hand over her mouth to cover a giggle. "And here was I thinking you were a bit of a balloon."

"A balloon?"

Her face was full of mirth and she held his gaze as her lips twitched. *What the hell was she on about?* Just his luck to sit next to someone who was two bricks short of a load.

"Sorry, I keep forgetting I'm not in Scotland. A balloon…" She tipped her head to the side and he read the mirth in her expression. "Ah . . . it's someone who thinks they are pretty damn good. After all, I did catch you checking out my wee arse." When he looked at her blankly, she leaned forward and pointed behind her. Her bare leg pressed against his thigh as she twisted in the seat.

"My backside!"

"Oh." He wasn't quite sure if she was complaining or teasing him, and for a fleeting moment he was tempted to make a smart reply about her butt. But her Scottish burr made it impossible to read her tone, and he didn't want to offend her. He moved away from the warmth of her leg, which was still connecting with his. She straightened and settled back in her seat. Her chin was propped in her hand on the divider between them as she continued to read the list over his shoulder.

"What were you going to add to my list?"

"I don't know you, so I hope you won't be offended." She unclipped her belt, flipped back the arm of the seat, and slid across to the middle seat so she could get a better look at his screen.

"You have my interest," he said waiting as the warmth of her bare shoulder pressed into his shirt. She concentrated for a moment, and he watched as her gaze flicked down his typed list before she placed her hand over her mouth and covered a giggle. "I'm sorry." She snorted and then burst out laughing. "I can't believe you've written a list. I don't think I've ever written one in my life. So my suggestion would be to stop writing lists and start doing some of it!"

Tom leaned over and typed # 11 . . . stop making lists. He looked over at the woman sitting next to him who was watching him closely. Her deep brown eyes were fringed by thick dark lashes and her expression still brimmed with mirth. The shadows around her eyes had faded a little after her nap. They had been in the air for four hours and she'd slept soundly the whole time.

"I hope I haven't insulted you. I'm pretty good at doing that, or so my family tells me," she said. "They say I should learn to think before I open my mouth."

Tom snapped his laptop shut and leaned forward to put it in the carry bag. He bumped his head on the back of the seat in front of him and had to bend sideways to retrieve the bag.

Christ, they made these seats for midgets, not six foot plus tall men.

He turned his attention back to Brianna when the laptop was safely stowed.

"No. No offense taken. Not at all. Maybe, as you suggest, I do need to lighten up a bit." He looked back at her. "After all…it's on the list."

"Well, I'm the person to do it. And you have the pleasure of my company for another sixteen hours unless you are only going to Singapore?"

"No, I'm going all the way through to Rome." He surprised himself sharing information with a chance-met stranger. She loosened his tongue with her constant questions and he'd quite enjoyed her banter about his list making. "I'm going to Italy mainly for business."

"So, let's try again," she said with a smile and held out her hand. "I'm Brianna."

"Tomas." He took her hand and held it a little longer than he normally would have, as unexpected warmth shot up his arm.

"So are you a businessman or holidaying?" Brianna pulled her hand out of his and reached over and touched his narrow navy-blue tie. "The suit and the computer. I had you picked for a business traveller when I saw you in the coffee shop. In fact, I'm surprised to see you slumming it back here in economy. You looked like you should be up front in business, not in cattle class."

"Waste of money. Why pay thousands of dollars extra for a seat to get to the same destination for a glass or two of champagne."

"Ah. I bet you work in finance."

Another woman on the make. That's the last thing he needed next to him for eighteen hours. It was time to pull back and stop acting like the "right balloon" she had pegged him as. He gave her a non-committal nod. "And I have some work I must finish."

He'd just put the laptop away, so he pulled out the newspaper he'd already read from back to front out of the seat pocket. He wasn't worried about hurting the feelings of someone he'd never see again, and glanced across at her as he opened the newspaper and was surprised to see a huge grin plastered on her face. Her opinion of him was written in her expression.

"Okay, I'll leave you in peace and stop the twenty questions."

She slid back to the window seat and placed the headphones over her ears and reached forward to fiddle with the control of the small viewing screen on the back of the seat in front of her. Even though he'd ended the conversation, Tom decided he had been dismissed. He leaned back in his seat and closed his eyes. This was going to be a long flight . . . maybe he should have spent the extra and flown business class. He could afford it, but old habits die hard.

***

The voice of the captain announcing they were commencing the descent into Singapore roused Brianna from a deep sleep. She rubbed her eyes with the backs of her hands and pulled the earphones out. They'd slipped across her face and were now snagged in her hair.

"Damn," she said softly. Tugging at them only made it worse. She tried to untangle the hair caught around the posts, but they snagged even more tightly. Glancing over at Tom, she was pleased to see he was awake and typing on the keyboard.

179

"Could I have some help here, please?"

Tom looked up from his screen and then closed the lid and slipped the computer into the seat pocket in front of him. He moved closer and lifted her hands away from the tangled hair and cable, and placed them in her lap.

"You let go, I'll do it. You certainly have it tangled."

"Ow," she cried. He unwound a strand of dark hair from the cable on the earphones and she closed her eyes.

"Sorry, I'll try to be gentle. Relax."

Brianna leaned forward, and warm, gentle fingers brushed against her cheek. His hands smelled like citrus, and she smiled to herself as he tried to untangle the cord from her hair. She'd noticed his manicured nails when he was typing his list earlier.

"Move closer."

She dropped her head lower and leaned across into his shoulder to help him. Peering down, she had a clear view of taut thighs encased in trousers with sharp creases and a pair of polished shoes, and a frisson of attraction skipped her heart rate up a notch.

"There you go."

She sighed with relief when he handed her the earphones. After putting them back in the seat pocket, she ran her fingers through the loosened hair and tried to wind it back into her braid.

"Thank you so much." She looked up and smiled at him." For a while there, I was thinking I would be leaving the plane with them stuck in my hair. I'm overdue for a trim."

She'd planned to get her hair cut in Sydney, but the letter and the rush to change her travel arrangements and book the flight to Rome had interfered with *all* her plans. Not that planning was one of her strengths. She'd been lucky the travel agent had been able to book her all the way to Lipari with ease. All she had to do now was not lose her itinerary. Luckily the Burrough Medical Service back home in Edinburgh had given her a year's leave to finish her book, and she'd planned to stay in Australia for at least half of that. The deadline from the publisher was creeping closer every day and she'd started to panic. Most of her advance had been spent on travel, so she had to make the deadline. She'd need the rest of the money to sort out her current problem.

Hopefully this cottage on Lipari would have somewhere she could sit and write, and get her first draft finished and back to the publisher. Tears pricked her eyes as she thought of that lonely unkempt grave back in Sydney. She'd managed not to think about it since she'd woken from her nap, and she sighed as the grief filled her chest. Brushing the tears away with the back of her hand, she glanced up and saw Tomas watching her. "Sorry, I was miles away. Did you say something?"

"Only that it would be a shame to cut your hair. It's beautiful."

"Are you hitting on me?" As soon as the words left her mouth, she regretted them.

"Certainly not." His voice was frosty and he stared at her. "I don't need to hit on women."

She looked at him as he lounged back in the seat. His dark hair deepened his tanned skin and his cold gaze was fixed on her. An observer may have been fooled by the relaxed and casual position, but there was nothing casual in his unswerving observation of her. A flicker of discomfort shimmied down her spine.

"No matter. I won't be insulted." She forced her lips into an apologetic smile. "Sorry, Tom . . . is it okay if I call you Tom? Look, I was teasing. I grew up in a family with a brothers and lots of male cousins, and I protected myself through childhood by tormenting them before they could get at me. I guess it comes naturally, and I usually lead with my mouth and then my brain kicks into gear." She placed her hand on his arm and then pulled it back when he dropped his gaze down to it. His mouth was set in a cold, straight line.

"Look, I didn't mean to insult you. If someone wants to hit on me, that's flattering, but I expect honesty. And like I told you before, I always babble on too much. So if you want some peace and quiet on the next leg you can always change seats." She pointed to the vacant seat across the aisle.

"There's no need for that," he said. "Besides, we've landed. We're in Singapore"

The wheels bounced onto the tarmac and she glanced out of the window to see the puff of smoke as the rubber hit the ground. Relief coursed through her body and all thoughts of Rosa, the inheritance, and her deadlines flew from her mind.

"Oh wow, we've landed! And I didn't even have to worry. I hate landing . . . it's not the flying. I usually put the music on and close my eyes and ignore it, but you took my mind off it. Thanks so much." She looked up and caught a bemused look on his face. "Woops, I'm prattling on again, aren't I? I told you I talk too much. If you get sick of me babbling, tell me to put a sock in it."

A slow smile spread across Tom's face and she grinned up at him when he shook his head at her. Relief coursed through her. That was one less thing she had to worry about.

"Look, I'm sorry for being a pain. It's been a big week. I'm sure you'll keep me entertained and the rest of the flight will pass very quickly."

"How about you buy me a cup of tea to apologise for being rude? I'm sure we can get a decent cup in the airport somewhere." She smiled up at him and although the daunting stare had disappeared, she sensed his reluctance. "Don't worry, no strings attached."

"Sounds like a plan."

Leaning forward, she checked her money belt was secure and tightened it around her waist. She was not going to lose anything else, especially while they were in Singapore. They disembarked and strolled through the retail area of the airport, and Brianna looked around in appreciation at the huge gardens down the centre of the concourse. Tropical orchids of every imaginable colour cascaded in garlands from lush foliage and the perfume overlaid the usual sterile, artificial smell of most airports. As they walked on, a large display of tropical and temperate orchids hung into a pond filled with bright orange, red, and yellow koi.

"How amazing is that?" she exclaimed. "That's one thing I'm looking forward to in Italy—the gardens. Are you a gardener, Tom?"

He gave her a reluctant smile. "No, I live in an apartment and any plant I ever had died from neglect."

"Well, that's another thing for your list." She tipped her head to the side and wrinkled her nose at him. "No, scrub that. Not exciting enough. You can have a garden when you're old." She grabbed his arm and dragged him into the Starbucks at the edge of the orchid garden and slid onto the padded bench seat along the wall. "I hope Starbucks is up to your coffee tastes."

"Starbucks in Singapore. Hmm . . . we'll see. Okay, I'm buying. How do you like your coffee?" he asked.

"Tea, please," she said and leaned back against the soft padded back of the seat. She was stiff and sore and they'd only travelled for eight hours. The second leg of the flight was another twelve hours and her body was telling her she'd spent too much time in planes in the last week.

Tom stood at the end of the long queue at the counter. Even as he waited in the crowd, his bearing showed what her adopted mother referred to as "good breeding." When he stepped forward to be served, she had a clear view of him, and Brianna smiled to herself. He was tall and broad shouldered, and held himself straight. His eyes were bright and his cheeks had the fresh glow of good health, of someone who looked after himself. Her gaze travelled down from his wide shoulders to his broad chest and his snug-fitting white business shirt. He'd shed the jacket on the jet bridge as the humidity had hit them and rolled his sleeves up to his elbows. Long legs ended in a nice butt. Even in the suit pants. She looked up and caught his cool glance before he turned back to the counter. The heat rose in her cheeks.

He might be a looker, but he needs to lighten up.

She wasn't going to let him get away with the cool responses and grinned at him when he placed a tray loaded with a variety of food on the table. She'd get a laugh out of him if it took the whole damn trip.

What's good for the goose is good for the gander. "Sprung. We're even now."

He raised his eyebrows without speaking, but it was clear he understood what she was referring to.

"Okay, thanks. I owe you a meal, or several meals by the look of this," she said. He sat and reached for his coffee and leaned back, silently watching the hustle and bustle of Changi airport go past them as Brianna demolished most of the food.

"I won't need to eat again till Italy." She smothered a burp and giggled. "Oops. Sorry . . . bad manners. My mother would be horrified."

He looked across at her and she held his gaze. Even though he didn't smile much, when he did, the crinkly smile lines around his deep blue eyes softened his angular face. Even though she'd only met him eight hours ago, she still felt comfortable with him and sensed his grumpiness was a bit of a shield.

She tipped her head to the side and tapped her finger on her chin.

"Tell me a little about you, Tom. Where's home for you? Do you live in the city or are you from the outback?"

"No, certainly not the outback. I grew up in small rural city, Armidale. It's inland from the north coast. I went to Sydney to university and then back to the country after I graduated." He looked at her. "What about you? How long were you in Australia?"

"Ach, my wee accent has given me away as a tourist, then?" she said, exaggerating her Scottish lilt.

"Just a little."

Finally she'd got another smile out of him

"Well, I'd only been in Australia a few days when I received—" She hesitated. Even though she could babble on like a brook, she was circumspect about giving personal details to strangers. And he was a stranger. For all she knew, he could be setting her up. Her family always told her she trusted too easily and wore her heart on her sleeve. "I received some sudden family news that meant an unexpected trip to

Italy. Good news. So no, I have no idea where your city is. I visited Sydney and that was it."

"What about your boyfriend? Weren't you travelling together?"

"My boyfriend?"

"The guy at the airport . . . with . . . er . . . with the hair."

"God, no. Phil's my brother. He's been over here for six months and he'd just flown back in from Bali. It was an absolute coincidence we were at the airport at the same time. We were going to travel around Australia together for a few months. No boyfriends or husbands in my life. I'm a career woman through and through."

She looked down at her khaki shorts and T-shirt. "Even though I look like a tourist, I do have some work to do, and I was going to settle at my sister's place after a wee trip around."

"What sort of work?"

"Oh, a bit of work I can do anywhere. Now we were talking about you. Tell me why you're going to Italy seeing as you're not the big financial businessman who travels in business class." She sensed his hesitation and was interested to see if he would answer her question.

"I'm going over to help my aunt. My uncle died a few months ago and she has a business to run. I am going to help out for a while. See a bit of the country and have a bit of a holiday."

"What do you do? No, don't tell me, let me think about it and then we'll play twenty questions on the plane to pass the time." She looked down at her watch and slumped her shoulders. "Jeez, after all we've got another twelve more hours to fill in."

***

Brianna shifted in the window seat and leaned her head against the recess around the window. It was pitch dark outside and the only thing to look at was the light flashing on the end of the wing. Tom sat up in his aisle seat, his back straight and his arms crossed in front of him. He looked down at the vacant seat between them. Somehow Brianna had managed to fill it with magazines, food wrappers, and a calico money belt. He reached over and rescued her passport, which was about to slip out of the belt onto the floor, and handed it to her.

"You might need this," he said.

She tipped her head to the side and looked back at him for a long moment before speaking, her expression serious for once and he took the opportunity to study her deep brown eyes. They were flecked with gold and her eyelashes were dark and lush, and he was sure it was all natural. She wore no other makeup. A sudden shaft of desire shot through him and he held her gaze. His eyes travelled down her face to her throat and to the soft swell of her breasts beneath her snug T-shirt. Brianna was the first to look away and bent down and slipped her passport back into the belt before leaning forward and slipping it over her head

"Thanks, the belt was sticking into me and kept me awake. That's the last thing I need to lose, isn't it?"

"Yes, you will need your passport."

"I'm hopeless. Always seem to lose things," she said before pushing her long legs out as far as she could to reach her arms above her head and held the back of the seat. "My family has given up on me. They know not to buy me anything expensive because I always lose it."

Tom lifted his gaze from the T-shirt stretched tight against her small firm breasts.

He changed the subject. "Sounds like you come from a big family? Happy childhood?"

"Happy enough." Her voice was a little sad.

"Brothers and sisters?"

"One sister and one brothers, both married, and a tribe of nephews and nieces."

Brianna put her head to the side and tapped her finger on her cheek, moving his attention from her family. "Now, my turn. Let me guess what you do. You said you went to university?"

He nodded.

"A lawyer?"

This time, Tom shook his head.

"Shame. Okay, your turn."

***

Three hours later, a light meal had been served and cleared, and now the cabin was dim again. The movement in the plane had slowed as passengers slept and the cabin staff came through with the occasional offer of water. Tom's body clock was out of sync and he was wide awake.

Neither he nor Brianna had been able to guess the other's profession, and they had exhausted their twenty questions. Tom wouldn't budge and was enjoying the frustration he could see building in Brianna as she ticked off careers.

She was getting ridiculous now and was whispering her way through the alphabet. When she got to zookeeper and he shook his head, she turned to him and took his face between her hands. Her fingers were warm against his skin, and he resisted the temptation to reach up and hold them there. "I've been guessing for three hours now and I am not going to be able to get to sleep until I know. So you tell me and I'll tell you. Deal?"

"Deal, you go first."

"No, you go first."

"You go first… okay… rock, paper, scissors…"

Brianna raised her eyebrows as they put out their fists and fingers and Tom lost.

"Well, come on…spill."

"I am—" he paused for a moment "—a bursar."

"I knew it, I knew it," she squealed and then looked around at the other passengers sleeping and put her hand over her mouth. "I was right then when I guessed accountant." She put on a mock pout. "You didn't play fair. I guessed that straight after lawyer."

"Okay," Tom said. "I'm sorry, but it wasn't exactly what I do. A bursar is a financial administrator. I guess the difference is I don't play with numbers anymore, I manage the staff. Now it's your turn." He was very interested to hear what she did. "I've exhausted every possible profession—" He widened his eyes in mock horror "—barring the oldest profession in the world."

She made him wait for a full minute before she answered. "I've taken twelve months' leave from my job."

He tipped his head to the side waiting for her to continue. "And?"

"I'm a clinical psychologist. I work mainly with couples with relationship problems."

Tom was cross with himself. That'd be right. Of all people to get chatty with, he had to pick a psychologist. He thought back over their conversation—he'd not mentioned anything private that he could remember. He didn't have relationship problems, just preferred to keep his life private and not share his feelings with anyone. So much for the free-spirited Scottish lass he'd thought was interested in his family.

He picked up his sunglasses and fitted the headphones into his ears. She could go and find someone else to psychoanalyse. "I think I'll sleep for the rest of the flight. Good night, Brianna."

Chapter Four

"Pompous jerk," thought Brianna. She'd sat there stewing over his reaction for the three hours he'd slept, or pretended to sleep, because he'd fidgeted the whole time and she knew he was awake and was avoiding talking to her. Unable to sleep, she was now cross and tired and she let her thoughts go back to her mother's grave in Sydney. Instead of wasting time exchanging pleasantries with Tomas, she should have been planning how she was going to sort out her problems when she got to the island.

"Just water, please." Tom smiled at the steward as he poured chilled water into a cup and placed it onto the tray in front of him.

Brianna took a sip of her red wine and looked out the window. She was so angry he'd turned from her when she had revealed her profession. She'd had a glass of wine hoping it would put her to sleep, but it had the opposite reaction and now the thoughts were scurrying around in her head again. Her throat tightened and she gripped the wine glass as she stared into the dark. According to the flight screen on the back of the seat, they were flying over the Himalayas, but it was pitch dark outside.

Bloody stuffed shirt. She settled down into her seat and sipped on her wine determined to ignore him. God, if she told him her book was about sex therapy he'd probably have a conniption and request another seat. The disappointing thing was that she'd thought they'd hit it off. For someone in her profession, she was such a lousy judge of character. She'd been enjoying their playful conversation and the flight had passed quickly. As soon as he found out she was a psychologist, he'd turned away from her and pretended to sleep. At least she'd managed to forget about her mother and the inheritance and all the other problems looming in front of her. Thank God she hadn't prattled on about that. One thing to be grateful for, at least.

She glanced at her watch and did the time conversion. They were still four hours from Rome. She put her wine glass on the tray and tucked the pillow under her head, determined to get some sleep. It seemed like minutes later and she woke as the captain's voice came over the announcement system. "Ladies and gentlemen, we are making our final approach to Rome."

Her eyes flew open and she sat up straight in her seat, clenching her fingers together in her lap. "Oh, shit, I've left it too late. Inhale, exhale. Simplicity of breath. Inhale, exhale," she muttered under her breath. She closed her eyes again, ready to meditate her way through her fear and ignore the actual landing.

Inner peace and enlightenment. Breathe. Inhale. Exhale. Breathe. Inhale. Exhale.

A tentative hand tapped on her shoulder and she opened her eyes. Tom's nose was about an inch away from hers.

"Are you all right?" He was frowning and those blue eyes were full of concern.

"No, I'm not bloody all right. We're about to land."

"Oh, that's all right then. I thought you were still angry with me."

Brianna turned to him as the anger burned back up from her stomach. He might have taken the time to get to know her a little bit on this flight, he might have seen her with Phil in carefree mode, and he might have played word games with her, but this uptight *eejit* had no idea about her temper.

Tipping her head to one side, she allowed a sweet smile to cross her face and unclenched her fingers and placed her hand on his arm. She gripped it and allowed her nails to bite into his skin.

"Cross with you? Now why would I be cross with a perfect human being like you? Tom, I'm so glad I met you on this flight. I will strive to be like you for the rest of my days. And I will also start making a list so that I don't upset stuffy guys who sit next to me and think I am psycho-analysing them when I'm just trying to be friendly." She waited for him to turn away and ignore her.

I've overdone it this time, but by God, I am so sick of being judged.

All her life, she'd tried to be the daughter, her adopted mother, Jennifer, had expected her to be. She'd failed miserably. The hope of meeting her birth mother had finally died in a lonely cemetery and the events of the last few days had overwhelmed her. This poor guy had been the one to wear her temper. Before she could apologise, Tom reached into the seat pocket and pulled out his computer. His face was without expression and he didn't speak.

Shit, I've pushed his buttons too much this time. The sooner I get off this plane the better.

Tom tapped away at the keys for a few seconds and turned the screen to face her so she could read it. He had added number twelve to his list. She read it and she shook her head and smiled at him.

#12 Don't insult beautiful clinical psychologists on planes. Sorry for being such a jerk.

A row of little smiley emoticons was at the end of the typed words.

Brianna burst out laughing. "Put the computer away. The seat belt sign just came on."

The intercom crackled and the captain's voice announced the imminent landing. "Cabin crew, prepare for descent."

Tom closed his computer and slid it into the seat pocket before reaching over and taking her hand. "I really am sorry. Apology accepted?"

"Okay. I'm sorry, too." She squeezed his hand, grateful for the comfort he was giving her. "I've had a pretty emotional week and you wore it. And I was nervous about the landing."

Tom smiled and pointed out the window. *"Benvenuti all' Aeroporto Internazionale Leonardo da Vinci di Fiumicin,"* he said in perfect Italian

She looked out the window just as the wheels hit the tarmac.

"Hey, two landings and I missed both of them." She looked down at his hand, which was squeezing hers back. "Thanks to you. And I'll take back that stuffy guy comment. You're forgiven."

Brianna was amazed at his perfect Italian, or it had sounded perfect to her. "Where did you learn to speak such perfect Italian?" She turned and looked earnestly at him. "And I am interested as a friend. I'm not in psychoanalysis mode."

"My mother was born on Lipari Island . . . it's off Sicily. That's where my aunt still lives. She was already married when their parents emigrated to Australia, so she stayed there. She's a lot older than my mother, and now she's widowed. She needed some help, so I volunteered." He laughed and shook his head. "I might add, to the great amazement of my entire family. You picked me well. I am a boring balloon. So to answer your original question, we all learned to speak Italian at our mother's knee. She wanted us to speak both languages."

"No shit! That is amazing." She put her hand over her mouth. "Oh, I don't mean amazing you speak Italian. I mean . . . it's amazing you're going to Lipari." She ran her hand through her loose hair." "So am I . . .I mean . . .Lipari Island. That's where I'm going too."

Tom smiled at her. "Are you catching the ferry across from Naples?"

"Yes, I'm catching the train to Naples tomorrow and then getting the midday ferry across on Tuesday."

Lipari Island was a very small place. She'd looked it up on Google Earth. It would be great to know someone there who could speak Italian because she had a feeling the inheritance situation may become a little messy, and if she was honest, she was pleased she wouldn't be saying goodbye to Tom when they got off the plane. "What about you?"

"I'm flying to Naples tonight and then catching the Tuesday ferry. Looks like we'll catch up then. Where are you staying in Naples?"

Oh. My. God. Brianna stared at him and let her mouth drop open as a crazy idea hit her. She shut it and covered it with her hand as she stared at him.

Maybe . . . just maybe . . . the answer to her problem had been sitting next to her all the way to Italy. An over six foot perfectly believable answer who should be able to convince anyone he was her husband-to-be. All she had to do was get him to agree to it. Thoughts scurried around in her head.

"Brianna?" He looked at her quizzically.

She gave him the name of the hotel she was staying at in Naples as questions flew around her mind. "Sorry, I don't know where it is. I've lost the address, but I am sure the taxi drivers will know where to go." She closed her eyes. Yet another thing in her rucksack, although Phil would have retrieved it by now.

They made arrangements to share a taxi to the port on Tuesday morning and he added the name of her hotel into his schedule on his laptop.

"Tom?" Her heart was in her throat. She was about to make a huge fool of herself. He turned to her and frowned as she chewed her lip nervously.

"Yes?"

Bloody hell, could she do this?

She reached up and kissed him lightly, and as her lips brushed his stubbled cheek a tingle shot down her spine and she shivered.

Yes, it was about her only solution.

"Tom? Ah . . . Tom, would you consider marrying me?"

"What?" He looked at her for a moment. If it hadn't been so serious, the look on his face would have been enough to make her burst out laughing.

"You're quite serious, aren't you, Brianna?"

"Yes, I'm serious." The passengers around them began to stand and make their way down the aisle. He frowned and kept looking at her as though she was crazy.

"Look, just forget it for the time being. I'll tell you all about it when we catch the ferry on Tuesday. Okay? I'm not crazy. I'll have a proposition for you then."

Brianna stood and pushed past him, past caring that her backside was in his face as she stepped into the aisle.

"Just think about it. I'll see you later." She hurried down the aisle to where her laptop was stowed, anxious to get away from him before he could say no.

Problem number two. If Tom did say yes—and it was a long shot—if he did say yes, the next problem would be finding some way to repay him.

Chapter Five

Tom had booked a taxi through the concierge when he checked out from the hotel and now he gave the driver the address of Brianna's hotel. Unexpected anticipation curled in his stomach. He'd enjoyed exploring Naples and visiting Pompeii, and now he was looking forward to Lipari. He wondered how Brianna had spent the past couple of days. No doubt he would hear about it all the way to the island. And hear more about her crazy proposal.

He shook his head. This trip was far removed from his expectations. He was used to things going exactly as he'd planned. Maybe that's where he'd been going wrong? Once he found out why she needed a husband he would decide if she was plain crazy or if it was her ideas made her seem that way.

He'd slept soundly on Sunday night when he'd arrived on the flight from Rome and stepped out early on Monday to explore. No time to succumb to jet lag. Tomas was determined to enjoy every moment. Being able to speak the language had eased his way in Naples considerably, and he'd taken to the city like a native and had the strangest feeling of coming home. Their mother had encouraged them to appreciate their Italian heritage throughout their childhood, but apart from learning the language at home and then polishing it at university, he'd never been much interested in Italian culture. He enjoyed his mother's Italian cooking and he made sure he ate at home as often as he could, but now he was giving some thought to her belief that genetic memory played a big part in a person's cultural make up. He could get to like this place. He'd even become accustomed to the aroma of fish and garlic that pervaded every street.

It was less than a week since he'd left his office and already it felt like a different life. He'd not planned his day and had wandered around Naples as the mood had caught him and experienced the colours, flavours, and delights of this amazing city, visiting the Norman Castle, *Nuovo* and the *Castello del l'Ovo*. He'd taken the whole afternoon to spend time in the famous *Duomo* and the *Gesu Nuovo Church*. Even if he'd had to turn around and go home today, the richness of his experience in Naples had satisfied him already and he was looking forward to getting to Lipari Island.

Being alone in Italy had been most conducive to thinking, and as he'd explored, he'd given a lot of thought to what he was really doing here. The only downside had been the call from Nick.

"Hey, how's Italy?" he'd asked.

"Great," said Tom. "As much as I've seen in one day. I just got here."

"Rang to give you a heads up, mate."

"Heads up?"

"Mama and Aunt Carmen. They've been matchmaking. Looks like a bevy of hot Italian beauties may be lined up waiting for you at Aunt Carmen's apartment."

"Oh no. Please tell me you're kidding."

"Well, there's at least one coming for dinner the night you arrive. Some friend of the family. I got that much out of Mama after you left. Now that one of us is married, they're determined to set you up next."

"Thanks for the warning, appreciate it."

Tom groaned and finished the call. Nick's warning was welcome and he'd have to have a quiet word with his aunt. He was here to work . . . and then he smiled as he remembered the list he'd written on the flight. There would be time for some fun, but on his terms not anyone else's.

A blaring horn interrupted his thoughts and he grabbed for the door as the taxi driver wrenched the wheel to avoid yet another collision. One thing he would never get used to in Naples was the traffic. He closed his eyes and prayed he'd stay alive long enough to get to the ferry, as the taxi driver continued through the heavy traffic, beeping his way to their destination.

***

The phone line was filled with static and Brianna ran her free hand through her hair in frustration, before picking up the phrase book once more. It had taken the secretary from the Liparian law firm, *Antoniolli and Bruni*, two days to return her call. Luckily Phil had managed to get her rucksack back from the taxi company and she'd transferred their phone number to her laptop. At the rate she was spending money on phone calls, she'd have no money left to stay on Lipari for long.

Let alone pay someone to be her fiancé.

She had called the law firm twice yesterday, only to be told *Signore* Antoniolli was out and would call as soon as he returned. Anyway, that was what she thought the secretary was telling her. The language barrier on the phone was problematic. It was fine when you were face to face with someone. A nod and a smile and a phrase book had eased her way through the city these last couple of days.

Now, thanks to the dense secretary at *Antoniolli and Bruni*, she was running late for checkout. Tom would be waiting in a taxi and the silly woman on the other end wouldn't even try to understand. Brianna was using the phrase book in an attempt to communicate with the woman.

"*Il mio nome è Brianna. Signorina* Brianna, not *Signore* Brian. Look, I'll be there tomorrow." She scrabbled through the pages. "*Domani*, okay?"

The woman finally seemed to understand, and Brianna terminated the connection and headed for the elevator. Thank goodness she'd packed early and sent her bags down. Striding across to the checkout, she scanned the foyer for Tom and breathed a sigh of relief when he wasn't waiting.

At least she wasn't late. One thing had gone her way this

morning and her checkout followed without a problem. Moving across to the glassed entrance she waited and tried not to worry about the conversation with the secretary. She doubted if the woman had understood her, and she was going to have to turn up on spec tomorrow. Surely someone there would be able to translate. She'd have to wait and see.

A white taxi sped into the drop off area at the front of the hotel and screeched to a halt. Tom leaned across and spoke to the driver before he opened the door and stepped out.

A warm feeling shot through her when he walked across the foyer toward her. Faded jeans clung to powerful thighs that the suit pants hadn't done any justice to at all, and a loose T-shirt proclaimed *Real Men Wear Jeans*.

Brianna stood on her toes and greeted him with a kiss on his smooth, clean-shaven cheek, and inhaled expensive cologne. "Mm, yummy . . . been shopping?"

He smiled down at her, looking relaxed and more carefree than the formal man she had shared the flight with. He gestured down to his clothes. "These old rags? Na. Had 'em forever."

"No, I meant the *Silvestri*. I know my colognes."

"Well, I did fit in time for some shopping between sightseeing." He stepped back and looked at her. "It's a beautiful city. How about you? Did you get some sightseeing in?"

Brianna returned his steady gaze. His hair was mussed and his eyes were bright.

Much happier than the stranger on the plane. She'd had glimpses of this man as they had shared stories and was pleased to see how happy and relaxed he appeared.

"No. I stayed around here. Caught up on some work and tried to sort some business stuff out. With no luck, I'm afraid." She reached over and held his wrist up and looked down at his watch. "Come on, I'll tell you all about it on the ferry. We're running out of time."

Tom raised his eyebrows at her and grinned. "That's my line."

When the taxi dropped them off at the ferry terminal, she watched thoughtfully as Tom conversed with the driver in fluent Italian when he paid the fare. His snug jeans hugged his rear. He was in pretty good shape for someone who sat behind a desk all day.

Go slow. Italy might be the place for romance, but she needed him to pretend to be her fiancé first.

Forget the romance. You don't need it, girl.

***

The large inter-island ferry departed late from the busy marina and when they were finally underway, Tom stood beside her on the deck as Naples disappeared into the distance. It was a five-hour trip and they would dock about eight in the evening. Brianna planned to find a hotel room when they got there. In her usual 'trust in the gods' fashion, she hadn't booked, but she wasn't going to let that slip. Tom was going straight to his aunt's apartment. "I'll spend a couple of days there with her and then find myself an apartment."

They stood together and watched the Italian shoreline disappear in the heat haze. The smell of diesel and the cool spray forced them into the saloon of the ferry with the rest of the passengers. All of the seats were taken and they stood along the wall of the large cabin, occasionally grabbing the safety bar around the wall as the ferry ploughed through the rough swell.

"Drink?" Tom asked.

"Yes, please. I packed some snacks because I read there's not much food available on the ferry, but there is a bar."

Tom rejoined her with a bottle of red wine and a couple of plastic cups. They moved through to the smaller lounge area where there was a vacant table and settled comfortably. Brianna delved into a plastic bag and spread some cheese and crackers on a plastic plate.

"Miss Organised," Tom said with a smile.

"See, some of your organising must have rubbed off on me because I'm usually pretty hopeless at thinking ahead. Don't get too used to it." She smiled apologetically. "The next couple of days are going to be a testament to that." Even though she'd been cross at him and his reaction—or more his lack of reaction when she'd proposed to him—she was grateful he hadn't mentioned her crazy proposal yet. "Can I tell you a story?"

"Certainly." Although he agreed, two small frown lines appeared between his eyebrows and she hastened to explain.

"I've got an appointment to see a lawyer tomorrow in Lipari to sort out some personal business." They both reached for their glasses at the same moment and their hands brushed. She smiled at him as the nerve endings tingled in her fingertips. "You know how I told you I come from a big family?"

He nodded again and held her gaze.

"Well, I'm adopted and I lived in Scotland with my adoptive family for most of my life. I tried to find my birth parents in my late teens, and Dad was understanding, but I think it bothered Mum a bit. She's been pretty upset with me about a few things."

"And did you find them?"

"Not then, and I got over it for a while. I went off to university and started my career and worked for a few years in England before going back home to Edinburgh to finish my Master's degree. Then I did my clinical training and started work."

Tom looked at her intently. "How old are you? You don't look old enough to have done all that."

"Thirty-one. I was always the odd one out with my olive skin and dark hair in a family of freckled redheads. Now I know it's my Italian background."

"You've found your family, then? That's why you're going to Lipari?" He spoke slowly. "Has that got anything to do with wanting to marry me?"

Brianna laughed. "Oh Tom. I don't want to marry you. I don't want to marry anybody . . . ever. But I have to, or at least I need a fiancé."

Before he could answer she rushed on, trying to speak clearly.

She knew her accent made her difficult to understand when she got emotional.

And she was not going to get emotional.

"I'd only just arrived in Sydney when I got a letter from an Italian law firm. It's chased me around the world. Scotland to England, and then it got emailed it to me when I was at the hotel in Sydney. It said my birth mother was recently deceased and I'm the beneficiary of her cottage in Lipari, but I have to claim it by the end of the month, a couple of days from now."

"You've certainly cut it close."

"That's why I had to cancel all my plans and fly over straight away. I have until this Friday to claim the cottage. There are some conditions attached to the inheritance."

"What sort of conditions?"

"That's another favour I want to ask you. I can't get through to them at the law office. I've had five different conversations with them, twice in Sydney and three times from Naples." She looked up at him, hoping fervently he would be happy to help her out. "How would you feel about coming with me and translating for me at the lawyer's tomorrow morning? You do speak the language like a native."

A shaft of red sunlight hit the wall behind him and she jumped up and grabbed his hand. "Come on. The sun's setting over the Tyrrhenian Sea. We can't miss that."

He gathered up the cups and leftover food, and put them back into the plastic bag she'd left on the seat and then followed her out to the deck. The breeze was cool and they stood close together as the sun dropped low in the sky. One by one, the other passengers gave in to the cold breeze and headed back into the warmth of the saloon. Brianna shivered and rubbed her arms.

"I didn't think to pack a coat. Summer in the Mediterranean, I thought it would be warmer."

"It's always cool out on the water." Tom removed his jacket and placed it around her shoulders. Her skin absorbed the lingering warmth from his jacket. His fingers brushed her throat as he pulled it around her and she shivered again. *But not from the cold.*

"Happy to stay out here till sunset? It's not far off now," he said. He stood behind her and put his arms loosely around her grasping the rail in front of them. She appreciated the warmth of his body blocking the chilly breeze blowing across the deck. They watched as the blood-red rays of the setting sun tinged the clouds with shades of colour ranging from the palest pink to silver. The last sliver of the orb dropped behind the water to the west and the wind dropped almost immediately.

"Would all their colours from the sunset take, from something of material sublime, rather than shadow our own soul's day-time in the dark void of night," Tom murmured.

"John Keats? You are full of surprises, Mr Bursar." Brianna looked back at him and the wind caught her loose strands of hair and blew it into his face.

"Sorry." She turned around, reached up, and removed the hair stuck to his cheek and was surprised by an intent look on his face before he dipped his head and caught her lips with the soft warmth of his. It caught her by surprise, and she stood stiff in his arms not sure how to respond. By the time she'd come to terms with it, he'd pulled back.

"You looked sad," he said with a smile. "And I couldn't resist trying to cheer you up. And, yes, I'll help you out. I'll come along to the lawyer and translate. Now, come back inside where it's warmer and you can tell me more about this visit to the lawyer's office and what you need me to find out." Tom held out his arm and waited for her to take it. "Oh, and perhaps while we're talking, maybe you can tell me if this has anything to do with your crazy proposal on the plane."

Brianna took his arm and looked up into serious blue eyes. She had a feeling she'd been set up. Sucked in by poetry and a kiss.

##

The last hour of the trip was rough and Brianna's stomach roiled as the ferry ploughed through the waves. A number of times she'd thought she would have to run for the bathroom, but fought it back. And it wasn't because of the conversation they'd just had. She blamed the cheese, wine, and the rough seas.

When she had come clean and told him why she needed a fake fiancé, he'd sat back without speaking for a few minutes and looked at her with narrowed eyes.

"For how long?"

"I don't know any more until I see the lawyer, and that's why I need you to translate so I get all the facts right."

"So, let me get this straight." His eyes were fixed on her face. "You need someone to pretend to be your fiancé so you can inherit your real mother's house, but you don't know anything more than that?"

She gulped and nodded. He was looking at her as though she was a wayward child.

Leaning forward, he nodded at her and a strange smile tilted his lips. "I think I can accommodate you. It might suit me fine to turn up with a fiancée on my arm."

Much to Brianna's amazement, he seemed to be considering her proposal and didn't tell her she was mad. She still couldn't believe it. If it wasn't for the look on his face, she might have said he felt sorry for her. She looked up into his closed face as he ran his hair through his short, cropped dark hair. There was no pity there.

"So you thought you'd call in to the local employment agency and hire an actor?" He shook his head, obviously unable to believe anyone could be so stupid.

"No, I wasn't. There's no need to be rude," she snapped as her temper began to build. "It's my problem and I would have thought of something. You don't have to do it, Tom."

"Something?" He laughed. "Anyway, I keep my word. I've agreed to help you out and I will. I don't want any surprises when we get there. I want the complete truth."

"There's no more to tell. I apparently need a husband before I can inherit the cottage, and the why remains a mystery. That's what I'll . . . we'll . . . be finding out tomorrow."

Diesel fumes filled the saloon and Tom got up and closed the door to the deck. They sat without speaking as the ferry pounded through the heavy seas around the Aeolian Islands, before turning into a quiet harbour. The waves calmed and she began to feel better as the ferry glided across the still water. The moonlight shone on the rainbow slick of the oily water as the ferry berthed at the marina on Lipari Island

They presented their tickets and collected their bags from the luggage bay and disembarked. Brianna was grateful for Tom's hand underneath her elbow as they walked down the slippery ramp to the boardwalk dragging their suitcases behind them. Despite his arrogance, he could be polite and thoughtful.

When it suited him.

He slung both their laptop bags across his shoulders so Brianna could hold the railing with her other hand. As soon as they stepped onto the boardwalk her stomach settled and her mood improved.

Things would work out. Something would happen. It always had for her.

The narrow ramp led across to a cobblestoned corso covered with stalls, and a night market festooned with fairy lights was in full swing. She looked up in delight at bunches of wildflowers hanging in garlands around the first two stalls.

"Oh, look at those gorgeous colours!" Leaning her suitcase against a stone wall, she scrabbled in her money belt and instructed Tom to mind her bag. She made her purchase and walked back over to him, holding the sweet smelling flowers up to her face. "Come on, let's explore," she said excitedly.

He shook his head with a frown.

"We'll take your bag to your hotel first so you don't have to cart your luggage around. Where are you staying?"

She swallowed and looked up at him. "Don't know yet. Wherever I can find a hotel room, I suppose."

"You mean you haven't booked anywhere?" The exasperation was clear on his face and she glared at him.

Who did he think he was?

"Chill out, it's not your worry. After I've looked at the market, I'll go and find something. Don't be such a stuffed shirt. I'm in Italy and I plan to enjoy every second, no matter what happens."

"Brianna," he said in a condescending tone. "There are times to be responsible and then you can have fun. You'll enjoy yourself even more."

"Who says?" She put her hands on her hips and stood nose to nose with him. Or at least she attempted to. It was more nose to chest. She was tall and he still towered over her.

"I say," he said firmly. "Now, come on, we'll find you a hotel."

"But . . . " She stumbled over her words and tried to think of a suitable retort, but he took her arm and marched her up the hill away from the tempting market stalls. A small brightly-lit hotel was situated at the top overlooking the wharf and he ushered her through the doorway.

"You book in. Then we can get something to eat, and then I'll find my aunt's apartment." He gave her a tight smile. "That way I'll know where to find you so I can accompany you to your appointment tomorrow."

She glared at him without replying.

Accompany me to my appointment. Jesus, how about you come with me.?

"That's if you're still talking to me and want me to translate for you," he said as a grin crossed his face. "Oh, and if you still need that fiancé."

She gritted her teeth and made her way to the counter to ask if there was a room. If she wanted him to help her, she was going to have to put up with him taking charge, and that did not sit well with her.

When the young girl on reception told her she was lucky to get the last room because it was festival time on the island, she nodded and filled in the registration form, determined not to let Tom know he was right. Being independent had never failed her before, and she was certainly not going to start relying on someone now to get her organised. And she hadn't expected, or appreciated, the warm fuzzy feeling that had filled her chest when he'd shortened her name. Putting the key in her pocket, she walked across to him, leaving her bags at the reception counter.

"All sorted," she said forcing a carefree tone into her voice. "Don't worry about staying with me. I'm going to grab something to eat at the market and have a bit of a look around. There's no appointment time set for tomorrow, so turn up here whenever it suits you."

Regret settled in her stomach like a brick when he simply nodded at her, and handed her the laptop bag, his face expressionless. She watched until the dark swallowed him, and then asked the receptionist if she could arrange to have her luggage sent up. Forcing a jauntiness she didn't feel into her step, she headed down the hill to the night market. Even though he pushed her buttons, Tom's sense of responsibility had made things a little easier.

She could get quite comfortable having him around, despite his smartarse attitude.

Chapter Six

Tom's quiet swearing was muffled by the music and noise of the market as he headed back down the hill. He'd be damned if he was going to turn around and check if she was all right. She was *not* his responsibility.

God, she hadn't even booked a room, he thought. Talk about irresponsible. He didn't need any complications in his life. He was here to enjoy himself and not worry about someone who couldn't organise themselves. "Well, stop worrying about a grown woman you just met who is quite capable of looking after herself," said the little devil in his thoughts.

"Shit." He didn't think she could look after herself. If the conversation he had overheard with her brother was anything to go by, she couldn't even look after her possessions. And he knew what his real problem was—he found her way too attractive and too fascinating for his own good. When she'd buried her face in those bloody flowers and looked up at him, he'd been tempted to kiss her again. And that was the last thing he needed. Why on earth had he kissed her on the boat?

Sprouting Keats and kissing her?

She'd already said she thought he was a right . . . what did she call him? A right balloon. Well, he'd confirmed it for her now. He hadn't even thought about it before he'd kissed her. It'd just happened, and he was damned if he was going to lose sleep over a single kiss. In fact, he'd probably lose sleep because he couldn't get her out of his mind. And not just her problems either. The warmth of her body lingered on his skin and his heart gave a little jump.

"Nothing wrong with a good time," said the little voice. "After all, you *are* here to start your new life.

He reached the end of the street and turned right. The cathedral was on the left as he remembered, and then he passed the *Museo Archeologico* before turning back toward the harbour where Carmen's apartment was located adjacent to the small marina she and Uncle Renzo had inherited from his grandparents.

A wave of nostalgia washed over him as he turned into the street and headed toward the bright blue door of Aunt Carmen's apartment. He had played in this street as a child with his brothers and sisters when they had visited from Australia. The balcony on the first floor still had the same table and chairs and hanging plants of his childhood memories. His parents and aunt and uncle had sat up there in the early evening and watched them all playing in the street below. He shrugged off thoughts of his new Scottish friend and her problems. Dealing with his reaction to Brianna could wait till tomorrow. He had his own life to sort out first.

The entry to the apartment was at street level overlooking the marina and the office was next door. The signage to the business was faded, and there was no information about opening hours or services available. Even as he raised his hand to ring the bell, his mind ticked over. True, he knew very little about running a marina, but good business practice carried across, no matter what the enterprise was. He would have to talk to the staff about getting some advertising out there for catching the passing tourist trade.

Before he could press the buzzer, the door opened and he was assailed by the overpowering smell of rose perfume and an excited squeal. He dropped his suitcase and held out his arms as Aunt Carmen reached out, and grabbed his cheeks with her soft, plump hands, pulling his head down for an exuberant kiss on both sides of his face.

"Oh, Tomas, look how you have grown!"

He grinned. Of course he had—he hadn't visited Lipari Island since he was a teenager. It had been years since he'd last seen his aunt, but his childhood memories of spending time with Carmen and Renzo were wonderful. Before his father had taken the professorship in Armidale, his parents had travelled the world, and he had spent several summers on this beautiful island with his family. But it had been fifteen years since his last visit and now Uncle Renzo had passed on. Tom took his aunt's arm and stood back. She had aged and he was pleased he could help out and keep the business in the family.

"It is wonderful to be here, Aunt Carmen. "

"Come in, come in. I have someone I want you to meet." She chattered on as she led him into the small entry foyer. Tom picked up his bags and followed her down the narrow hallway.

"Put your bags in my room. You will be sleeping in the pull-down bed in the living room until I leave."

"Leave?"

"I am going on a trip. You will need somewhere to sleep, so you will have my bed after I leave tomorrow."

She led him into her bedroom, and Tom closed his eyes as the smell of roses mixed with camphor and mould hit him. Opening them and looking around, his stomach sank. The walls were papered in huge pink roses and on the east-facing wall a small shrine protruded out into the middle of the room. Tom placed his bags next to the table, which was filled with candles, rosaries, holy cards, and a huge photograph of Uncle Renzo. Incense burned in a small brass receptacle and his stomach moved toward his throat at the mix of the cloying smells.

"You will be able to pray in here as well." Aunt Carmen beamed at him and pointed to the prayer cushion on the floor.

Tom thought of his minimalist apartment back home overlooking the park in Armidale, with its white walls and lightly polished floors. And he hadn't been to a church since his mother had dragged him along to his confirmation over twenty years ago.

"Ah, yes. Thank you, but I will be staying with my…er…fiancé."

Aunt Carmen's face fell. "Your fiancé?"

"Yes, Brianna and I became engaged on the trip over." There was no need to tell his aunt they'd only met on the trip over as well. No one needed to know the background of this fake engagement it looked like he had decided to agree to and he'd sort out something to tell his family when he thought of it.

"If you're talking to Mama, please don't mention it yet. We haven't told anyone." Tom swallowed. "You're the first to know, Aunt Carmen."

"And I'm the second."

As they walked into the small kitchen, a young woman stood and held her hand out to Tom. Dressed in a low-cut red dress, which showed her ample cleavage, she looked him up and down and he sensed he was found wanting.

"Tomas, this is Helena. She will be your secretary in the office from tomorrow."

"Oh, good." Tom took her hand and shook it. "You can show me around and help me get set up."

"No," she said, boredom lacing her voice. "It is my first day too."

Tom turned to his aunt and she shrugged. "Ah, I thought it would be nice for you to have someone in the office with you… and Helena is my friend's daughter and she was looking for a job."

"Oh, I see." Tom wondered if Helena was one of the women Nick had mentioned on the phone.

Aunt Carmen gestured for him to sit at the table. Despite the smells in the rest of the apartment, the aroma coming from the pots on the stove was mouth-watering.

As his aunt served their meal, Tom tried to converse with Helena, but she had picked up a nail file and was filing her long red fingernails with disinterest and avoided looking at him. After a few questions to her, which she ignored, he turned to his aunt and caught her up with the family news. It was difficult to focus on the conversation, and he tried to keep his thoughts away from Brianna, but all he could see was the cross look on her face when he'd left her at the hotel. As well as those legs that went forever, Christ, he was the one who should be cross. Bloody crazy scheme and now he'd committed to it by telling his aunt he had a fiancé.

"Well, Tomas?" He realised his aunt had asked him a question.

"Are you staying here tonight? You have brought your luggage, but not your fiancé?"

"Sorry, Aunt Carmen, I must be a bit jet lagged. I'll stay here tonight with you and then Brianna and I will look for an apartment tomorrow."

God, this was becoming more complicated by the minute. Why the hell had he promised to help Brianna out?

***

Brianna sat in the warm sun, her back against the whitewashed wall of the small hotel where she'd spent the night. Her booted feet were crossed in front of her and the sun warmed her bare legs. A good night's sleep had put her in a much better frame of mind. Things were looking up. Tom would translate for her, and until she saw what the deal was with the inheritance, the lawyers would see she had a husband in the making.

She owed Tom an apology for losing her temper and being a smart-mouthed bitch last night. After all, there was really no reason for him to help her out. It wasn't as if they were even friends. She wondered why he'd agreed.

I'll hold my temper in and not say a thing, even when he does act like a jerk. She grinned when she remembered how he'd reacted last night and left her standing there. She hadn't stayed long at the market, just wandered around the cobbled streets wondering whether her mother had ever walked on the same streets at some time in her life.

She sighed. There was so much to find out and so many questions to be answered.

If Tom hadn't been coming with her this morning, she would have been in a right state by now. But knowing he'd be there had eased her mind a little. She'd slept soundly and was looking forward to sorting out the legal details, and hopefully seeing her mother's cottage. Maybe they'd even have some pictures and personal effects, something to help her know her mother.

"*Cassetta*," she corrected herself. Time to start learning the language.

It was a moment she'd waited a long time for, and she couldn't believe how close she'd come to losing it. If she hadn't made the call from Sydney saying she would be here by the end of the week, she would have missed out and the house would have gone to someone else. So there had to be more family somewhere. A shiver of excitement rippled through her. She'd tried for so long to find out about her mother. She wondered if Rosa had been born here or if she had moved here alone. It wouldn't be long now and all would be revealed . . . hopefully.

She sighed. The news about the inheritance had been totally unexpected and she hadn't had much time to think about what it was going to mean for her life. There were some big changes coming, of that she was sure.

The crunch of footsteps on the white gravel leading to the hotel entrance caught her attention, and she looked across the brightly coloured garden. Tom was striding through the gate and she pushed herself to her feet as he crossed the small patch of lawn toward her.

"Good morning." She injected as much enthusiasm as she could into her voice. "Isn't it the most sparkly day?" Lifting her arm, she shaded her eyes and pointed to the harbour where teenagers were tacking across the ruffled water in small yachts with madly flapping sails. "Look."

The morning sunlight reflected off the small waves stirred up by the light breeze as the yachts bounced along. The shrill cries of the young sailors carried across the water and were overlaid by the deep booming of the morning ferry's horn as it pulled away from the wharf for the trip back to the mainland.

"It certainly is a beautiful morning," said Tom. Despite agreeing with her, his voice was clipped, and she sensed he was still cross with her. They stood together for a moment watching the boats whiz across the bay before he turned toward the road without speaking again.

"I love this island already," Brianna said as she followed Tom out through the gate. "Everyone is so friendly. I chatted to at least half a dozen people as I waited," she added with a smile. "Well, I talked to them anyway. I didn't understand a word they said, but they were all very friendly." She held up her guidebook. "But I'm learning phrases."

Tom walked along beside her quietly as they climbed the hill to the main part of the small town, and she tried to keep a conversation going. That is if one-sided prattle with monosyllabic replies could be called conversation. If he was cross with her he could go to hell and she would cope. No one was going to spoil the day she found out about her mother. Something would happen. Trust in the universe.

"How is your aunt?"

"Well." He surprised her with not only an answer, but it was accompanied with a smile. "Aunt Carmen is a smaller version of my mother, but just as vivacious."

"I love that word," said Brianna. "Do you know the Italian for it?"

Tom glanced across at her, but she couldn't read his expression in the shadows of the shaded street.

"Very close to the English. *Vivace*."

"*Vivace*." The word rolled off her tongue, and she tried to stop her Scottish burr. "I'm picking up the language." When he didn't reply, she glanced back at him. "Even though she is *vivace*, is everything else okay? You looked like the weight of the world was on your shoulders as you came in the gate. Or is it because you are still cross with me?" She needed to clear the air before they got to the lawyer's office. After all, they were playing the role of an engaged couple in love.

He stopped and answered her with a sort of humph.

"And no, I'm not psycho-analysing you," she said. "You have to get over that perception. I've been good at picking up people's feelings since I was a child, and all my friends used to spill their souls to me. It's one of the reasons I went into psychology."

She grabbed his arm and pulled him to a stop beside her. 'Tom!'

"I'm not cross with you," he said.

"Well now, if you're not cross with me, at least be up front with me. I can tell there is something bugging you. Have you changed your mind about coming with me? Are you worried about me taking advantage of you? Are you scared you're going to appear in my book?" She stared up at him. "But for goodness sake talk to me. Get it over with and then I can sort something else out."

God, how on earth would she really cope without any knowledge of Italian? She'd had enough trouble with the secretary on the phone. She'd rushed to get here and she hadn't even thought to buy a phrase book, and her trusty guide book only had the most basic phrases in it. Then she saw the funny side of it and giggled . . . at least she could say hello and goodbye and where's the toilet?

"No, I made a commitment to you," Tom said and she smothered a smile. They were a fine pair. She couldn't speak Italian and his language was so formal.

"I'm coming with you, and no, I'm not worried that you will take advantage of me." He started walking up the hill and looked back at her over his shoulder. "And I hadn't even given any thought to appearing in your book. I'm certainly not interesting enough to appear in a psychology book."

But his formal language might come in very handy in the lawyer's office, she thought.

"I'm thinking about how we'll handle it. I'm sorry if I don't indulge in mindless chatter just for the sake of having a conversation."

The comment wiped away the grin that had been pulling at her mouth, and turned it into a cough.

Mindless chatter, indeed. Well, she could play intellectual, no conversation games, too.

If only she didn't find him so damned attractive it would be a lot easier. Every time he stood close to her, she got a whiff of his citrusy aftershave, and a sharp insistent tug of desire shot through her. *Again.*

"Aunt Carmen had prepared a room for me and wants me to

move in, but her place is no bigger than a shoe box. She had to move some furniture to get the fold-out bed down for me last night." He laughed and rubbed his back. "My feet hung over the end of the bed all night." As soon as we see your lawyer, I have to get back to the marina. My aunt is leaving for the mainland. I'd like you to come too because she wants to meet my fiancé."

Brianna stopped and Tom turned around and looked at her with exasperation.

"Jeez, you told somebody we were engaged?" she said. "It would be best if we keep it as quiet as possible."

"Yes, but it's a two-way street. It suits me well to have a fiancée too."

Relief coursed through Brianna. If he needed her as much as she needed him, there was a better chance of it all working out. She walked around in front of him and stood on her tiptoes. Ever since he'd come through the gate, she'd been watching his mouth when he spoke. Now she gave in to the impulsive urge that had been tugging at her and reached up and kissed him.

"Happy engagement."

Ignoring the warmth that filled her as she touched his lips, she pulled back and smiled at him before taking his hand. "Come on then, we'll get my legal stuff over and sorted and then we'll ask around in town and see if we can find you somewhere to live on the way back to your aunt's." She squeezed his hand. "I was so worried you'd changed your mind about coming with me."

"I don't go back on my word. You can trust me."

##

Brianna wiped her forearm across her forehead. When they stepped into the town square from the cool shade of the buildings in the back streets, the mid-morning sun was belting down. She reached up with one finger and wiped a line of perspiration from Tom's top lip.

"I thought an Aussie boy would be used to the heat."

"I live in the highlands. Cold winters and temperate summers."

She reached into her bag and then dabbed at her face with a tissue. "We're a fine pair. You know what they say about mad dogs and Englishmen. Make it a Scotswoman!"

"Which way?" asked Tom. Old brick buildings lined the footpath around the edge of the square.

Brianna swallowed nervously and looked around. "Umm . . . I'm not quite sure."

She pointed across the square. "Maybe that way?"

Tom looked back at her with a quizzical smile. "What's the address?"

"I don't actually know."

He turned with his hands on his hips. "You don't know? You've travelled across the world and you don't know where you're going?"

Despite his body language indicating otherwise, his voice was patient and it really annoyed her. "Of course I do. I know the name of the firm. It's *Antoniolli and Bruni*. I just don't have the address."

"Wasn't it on the letter they sent you?"

"Yes, Mr Twenty Questions. It was . . . but I . . . ah . . . I haven't got it with me." Irritation burned in her stomach when Tom looked at her, disbelief written all over his face.

"Well, we'll have to go back and get it." He grabbed her shoulders and turned her back toward her hotel, and looked at her with those sexy lips set in a straight line when she didn't start walking.

"Hurry up, or we'll be late," he said patiently.

"No we won't. I don't have an appointment either, remember." Sarcasm laced her voice while she tried to forget about how his lips had felt on hers. "And I suppose you're never late for anything, are you? I'd take bets on that."

"Look, do you want me to help you with this or not? I can quite easily spend my time finding an apartment. I'm happy to help, but I can't unless we actually get there."

"I'm sorry. Look, I didn't mean to snap. It's just you are so bloody perfect. I know where to go, we simply have to ask someone

216

where it is because I . . . lost the letter." Her face heated when the realisation dawned on his face.

"Lost it? Where?"

"It's in Sydney. It's a long story." She looked around and noticed a small store across the street. "It's not a problem. I'll sort it out."

Leaving him standing on the footpath, Brianna stepped into the grocery store and smiled at the short, stout woman behind the counter. Garlands of flowers hung in profusion along each side of the counter, and strands of garlic bulbs were threaded along the front of the counter. Jars of plump olives in all sorts of different coloured marinades tempted her. A huge tub full of the biggest avocadoes she had ever seen sat by the counter. For a moment she stood and inhaled the mixture of aromas, and then Tom's shadow filled the doorway and she scurried over to the counter.

"Ah . . . er . . . excuse me . . . er . . . *scusi.*" She was determined to show him she could do this without his help. The woman smiled at her. "Er... I need to find . . . Mr Antoniollo . . . and er . . . *Signore* Bruni?

The woman tilted her head to the side *"Quale?"*

"Ah . . . *Signore* Antoniolli . . . the lawyer?"

The woman shrugged her shoulders and lifted both hands, palms turned upward in that expressive Mediterranean way. Tom stepped up behind her and placed his hand gently on her bare shoulder. Her skin burned under his hand as the nerve endings fired. He spoke in rapid Italian to the little lady, and Brianna looked at him in confusion when he said avocado.

What the hell was he doing?

She stepped away from his hand. The woman laughed and replied *"Ah . . . si, avocatto."*

She stepped around the counter and took Tom by the hand, leading him across to the door before she pointed up the hill and appeared to give him directions with much waving of her free arm.

"Grazie." Tom reached into his pocket and slipped some money into the woman's hand before turning to Brianna.

"Come on, *Signores* Antoniolli and Bruni are up the hill and around the corner. His eyes crinkled at the edges. "And, Brianna, we may even be early for your non-appointment. They don't open until eleven o'clock."

##

The foyer of the law firm was a tiny room closed in with dark timber lining. A secretary sat at a small desk typing on an old-fashioned typewriter. Her fingers clattered on the keys and the bell rang when she pressed the carriage return with a flourish as she reached the end of a line. Brianna was fascinated to think that in this day and age they would have an old manual typewriter. And the old telephone handset on the desk was an old fashioned one with the numbers in a circular dial on the front.

Tom placed his hand on her back and the warmth shooting up her spine took her thoughts away from typewriters and telephones.

"Would you like me to handle this?" he asked.

She didn't need the warmth of his hand through the thin material of her spaghetti-strapped T-shirt. Her shoulder was still tingling from where he had placed his hand on her bare skin in the shop where she thought he'd had too much sun and had been buying avocados. She'd soon realised what was happening. *Avocatto* meant lawyer.

Vivace and *avocatto*. She was picking up the language quickly. At this rate, she'd be fluent by the end of the week and wouldn't need Tom to translate.

"Thank you." She didn't want to appear rude. After all, he was helping her and she would certainly find this much more difficult if she hadn't had the good fortune to meet him on the plane. Maybe he wasn't such a stuffed shirt after all. There was something to be said for being organised and planning ahead. He'd made her morning a lot easier. If it wasn't for him, she'd still be wandering around trying to find the blasted law firm. Reaching up, she took his hand and squeezed it gently.

His fingers gripped hers and those sexy, crinkly lines appeared around his eyes.

"My pleasure. We'll get you organised in no time."

She laughed softly before she replied. "Don't hold your breath. My family has been trying to do that for thirty years." She tilted her head to the side. "They don't call me Brianna. They call me lightning."

Before he could reply, the office door opened and a small man with white hair and a deeply lined face reached out and grabbed Tom's hand and shook it vigorously.

"*Signore Ballantyne, benvenuto . . . benvenuto.* He peered over the top of his little round glasses at Brianna and smiled at her. "*Signora Ballantyne?*"

He nodded his head and he kept smiling as he pumped Tom's hand. Tom began to speak, and the old lawyer raised his hand and stopped him.

"*Un momento.*"

He turned to the secretary, and pointed to the telephone. "*Signore Caranto,*" he said before ushering them ahead of him into his office.

A small lamp on the side of the desk shone onto the huge timber desk and provided the only light in the dim office. The heavy dark drapes were drawn, blocking out the morning sunshine. Brianna wrinkled her nose. The smell of mould was overpowering and she blinked her eyes trying to ignore the claustrophobia that crept over her. The elderly lawyer ushered them to seats in front of the desk, and Tom waited till she was seated before taking the chair beside her.

Tom and the elderly lawyer chatted for some minutes, and Brianna gave up trying to follow the gist of the fast-paced conversation, but it all seemed very social. There was a tap on the door and the secretary appeared with a tray of coffee and biscuits. All was quiet as she poured coffee for them.

Tom glanced across at her and when she returned his gaze, Brianna caught sight of another elderly man who must have followed the secretary into the room. He sat silently across the room in a chair in the dark corner. She nudged Tom and a look of surprise crossed his face as he also realised there was a fourth person in the room

Probably Mr . . . no, start thinking Italian, she corrected herself.

Probably *Signore* Bruni.

Signore Antoniolli paid no attention to the other lawyer and did not introduce him. He stood and crossed the room to a huge wooden filing cabinet and pulled out a sheaf of paper tied with string before launching into a lengthy conversation with Tom.

Tom participated in the discussion, intense concentration etched on his face. He seemed to be doing a lot of frowning, and the smile crinkles she loved looking at were replaced by deep lines on his forehead. Occasionally, he put up his hand to pause *Signore* Antoniolli and pointed to Brianna and asked a question of the lawyer.

She looked from one to the other and then placed her hand on Tom's arm. She wanted to know what was being said. Tom shook his head and the elderly lawyer frowned at her. A flash of white caught her eye and she looked across to the corner as the other lawyer wiped a tear from his eye. Absorbed in watching the old man wipe his eyes, she jumped when Tom reached out and placed his arm around her shoulder and pulled her close to him.

He leaned down and placed his lips against hers before she could move. "What the f—," she whispered against his lips.

"Just follow my lead," he murmured into her mouth.

"Kissing men, crying lawyers. This is bizarre," she muttered and Tom frowned at her.

She sat straight in her chair and flicked her braid over her shoulder. She concentrated and tried to follow the conversation. Signore Antoniolli directed a comment to the man in the corner, and he gave a cry of distress and jumped out of his chair, launching himself at her. He leaned over and hugged her tightly from behind, his papery skin rubbed against her cheek before he stood and wiped his eyes once again.

"*Più tardi*," he said as he walked to the door and left pulling it shut behind him.

Brianna turned to Tom, absolutely bewildered. "What the hell was that all about? Translate please."

"Later."

"No, now," she said in a furious whisper. "Tell me *now*."

Tom looked at her patiently. "It means later. *Più tardi* means later."

"Oh," she replied sheepishly. "Thank you."

The conversation continued around her and the lawyer slid some papers over for her to sign. She choked back a laugh when he passed her a fountain pen and gestured to the ink well. She looked up at Tom and he nodded.

"It's an acceptance of the conditions of the inheritance. You dip the nib in the ink," said Tom when she looked blankly at the old-fashioned pen.

"I know." She clenched her jaw. "What am I signing? Shouldn't I know first? Do I have to do it right now?"

"It's an acceptance of the deeds of your mother's house. It's called *la Casa Bianca* . . . the White House. The conditions are straightforward, but you need to sign them today." He dropped his voice to a whisper. "You've just made it by the skin of your teeth, Brianna. If you'd been one day later, the time for you to claim your inheritance would have run out and you would have had a huge legal battle on your hands."

"Oh," she said in a small voice. Tears filled her eyes and her chest tightened as emotion welled through her. Her hands shook as she dipped the pen in the ink well.

My mother. My real mother. Rosa's house.

She fought to stop her chin quivering as she signed the paper with shaking hands.

She'd had no idea it could be sorted so quickly. The lawyer smiled hugely when she pushed the papers across the desk to him. He went to a cupboard and pulled out a heavy brass key and handed it to

Tom. Brianna's throat tightened and she swallowed. Her chest was heavy and this stuffy room was closing in on her

I have to get outside.

"Congratulazioni." Signore Antoniolli shook Tom's hand and then hers, before he ushered them through the door. *"Fino a domani."*

Brianna quickly walked out and Tom followed. The midday sunshine was bright and she covered her eyes, blinking back tears.

"Are you all right?"

"No," she said taking deep gulps of the welcome fresh air. "I'm starting to realise this is all true. It was an adventure when I got that letter and now—" she reached across and took the old key from Tom, "— I am holding the key to my mother's house."

She burst into tears, unable to hold the emotion back any longer.

***

Tom looked down at Brianna as she sobbed and grasped the large key to her chest. He stepped over and put his arms around her and patted her awkwardly on the back. The loose hair that constantly unwound from her braid tickled his nose and the softness of her breasts pressed into his chest. He had been privy to Brianna's emotion since she had first squeezed past him on the plane. She was open and honest, and didn't seem to hold back no matter how she was feeling.

Even when she thought I was a jerk.

She leaned into him closely for a few seconds and then she stepped back with a muffled sniff, before childishly wiping her nose with the back of her hand. She held the key and turned it over and over, rubbing her long slender fingers against the gnarled edge. His heart kicked in sympathy as the tears rolled down her cheeks.

She wiped them away. "Okay, Mr Italian speaker. Take me to my house." She smiled up at him through her tears. "I'm sure you asked for the address?"

Tom looked down at her.

"Yes, *Signore* Antoniolli gave me the address. It's actually in the next village and we have to catch the bus. The village is called

Cannetto."

He ran his hand through his hair and turned away from her for a moment to gather his thoughts.

How the hell was she going to take the rest of the news he had to tell her?

The content of the conversation that had taken place in the office would floor her. It still floored him and he needed to take some time to digest what he had done himself.

He grabbed her hand and led her across the street. He'd really become a part of Brianna's adventures and had given little thought to the reason for his own visit. He had to get back to the marina later in the day, and he had to remember his commitments there. This feisty woman was in the forefront of his mind and he needed to pull back.

"Before we catch the bus, we need to sit down and have a coffee so I can tell you what happened. There were a . . . er . . . a few more legal things we have to organise."

"There's a café over there by the square." She pointed past the fountain to an outdoor café. "Come on, I want to hear everything." Keeping his hand gripped tightly in hers, Brianna marched toward the middle of the square, her boots pounding on the cobblestones as she dragged him along behind her. He glanced down and was far enough behind to admire the long tanned legs beneath her shorts before he caught up to her.

Tom shook his head. He had never before met a woman who was so sure of herself, yet so soft and emotional at the same time. She had layer upon layer of resilience, and he was getting a fascinating glimpse of her character each time she was presented with a challenge.

"And who was that crazy old man who grabbed me on his way out of the office?" she asked as they passed an old fountain with a statue of Neptune extending his arms in a lordly gesture of stilling the waters. "That was downright creepy. Strangest law firm I've ever been in."

"Ah… he was—" Tom cleared his throat, at a loss for words.

Just tell her.

"He's your grandfather."

Brianna stopped abruptly and Tom bumped into her almost pushing them both into the fountain.

"What did you say?"

"I said he is your grandfather. Come on, I'll tell you everything when we sit down."

By the time, they sat down and their coffee was brought to the table, Brianna appeared more composed. Her tanned face was unusually pale, and a little freckle he hadn't noticed before stood out on the side of her cheek. He reached over and took her hands in his, and a jolt of pleasure ran through him when she responded and tightly linked her fingers through his.

"*Signore* Antoniolli filled me in on your family background and the strict conditions of your inheritance. Now, tell me what you know first so I don't repeat it all."

Being devious didn't come naturally to him. He needed to be sure she hadn't known the conditions of the will and he wasn't being conned. He remembered Nick telling him on many occasions that he was a soft touch. Too many women had tried to dupe him, making him look the fool.

"Hello?" Brianna tugged on his arm.

"Oh, sorry. Where were we?" He straightened in his chair and brought his mind back to the present. "Now, tell me what you know about your Liparian family."

"My Liparian family?"

Her Scottish burr and the Italian words were an interesting mix. He could listen to her soothing accent all day.

"Nothing, zero, zilch, I know nothing. The first I knew was the letter I got in Australia and when I rang the number they asked for Brian." She pulled one hand back from his and grabbed her braid. He was starting to recognise this was a sign she was nervous.

He took a deep breath wondering why the hell he'd done what he had.

Was he crazy? He'd had taken a lot upon himself in the lawyer's office and was more than a bit wary of her reaction, to say the least. Maybe he should have run it by her first, but he didn't want to give the lawyer any inkling that things weren't as he thought.

He'd come over here to loosen up and certainly hadn't expected to get married as soon as he arrived. Taking a deep breath, he prepared to tell her what he'd just promised the lawyer.

Chapter Seven

"You what?" Brianna looked at Tom wondering if he was the crazy one. "Did you just say we are getting married?" She pulled a tissue from her bag and wiped the last of her tears away.

Tom nodded.

"And you did say tomorrow?"

When he nodded a second time without speaking, she pushed her chair back and stood up.

"Whoa. I said I needed a fiancé, not a bloody husband." She strode out for the bus top across the square, not caring if he followed her or not.

"Brianna, wait." Tom hurried after her, catching her as she reached the bus stop. "Don't go getting yourself all worked up."

She looked up at the sign above the bus stop at the far end of the square. She could read the sign to the towns the bus visited and it said Cannetto so she was in the right place. At the moment, she didn't care if Tom was with her or not. Her temper was firing and she was having trouble being polite.

"Worked up? I asked you to pretend to be my fiancé and before I know it you've organised a whole bloody wedding with my lawyer without one word to me."

"Will you listen to me?" He spoke loudly as he grabbed her arm and she looked down with disdain. There was no one around to overhear them in the square was deserted. "Unless you signed that document today and also proved you were married, there was no way you would have got your mother's house. As it was, I had to do some quick thinking and assure him we were getting married straight away or you would have missed your chance."

She leaned against the warm brick wall and folded her arms and watched Tom. Her temper faded away and was replaced by a glimmer of sympathy as she appreciated what he'd done. Before she could speak the bus appeared around the corner and Tom put his hand out and held it as they walked over to the bus. After they boarded, he followed her to the back of the bus where there were two vacant seats.

Her shoulder rubbed against his as the old bus trundled up the steep hill to Cannetto, the village closest to Lipari. The spectacular view across the water from the top of the cliff filled the window as the bus lurched close to the edge of a big drop. Neither the sapphire-blue waters of the Mediterranean nor the profusion of wildflowers growing down the side of the cliff could hold her attention while she tried to process what Tom had just told her.

I have a grandfather and he wants to see me this afternoon.

And I have a house.

And Tom and I are getting married.

A giggle bubbled up from her chest and she fought to control it. He sat there beside her with no expression. He was a master at hiding what he was thinking, although he had been very intense when he'd held her hand and told her what had ensued in the lawyer's office. For some reason, she could see the humorous side of what he'd done. She choked it back and the tears welled in her eyes. He reached over and patted her arm.

"It's okay. I'll help you sort it out."

She leaned forward, her shoulders shaking from crying, and put her hands over her face. Tom rubbed her back, his warm hand etched soothing circles through her thin T-shirt, and her skin sizzled beneath his fingers.

"Come on." His voice sounded strained. "It's okay. We'll figure out a way to get around it. There's no need to cry." Brianna straightened up and looked across at him.

"I've had some amazing friends in my life and lots of people have done good things for me, but no one has ever stepped up for me like you did today." She leaned across and somehow his arm ended up around her and she was against his chest. "What you did was the most gracious and amazing thing. Now tell me all the details."

She laughed with sheer delight when he'd repeated what had been discussed in Signore Antoniolli's office. Then in his organised fashion he ticked off the things they needed: an *Atto Notorio* filled in at the town hall and faxed to the consulate, a statutory declaration, and their birth certificates. He had been amazed when she said she had a copy of her birth certificate in her travel documents.

"I carried it with me to Australia, in case I needed proof of identity over there. But surely he knows your aunt. It's such a small island. Wouldn't he have known you were coming over anyway? Is it too much of a coincidence?" She chewed her bottom lip.

"No." Tom paused for a moment. "There is something a bit tricky there, but nothing you need to worry about yet. I'll explain later, but he definitely didn't know either of us were coming until they rang him today." He leaned in closer, and Brianna got a whiff of his aftershave and stared back at him fascinated by the black rims around his deep blue irises. She hadn't noticed before what beautiful eyes he had.

"I knew I was taking a big risk telling him we were about to get married, but I couldn't risk telling you in the office, because he might have been a bit suspicious. Especially with your grandfather there."

"So—" She dragged her attention back to what he was saying. "You said we would be getting married soon just so I wouldn't lose the house? Why would you do that for me? It's not like you even really know me." She looked up at him as gratitude overwhelmed her. "I thought maybe being engaged would be enough. I really didn't expect I would have to be married."

"The terms of the will are explicit. Once the marriage certificate is signed, the inheritance will be completed. In the meantime, he let you have the key so you can have a look at the place."

She shook her head and tried to shake off the feeling she was in a dream. Even though she had known from the letter the inheritance all hinged on her being married, deep down she hadn't really thought it would happen.

"Bri."

He shortened her name and she liked the roll of the abbreviation in his deep voice.

"All I could think of was my family and what it would be like not to have known my own mother. And I knew you now had the opportunity to find out about your own birth mother." He shook his head, a rueful expression on his face. "You don't know me very well, but let me tell you, never have I made a decision so quickly in my life."

"I'm still not sure it's the right thing to do, but I guess we're sort of stuck with each other till we get this sorted."

Looking up into his face, she was taken aback by his expression. Something serious, something much deeper than a friendship was in his gaze and her heart pounded a warning.

She sat back in her seat, pulling away from the arm still loose around her shoulder. "Okay, it's time we made an agreement here. We can't risk doing it through the lawyer, so we'll have to draw up something and sign it together."

"Cross our hearts and hope to die? In blood." He grinned unapologetically. "Sorry, I have brothers."

"Talk about loosening up. Must be the Mediterranean air. Don't be flippant." She shook her head and grinned back at him. "I appreciate what you've done, but we do need some sort of agreement. For all you know, I might demand half your money when we annul the marriage."

"That's a good idea," he said, the grin still on his face. "You never know, I might want half your cottage in six months."

Brianna looked at him curiously. When he dropped the serious face, Tom had quite a sense of humour. Before she could reply, an elderly woman stood and pulled the bell rope and the bus stopped in the middle of a cobblestoned square in Cannetto.

"We're here," said Brianna. "Come on."

***

They stood on the crest of the hill on the northern side of the village. Tom had sought directions from the bus driver who had told them to follow the road through to the other side of the little village.

"It's magnificent." Brianna took a deep breath and stood staring out over the sea.

Mount Stombroli lay seven miles to the north across the Tyrrhenian Sea. Clouds of smoke hung over the volcanic island and contrasted with the deep blue sky and the azure waters of the sea. From the side of the road, the hill ran steeply down to a magnificent white beach.

"Oh, I do hope we can see the water from the cottage."

"Come on, let's find this place and then all your questions will be answered." Tom tugged at her hand and they walked up the steep hill.

"Are you sure he gave you the right directions?" Brianna asked stopping and pulling a water bottle from her bag after they had climbed for another ten minutes.

"Yes, I am sure. It should be around the next bend."

She skipped ahead of him and he smiled to himself. From a distance, she looked like a teenager with her long gangly legs and her dark braid flying in the breeze as her excitement at seeing her mother's house spurred her along.

A whitewashed villa sprawled down the hill at the end of the road. The vista of the sea formed a scenic backdrop to the waves breaking gently on the pebbled beach far below them.

"Is this it?" He strode down the hill and caught up to Brianna who stood at a locked wrought iron gate. Tom peered over the top of the intricately scrolled metal into a paved courtyard with a small fountain in the middle. Wind chimes tinkled and the soft sound of the cascading water greeted them from inside.

"This is it. La Casa Bianca." Tom held the key out. "The White House."

"But . . . but . . . it's not a cottage. It's a lot posher than I

230

imagined. I thought it was going to be a wee cottage." Bianca's hand shook as she inserted the large key Mr Antoniolli had given them. To Tom's surprise the gate opened noiselessly on the first turn of the key and they stepped through.

"Oh, my God. Look at this." Bianca turned to him, wide-eyed. "Is this really the right place? Is this my mother's place? Did the lawyer say it's really going to be mine?"

"Twenty questions again, Bri?" He couldn't help grinning at her delight and stood back as she whirled around and took off to the side of the building.

He followed her slowly, allowing her time to have her first look alone.

It wasn't a cottage. It was a small villa that was well cared for, and it was obvious from the pots of pink and red geraniums spilling down the sides of the wall overlooking the sea that someone still maintained it on a regular basis. The windows shone, and the pungent smell of thyme growing in the cracks between the cobblestones floated in the still air as it crushed beneath his feet.

Brianna stood at the wall overlooking the white pebbled beach far below, with her back to him, hands gripping the bricks tightly, her shoulders shaking. The unpredictability of this woman left him guessing most of the time. The emotions she showed freely confused him. He hesitated, unsure if she was laughing or crying this time, and then walked across and stood next to her. He breathed in deeply, as the heady aroma of the geraniums and herbs filled his senses and followed her gaze. Below the whitewashed brick edge of the balcony, a steep hill covered in yellow wildflowers led down to the shoreline. There was another small gate at the side of the balcony opening to a rough stone path that meandered along the cliff down to the water.

"I know I'm being emotional." She turned and smiled shakily up at him through her tears. "But it's so amazing. Pinch me, Tom. Tell me this is real. I'm not dreaming?"

He patted her on the arm. God, he'd run a mile when his sisters had gone through their teenage emotional stage and he'd didn't know how to react to Brianna. "Okay?"

She turned into him and he held his arms out. She buried her wet face in his chest, taking gulping sobs as he rubbed her back. Her whole body was shaking. This time there was no laughter. The loose hair from her braid tickled his nose, and as he turned his head to the side, he inhaled the sweet jasmine scent of her hair.

"I don't know if I can even go inside. I thought I could do this. I had childhood strange childhood. Even though I love Mum and Dad, and Phil, and Susie to pieces, I never truly belonged in the family. When I got the letter, the thought of Italy and a little cottage took over. But Tom—" She pulled back and he looked down into her red-blotched face—"this is my mother's house, my real flesh and blood mother who gave birth to me, and now I know she's dead and I'll never see her, but I feel like I've come home. This is where I belong."

Tom's eyes pricked at the mix of grief and happiness on her face.

"Are you going to be all right to meet your grandfather later? You don't have to do it all in one day."

"Yes," she said dragging in a deep breath. She touched his shirt, which was damp from her tears. "Thank you, you're a good man. Now come with me while I explore my mother's home, my new home."

The same large key opened the ornate metal screen door leading into the villa from the back courtyard. Like the outside of the house, the interior was clean and well maintained. Even though it was empty, it was not musty and had a welcoming feel. Tom followed Brianna as she walked slowly from room to room. The villa was spacious and the two bedrooms, small bathroom, and living area adjoining the tiny kitchen were bursting with colour. Pottery, rugs, and paintings in bold, bright colours contrasted with the stark white walls and the white tiled floors. Each room had an external door opening out to the balcony, which wrapped around the whole house.

Brianna was quiet as they looked around. She stopped in the

living room and ran her hand along the back of the deep sofa and stood looking out over the water. Every room faced the sea. Comfortable chairs sat by the large windows and brightly covered shawls and throw rugs graced every piece of furniture. The afternoon sunlight streamed in onto the tiled floor. She slowly pulled open a cupboard door in one of the bedrooms and sighed softly.

"Oh my God. Look, Tom, all my mother's things are still here. It's like an Aladdin's cave."

She opened doors and cupboards until it overwhelmed her. Her throat clogged with tears and she decided to wait until she moved in before she examined the rest of the possessions her mother had left in the house.

"Come on, let's head back to Lipari," she said. "It's a bit much to take in all at once, and there have been enough tears for one day." She caught Tom's hand as he passed her the key to lock the door.

"Tom . . ."

He gazed down into her face, her eyes bright but clear of tears.

"Yes? What's wrong?"

"I've been thinking. Look, I'm still getting my head around all this. After we get married—" She stopped and giggled—"Shite, can you believe I said that? I really feel like I am dreaming."

"Yes?"

"You know you'll have to move in here with me. You said your aunt's apartment was too small. We'll have to keep up the appearance of being married so you can't go finding an apartment. But now I've seen it and felt it . . . there's no way I'm letting this opportunity go." She met and held his gaze. "Not because it's a lovely little villa perched on top of an island in the Mediterranean, but because it was my mother's." She grabbed both his hands and looked at him, her eyes wide. "What do you think, Tom? There are two bedrooms. There's the bus down to Lipari every day, although if it wasn't for the hills, the villages are close enough to walk between."

Tom's gut clenched. Her wide green eyes were bright with

happiness. It made sense and he did need somewhere to live, and if they were going to go through with this marriage, they would have to make it appear real or it would be for nothing. But he wasn't sure, things were going way too fast for his liking, even though he'd told the lawyer they'd get married, he hadn't really expected it would happen.

"What do you think? Could you agree to live with me for a few months? Could you stand it?" She spoke fast and her words ran together. "I'll be busy writing my book, and I promise to leave you in peace and give you some space."

Looking down at her, a surge of affection rushed through him and he smiled.

"I think I could stand it, and I am very grateful for the offer." He reached across and wiped a single tear from her cheek with the pad of his thumb. "After all, you don't really know me."

"How about a simple agreement, sealed with a kiss." He bent his head and briefly pressed his mouth on her trembling lips. He pulled back as a surge of desire headed straight to his groin.

He turned away before she could glance down and see the effect of that single kiss.

"You lock up," he said gruffly. "I'll wait out here. We'll go down to Lipari and you can meet my aunt."

She looked at him with a knowing glance, and he cursed inwardly as she turned to the door. It was obvious she knew why he'd turned away, even though he'd tried to change the subject.

It was a shame the island was so small. There was no way they could get a legal agreement drawn up and keep it quiet. They would have to draw up a gentlemen's agreement. It could jeopardise her inheritance if they got it done on the island. He'd surprised himself when he had told Mr Antoniolli they had waited before they came to Italy to get married. There was nothing in it for him, but it would solve the problem of his matchmaking aunt. And that was almost payment enough for what he was about to do, for a perfect stranger.

Chapter Eight

Brianna's nerves got the better of her as they waited outside the Aunt Carmen's apartment. She paced up and down the narrow footpath as Tom rang the doorbell a second time.

"Maybe, she's not home?" she said hopefully.

"She's expecting us." Tom reached out and took her hand. "Come on, she might be down in the office." A surge of warmth shot up Brianna's arm at his touch as he pulled her along. She wasn't used to having a reaction like this when a man touched her casually.

He wasn't her usual type and she pushed her emotions aside and tried to think logically. She was obviously a bit fragile with all the family stuff happening.

That's all it was.

They walked down a narrow path at the side of the building and walked along a short wharf back to the office. An elderly woman in a bright pink dress had her arms around a woman sitting at the desk. As they entered the room, the younger woman stood and pointed at Tom.

"Sto lasciando questo lavoro"

She picked up her elegant leather bag and slung it over her shoulder and walked across to Brianna. Dressed in what appeared to be a designer suit and four inch heels, she towered over Brianna who was still dressed in her shorts, T-shirt, and sturdy walking boots.

"Pah, she looks like *ze* boy anyway. You will be sorry you didn't marry me. You could have had a real woman."

Brianna's heart plummeted and she looked from Tom to the elderly woman in confusion. Tom already had a girlfriend here? He hadn't even mentioned her.

At least the house was signed over, but they still had to go through with the marriage before it was final. And from his conversation earlier, she knew Tom was having second thoughts and now she knew why.

"Tom?"

"Don't worry, I'll explain later. Helena just quit her job." His face was flushed and she could see the pulse beating in his cheek. She pulled her hand out of his and turned away.

"Brianna, this is my Aunt Carmen."

The old woman enfolded her in a close hug and Brianna blinked to clear the tears pricking behind her eyelids

"I am very happy to meet you, Aunt Carmen. May I call you that?" She rushed on, not sure what she was trying to prove, but it was a way to get Tom's intentions out in the open.

"Are you able to delay your trip? I would love you to stay for our wedding."

*****

Tom sat in the work yard of the marina looking out across the small harbour, watching Matteo, the young labourer, sand down the hull of a hire boat. Apart from the recently departed secretary, there were no other employees.

"Shit," he muttered. "Double shit."

Aunt Carmen had spent the better part of the afternoon showing him through the office and the overflowing boxes that comprised her financial records. When he asked if she had a computer, she had simply shaken her head and pointed to the boxes and handwritten ledgers on the table. The record keeping of the business was in such a mess that it would take him weeks to sort it out. If he'd known how bad it was, he would never have bought the business. In fact, he probably would never have come to Italy. For a moment he wished he was back in his organised office at the university with his own apartment to go home to.

He'd had no idea that the business records were in such an archaic state. The information her accountant had sent over to him had seemed to indicate there was some sort of computer system in place. But no, it was all handwritten. He would buy a computer and hire a new secretary who would enter data until at least this year's records were in some sort of system.

"Shit," he said again.

That is if there were any records. There didn't appear to be any activity. It seemed the hire boat business had died along with Uncle Renzo last year. All he had was a couple of old boats and one workman. No tourist trade, no hire boats, no day trips.

His aunt had been delighted to meet Brianna and had agreed to delay her departure until after the wedding. He certainly didn't want to upset her with questions about the marina; he'd just have to get on with it the best he could.

God, he had so much on his mind.

The look on Brianna's face when Helena had been so rude to her was something he couldn't shake from his mind. He'd have to explain to her late he didn't even know the woman. She'd made it sound as though they'd practically been engaged.

How did every part of his life get so complicated in a few short days?

He looked down at the cell phone in his hand. There were a couple of calls he had to make. Or maybe he'd just call Nick? He stared at his phone wondering what the hell he was going to tell his family. They'd think he'd gone mad.

"Okay . . . deep breath. Which one?"

He shook his head. He was going bonkers sitting here talking to himself. Choosing the easy option, he punched in the speed dial for Nick.

After a long silence the international connection clicked through and he waited for Nick to pick up, hoping at the same time he wouldn't. He thought he was crazy and he knew his brother would give it to him. Perspiration trickled into his eyes, and he used the back of his hand to wipe his brow. He remembered how Brianna had soaked his shirt with her tears when she'd seen her mother's villa.

I'm doing the right thing.

"Tomas." Nick's voice replaced the buzzing ringtone. "You

there, bro?" said Nick

"Hello, Nick, it's Tom."

"Yeah, I know, you mutt. I have caller ID. How's *la dolce vita*?"

"The what?"

"The sweet life. With all those gorgeous Italian girls Aunt Carmen has surely introduced you to already."

Tom looked out over the marina at the coloured sails fluttering in the breeze and the two small skiffs racing each other across the harbour. The hulls of the small craft slapped on top of the waves and the call of the spectators on the shore encouraged them to go faster.

"Great, all good. I got here in one piece and Aunt Carmen is as delightful as ever, although I have my work cut out with the business. Her accountant was less than honest in his outline of the financial system."

"It'll do you good to get some Italian sun and relax away from your computer for a change."

"Ah, Nick . . ."

"What's up?"

"Ah . . ."

"What's the matter? Is everything okay?"

Tom paused and a frisson of excitement tingled down his spine and he cleared his throat. "I rang to see if you and Lissy were settled in to your new jobs in Auckland . . . er . . . and to tell you I'm getting married tomorrow."

For a full minute, there was silence, and Tom looked at the screen thinking the connection had dropped and was about to press end and redial when Nick's voice roared through the phone.

"Are you taking the piss out of me? What do you mean you're getting married? And I thought I heard you say tomorrow!" Tom could hear Lissy in the background.

"Long story, Nick. It's all good. I'll send you an email when I get my internet connection all sorted. The service is unreliable over here. Do me a favour, tell Mama I have some news, and tell everyone

I'll call in a couple of days. I'll try and get Aunt Carmen to hold off ringing Mama, but I know what they're like. I didn't want her ringing before I got a chance to call. I'll talk to you in a few days. Okay?"

He spoke over Nick as his brother continued to protest. "*Ciao.* Give my love to Lissy."

His phone rang almost as soon as he disconnected the call.

"What the f—. All right, Lis . . . okay, I'll calm down." Nick's voice roared through the phone. "Tom, I swear if you don't tell me what's going on, I'll jump a plane and come there. What do you mean you're getting married? Are you kidding me?"

"Calm down. It's all above board. I'm helping out a friend out with a legal issue. She has to be married for an inheritance and I'm helping out, but keep that quiet. That's between you and me. According to the lawyer, there's already a bit of bad blood between the families and I don't want it to get around."

Nick's curse came down the phone, and Tom held it away, but the deep tones of his brother's voice came through even with the phone held away from his ear.

"What friend? You don't have any friends."

"Thanks, mate. I'll remember that one."

"Oh, Christ, Tom, you know what I mean. You don't have any friends in Italy."

"It's all right. We sealed an agreement this morning and it's only for a few months."

He closed his eyes as Nick continued questioning him and remembered the feel of Brianna's open lips beneath his as they had sealed the agreement. Her lips had been soft against his and had clung for a few seconds longer than he'd intended.

"Five minutes you've been away from home. Tom . . . you are such a soft touch . . . haven't you learned anything yet? You think you are going to get bloody married just to help out some stranger on the make? Mate, she saw you coming."

Hot anger burned up from his stomach. He was sick of being the responsible brother.

"Don't treat me like a fool." His voice was cold and it seemed to get through to his brother straightaway.

"Oh for God's sake. Be careful. Don't go getting yourself into anything messy."

Tom smiled to himself. "Don't worry, mate. It's not messy," he said as his temper cooled. "I'll call you in a couple of days, but first can you please tell Mama what's happening in case Aunt Carmen decides to ring her. She's going to witness the ceremony."

He ended the call and leaned back against the wall before glancing at the time on his phone. It was almost time to meet Brianna at the small café. He grinned to himself and shook his head. She was hopeless. Her cell phone charger had disappeared and she couldn't charge her phone so she was going to email the news of her inheritance to her family in Scotland from the public computer in the small café in the square. Only about the inheritance—she'd decided not to tell them about the marriage until it was all over. "The less family involved the better," she'd said.

It was shame he'd had to tell his family, but he knew Aunt Carmen wouldn't be able to keep a secret, and he couldn't tell her the truth in case it got back to the lawyer or Brianna's grandfather.

***

Brianna stood outside the café and watched Tom walk across the cobblestoned square toward her. Much to her surprise he was late. She'd finished emailing the family and knew there would be a flurry of emails in return when they found out she was in Italy, but she'd told them no details. It was now late in the afternoon and the village centre was deserted, the only sound the gushing of the water directed by Neptune in the fountain. She'd been waiting for Tom for over half an hour and was starting to wonder if he'd changed his mind. Ever since she'd met Aunt Carmen and the woman who was upset that she was marrying Tom, her mind had been in turmoil. And now she had to meet with her grandfather.

She squared her shoulders and bit down on her lip. This was going to be difficult.

Her grandfather. A flesh and blood relative.

It was so hard to believe. The strange old man in the lawyer's office had unnerved her and her stomach churned. Thank goodness Tom was coming also, so there could be no misunderstanding if her grandfather couldn't understand her English.

Tom stood beside one of the outside tables and waited for her to join him. She smiled at him when he pulled the chair out for her. He'd had his wee sulk on the plane when he'd thought she was psychoanalysing him, but the moodiness had left him since they'd arrived on the island.

The light breeze from the harbour blew his damp hair into disarray and she smiled. He was looking more relaxed every day. The formal suit he had worn to the lawyer's office this morning had been replaced by snug fitting jeans and a tight black T-shirt, and he looked like an Italian local with his dark hair and olive skin.

"You're looking very casual." She tipped her head to the side.

"I've been jet skiing. I've started on the list. One down, ten to go" A wide grin crossed his face. "Sorry I'm a bit late, but after I came back in Matteo wanted to show me the hire boats that need repairing. He wants to teach me how to do it and then we'll be able to hire them out again."

She shook her head, unable to picture it.

"Don't look so sceptical. I'm not totally a businessman. I can sand and fix a few little boats. And I can't face that office yet. And you know what? I've crossed two things off the list."

She smothered a laugh. Most of the boats in the harbour and dotted around the shoreline were not so little. "What's the second thing you've crossed off?"

"I haven't made a list since I got here."

Brianna sat back and looked at Tom and a funny feeling filled her chest. He was so damned attractive. If they didn't have all this hassle hanging over them, she would be tempted . . . But no, it would complicate matters too much. Which reminded her, they still had to come up with an agreement. She stifled a giggle—maybe they could put a sex clause in it.

They ordered their drinks and sat silent while the tourists disembarking from the afternoon ferry filled up the square.

"It is a beautiful place. And off the beaten tourist track. I'd never heard of Lipari until I received the letter from Mr . . . I mean *Signore* Antoniolli." Tom sipped his coffee and looked at her intently. "I have to get my head around this language if I'm going to stay here for a while."

"Do you think you'll stay for long?"

She shrugged. "Depends how it all pans out, I suppose. I know I've got the house, but it all rests on what happens with my…grandfather. I would really love to settle here for a while."

"Are you ready to meet him?"

"As much as I'll ever be, I suppose. I'm still trying to get used to having a real grandfather, like a blood relative." She sighed. "Just tell me a wee bit more about what the lawyer said."

"He said your grandfather was only happy for you to have the house once he assured him we were getting married on the island . . . and soon. I think he maybe doubtful about whether we are genuine or if we are just getting married for you to get your inheritance."

His face was serious and the doubt settled in Brianna's stomach.

"He seems to be an astute old thing. That's why I said we were getting married soon. It came out of nowhere."

"As long as you are sure you want to go through with this. What about your girlfriend?" She looked away from him and picked up the small teapot. Her hand shook as she poured her tea and waited for his answer. She'd waited for him to explain what that was all about, but he obviously wasn't going to mention it.

"Are you having second thoughts?" asked Tom.

She looked up and was surprised by the frown crinkling his forehead as though he would be disappointed if she changed her mind.

He was probably hoping she would.

"No. I'm worried about the huge favour you are doing for me. I can't understand why, especially when it's upset your girlfriend. Did you meet her in Australia?"

Tom looked at her and shook his head as he ran his hand though his hair in a frustrated gesture which was becoming quite familiar to her

"I don't have a girlfriend. She's Aunt Carmen's friend's daughter and for some reason she was expecting to get a job and a husband out of my visit. My aunt and her mother had obviously given here some expectations."

Tom reached over and took her hand and the usual heat rushed in.

"Honestly, I met her for the first time when I arrived at Aunt Carmen's after I dropped you at the hotel the other night." He pulled out his phone and checked the time. "It's almost time to meet him. Are you ready?"

Brianna jumped up and walked around the table. She stood behind Tom and draped her arms around his neck before bending down and kissing his cheek, letting her lips linger on his freshly shaved skin.

"Okay, even if I can't understand why, I guess we need to make this look genuine if we're going to go through with it." With a deep breath she inhaled the citrus tang of his aftershave and a spark of desire ran down her spine as he looked back at her. This tug of attraction hit her at the strangest times, and she decided to put it down to her overcharged emotions. That's what it was. It was plain relief, not attraction. And he *was* a good-looking guy, so that was a bonus. She pulled back from him and tugged at his hand. "Come on then, we'd better get going."

"There's one more thing you need to know before we go," he said slowly as he stood.

She looked up at him, the tone of his voice worrying her.

"Oh God, what now?" She pulled her braid over her shoulder and twirled the loose hair at the end through her fingers.

"Apparently, there is some bad blood between our families."

"Well, that's nothing we can't sort out," she said. "Family feuds have nothing to do with us. It's just as well you're here to translate for me. If he doesn't speak English, I'll keep looking at you lovingly while you speak for me." She smiled and was pleased when he continued to hold her hand firmly in his as they made their way across the square back to the office of Bruni and Antoniolli.

Tom pushed open the door to the lawyer's office and the secretary gestured for them to take a seat. It was a short time before they were ushered into Signore Antoniolli's office. Her grandfather was standing straight and tall, next to the lawyer.

Brianna looked up into his unsmiling face. His demeanour had changed since this morning's meeting when he had rushed out of the office, and her heart rate picked up. She forced a pleasant smile onto her face, determined not to let her nervousness show.

"*Buongiorno,*" said Tom holding out his hand. Her grandfather nodded and ignored Tom's proffered handshake.

Mr Antoniolli directed them all to a seat before leaving the three of them alone in his office. They sat together in the small office until the silence became uncomfortable. Brianna gripped Tom's hand as her grandfather looked from one to the other. Eventually, he locked a wary gaze on Tom's face and spoke for a few moments.

Tom leaned over to Brianna after he replied to the old man. "He said he is happy to meet with us. He has heard the wedding is to be next week and asks if he may come."

"Well, I suppose that will be okay." Brianna's voice shook and Tom looked at her with concern on his face.

"You're sure you're okay with that?"

"Yes, as long as he doesn't look like he's at a funeral rather than a wedding."

Tom turned to her grandfather and spoke briefly. The old man nodded and ran a shaking hand over his face. Tom translated for Brianna.

"I told him we'd let him know as soon as we have the documents sorted and book the ceremony."

"Tom . . ." Brianna tugged at his sleeve. "Ask him what I should call him?"

The old man turned to her, after Tom asked him and nodded. "*Nonno*." His voice was stern and his face was expressionless.

"Please ask him what his problem is." She didn't care what the answer was. She wanted everything out in the open, except the bit about the wedding being a sham, she thought.

A lengthy conversation ensued, and she watched the expressions play across Tom's face. She leaned into him when he placed his arm affectionately around her shoulders.

The old man stood and looked across at Brianna, blinking his faded eyes. Tears pricked at her eyes as she held his gaze and she didn't brush them away. She moved away from Tom's embrace and walked over to the old man, and took his hand. Reaching up, she brushed a soft kiss across the papery skin of his cheek.

"*Nonno,*" she said. He gripped her hand firmly, before he turned away and opened the door .

"Well?" She turned back to Tom as her grandfather left the room. He held his arms out to her and leaned into him, appreciating his understanding of the emotion coursing through her

"Your mother left the island suddenly and didn't come back for a long time. Apparently, she left with no explanation and they never knew she'd had a baby. He is still unsure if you are really his granddaughter, but he'll accept what the lawyers say while he makes more enquiries. He's also a bit suspicious about the wedding, and he wants to make sure we really go through with it. He wants to know why we waited until we came to Lipari to get married, and I had to do a bit of quick thinking. He's suspicious the whole thing is a scam."

Tom looked guilty and a wave of compassion swept over Brianna. "I'm sorry, Tom. Are you sure you want to go through with this?"

Brianna's heart almost stopped as he frowned. He looked at her for a few minutes and indecision crossed his face. She was sure he was about to change his mind. She caught her breath.

"If you've changed your mind, tell me. And tell me now. I am not going to risk this. I won't lose the chance to get to know my mother. Even though she's dead, I can still find out about her life and I can live where she lived."

"This whole deception has got out of hand. It's starting to involve too many other people." His voice was firm. "It's not just about an inheritance any more. People are going to get hurt. And we're lying."

"So what are you trying to say?" The panic built in her chest and she fought the disappointment that was clawing through her chest. "Are you trying to tell me you've changed your mind?"

"No, I gave you my word. I've made a commitment and I won't go back on it. But I think we need to draw up an agreement before we go through with it."

Brianna pushed away the confusion filling her. She had a lot of things to get her head around, including the feelings she was starting to have for Tom, but in the meantime she had a wedding to plan, whether he believed it or not.

Chapter Nine

Tom received some appreciative glances as he pushed his way through the throngs of casually dressed tourists crowding the morning market next to the harbour. He pulled at the collar of his shirt. It was the first time he'd worn a suit since arriving in Italy, and it was constricting his neck after T-shirts all week. He strode up the road past the houses that seemed to be glued to the steep hillside overlooking the azure sea. Terraced gardens with grape, olive, and lemon trees and various vegetables provided a brilliant foreground to the intense blue of the mid-morning sky. Scarlet geraniums in window boxes and pots spilled down the front of the houses and sweet fragrances hung in the still, hot air.

He paused at the entry of the small hotel at the top of the hill and wiped the perspiration from his face before pushing open the front door. The reception area was deserted, manned by a huge ginger cat draped along the counter. It swiped a lazy paw at him as he walked past the office. Tom stood next to the desk for five minutes before glancing at his watch. He tapped his fingers on the counter.

Come on, Brianna, we're going to be late.

God, he didn't even know which room she was in. Leaning over the cat, he looked at the large book on the desk, scanning down the room numbers. Number six. *Ballantyne*. The name stood out in elegant copperplate in the old-fashioned reservations book.

He climbed the stairs to the first floor and walked along until he reached her room at the end of the corridor. After tapping on the door, he crossed to the window that overlooked the square below, and he stood gazing down at the open-air market while he waited for her to open the door. After another five minutes had passed, he knocked again and a harried voice called through the door.

"All right, already . . . hold ye horses. I'm bloody coming."

Sweet. A ladylike bride.

He hadn't planned on a wife, let alone one whose language could get quite colourful at times. Five more minutes passed and he glanced at his watch. He eased himself into the cane chair by the window and waited patiently. Noticing a speck of dirt on his shoes, he pulled out his handkerchief and polished it off. Satisfied they were back to their glossy shine, he looked up and a pair of long bare legs filled his sight. He raised his eyes to the woman standing in front of the open door.

A vision in white confronted him. Brianna's olive skin accentuated the virginal white of the tight, short dress moulded to her figure like a second skin. Her feet were clad in a pair of barely there gold sandals, and her toenails were painted a soft pink. For the first time since he'd met her, her hair was loose and a torrent of black curls cascaded around her shoulders, one side pinned back by a small spray of red and yellow wildflowers.

His stomach contracted as though he'd been punched in the gut, and a frisson of desire shot straight to his groin.

"You're ready then?"

"Yes, I'm ready…I think." She smiled a shaky smile and reached over to tug the sleeve of his suit coat. "But don't you think you'll be too warm in a jacket?"

"It's a formal occasion. I thought a well-dressed groom was called for."

She reached up and brushed her lips across his cheek. "I'm sorry." She pulled back and looked at him. "I was only teasing, but you do realise how much I appreciate this?" A frown wrinkled her forehead. "God, how many men would meet someone on a plane and then marry them within the week?" She shook her head and looked at him in disbelief. "It's like a fairy-tale. I can't believe it. My mother's cottage turns out to be a villa. I have a real grandfather, even though he doesn't believe it yet. I really am starting to wonder about this. I always act without thinking, I know that."

Tom looked down at his watch and feigned displeasure to divert his attention from the beautiful woman in front of him. She was not the flighty girl he'd felt sorry for last week. The braids and the casual shorts had disappeared. This was a woman oozing sex appeal and his libido appreciated it. And now she was the one having second thoughts.

"Unless we leave straight away, there's not going to be a wedding." He reached into his pocket and withdrew a handwritten piece of paper. Even though he'd typed the agreement in his laptop, there hadn't been a printer anywhere in the marina and he'd had to resort to handwriting. "So we'd better talk this over and decide if we are going to sign this or if we call it quits now." Brianna turned to pull the door closed and he gulped. Tanned smooth skin disappeared into a plunging deep V at the base of her back, and his fingers itched to run down her spine. He shoved his hands in his pockets and walked in front of her along the corridor to the narrow staircase. She stopped at the top of the stairs and sat down on the top step.

"Show me." She took the paper from his hands and quickly read the words. "Oh God, I don't know. Am I crazy?" Brianna looked up at him as he sat down next to her on the wooden step. "On second thought, don't answer that. I am. I know I'm crazy. I should never have suggested this in the first place." Her bare shoulder pressed against his and he ignored the jolt of heat rocketing through his body.

"Oh shit, Tom, I just thought. We haven't got rings. So that solves it. We can't go ahead with it."

"Yes, we have," he said, patting his pocket. "I've got a ring for each of us." He leaned over and put his arm around her, and as she leaned into him, her hair tickled his nose. "If you are going to change your mind, you have about two minutes to decide."

"What do you think?" She turned to him and he looked down at her. Her eyes were wide and fill of trust.

She didn't really need to know what he was thinking at the moment because it had nothing to do with getting married and making the right decision. He was fighting the temptation to push her back into the carpeted hallway, put his lips on hers, and run his fingers along her bare shoulders.

But that wouldn't solve anything. It would only make matters worse. He removed his arm and cleared his throat, trying to regain his composure.

"I know," she said. "Let's make a list. Have you got a pen?"

Tom pulled a pen from the pocket inside his jacket. "What sort of list?"

"Of course you've got a pen. Who else would carry a pen to their wedding?" Brianna burst out laughing and he grinned back at her. "Okay. Pros and cons. And then if that doesn't work we'll vote."

He shook his head. "We can't vote with two. It wouldn't be fair to the loser."

"Shit, shit, shit." Brianna handed him back the agreement, leaned forward and put her elbows on her knees, and dropped her chin into her hands. "I honestly don't know what to do. It really isn't the right thing, is it?"

"Depends what we both want out of it. We're both going into it with our eyes open." Her uncertainty was hard to watch and he wanted to see her smile.

"We haven't even got time to make a list," she said.

"I know how to decide," he said keeping his voice serious.

He pushed himself to his feet and stepped down two of the stairs so his face was level with hers and then reached down and lifted one of her hands. He let go and lifted his other hand and held it in front of her.

"Rock, paper, scissors? Winner decides."

"Okay."

"Ready?" he said. She nodded.

"One, two, three . . . four!"

Tom laughed at both their palms extend flat in front of them. "Uh oh. A tie. What now?" he said. "Best of three?"

Brianna held her hand up to him and when he held it, she pulled herself to her feet."

"No, no more time for games." She turned to him, her eyes alight with laughter. "Give me the pen and paper. You convinced me. Hurry up or we'll be late." They both signed the agreement and Tom out the piece of paper back in his pocket.

"Come on, then. You're getting to know me. I hate being late, and I'm not going to be late for my own wedding."

***

It was cooler in the dim foyer of the town hall and the three guests waited quietly. Brianna was surprised to see an elderly lady, obviously Tom's aunt, chatting to *Signore* Antoniolli. It was a small town so of course they'd know each other.

Her grandfather stood to the side, and looked across at her without a glimmer of a smile on his face, his beetling brows almost meeting. She looked away, and Tom, God love him, took her hand and squeezed it. His wedding, he'd said. Well, it was her day, too, and if she followed her heart and remained true to herself, it would be her only wedding. Once they annulled the marriage, there was no way she was ever going to marry again, so she might as well make the most of this one.

Tom led her to the celebrant, and Brianna felt like she was distanced from the whole proceeding. Here she was getting married in an Italian town hall, surrounded by strangers, and not understanding a word of it. Nervousness settled deep in her chest like an ache.

She swallowed, but the tightness rose up into her throat. Determined not to cry, she bit down on the side of her cheek so hard she tasted blood. But she failed and the urge to burst into tears got stronger. Tom elbowed her and she looked across at him, tears threatening to spill over onto her cheeks. She shook her head and he elbowed her again and inclined his head to the celebrant who was standing there with an expectant look on his face

Even though the language was musical and pleasant to listen to, she'd stopped paying attention when her nerves had taken hold, and she had no idea what the man was saying. After a few moments, Tom leaned across to her. "He's waiting for you to say you will take me as your husband."

Her nervousness disappeared as she looked up into Tom's deep blue eyes. The sexy crinkles around his eyes deepened as he smiled down at her. He'd drilled the words into her memory and she had practised it over and over.

"Err . . . *i sarà*."

Aunt Carmen clapped and her grandfather nodded when the celebrant put their hands together and spoke solemnly.

"Si può baciare la sposa."

All thoughts of tears drifted away as Tom took her face between his hands and leaned his head toward hers. She held that sexy blue gaze with her own. He closed the distance between them. Desire rocked through her and her trembling legs threatened to give way. All she could think about was running her hands up underneath his shirt and touching his bare skin.

"Pay attention," Tom murmured against her mouth.

She opened her mouth to assure him that she was, and he kissed her, forestalling any protest from her.

Brianna sighed against his lips and looped her arms around his neck pulling him closer. Tom deepened the kiss and shivers skittered across her skin as he explored her mouth. She stiffened when he put his hand on her bare back to draw a lazy circle on her skin and his lips slid from her mouth to her cheek. Goose bumps rose on her arms. It was as if he'd read her mind. She'd been thinking about touching his skin and now his fingers were plating on her back.

He pulled back slowly and locked his gaze with hers. "Convincing enough?" he whispered. "Now you have your villa, Mrs Richards."

The warmth tingling through her body disappeared as if a bucket of cold water had been thrown over her. For a brief minute she'd closed her eyes and pretended it was for real. Now she shivered, her body as cold as his voice.

Blinking, she looked around at the small group surrounding

them. Tom kept a tight hold of her hand as a chorus of congratulations washed over them. His aunt chattered away to him in Italian and he pulled Brianna forward.

"*Zia*, this is Brianna, my wife."

Aunt Carmen kissed her soundly on both cheeks and gripped her hands.

Brianna looked across at her grandfather. A slight smile played about his mouth and he held her gaze and extended his old wrinkled hand to her. She took it and closed her eyes. She could smell garlic and hair cream on him, but didn't pull away as dry papery lips brushed her cheek. Unbidden tears filled her eyes, but before she could speak the old man turned away from her to Tom and shook his hand solemnly.

"*Più tardi,*" he said before tipping his hat and walking out of the room. She remembered the words from the lawyer's office yesterday.

Later.

"A meal, *si*?" Aunt Carmen glared at the back of the old man as he walked out of the door. "Pah, he has always been a stubborn old man."

Her expression changed to a beam when she turned to face them. "But it is your wedding and the rest of us will be so happy for you." She came over to Brianna and enfolded her in a close hug. "My sister would never forgive me if I did not make a fuss of you on your wedding day." She lifted her hands and placed gentle hands on each side of Brianna's face. Welcome to the family, *cara ragazza"*

Signore Antoniolli nodded and Brianna found herself swept out the door and into the hot sunshine. Aunt Carmen and the lawyer chattered non-stop as they crossed the square, and Tom still held her hand tightly. She looked at him. For someone who was playing a role, he was doing it pretty well.

"You can let go now, if you want."

He dropped her hand and she looked down at her hand as the sunlight glinted on her wedding ring.

"Jesus, Mary, and Joseph," she muttered under her breath. "What in the bloody hell have I done?"

Confusion overwhelmed her, and Tom cupped his hand beneath her elbow as they reached the restaurant. "Are you all right?"

"Yes, yes, I'm fine. It's just a bit hot." She grabbed a menu from the counter and fanned herself as they made their way through to the courtyard in the centre of the small restaurant. The waiter fussed around and seated the two women, and then poured them a glass of iced water. Aunt Carmen reached over and squeezed her hand. Her face had been wreathed in smiles since Brianna's grandfather had left them.

Brianna looked down at the small cake in the centre of the table as she sipped her drink. It was decorated with sugared flower petals, and had a plastic bride and groom stuck in the middle. She wondered who'd ordered it.

There was so much to process; it was as though she was in a dream. A week ago, she'd known none of these people, and now here she was sitting with a husband, his aunt, and the lawyer who had sent her that fateful letter.

Heat filled her cheeks and her hand shook as she fanned herself with the cardboard menu. "More water, please," she whispered.

Tom held her against him and placed the glass of water to her lips. She sipped gratefully and the faintness receded as fast as it had come.

"Sorry. I've been on a bit of an emotional roller coaster ever since I got that letter and it all just hit me."

Tom squeezed her hand, and kept his other arm around her bare shoulders while Aunt Carmen and *Signore* Antoniolli looked on affectionately

"You know, we didn't think this through very well," she whispered. "They're going to expect us to spend the night together."

"Brianna, my dear." He smiled and pushed the loose curls back from her forehead, before he whispered in her ear. "Don't worry. We don't have to please anyone except ourselves now that the marriage certificate is signed. Your mother's house is all yours and we have to keep a facade up for a few months until we get an annulment. It's as easy as that."

Gratitude overwhelmed her and for a moment she couldn't speak.

"Oh God, what a day. We did it." All she'd worried about was herself. What about Tom? How the hell had he got himself mixed up in her problems? She would be eternally grateful to him, but she hadn't given him much thought.

She grinned at him and reached over and straightened his suit jacket. "At least you got to wear your suit before it got packed away. A wedding wasn't on your list."

"What list? Do I look like a man who needs a list?"

She looked him up and down from his polished shoes to his crisp white shirt and straight tie and nodded with a grin.

"Aye, my man. You surely do."

"Well, I might now, but wait till you see Tom the boatman. He's the new happy-go-lucky, don't give a damn man."

She burst out laughing and grabbed his arm.

"I will be forever grateful, you know. Now, what can I do to help you out? How on earth can I ever repay you?"

"What do you know about boats?" he asked with a smile.

##

The meal continued into the afternoon, and Brianna ended up in her usual giggles when Signore Antoniolli decided to teach her some basic Italian. With the assistance of Tom's Italian and Aunt Carmen's English she learned several new phrases. Her working knowledge of the language now included more than *casa, vivace,* and *avocatto.*

Signore Antoniolli stood and raised his glass. *"Per cent'anni."*

Aunt Carmen nodded. "For one hundred years," she repeated in English.

"They are wishing us a happy marriage for one hundred years," Tom said.

Eventually, it became too warm to stay outdoors as the sun rose high in the sky above the open courtyard. Signore Antoniolli picked up his hat and cane, and swept into a deep bow before he took Brianna's hand in his.

"Congratulazioni, mia cara."

Aunt Carmen grabbed both Tom and Brianna in a close hug and then Signore Antoniolli escorted her out of the courtyard and down the cobblestoned street.

Tom sat back and sipped his wine and looked at Brianna, his face inscrutable.

Brianna sat back as well and looked across at him. "Well?"

"Well what?"

"What now?"

"I guess we have to decide where we are going to spend our wedding night." Tom put his wine glass down and frowned. "Are you too tired to get your things from the hotel and move up to the villa this afternoon, or do you want me to get another room at your hotel to keep appearances up?"

"You sure can't go back to your aunt's place." Brianna looked across at him and a wave of true affection swept over her. She grabbed both his hands in hers and turned his left hand over and looked down at his wedding ring.

"How did you get the rings so quickly?"

"Comes from being organised," he said with a smile. "And having contacts. Matteo's father owns the jewellery shop across the square."

"It's a beautiful ring and entirely appropriate. Thank you." She held her hand in front of her and the bright sunlight glinted off the Celtic love knots on the gold ring. "I'm not too tired and we have plenty of time left this afternoon to move into the villa. Come on, we'll go back to the hotel. I'll get changed and then we can spend the night at the house and decide how we are going to play this. I am worried my grandfather is still a wee bit suspicious. He didn't crack a smile the whole time he was there."

Tom stood and pulled her gently to her feet, and rested his chin on the top of her head.

"Did I tell you what a beautiful bride you are?"

"Thank you, but you don't have to. It's not as if I'm a real bride."

"But you are still a very beautiful bride."

Embarrassed by his words, she tried to play it down. He was so hard to figure out and she was not going to get sucked in by him.

"A bit different to my usual look, you mean," she said briskly. "Come on. It's time to go."

***

Later that afternoon, Tom stood on the balcony at the side of the villa. It was a beautiful home and full of vibrant colours. The atmosphere in the house suited Brianna's personality, and he wondered if she took after her mother. He had never met anyone so full of the joy of life and so open.

Shit. He cursed under his breath. *Pull back, mate.*

Although after a few days in Italy, he was pretty comfortable with the way things were shaping up. He stood on the balcony watching the sea darken as the sun disappeared. Grey waves were whipped up by the early evening breeze and the chill of the evening settled. He shivered and turned to go inside where Brianna was unpacking.

If it could be called unpacking.

He stood and watched, trying not to laugh. Her suitcase had exploded in the middle of the tiled floor of the living area.

"How did you manage to fit all of that into one bag?" he asked with a grin. Clothes and books, folders and papers, and a tangle of computer cables surrounded her on the floor. There was even a small printer peeking out from underneath a pile of underwear.

She looked up at him and laughed. "Told you I wasn't organised. Now you'll get to see it."

He kneeled down next to her on the tiled floor. "Can I help?

"It's okay, I'll tidy it up. I'm just looking for my PJs." She lowered her lashes. "Do I need them?" She paused and then looked up and held his gaze. "We haven't discussed the finer details of our agreement. After all, it is our wedding night."

Tom's stomach lurched and his mouth went dry. His heart pounded a slow heavy beat and the blood pumped through his limbs. He stood there looking at her until Brianna pushed herself to her feet and walked over to him, and placed her hands on his shoulders. She reached up and ran a butterfly kiss across his lips and he closed his eyes as the smell of jasmine from her loose hair assailed his senses.

"I know what we discussed, but our agreement was only sealed with a kiss, remember?" she said softly. "Keep the legal mumbo jumbo filed away for when we finish the marriage."

She looked earnestly up into his face and the tip of her small pink tongue touched her top lip.

Leaning over close to him, her voice was hesitant, but then her tongue touched his lips in invitation. "Will you come to bed with me, Tom?"

Tom's world tilted on its axis, but he held her shoulders and stepped back, putting some space between them. He bit down on the anger building in his chest as he tried to find the right words to say without losing his temper and hurting her feelings. He knew it was only gratitude on her part. No matter how much he wanted her, he didn't sleep with anyone out of gratitude. He shook his head slowly.

"I don't sleep with anyone because they think they owe me for a favour."

"No . . . listen to me, Tom. Hear me out. Looking at you makes me feel, well, you should . . . you should know. We're adults, and unless I'm reading you the wrong way, you're attracted to me as well. So we might as well share a bed and have some fun while we're here together." She put her hands on his shoulders and stood on tiptoes. "I know this isn't for real, and I know neither of us wants that, but it's the least I can do."

It was the second time she'd said that.

Tom lifted her hands from his shoulders and placed them by her side and walked across to the window. He was tempted to take her in his arms and kiss her, but he was determined to walk away from the temptation. It wasn't the way he wanted it to happen. Not because she felt she owed him something for a marriage certificate. If indeed it ever happened.

She looked up at him, and those green eyes that had been brimming with tears over the past week were alight with laughter, and her lips parted as she stared at him.

"I don't expect sexual favours because I have helped you out, Brianna."

She burst out laughing.

"Oh, God, Tom. You're so uptight. Look, I'll make you another deal. You helped me out. I'm more than happy for you to be my 'bidie-in,' and I'll help you get over your hang-ups."

"My what?"

"Oh, you know what I mean," she said with a dismissive wave of her hand.

"No, Miss Psychologist, I don't know what you mean. And how would you know if I have sexual hang-ups? You've known me less than a week and you don't know anything about me. And I don't know anything about you. That's the reason we need to take this slow." He glared at her. "If we take it anywhere at all."

"I think we need to make an agreement. For all I know you're after half my villa. We should have done that before. I'm surprised you didn't insist on it, *Mr Organised*."

"A legal agreement?"

"Yes, a legal agreement. Just in case I'm after your marina."

He laughed. "For what it's worth."

She turned away from him and her face was hidden in the shadows. "Just in case you think I might be on the make, we need to make an agreement. Between you and me, seeing we can't involve the lawyers. I'll go and get my laptop and you can type it up."

"No, thank you. We're not going to do that while we're both angry." Tom forced his anger down. "We'll sort out an agreement in the morning and we'll email it to our own lawyers. Okay?"

"Alright, then. I'm going to bed."

"Where shall I sleep?"

"I've put my stuff in the room near the bathroom," she said, her back still turned to him. "You can have the other one or the lounge. I don't give a shit."

"Brianna?"

She turned slowly and her face was closed, her Scottish burr clipped.

"What?"

"You are a very beautiful woman, but I don't think gratitude is a good basis for a sexual relationship."

"No matter, I've changed my mind anyway. We can live here together as strangers and when your visit's up, you can go on your merry way with all your finances intact. Our agreement will make sure you don't try to get half shares in *my* villa. After all, you don't trust me. Why should I trust you?"

She slammed the teapot into the sink. "Now, I'm going to bed." She stomped across the living room into the bedroom, and slammed the door.

"I do trust you," he said quietly.

"Whatever," came the muffled reply through the closed door.

Chapter Ten

The soughing of the waves washing back over the pebbly beach below the villa woke Tom before sunrise. His chest was heavy as he remembered the argument with Brianna.

God, he was so damn attracted to her and knew he'd hurt her feelings. It had taken him ages to get to sleep. Logic told him it was way too soon to get involved with her. He was still not ready to go down that path, no matter how much she tempted him.

He tended to avoided situations like this—he hated conflict and messy emotions. Give him a financial problem to nut out any day. When you didn't depend on anyone else you didn't have to deal with all the emotional crap that came with it. He much preferred his life to be organized and predictable.

So what the hell was he doing? He'd been with happy with the agreement as it stood, and then Brianna had to go and ruin it all last night. He hated not being in control.

Friends with benefits was not the way he operated.

He dozed back off and woke a while later when the bed creaked and moved. He rolled over to his side. Or rather, he attempted to roll over. A weight on his chest and legs prevented him from moving and he opened his eyes slowly. Tom groaned and immediately closed them. He kept them squeezed shut, hoping he was still asleep and this was a dream, but a little giggle and a tickle of hair on his bare chest convinced him he was awake and his wife of less than twenty-four hours was straddling his bare legs.

Brianna was perched on his thighs with her knees resting on each side of him on the crisp white sheets. "Open your eyes. I know you're awake.

Tom obeyed reluctantly. Her black curls tumbled in wild

disarray over her bare shoulders and skimmed the edge of the sheet she clutched over her loose T-shirt.

"Brianna, what . . . what the hell do you think are you doing? Stay there any longer and I won't be responsible for what happens." He closed his eyes, covered them with one hand and waited for her to leave.

No such luck. Or more to the point, he was about to get lucky.

"I'm apologising to you."

"Apologising?"

"Yes, I was a right cow last night."

He opened his eyes again and tried to pull the other side of the sheet up over his bare stomach.

"Don't say a word," she whispered.

He opened his mouth to speak. She leaned forward and placed her fingers over his mouth.

"Now I want your full attention for a wee while, and if I start babbling tell me to put a sock in it."

Tom was in no state to think about socks or anything else. His brain had joined the lower half of his anatomy. He nodded without opening his eyes, fighting between the fading desire for her to leave and the need to grab her and roll on top of her.

"That's good. Don't say a word, hear me out. I was a bitch last night. I was upset, but when I thought about it, I know I was unfair to you. You're the one doing the favour and it was mean of me to say I didn't trust you." She paused to take a breath. "Open your eyes, so I can see what you're thinking."

Tom obeyed and lay there looking up at her, calling on his sheer strength of will to kill the desire that was running rampant through his blood.

He failed.

"We're both adults. If I insulted you by offering to sleep with you again last night, I'm sorry, but the truth is I wanted you. Every time I looked at you yesterday, all I could think about was taking that suit off you and peeling your white shirt off. But I went about it the wrong way last night and then that stupid phone call upset me and—"

"You're babbling. Now listen to me." Tom swallowed as her fingers traced circles on his bare chest. "We've only known each other a few days, and we've landed ourselves in a situation. You know I trust you. If I didn't, I would never have offered to marry you. I don't want to take advantage of you and the situation."

She smiled at him and wriggled on his legs and he tried to keep his eyes away from the gentle swell of her breasts beneath her T-shirt.

"I don't think it would be taking advantage of me and isn't that what counts? It's more than gratitude. More like friends with benefits."

He sighed when she repeated the words that had been in his head a couple of minutes ago.

"We are friends, aren't we, Tom?" She lowered her voice to a sexy purr and the Scottish lilt in her voice sent desire rocketing through his entire body.

"Brianna, whatever we are . . . can we talk about it later?" The heat was moving between his face, his neck and he couldn't think straight.

"Now don't go getting in a *fankle*," she said.

"A what?"

"You know a tizzy, a right state."

"Ah, but Brianna, I'm already in a right state and . . . er . . . I don't have any clothes on." He tried to grab the sheet, which was crossed over her legs. Instead, she lifted the sheet and peeked underneath it. "Well, well, Tomas . . ." she said with a cheeky smile.

She leaned forward and her hair brushed his chest. She picked up his hand and moved it behind his head, closing his fingers around the black pine bed posts.

"What are you doing?"

"I'm saying sorry, seeing you don't want me to say thank you. It's the morning after our wedding. We had a civilised agreement which—" she said leaning forward and brushing his lips with hers "— we sealed with a kiss. I think we need to change the agreement. After all, we're both old enough to know what we want, aren't we?"

She sat back and lifted the sheet, peeked underneath again, and smiled down at him.

"Don't we, Tom?"

Tom couldn't move. The weight of her pressed onto his thighs, and he was sure he was about to lose it. He usually hated not being in control, but this situation was getting more enjoyable by the minute.

"I have a plan," she said and looked across at the bed table. Tom followed her quick glance and almost choked when he saw a row of foil packets placed in a neat line along the edge of the table. They hadn't been there the night before.

"Now . . . I'm *sorra* for losing my temper last night." Her Scottish burr became more pronounced as she spoke and he narrowed his eyes when the pink flush deepened high on her olive cheeks. He held her gaze and noticed her lips trembling slightly. Warmth filled his chest as he understood what she was playing at.

It's all an act.

She was as nervous as a virgin bride, scared he would reject what she was offering.

"Okay, tell me your plan." At least he could control his voice. He made a mammoth effort to sound calm and to ignore the woman who was trying her best to tempt him. As if reading his mind, she wriggled to get more comfortable and his calm flew out the window.

"First things, first," she said and reached over for one of the foil packets. "Are you happy for me to continue?"

"Yes," he managed to choke out.

"And we are going to rework our deal?"

Tom gulped and nodded as she lay beside him.

With a deep groan, he rolled over to face her. Cheeky eyes full of mirth met his. She opened her mouth to speak, but he pressed his lips against hers.

"No words," he murmured against her mouth. "Now, I'll show you *my* plan. Step one."

"I like your style," she murmured as he took the packet from her.

***

Tom woke much later in the morning. The sun had passed over to the other side of the villa and the room was dim. Instead of worry in his chest and a sexy weight on his legs waking him, Brianna's warm even breath puffed against his lips. Her hair tickled his nose and he opened his eyes as one of his favourite songs flitted through his thoughts.

I could stay lost in this moment forever.

He stroked his hand down her cheek and pushed her hair away from her face back onto the pillow. She sighed in her sleep and snuggled into him. His body responded, and he leaned closer to nuzzle his lips into her cheek.

"It's time we were up," he murmured.

A rhythmic creaking sound drifted in through the open window, and he lifted his head away from her hair and turned to the sound. The grating of a key in the metal gate on the back balcony followed. He shook Brianna's shoulder when he heard a voice call out, *"Allo? Allo?"*

"Brianna," he whispered. "There's somebody in the kitchen."

"What?" She sat up and smiled at him, her expression relaxed and contented.

"There's somebody in the kitchen." His words were confirmed by the running of water and the clanging of dishes in the sink. Then a quavering female voice burst into song.

"Bells will ring ting-a-ling-a-ling, Ting-a-ling-a-ling and you'll sing, "Vita bella"

Hearts will play tippy-tippy-tay

Tippy-tippy-tay like a gay tarantella"

"What's that noise? Who's in my house?" Brianna clutched the sheet, wrapping it around her as she climbed out of bed. She marched to the door, followed closely by Tom who grabbed his jeans from the floor and pulled them on. He put his hands on Brianna's shoulder and stepped past her. A short elderly woman with rosy cheeks and grey hair pulled tight into a bun grinned at them across the living room. She clapped her hands delightedly and laughed.

"Oh, so happy for you . . . so, so happy!"

"Ah, excuse me," said Brianna. "Who are you and where did you get the key to . . . er . . . my house?"

The woman shuffled across the tiles and met them at the doorway. She grabbed Brianna and kissed her on both cheeks, and Tom reached for the sheet when it started to slip.

"Oh, you are so like your mama." Tears welled in the woman's eyes.

"You *knew* my mother?"

"I am your *prozia Maria* and that foolish old man sent me here to spy on you," she said. "And to cook and clean," she added as an afterthought.

"Prozia?" Brianna turned to Tom with a quizzical look.

"Great aunt," he said.

He turned Brianna back into the room and a flush warmed his neck while he spoke to Maria. It would be obvious to anyone they'd been in bed together and Brianna's slumbrous eyes and flushed cheeks confirmed it. Even though they were technically married, guilt settled in his chest.

"We'll be out in a moment. Perhaps you could put some coffee on?"

"Nessuna fretta . . . no hurry. And I will cook for you *prima colazione."* A broad smile crossed her wrinkled face and she spread her arms wide. "You need to build up your energy again."

Wiping her eyes, she beamed at him with delight and turned back to the kitchen.

Tom nodded, bemused, and then followed Brianna to the bathroom attempting not to step on the bed sheet trailing along behind her. He closed the door quickly when she dropped the sheet. She stepped across to the shower and turned the jets on, at ease with her nudity. When she turned to him and held out her hand, he was tempted to forget all about the woman waiting in the kitchen.

"I have more family. She knew my mother. I am so, so happy." She looked across at him with a cheeky grin. "Want to wash my back?"

Tom gulped and resisted the invitation. He kept his gaze locked on her face trying to forget the feel of her bare body pressed against his minutes ago. "No, come on. We have to sort out what she's doing here."

"No one said the house came with a housekeeper and a cook," she said with a smile.

***

Ten minutes later, after they'd washed and dressed, the aroma of cooking enticed them to the kitchen. Maria clucked around, fussing until she was satisfied their plates were loaded with sausages stuffed with tomato and cheese. She filled a plate with delicate pastries from a basket in the kitchen and placed a large jug of what looked like crushed strawberry ice in the middle of the table.

Brianna leaned over the table and dipped her finger in and licked it.

"Mm. What is that?"

"*Granita* . . . from your strawberries." Aunt Maria pointed to the baskets hanging outside the kitchen window.

"My strawberries." Brianna turned to Tom with a delighted smile on her face.

After pouring fragrant coffee into three large mugs, Great Aunt Maria sat down at the table with them, and folded her hands across her ample stomach and beamed.

"He *ees* a stupid old man," she said in a firm voice. "And I will tell him so."

Tom looked across at Brianna, concern spiking through his chest. He was keen to see her reaction. After all, here was yet another family member she hadn't known about. She'd been burdened with so much over the past few days, and they hadn't even had a chance to talk about them ending up in bed this morning. All agreements had flown out the window and now he had no idea where things stood between then.

Or where he wanted them to stand.

He needn't have worried. Brianna pointed to the food laid out on the table.

"Thank you. Can I call you Aunt Maria?" A wide smile crossed Brianna's face. "I can't quite get used to having a family. You will have to tell me all about everyone. I can't wait to meet them. Do they live on Lipari?"

Aunt Maria had a working knowledge of English and with Tom translating between them, they managed to get the gist of what she had said about the foolish old man—Brianna's grandfather

"He no trust." She wagged a finger. "He thinks you only want *ze* house."

The guilt stuck in Tom's throat and he looked up and caught Brianna's eye. She shook her head imperceptibly.

"But I was not going to not tell him what I saw." She cackled with delight. "Now I can tell him *ze* truth and tell him what I saw."

She drained her coffee and smacked her lips.

"Sunday—at the big house. You will come for dinner and meet all the family. *Si?*"

Tom looked across at Brianna and she nodded enthusiastically.

"Si."

Aunt Maria gave Tom directions to find the big house in Lipari and what time to arrive. She gathered up her empty baskets after telling him she would be back each morning to prepare their evening meal. Tom and Brianna followed her to the door and waved to her as she wheeled her bicycle out the gate.

He turned to Brianna as Aunt Maria disappeared down the hill. The worry that had been niggling at him since he woke up came back in full force.

"Brianna. I think we need to have a chat about the terms of our agreement . . . now."

***

His less than subtle reminder of the need to discuss their

agreement, and right now, fired her temper. For Christ's sake, they'd had sex, she'd just met her second relative and found out she had a whole family on the island waiting to meet her and he wanted to have a chat *now*. Deep down, she knew her anger was fuelled by her unexpected reaction to being with him this morning, but she buried the thought as deep as she could. Her life was complicated enough without going there.

Now.

Determined to present a light 'things aren't serious' front to him, she pushed her chair back and came around the table and placed her hands on his shoulders. Bending her head, she brushed her lips lightly across his.

"Now, Tomas, why do we need to talk?" She looked at him from under her lashes and ran her hand down his chest. "We already have a signed agreement. The only difference is that sex is now part of it. So if you want to add a—what do you call it?—condition, codicil, post script or whatever, just do it and I'll initial it. I've apologised to you for being a bitch and nothing else has changed. Has it?"

He looked at her without speaking and she felt like a right cow again, but she was damned if he was going to see the effect he'd had on her. She needed to put those feelings away and think about it later.

"So," she continued. "We're married. My grandfather is satisfied. You have your work at the marina. I have my book to write, and we also get the benefit of great sex."

She patted his shoulder, feigning a confidence she didn't have and turned away before he could see her pursed lips. She was as nervous as hell about what he wanted. If he wanted out of the agreement already, she didn't know what she'd do. And not just because of her mother's villa. Gathering the dishes from the table, she walked across to the sink.

"Agreed?" she said evenly. She needed to be in control here.

When he didn't answer, she turned around and came face to face with him. He'd walked silently over to the sink in his bare feet. He placed his cup on the draining board, lined up neatly next to the other dishes. She waited for him to disagree, but he pushed his body against hers and bent his head. He wound her hair through his fingers and took her mouth in a hot kiss. Her head spun and she grasped at his shirt to keep her balance. Her back pressed into the cold stone of the sink and she moaned as his tongue plundered the depths of her mouth. Pulling back, he looked at her.

"We'll change the agreement. Friends with benefits."

Lost for words, Brianna stared at his back as he headed for the door. She reached up and placed her fingers against her lips. Control was back in Tom's hands.

And what hands they were.

Chapter Eleven

The hot morning sun burned Tom's skin as he rubbed the sandpaper up and down the bottom of the boat. Aunt Carmen had gone to Naples to visit her daughter, and he'd taken over the running of the marina. Matteo, the young boatman had shown him how to strip the paint and remove the old putty and caulking cotton in the boats lined up for re-caulking. He grinned to himself. If Nick and Alex could see him now they would give him a hard time. But the rhythmic motion of the sandpaper was what he needed to ease his temper this afternoon. It was much better than poring over the jumbled financial records. He'd borrowed Matteo's car and taken the boxes of financial records across to the villa. He had spread them out on an old table on the covered balcony, and it would give him something to focus on after dinner each night and stay away from Brianna.

He cursed himself for succumbing to her temptation so readily. The idea had been that he would come to Lipari and start living life on his terms, enjoy himself and he hadn't even been here a week and he had screwed up big time. But when he'd woken up with her in his arms this morning, a deep contentment had filled him.

For him it was always about more than just the sex, more than friends with benefits. And that's where he usually came unstuck. If that's all she was after, fine, she could damn well go without—he was not going to risk getting caught up in an emotional mess. He'd been there, and done that before. They'd added the friends with benefits clause to the agreement but she could run around the house naked for all he cared. He was not interested on those terms.

"Shit," he swore as he missed the timber and sliced his finger open on a bent nail.

Like hell he wasn't interested, but he was still going to ignore her. No way would he let her know the effect she was having on him. He wasn't going to risk being hurt again.

*****

Later that evening, Brianna looked over her wine glass at Tom as they sat on the terrace overlooking the sea, appreciating the aroma of the spaghetti sauce Aunt Maria had left bubbling on the stove. She'd left instructions for adding the seafood from the refrigerator and cooking the spaghetti, which made her feel very clever, having been able to put the simple meal together.

A fat moon hung low over the ocean and silver trails shimmered on the long lazy swells that pushed into the shore. The salty tang of the sea breeze mixed with the aroma coming from the kitchen.

"I've never been able to cook, you know," she said to Tom, determined to engage him in conversation. He had answered each of her questions in monosyllables since he'd arrived home from Lipari late in the afternoon, and he'd not initiated one conversation. He'd disappeared straight into the bathroom and come out half an hour later in clean clothes. Trying to hide how his lack of conversation was bothering her, she prattled on.

"Aunt Maria left very simple instructions so I hope it turns out."

"I'm sure it will." He raised the glass to his lips and stared out over the sea.

She couldn't hold back any longer. "Oh for pity's sake, stop acting like a spoiled wee child who can't get his own way."

He raised his eyebrows. For a moment she thought he wasn't going to answer. When he swallowed and his Adam's apple bobbed, she realised he was trying not to react to her goading.

"I think you have a bit of growing up to do, speaking of 'wee' children," he said, picking up the carafe and gesturing to her glass. Brianna burned up, not liking the look on his face nor the tone of his voice. She ignored his offer.

Why?" she asked. "Because I'm honest about my feelings and I know what I want and I go for it?"

His mouth, the same mouth that had taken her to paradise and back that very morning, turned up in a patient smile.

"No, because you can't accept that when I'm being honest about my feelings, I'm entitled to my opinion. I think if we sleep together it's going to stuff up our arrangement. That's the way I feel and you'll have to accept it because you won't change my mind."

The warmth of a flush burned its way up her neck and she blessed her olive complexion. How dare he try to make her feel bad about seducing him this morning?

"I don't recall you thinking that way earlier," she said coldly. "In fact, I recall you were a more than willing participant." She locked her gaze with his and was pleased to see a pulse flicked in his cheek and twin spots of colour darkened his skin. "And you added the friends with benefits bit to the agreement."

"So we've got all bases covered then," he said. "If you're happy for me to keep living here, I'll be most grateful. I'll sort out the finances, you can write your book, and when the right time comes, I'll head back to Australia or wherever the mood takes me. You'll have your villa and we'll both be happy."

"Fine." She tossed her head. "That suits me fine too." She was still a bit unnerved, never having felt so connected with anyone before. He'd ignored her mention of the 'benefits' but she'd be damned if she's bring up the sex again.

They both sat there glaring at each other until a bubble of mirth escaped from Brianna's mouth.

"I'm sorry." She put her hand up to her quivering lips. "I've never been able to stay mad. I *always* lose an argument. My brother and sister always won and I had to do their chores because they would bet me I couldn't keep a straight face."

Finally, Tom smiled back at her. "It's not such a bad thing. I was always the serious one in our family. Must be a personality type I inherited."

He stood and came and kneeled beside her chair, and picked up her hand. A frisson of warmth ran up her arm. "You bring out the worst in me, Brianna. Do you think you can put up with me *and* my hang-ups for a few months?"

"Oh, Tom, you don't have any hang-ups. And there's nothing to put up with. There's not a lot you don't know about me." Brianna looked down at his hand and ran her thumb over a cut on his finger. "Look, I'll be honest. I don't do emotion well. I do sex, I am a loyal friend, but I don't do emotion." She laughed when she saw the expression of his face. "It's okay, I have a very happy life, and I live it on my terms. Now, let's make a new deal."

"Agreement version three? Let me go and get the piece of paper."

Brianna laughed and shook her head. "Forget the paper. Stay living here with me. I need to convince that cantankerous old grandfather of mine that I really am his granddaughter and this house is mine. I want it and I'm going to keep it. I want to find out as much as I can about my mother and why she gave me up. There's all that stuff of hers I haven't even looked at yet." She squeezed his hand. "And I'll help you chill out and we'll work on your list and have a great time together, and then you can pay me back." She burst out laughing at the sceptical look on his face. "You are so easy to read. Don't worry, there's no sex in my equation."

"I'll need to pay you back for giving me a roof over my head."

"Help me get organised so I can finish my book and make the deadline."

"But I'm no writer. I have no idea how to go about writing a book."

"I can do the writing . . . it's the time management, and as much as I hate to admit it to you, some list making would speed up my output. I tend to stuff around and miss most of my deadlines. This is my last chance before I'm in breach of my contract." She dropped her head.

"And I've already spent the advance."

He nodded. "Is it a psychology text book?"

"You could say that." She avoided a direct answer. He wasn't quite ready for the subject matter of her book. She didn't want him running away yet; she needed him to stay around until her grandfather accepted her and she was sure she could keep the villa. Plus, she was getting quite used to having him around.

"And Tom, one more wee favour?" She reached up and ran her fingers down the side of his face. "You know, I really, really want this house. You don't know how much it means to me to have the opportunity to find out about my real mother. So when we see my grandfather, would you keep up the 'loving husband, so much in love with me, you can't keep your hands off me' act?"

He let go of her hand and stood and moved away to the edge of the balcony.

"As long as you keep your side of the bargain. No more early morning visits to make it real."

"I promise. No more friends with benefits." She tipped her head to the side. "I'll wait until *you* ask."

He rolled his eyes at her.

"You, madam, are incorrigible and I can smell burning sauce."

With a squeal she ran into the kitchen and whipped the saucepan off the stove before it boiled over.

***

Tom sat back and wiped his mouth with the linen napkin. Brianna had set up a small dining table out on the balcony and they made plans for her writing routine while they ate the *spaghetti marinara*.

"Now we've got your writing space organised, do you think you might need to get Internet access here?"

She shook her head. "No, too much temptation to chat instead of writing. I'll come to Lipari with you to the Internet café when I need to contact my publisher."

He was surprised at her self-discipline. She tipped her head forward and flicked her thick braid over her shoulder. It was less tempting for him with her hair tied back, but he still remembered how the tendrils had brushed against his bare skin. As it was, he was having a hard enough time forgetting how her skin felt, the taste of her, and how she'd pulsed around him. He swallowed and desperately tried to think of something other than reaching for her and kissing her exposed neck. He grasped at the first thing that came into his mind.

"Oh, by the way, your aunt sent a message to the marina and said someone will pick us up here on Sunday for the dinner at your grandfather's place."

Brianna sat with her chin propped in her hands gazing out over the water, her eyes reflecting the moonlight and she spoke softly. "I'm a bit nervous about meeting him again, you know. He is such a sad man." Her body was outlined in the soft moonlight and the gentle swell of her breast under the loose T-shirt drew his gaze.

Tom stood suddenly and dropped his napkin to the table fighting the surge of desire pulsing through him.

"I'm going to bed." His chair scraped on the tiled balcony. If he didn't leave now, he was going to do something he'd regret and break every damn promise he'd made to himself. "Good night."

"Good night, Tom."

He lay on his back for a long time, watching the moonlight play across the ceiling, angry at himself and frustrated, wondering what sort of a fool he was. He'd never been so fascinated by a woman. She'd breathed life into every minute of the day. She was willing and had made her position as clear as day so why was he hesitating?

He didn't need that emotional stuff. It sounded too much like commitment to him and he wasn't going anywhere near that.

***

"You can have the bathroom first," Brianna called out from the room she'd set up with a table and her laptop. Tom stripped off his sweat-soaked work shirt and threw it into the old stone tub in the laundry room off the back balcony. In less than a week they had settled into a routine and there'd been no major fireworks between them. And he'd managed to keep his hands off her.

Aunt Carmen was still in Naples and he'd spent the past four days working on the boats. Instead of catching the old bus back to Cannetto today, he'd left early and walked along the cliff path between the villages. The view was spectacular and he'd promised himself a trip to climb the volcano, which puffed out white smoke all day. Another one off the list.

"Thanks," he called back. "I'll be quick. Maria said we'll get picked up about five."

He stripped off, surprised by the deep tan he'd acquired in a few days. He shaved for the first time in a week. Brianna had been quieter than usual the past couple of nights and he suspected she was nervous about meeting her grandfather again. Either that or it was sexual frustration. He knew all about that. He couldn't get her out of his mind, and knowing she was just through the wall in the next room each night was killing him.

He turned the water off in the shower and jumped as the door opened before he could reach for a towel. And then he realised there were no towels hanging on the rail.

"Sorry, I took the towels out this morning and washed them." Brianna stepped into the bathroom and handed him a clean towel, and broke into a huge grin when he grabbed it and wrapped it around his hips.

"Wow, great tan." She turned and headed for the door." Don't be embarrassed. I've seen it all before." Gently closing the door, she laughed. "I've got a brother, remember."

Tom shook his head. She was so confident and so full of the joy of life, he had no doubt she would have her grandfather and the rest of her family under her spell before the night was out.

Christ knows, she's got me sucked right in.

The most explosive sex of his life had left him wanting more.

Once he finally got to sleep each night, he dreamed about her and those magic hands. It took all his will power to stop himself from knocking on her door, climbing into bed with her, and taking up where his imagination had left off.

Earlier in the week she'd shared some of her work with him and he'd seen another side of her. He'd wandered over to her desk to help her with a printer jam and read the chapter list on a piece of paper stuck in the printer.

This giggly, free-spirited girl was writing a textbook on sex therapy. He shook his head and smiled. A couple of weeks ago he would have run a mile but their conversations had shown him a different side to her and he'd developed a respect for her knowledge and her obvious clinical experience. Her exuberance for her subject had impressed him and she'd challenged him with some questionnaires and shown him the fun side of being psycho-analysed by her. It had got him thinking and he'd mulled over the couple of failed relationships in his past as he'd worked out in the fresh air this week. Like everything he did, he'd focused on them too much before they had developed. His total approach was wrong.

No more.

Half an hour later, Tom and Brianna waited together on the balcony for the promised lift. A small crescent moon hung low over the horizon. The pungent aroma of herbs surrounded them, crushed underfoot as they crossed the stone path.

"Do you know who's picking us up? Do you think it will be him?" She ran her fingers through her loose curls, a sure sign she was nervous. "My grandfather . . . *Nonno*, I mean."

"I don't know. Maria said to be ready at five."

She smoothed her dress down with nervous hands. A deep plunging back left her tanned skin bare. Tom put his arm around her and tried to ignore the jolt that went straight to his groin when he touched her warm, satiny skin. Her loose curls tumbled over her bare shoulders and she smelled of coconut. "It'll be fine. I'll be the loving husband and

I'll watch out for you. If he gets nasty, we'll come home early, even if we have to walk."

She snuggled into him. "You are a good man, Tom Richards."

The purring of a car motor coming slowly up the hill caught Tom's attention and he whistled in appreciation. He gently turned her around and pointed to the car silhouetted by the setting sun.

"Not bad," he said. "Not bad at all."

"What is it?" she asked.

"A C-class Mercedes Benz coupe. Very nice." He had considered one of them before purchasing his latest BMW back home.

She shrugged. "A car's a car."

"Oh, you Philistine. It's a thing of beauty." He laughed. "I can see I need to educate you. Just because I've been depending on that old rattle trap of a bus to get around, I still appreciate a fine motor, and you and I are about to have a ride in one of the best."

The large white car drew to a halt beside them, and Tom glanced across at Brianna. She choked back a laugh when a middle-aged man wearing a chauffeur's uniform and a cap with a gold insignia stepped out of the car and bowed to them.

"*Signore, Signorina.*" He opened the back door and gestured for them to enter. Brianna slid in and Tom joined her and placed his arm around her.

"You never know, the hired help may have been sent to spy on you, too," he whispered with a smile. Besides it was an innocent opportunity to touch her.

"Why would my *nonno* send a hired car to pick us up?" she whispered back.

"I'm not so sure it's a hired car. I think we may be in for some surprises tonight, so best prepare yourself." He squeezed her shoulder appreciating the way she tucked in under his arm. A warm contentment filled him. The driver turned the car around in the drive and headed down the hill toward Lipari. They cruised through the town and climbed the hill to the west, where a large villa on top of the ridge was bathed in light.

"Holy Moses, don't tell me that's my grandfather's house."

"I think it's more than a house."

Brianna reached over and gripped his hand. "I don't know if I can do this."

"You'll be fine. Remember how sweet Aunt Maria is . . . and I'll be with you to look out for you."

The car turned through a large set of ornate gates that opened automatically when they approached and then down a sweeping driveway flanked by a low hedge. Bright spotlights highlighted ornate statues of gods and goddesses placed at regular intervals.

The car drew to a halt in front of a small fountain, and the chauffeur opened the door on the passenger side. Brianna slid across the black leather seat, hitching her dress down over her long, bare legs. Tom followed, pleased she'd discarded her usual garb of khaki cargo pants and T-shirts. Apart from their wedding it was only the second time he'd seen her in a dress. With legs like that, legs that went forever, she should wear dresses every day.

"Quit gawking and be a good husband." She grabbed his arm and pulled him closer just as Aunt Maria came running down the steps to greet them.

"*Benvenuto*." She clutched at Tom's arm and pulled him down and kissed both his cheeks.

"And my *cara nipote*."Aunt Maria looped her arm through Brianna's. "Now you come and meet your *famiglia*."

Tom hurried to catch up to them and took Brianna's other arm. He straightened his back, stiffening his resolve to protect his 'wife' from any unpleasantness that may ensue. Maria led them through a marble foyer with a massive chandelier hanging from a domed ceiling.

"Close your mouth, Bri." He leaned over and jabbed her in the ribs.

They followed Maria and passed through whitewashed arches and over cool ceramic floors until they reached the back of the house.

The view looked out over the mountainous interior of the volcanic island. A solarium, a tennis court, and a lawn for playing bocce were surrounded by a large garden of citrus and olive trees.

"It's like something from the movies," she whispered. "Is this really *his* place?" She frowned as she looked across the garden.

"We'll soon find out."

"I can't understand this. What's the big deal with him wanting my little house?"

Aunt Maria stepped out into a shady arbour where dozens of people of all ages stood around chatting. Tom held Brianna back and pulled her close. He closed his eyes and listened. It reminded him of home, and for a brief moment he missed his boisterous family.

"What's wrong?"

"Nothing," he said lowering his head and kissing her briefly on the lips. "Just playing the loving husband."

Brianna reached up and touched his face and looked adoringly into his eyes as Aunt Maria led them across to her *nonno*.

"*Signore* Caranto." Tom stepped forward and held out his hand, and was pleased to see the old man smile. His hand was pumped enthusiastically and Tom pulled Brianna forward with his free hand.

"Brianna, say hello to your grandfather."

He held his breath as the old man and his granddaughter stood and took stock of each other. Eventually the old man nodded and held his arm out to her.

"*Nonno.*" She nodded and linked her arm through his and held her other hand out to Tom. He gripped it tightly and followed them out to the waiting crowd.

Two hours later, Tom stepped into a dim corner of the lawn and sipped his drink. Brianna had kissed him, touched his arm, ran her fingers up his back, ruffled his hair and gripped his thigh on numerous occasions throughout the meal, and the old man had not taken his sharp gaze from them for one minute.

His body was humming and the blood was pumping through at a

rate of knots. He needed some space and some fresh air. His attention was caught by Brianna's familiar laugh drifting across the garden.

Jeez, even the sound of her voice gave him a hard on.

He closed his eyes and gathered his thoughts, trying to dispel the desire shooting through his body. Playing the loving husband was not such a good idea. It had played havoc with his self-control all night. He'd squirmed like an adolescent right through dinner as he'd been introduced to cousin after cousin.

A whiff of coconut alerted him to her presence. He opened his eyes and his gaze was captured and held. Brianna pressed against him and looped her arms around his neck, her bare thigh brushing against his leg.

He groaned and she reached up and pressed her lips against his. "One last convincing display and we've done it," she murmured against his mouth. "Look at him, standing up on the balcony. The old man hasn't taken his eyes off us all night."

"I guess I can act like a besotted husband for a few more minutes." Her lips parted and he kissed her soundly, his tongue delving into her mouth. When he could take no more, he pulled away and gently turned her back to the lawn where her newly met cousins were taking their leave.

##

Tom and Brianna made their farewells and fielded many invitations to dinner at different villages around the island. There was no doubt the long lost granddaughter was a success and had been welcomed by the rest of the family with open arms. It was a damn shame the old fellow was still so reserved.

The driver was waiting for them in the car, and Tom held the door for Brianna as she stepped into the back seat. For a moment, he thought of traveling in the front to put a bit of distance between them. He slid in next to her and sat next to the window as far from her as he could. Brianna didn't appear to notice his lack of conversation, and chattered all the way home. He was grateful to have his attention taken away from the raging hard on that had been with him for most of the night.

"And I found out what the problem is between your Aunt Carmen and *Nonno*." The affectionate term for her grandfather came naturally now and he smiled when she lowered her voice to a whisper. "Apparently, they had a thing before your uncle came along and swept her off her feet . . . and they haven't spoken since."

"That explains why he didn't come to lunch after we got married," Tom said. He jumped when Brianna reached across and put her hand on his thigh.

"And not only that. I am so excited."

You and me both, thought Tom. He removed her hand from his thigh and put it back in her lap, but she didn't seem to notice.

"Bella—she's Aunt Maria's youngest—told me a little bit about my mother. She was close to her before she left the island. Apparently, when she came back, the villa was a holiday base for her."

"Maybe she left because she was pregnant with you?"

"Maybe." Her voice was wistful. "There's still an awful lot I don't know." She touched his leg again. "Now how about you? Did you have fun tonight?"

"I suppose that's one way of putting it," he said and tipped his head back and closed his eyes. She pulled her hand back as though it was burned.

The rest of the short journey home was completed without another word exchanged. They waved the driver off and crossed the courtyard to the gate. Brianna took the key from her bag, handed it to Tom, and stood beside him while he turned it in the lock. The gate creaked open. The sexual tension in the air was so thick he found it difficult to catch his breath. He bent and removed his loafers and placed them neatly by the door. She strolled ahead of him and reached for the light switch. He caught her hand.

"Leave the lights off."

Brianna turned and looked at him, her eyes wide. She didn't

speak and made no move toward him. Pulling her hard against him, he ran his hands down her bare back. When she reached up and grabbed his hair and leaned into him, her lips were a breath away from his. He lowered his head, and her lips opened beneath his, her hands moving beneath his shirt. Tom groaned as her nails raked down his back. Desire overwhelmed him and he deepened the kiss, wanting, needing his mouth on hers.

"You are the most beautiful woman I have ever known," he murmured against her mouth. "You've bewitched me. You're in my blood."

His voice was low and husky, and it was as though someone else was speaking. A spark of mutual need passed between them and her heart pounded against his chest. She leaned against him for a moment and then lifted her head and smiled up at him as he lowered his mouth to hers again.

***

Brianna accepted Tom's kiss and wondered if he could feel the thumping of her heart. He kissed her slowly, and she tried to catch her breath as his lips moved gently against hers. Before she could take a breath, he lifted her in his arms and she wrapped her legs around him. She laughed as he walked into her bedroom.

He put her on the bed and looked down at her.

"Wait," she murmured.

He stiffened and she laughed and pointed to the bedside table. "In the top drawer."

Within seconds, the foil packet discarded on the floor with his clothes and Brianna chuckled. "Mr Neat and Tidy forgot to fold his clothes."

"I don't think he'll need them for a while," he said and reached for her again.

284

Chapter Twelve

Brianna pushed her hair back from her face and wiped the perspiration from her brow with the back of her arm. She stood, stretched, and cracked her knuckles. God, her back was sore. She'd been sitting at the desk for five hours, but she had finished the three chapters her publisher had requested. The first draft of the whole book was almost complete and she hoped to get it away by the end of the week. She'd followed the schedule Tom had written out for her to the minute, determined to show him she could be organised and wasn't a complete airhead.

Why she wanted to impress him with her efficiency, she couldn't explain. She didn't want to be super organised like him, although she had to admit the Tom who was spending each day at the marina was way more relaxed than the man she'd met on the plane.

Smiling to herself, she thought of the routine they had fallen into over the past couple of months. Aunt Carmen had gone off to Naples again visiting friends now she had sold the business. Tom had taken over the day-to-day running of the boats, but the financial records were still piled on the table on the balcony.

He'd moved into her bedroom after the night at *Nonno's* villa. Their days were spent working and their nights were full of passion. She smiled and plugged in her external hard drive—another lesson she'd learned from him. The external drive whirred as she stared through the window with her chin propped in her hand. A cloud of dust down the hill caught her attention. She stood and peered out the window to see who was coming. What the hell was it?

She stepped out onto the balcony and an old rusty bicycle appeared over the crest of the hill. White teeth in a tanned face surrounded by unruly black hair flashed at her in a wide grin at her as the old bicycle creaked closer. The front wheel wobbled from side to side as Tom rode up the hill toward the villa. Brianna put her hand over her mouth, waiting for the inevitable fall. She giggled at the intense concentration on his face as he fought to control the wobble.

Another thing to tick off his crazy list.

He pushed the last twenty yards with a loud whoop. She ran to the front gate and opened it so he could ride through without stopping. She ran to him and hugged him after he'd propped the bike against the wall.

"You did it! Where on earth did you find the old bike?"

"Ah . . . your grandfather gave it to me." He avoided looking at her.

She pulled back and her heart plummeted. "What were you doing there? How come I wasn't invited?" No matter how hard she tried, her relationship with her *Nonno* was going nowhere. He was still very reserved with her and their meetings were always tense.

"Maria wanted me to see him about some of her business and it was in an old shed at the back of his villa."

"And he gave it to you?"

"Well, I offered to buy it."

But no matter how cross she was with Tom for visiting her grandfather without her, she still laughed.

"You paid for it? It's almost a relic. It should be in that museum near Aunt Carmen's. He's so filthy rich, I can't believe he made you pay for it."

He stood straight and smiled a devastating smile.

"Bri, come here." He reached out and pulled her into a close hug. "He's not a bad old stick. You have to make more of an effort with him."

"I've done as much as I can, Tom. It's him, he just won't accept *me*." She looked up at him and all mirth had fled. Being unable to connect with her grandfather upset her a lot, more than she was going to let on. She'd tried to speak to him about her mother and he'd used the language barrier, and the only information Aunt Maria would share was how they had been close, but not close enough to know her secrets. The few possessions of her mother's in the house had not given any clue to Rosa's life.

"When he's not got his eagle eye on us, he just ignores me. I might as well go back to Scotland when I finish the book."

"I thought you were keen to stay here." He raised a quizzical brow. She swallowed and warmth suffused her face. She avoided his gaze and turned away, walking back to the kitchen.

"I am but I have to earn a living." There was no way Tom was going to know she'd thought about staying on the island after the book was done so she could stay here with him. She quickly changed the subject. "Now what's for dinner? I was working when Aunt Maria left, so dinner's a surprise."

Brianna looked up at him as he followed her into the kitchen. He had a silly grin plastered on his face and folded his arms across his chest. "I crossed another thing off the list today and you haven't even noticed." He dropped his knapsack and bent to pull out a piece of paper. Her gaze wandered to his tight butt. A few weeks of manual work and he was in good shape.

"Well, two more things." He waved the paper in her face. "And if you count tomorrow . . . three things."

"What else have you done?" God, she thought, talk about a role reversal. She was turning into a mother hen.

"Close your eyes," he said.

"Why?"

"Trust me, Bri." His deep voice sent a thrill through her. "Close your eyes."

She did as he asked and stood quietly until the warmth of his breath fanned her face.

"Now you can open them." All she could see was a riot of black curls in front of her. His hair had grown and was becoming more unruly every day.

"I took my specs off. I can't see a thing. Tell me?"

With a flourish, he pushed his hair back and she gasped.

"Freakin' hell. I don't believe it."

A small gold ring worthy of a pirate hung from his left ear lobe.

"Jesus, Mary and Joseph. Tom, you did it." She bent over and doubled up laughing uncontrollably. He stood there with a grin on his face.

"Yes, I did it and it hurt."

"Well, why did you do it, you silly man?"

"Because it was on my list. And I can always take it out when I go back home."

Her mood plummeted and she realised they would go their separate ways eventually. She couldn't stay here forever. They'd divorce and he would be out of her life.

"Come here. He wrapped his arms around her, and rested his chin on the top of her head. "Why the sad face? Does the earring look that bad?" He tried to get her to smile.

"I know it's almost over . . . and we've had such fun. I'm going to miss you." She spread her arms wide and spun around out of his arms. "And all this."

"It doesn't have to end, Bri. We could always stay here."

She laughed. "Don't tease me. I said I was going home when I finished the book and I am."

He gripped her upper arms and his hands were warm as he pulled her hard against her chest. "Now tell me you aren't going to miss this?"

Warm lips slid across her check and he blew in her ear. Goose bumps skittered down her arms and she shivered.

"I need a shower," he murmured close to her ear. "Come and wash my back?"

She stepped back and looked deep into those blue eyes, unable to resist him.

God, she had no will power when he was around her.

"I have to finish backing up my work," she said, her breathing ragged.

"What are you up to? Tantric sex or erogenous zones?" He kissed her neck as his hands wandered lower.

Aroused, but preoccupied with her thoughts, she pushed his hands away. Turning her back to him, she walked across to the large window and gazed out over the sea. "Go have a shower. I'll back up my work and check what Italian delight is in the refrigerator for dinner." She watched as he peeled his T-shirt off. A shaft of heat lodged between her thighs. "And then I'll come and wash your back."

She headed for the computer and then remembered what he'd said. "What was next on the list?"

"We're both taking the day off tomorrow and climbing a volcano."

She shook her head in disbelief. She'd created a monster . . . or at the very least a dare devil.

"I suppose I can spare a day to explore with you, and Tom, I so appreciate what you've done to help me. You'll have that list completely checked off before you know it."

***

Tom turned the shower on full blast and stepped in. For a moment, he was tempted to turn it to cold—to quell his desire and then decided he wasn't going to. He would wait for Brianna to join him and then afterward he was going to talk to her, uninterrupted by the desire that exploded when they were in the same room. Sharing her bed since the night of the dinner at her grandfather's villa had been amazing, and although they had spent many pleasurable nights and mornings, they'd avoided any discussion of the future.

A future he could not envision without her now.

It was time for a serious talk. The past couple of months had been the happiest he'd ever been, and he'd be damned if he was going to let her go. She'd let her guard down before. Now it was time to convince her they had a future together.

He stood under the sharp needles of spray and tipped his head back letting the warm water run down his body. The door of the bathroom opened. She was going to join him after all. The earring must have made him irresistible.

Brianna appeared in the bathroom, her face drained of colour and he knew immediately something was very wrong. His gaze dropped to his phone clutched in her hand.

"Tom . . . it's . . . it's your mother on the phone. She wants to talk to you. There's been an accident."

His stomach clenched as he stepped out of the shower, grabbing a towel as he reached for the phone.

"A car accident." Her voice broke and tears rolled down her cheeks. "Your brother's fiancée."

Chapter Thirteen

The ferry receded into the distance and Brianna touched a hand to her lips. Despite his grief, Tom had held her close and kissed her for a long time before boarding the ferry. Her skin still tingled where he'd gripped her. He'd pushed her away gently and stared down at her, rubbing his hands up and down her sides, as though he was reluctant to let go.

"Promise me you'll be here when I come back?" he asked.

"I've still got three chapters to do before I go home."

"I'll be back in a week or so. No longer."

She stood on tiptoes and kissed him again, and pushed him toward the boarding ramp as the ferry horn warned that departure was imminent.

"Are you sure you are going to be all right by yourself?" His brow creased in a worried frown.

"I've lived alone for ten years. I'll be fine. You worry about taking care of yourself and your family. Ring me when you arrive."

"Don't forget to charge your phone," he said with the first glimmer of a smile since the phone call from his mother. He held her gaze until the ferry accelerated with a churning of water and disappeared around the headland.

After saying goodbye she made her way to the Internet café, where she emailed her completed chapters to the publisher and answered the many emails waiting for her. She smiled at the messages from her family.

Brianna. We know you are a bad letter writer, but at least email and tell us you're still in Italy?

She replied to her mother and sent messages to Phil and her sister, and to as many friends she could find in her address book.

Finally she admitted to herself she was avoiding going home to the empty villa. It wouldn't be the same by herself. Placing her back-up drive in her knapsack and checking she had water in her drink bottle, she decided to walk home along the cliff path between the villages.

Thoughts crowded her mind as she wandered along the path, the warm sun beating down on her head. A mass of wildflowers covered the cliff down to the rocky beach below, and she paused to pick one every so often until she had a small posy in her hands. At the halfway point, she rounded a headland and Mt. Stromboli appeared before her, rising majestically out of the ocean, plumes of smoke puffing from the live volcano.

Tears filled her eyes. She sat on the grass and she wiped them away angrily. They should have been over there today, climbing the volcano together and crossing another thing off Tom's stupid list.

Life sucked, it really did.

Her heart went out to Tom's brother. Losing his fiancée so young would be so hard to bear. Even though she didn't know him, she knew from the way Tom spoke, he thought the world of him and no one deserved the grief he was going through. She was missing Tom so much already. She had to get her act together. It would be good practice for when she went back home. Okay, so she'd miss him for a while and then she'd get on with her life.

She didn't need this emotional crap.

She'd got on quite well by herself over the last ten years. She had a great job, she had friends and her adopted family was always there for her...and now she had a second family as well. Always a free spirit and that's the way she wanted to stay. Families were too complicated. She wasn't going to get tied up with anyone for life.

She wiped away the tears that wouldn't stop falling and then picked up her knapsack and marched toward Cannetto. There was a book to be finished and she would edit it as quickly as she could. When Tom came back, they would do their Stromboli trip and then she would go back to Scotland and get on with her life . . . alone.

Italy had been a nice interlude, even if she hadn't found out much about her mother. At least she knew where she came from, and she had a nice villa for her vacation every year.

She walked up the hill to the villa and groaned when she reached the crest.

Oh shit, not today.

The white Mercedes was parked outside the gate and her grandfather stood stiffly beside it. Brianna slowly covered the distance between them and stood next to him. He gestured to the driver and the uniformed man went around to the back, opened the trunk, and lifted out a large cardboard box.

The old man nodded at her. "Brianna." His voice made her name sound so musical.

"Nonno." She nodded back and stood waiting to see what he wanted.

"I come in?"

"I suppose. If you want." She shrugged and turned to the ornate metal gate. If he wasn't prepared to make an effort, she was just about ready to give up. She pulled the key from her knapsack, and was surprised when he held out his hand and took the key, opening the gate for her. The driver followed them in, and her grandfather gestured for him to put the box on the table and wait outside.

Brianna waited for him to speak first. She was in no mood for any more emotional stuff. He could say what he wanted and leave, although her gaze kept flicking to the box the driver had placed on the table.

He surprised her again by walking over to the sink and filling the coffeepot and putting it on the stove. He knew his way around; it was obvious he'd been here before. She sat and waited, and didn't speak, but surprisingly the silence was not uncomfortable.

The tantalising aroma of coffee wafted past her nose as he brought the coffee pot to the table and then went to the cupboard and removed the biscuit tin Maria kept filled for them. He carefully poured the coffee, and pushed the cream and sugar and a plate of biscuits in front of her.

She looked up and her stomach clenched when she saw his lips quivering. She dropped her head as tears filled her eyes and threatened to spill.

"*Mia caro . . .*" His voice quavered.

She was *not* going to make this easy for him and she lifted her head, holding his gaze refusing to let the tears fall. Finally, her shoulders sagged and she pointed to the box.

"What is it?"

He smiled and spoke in broken English.

"Your mama, she must have loved you very much. But your father go. It was a . . . how you say…shame?"

"Disgrace?" She filled in the missing word.

"*Si* . . . disgrace. She no tell us . . . her mama and I. She went away for years and when she come back, we still not know about you."

"Not until she die . . ." He wiped his eyes with a shaking finger, and Brianna wished Tom was here with her.

"And I get box from bank in Naples. She send there when she get sick."

Brianna stopped fighting the tears. Her throat ached too much and they rolled down her cheeks. It was only a few months now since her mother had died. She'd had thirty years to find her and she'd failed. Smashing her hand down on the table, the cups rattled in their saucers.

"Why didn't you tell me this sooner?" She put her head down on the table and buried her face in her arms as the tears came. "You've known the whole time I was your granddaughter? I thought you doubted me." Wrenching sobs overtook her and she struggled for breath. A soft gnarled hand rubbed her arm as her grandfather reached over and touched her. For the first time in her life someone of her own flesh and blood comforted her and warmth filled her chest.

"She was good daughter . . . and she would have love you very much."

"Yeah, sure," said Brianna. "I would rather have known her than had this." She sat up and gestured to the house around them.

"You see." He patted the box. "I wait outside. You come see me."

##

He stood and walked from the house, and moments later the metal gate clanged shut behind him. Then there was only the whisper of the sea caressing the sand below the hill.

Brianna didn't move. She stared at the box for five minutes as though there were a cobra inside ready to strike the minute she opened it. Her fingers tingled in anticipation, but trepidation took over. She went over to the sink, filled a glass with water, and sat at the table. She reached out and ran her fingers along the edge of the box.

Lifting the lid, she put it aside and waited a moment.

Oh God, I wish Tom was here. It would be so much easier. And then she got cross with herself for wanting him.

A lavender scent drifted across her nostrils and tempted her. She stood and peeked into the large cardboard box. Inside was a smaller box tied with mauve ribbon. She reached in and lifted it out, surprised at its weight.

Her name was written across the top of the lid, and for a moment she thought it was her own handwriting. Shaking her head in confusion, she looked closely and realised that although the writing was very similar to hers, some of the letters were formed with ornate loops, which she didn't use.

She undid the ribbon and removed the lid. A soft gasp escaped her lips. More than two dozen small packages were neatly labelled with each year from her birth up until one year ago.

She picked up one package at random and three photographs fell out. The top one was a photograph of her graduation, standing with her adoptive parents outside Edinburgh University.

She remembered the day well. Jennifer and Jim had seemed so proud that day and had insisted on a photograph, asking a passer-by to snap them before they went to a hotel in the Lawnmarket for a celebratory lunch. She turned the photo over and recognised Jennifer's handwriting.

Brianna, Jim and Jennifer. Graduation, 2002.

Photograph after photograph chronicled her life. All the milestones, each birthday and Christmas, and many random shots of her playing the fool. She smiled as the memories came flooding back. Each photograph captured the essence of her and the happiness of her family life.

Bloody hell.

She didn't know whether to be ecstatic or devastated that her mother *had* known her. Why in the hell hadn't she contacted her, especially when Brianna had tried so hard to find her?

Angrily picking up the photographs, she went to throw them back in the box and give them back to her *nonno*. She knew enough now. Her mother had known all about her, she'd left her a villa, but didn't care enough about her to even contact her. At the bottom of the box, was an envelope with *Brianna* written across the front in the same stylish handwriting. The lavender paper was delicate, and the folds were creased as though it had been read and refolded many times. She reached for it and unfolded it with shaking fingers, and started to read before she could think.

Chapter Fourteen

Tom bowed his head and kept his arm firmly around Alex's back as the pallbearers brought Emily's coffin down the wide aisle of the church. The last time he'd stood at his brother's side it had been a joyous occasion at Nick's wedding.

Now, he looked across and caught Nick's eye, and a silent message of support passed between them. They linked hands behind Alex as their younger brother's shoulders shook and the grief of his fiancée's death overwhelmed him. The music swelled as Emily's father and brothers brought the coffin down the middle aisle of the church toward the vestibule and the waiting hearse.

Tom swallowed his grief and focused his thoughts on Brianna. If this had happened to him, he was sure he wouldn't survive it. The depths of his feelings for her hit him like a punch in his chest. He loved her, and by God, he was not going to let her go. He had to get back to Lipari Island and convince her that they had something special. It shouldn't be treated flippantly and discarded.

The situation and the grief had firmed his resolve. Brianna was his wife and they were right for each other. Her joy of life brought out the best in him, and he knew he was good for her. They laughed constantly and all their time together, even from those first few hours on the plane had been special. For the first time in his life, he loved a woman . . . unconditionally. He was confident he could convince her to marry him, for real this time.

"Come on, mate." He leaned over to his younger brother. "Time to go outside."

The three brothers followed Emily's mother and sister to the door and stood quietly in the little churchyard as the coffin slid into the back of a hearse.

***

Tom stood alone at the window of his parent's large living room and the noise of muted conversations washed over him. Tessa had offered the use of their home for the wake and he knew Emily's family appreciated the gesture.

"Tom?"

Warm fingers squeezed his arm and he turned to see Lissy standing next to him.

"We're all so pleased you were able to get home in time for the funeral," she said. "You'll be tired after the flight and today, well, today has been so very hard for everybody."

"Of course I came. We all had to be here for Alex."

Although she smiled, her eyes filled with tears. "It really brings the uncertainty of life home with a vengeance when someone is taken so young."

Tom hugged Lissy and held her close for a moment. "Where's Nick?"

"He's out with Alex saying goodbye to Emily's parents." She stepped back and patted her swelling abdomen. "He wanted me to stay inside. He wraps me in cotton wool."

"I haven't offered my congratulations. I'm very happy for both of you."

"We weren't going to share the news till we were all together at Christmas, but well . . . everyone can see it for themselves now." She looked up at Tom, her eyes wide and shook her head. "And you . . . look at you. You look amazing, so healthy and relaxed."

He laughed grimly. "Come on, Lissy, be honest. I'm not such a stuffed shirt anymore."

"No, I didn't mean that. It's just the hair and the tan and the earring. Well . . . we—" she stumbled over her words "Let's say we nearly didn't recognise you at the airport. You look so different. Out of the three brothers, I never thought you'd turn into the bad boy." She reached up and her hand was warm against his neck as she flicked his earring. "But the main thing is, despite our grief today, you look happy. Tell me about Brianna."

Tom thought about the best way to describe her.

"Brianna is full of life. She sees the good in every situation and she makes me laugh. It's been a tough few months for her in some ways—she's tried to find out about her mother, but there seems to be a real secret there—but she's a real Pollyanna." He touched the black curls tumbling past his collar. "She makes me laugh at myself and I've done things I would never have thought of doing before. I've loved every moment of it."

Lissy laughed. "Too much information."

"Oh, God no." He hurried to correct himself. "I've done physical things . . . fun things."

"You're getting me more intrigued by the minute." She smiled at him and turned to Tessa who had walked over to join them.

"Tessa," she said. "Your son is filling me on the details of his sex life."

Tessa raised an eyebrow at her son and he hurried to correct Lissy.

"No . . . I meant I've done a lot more Nick sort of things. I've jet skied, and we're going to climb Mt. Stromboli. It's a volcano."

"And I think you have finally fallen in love with life," said Tessa. "It is so sad that we get to see your happiness when tragedy strikes."

Tom reached out for his mother and they stood in a close embrace for a few minutes before he pulled away.

"Can I get you a drink, Lissy?"

"A cup of tea, please."

Nick and Alex walked in together as he was pouring Lissy's tea. He looked across at his younger brother and his stomach clenched. He felt so bloody helpless—there was nothing they could do to help, except deliver meaningless platitudes. Nick and Alex crossed the room and joined him. Nick poured a coffee and gave it to Alex who looked at his as if he didn't know what to do with it.

"This is for Lissy." Tom handed the tea to Nick. It was time to give Nick a break—it would have been tough supporting Alex at the cemetery. He took Alex's arm and led him over to the window, searching for words, any words. But he came up with nothing.

"Don't worry, it's all been said," Alex said as if understanding his brother's search for comforting words. He put the cup on to the windowsill and coffee slopped all over the white glossy paint. "Don't try. It means nothing. Nothing will bring her back."

He stared out over the lawn and it seemed to give him comfort to speak.

"Did Nick tell you we were moving?"

Tom shook his head.

"Straight after the wedding. Only three months to go." Alex's voice shook and Tom's stomach gripped with an aching hollowness. He could not comprehend what Alex was going through. He and Emily had been together since high school.

Tom closed his eyes for a moment. At Nick and Lissy's wedding he had danced with Emily, and she had brushed her lips across his cheek and told him she was sure he would find his love in Italy. Now she would never know she'd been right.

"I got a transfer with the law firm. A big environmental job up in Brisbane." Alex's eyes filled with tears, and Tom put his arm around his brother as his voice broke.

"We've already bought a house up there and now she's gone. Bloody stoned truck driver. I could kill the bastard with my bare hands."

He let Alex vent his grief and held him close. Alex's shoulders shuddered as he drew in deep, ragged breaths.

"He's been charged. He was high on bloody uppers and went straight through the intersection. He didn't even see her coming."

Tom turned to Nick and inclined his head. Lissy came straight over with a box of tissues and Tom led Alex out to the veranda as grief consumed him.

He sat next to him, dry-eyed, staring out over the lawn focusing on all the good times they'd had in this garden when they were growing up. Life ebbed and flowed at the hands of fate. He firmed his resolve. He was not going to give up on Brianna.

Nick came out with a bottle of whisky and three glasses and crouched in front of Alex.

"It's not a permanent solution, mate, but I think a little inebriation may go a long way tonight."

He raised his eyebrows at Tom and filled three large glasses with whisky when Tom nodded his agreement. Alex picked the crystal tumbler and held it up to the late afternoon sun. A shaft of light hit the crystal and fractured into a rainbow of colours on the wall beside them.

"To my Em." He choked and drained the glass in one swallow and sat back and closed his eyes. He held his empty glass out to Nick for a refill.

Many drinks later the bottle sat empty on the table beside Tom and Nick. Alex had collapsed an hour ago and they'd carried him to his room assisted by their father. Tessa had fussed around, removed his shoes, and tucked him in like a young child. She sat on a chair next to the bed, holding Alex's hand between her own as the tears rolled down her cheeks. She looked at her other two sons and smiled sadly, motioning for them to leave.

"I'll sit with Alex for a while," she whispered.

Tom's eyes pricked and a lump formed in his throat.

Tom and Nick returned to the veranda and Lissy was sitting waiting for them with a pizza box. Nick sat down and pulled her onto his lap and buried his face in her red gold curls.

"I don't think I could eat anything," said Tom. "Another drink will do."

"Eat," instructed Lissy.

"Yes, ma'am."

***

301

Tom was grateful Lissy had forced them to eat last night even though the pizza gave him indigestion. He woke up with a dry mouth and his breath smelled of whisky, but he didn't have too bad a headache, which was just as well as he had a big day ahead of him. He glanced across at the clock and did the time conversion in his head and reached for his cell phone to call Brianna and tell her he was on his way home.

Home.

He smiled.

What was the old saying? Home is where the heart is.

The call went straight to her message service and he shook his head. She'd let the battery run down again. He had more than her organisational skills to work on.

He had a quick shower, pulled on some fresh clothes, and headed downstairs. Nick and Tessa were sitting at the kitchen table chatting quietly. He made himself a quick cup of tea and sat down with them.

"Alex?" he asked.

"Still asleep," said Tessa.

"He'll have a very sore head when he wakes up," said Nick. "What are your plans today? I thought we might take him out somewhere."

Tessa placed her hand on Nick's arm and looked across at Tom. "I think it would be better if we left him alone today and didn't organise anything him. Just be here if he wants us. He needs to find his own comfort."

Tom looked across at his mother and brother. "I'm going back to Lipari tonight."

Nick appeared startled but Tessa smiled at him with a knowing look on her face.

"You can't stay here for more than two days?" asked Nick.

"No, I have something important to do."

Chapter Fifteen

Brianna looked at the missed calls displayed on the screen of her cell phone and closed her eyes. Tom had tried to call every hour for the past twelve hours before he'd given up. *At least he'll think I've let the phone die*, she thought and that gave her a small measure of comfort. The nagging feeling she'd made a big mistake tugged at her thoughts and she tried to block it. She focused on the bumping of the train wheels as they clattered rhythmically on the track. It had been cruel to leave before he came back. He'd been so upset when he left and she'd had a glimpse of the love he had for his family. But she had no choice.

Let him go. Let him go. Let him go.

Staring out the window, she looked at the mist still lingering in the valleys despite the lateness of the morning. Summer in Scotland was nothing like Lipari Island. Shivering, she pulled her wool coat around her shoulders and tucked her scarf around her bare neck. She glanced down at her hands and smiled, thinking how out of place her tanned skin looked.

She'd left the island three days ago. The ferry to Naples, three flights, and now the final leg of her journey by train, and she was almost home. Not home to her flat in Edinburgh but home to her parents in Aviemore where she'd grown up in the snow-covered highlands of Scotland.

Ready to confront Jennifer—she couldn't think of her as Mum any more—not after the discovery she'd made in Lipari, she was trying to figure out what to say, what to ask to understand the enormity of what Jennifer and her mother Rosa had done. Her *nonno* had held her and she'd sobbed in his arms after reading the letter her mother had written before she died, and now she was going to confront Jennifer with the secret she had kept for over thirty years. No wonder she hadn't never felt love from her adopted mother. In a way she felt sorry for Jennifer. It must have been hard for her, sharing her adopted daughter with her birth mother and having to keep it a secret.

The train pulled into Kingussie station and she gathered her bags. Aviemore was next.

An hour later she pushed open the gate to her parents' retirement cottage and was pleased to see clothes flapping in the breeze. She'd been so determined to confront them, she hadn't even given thought to them being away on one of their regular trips.

Her phone rang when she was pushing open the front door. She pulled it from her pocket and sighed as she glanced down at the caller ID. She hit the off button and let Tom's call go to voicemail with a sigh, knowing she would have to talk to him sooner or later, but first she had to get her head around this mess.

"Brianna." She jumped as her father's voice boomed from the living room. "What a wonderful surprise." She slipped into his embrace and inhaled the familiar aroma of his pipe tobacco.

"Your mother's in the back garden. She'll be so happy to see you. She was only bemoaning the lack of emails from you this morning." He cupped her cheek in his large rough hands, his fingers scratchy against her skin. "Is everything okay, love? You look a wee bit unhappy."

She nodded and followed him through the back door, clenching her fists as a sharp ache lodged in her throat. These people had welcomed her to their family as a newborn baby and she should be grateful to them for the loving home they'd provided. Jennifer was on her knees weeding the vegetable patch. As much as she didn't want to hurt her parents, she needed to have it out. They owed her an explanation.

She closed her eyes and wished she were back on the island sitting on the balcony sharing a drink with Tom.

Blast you, Tom. Get out of my head. I am not going to depend on you.

Jennifer stood and pulled off her gardening gloves. It was apparent by the look on her face that she had read Brianna's expression and knew why she had come home.

"Time for a chat. We have a lot of talking to do," Brianna said.

***

An hour passed, much tea was consumed, and her parents convinced her the secrecy had been at Rosa's request.

"Love, she could see how happy you were and then she didn't want to mess with your head. All she wanted was for you to be happy and you have been, haven't you?" Jennifer put her teacup down and squeezed her daughter's hands. "We tried to persuade her, especially at the end when we knew she didn't have long, but she wouldn't have it."

"Did she tell you about the villa? Did you know she was leaving it to me?"

Jennifer shook her head. "She spoke toward the end about how if you ever married, she would leave it to you. I don't understand how you've got the villa now. She made it quite clear she wouldn't leave it to you unless you were married. She never forgave your father for leaving her as a single mother and she swore she would do as much as she could to make sure you married and settled. She wanted to provide for you, but I guess she put her own take on what happiness was. She became very bitter in the end. "

Brianna gave a short laugh and held out left hand and flashed her wedding ring. "She didn't change her mind. I got married a week after I arrived on Lipari Island."

The look on her parents' faces was priceless and Brianna gave a bitter laugh.

"And now I have to get out of it and try and keep the villa. Do we have a good lawyer?"

Her phone buzzed and she groaned, putting her head down on her arms on the table. Her voice was muffled.

"It's all too bloody complicated."

Chapter Sixteen

Tom sat alone on the balcony of Brianna's villa watching the sunrise over the sea before he started work. Silver and pink tinged the low line of clouds hovering above the horizon. It promised to be another clear and beautiful day, but he was not going to the marina. Aunt Carmen had returned from Naples and he'd promised himself he would make a start on deciphering the finances today. He couldn't believe the change in himself. A few months ago, he would have had the books balanced and computerised even if it had meant staying up all night. Now he preferred to spend his nights in Brianna's bed, and he gave little thought to his stocks and shares. They were in the hands of his broker and he trusted him to make the decisions for him.

Loneliness settled in his chest. It had sat there like a stone for the three days since he had returned to the empty villa. Luckily, Brianna had left the key for him and a brief note saying she was going back to Edinburgh and would be in touch. The disappointment had overwhelmed him, but he knew there must be a good reason for her sudden departure. Everything had been fine between them when he'd left and she had promised to stay, so something had happened. He knew he loved her and he was not going to doubt that she loved him, too. It was only a matter of time until she admitted it to herself and he had planned his strategy.

He'd reverted to list making and he hoped she appreciated it. The time had come to implement it. He pulled out his phone and checked the time. Seven a.m. here, five a.m. in Edinburgh. He knew she was not picking up his calls, because it rang out before going to her voicemail.

Time to wake up, Brianna.

He pressed send and put his phone away before pulling out the first box of papers.

Two hours later, he was sitting in the kitchen, receipts and journals spread chaotically across the table when his phone beeped.

I am.

Tom jumped to his feet and punched the air with a loud 'Yes.' Aunt Maria had arrived earlier and now she ran in from the balcony where she was watering the potted plants. "You have finished the books?" she asked.

Tom grabbed her and danced around the room. "No, but I will soon."

Aunt Maria shook her head and went back into the kitchen and Tom picked up his phone.

He typed another text

 #1 I got my earring, remember?

He waited and a beep signalled the reply.

I remember.

His fingers flew over the keypad.

#2 Jet skied and didn't drown. He waited for a reply but all was quiet. He turned back to the tattered ledgers spread across the table and lasted for another two hours until the call of the boats and the fresh air won.

The phone remained silent.

***

Brianna was sitting in the office of the chief executive officer of the Burrough Medical Service waiting for her boss to finish his call. She stared out the window at the steady rain, grateful for the warmth of the air conditioning in the office. Glancing down at the phone in her hand, she closed her eyes and smiled. A picture of Tom riding a jet ski around Lipari harbour, his long black curls tangling in the breeze, his muscles flexing as he steered through the waves was implanted in her mind. And of course, the earring would be glinting in the bright sunshine.

Damn him, she thought.

"So, Brianna, you've finished the book?" her boss asked. "A lot earlier than you'd planned."

"Yes, Mick. A new me. I met someone who helped me with my time management skills." She smiled at him. "So here I am, ready to come back to work a bit earlier."

"I'd be more than happy for you to cancel your leave." Mick steepled his fingers under his chin and frowned. "But your replacement is on a six-month contract and that doesn't finish for another eight weeks. So I'm going to have to keep you on leave for at least another two months."

Brianna looked across at the window and thought for a moment. "What about in one of the other branches? Any other openings to fill in for a couple of months? I'm happy to travel."

Mick shook his head. "Things are tight at the moment. Government budget cuts, and it's getting worse by the day." He looked down at his watch. "I'm sorry, I have another appointment. So we'll expect you back in eight weeks?"

Brianna stood and her phone beeped. She ignored it and gave her full attention to her boss. "Not a problem. It was worth a try. I might even start another book."

She walked out of the office and picked up her umbrella from the circular bin at the front door.

The fates were conspiring against her.

No way was she going back to Lipari while Tom was there. She was running scared, but she knew he was going to try and convince her to make it a real marriage. It was not fair—she was only emotional because of the situation with her mother.

She was not in love with Tom. She didn't do relationships. They don't last.

Her conscience nagged. She was so confused she didn't know what she wanted.

Her phone beeped again while she was on the bus and being pigheaded she decided to ignore it. He was persistent—went with his personality type. Closing her eyes so she couldn't see the phone tempting her from the side of her bag, she tried to make a plan.

No success.

What the hell was she going to do in Edinburgh stuck in her tiny apartment for eight weeks? She was so *not* going to be tempted back to the island by some stupid text messages. The phone beeped again. She shoved it down into her bag and sighed.

He knew how she felt and if he carried on like this he was going to get hurt. Yes, he was a great friend and she loved him like a friend. He was fun to be with and they were explosive in the bedroom. But he was only a friend.

I don't do love and happy ever after. And she knew deep in her heart he would be happy with no less.

Why can't things stay the way they were?

She chewed on her lip and the phone beeped again and she pulled it angrily out of her bag.

#3 I had fun.

So did I Tomas, so did I.

#4 Your kitchen is a mess and my clothes are on the floor. Aunt Maria won't pick them up.

Brianna burst out laughing and typed a response.

I don't like mess.

His answer came straight back.

#5. Got roaring drunk last week. Never again . . . been there, done that.

The bus drew to a halt and she realised they were at her stop. She grabbed her bag and umbrella, getting to the automatic door just as it began to close.

She jumped through the door and dropped her umbrella. When she bent to pick it up her cell phone flew out of her bag and landed in a puddle.

"Shit, shit, shit. Oh, no." Distress pierced her chest and she scrabbled around in the pouring rain. The phone was sodden and she wiped it with her coat. Glancing around, the bright lights of a tearoom beckoned and she pushed open the door, grateful for the warmth inside. With shaking fingers, she slid the loose back section of the phone back into place and pressed the power button, breathing a huge sigh of relief as the phone powered on.

The waitress waited for her order while she scanned her message box.

Three new messages.

She looked up at the waitress, laughing, and ordered a pot of tea and scones.

"Glad to see the rain hasn't upset you, lovey," the woman said.

Brianna opened her inbox.

 # 6 Didn't insult anyone on the flight back. No beautiful clinical psychologists.

Beautiful. A warm feeling stole over her and she closed her eyes. He told me I was beautiful all the time. What did he say before he left? 'You've bewitched me. You're in my blood.'

The waitress placed a steaming pot of tea and a plate of scones loaded with jam and cream in front of her. Comfort food. She looked down at the next message.

 # 7 Fall in love. Wasn't on the first list, but it happened

Oh Jesus, don't do this to me, Tom.

The phone beeped again. What the hell was the next message going to say?

Call me. Temporary staff member happy to leave now.

It was a lifeline from Mick. Disappointment surged through her. Her finger hovered over the buttons.

Chapter Seventeen

Tom pushed his bicycle through the gate of Brianna's grandfather's villa. He'd been invited up for a late lunch and was interested to find out what the old fellow wanted. The invitation had been more like a command. A brief note delivered yesterday by his driver, with a date and time in the mid-afternoon next to *'pranzo.'* Lunch. Friday, three o'clock.

Even though he'd taken a change of clothes and showered at the marina, he was hot by the time he parked his bike outside the luxurious villa. He wondered how cold it was in Scotland.

His phone had remained deathly silent since his seventh text and he had begun to worry he'd pushed her too far. Swallowing the doubt plaguing him, he rang the bell on the ornate door and waited to be summoned inside. It had been two days since his last text and it was about time he took the final step of his campaign.

"Benvenuto, figlio mio." *Signore* Caranto greeted him at the door himself.

"Still no Brianna?" the old man asked. Tom shook his head wondered how much her grandfather knew, but he didn't answer until they were seated in the salon. *Signore* Caranto poured a large glass of red wine for each of them.

"I'm waiting for a message from her." He couldn't help himself and pulled his phone out but the screen was clear. *"Scusi."* Scrolling down to the inbox, he checked in case a message had filed itself. Nothing.

Signore Caranto looked him with sympathy. "She will come back. She love you."

Tom's head flew up.

"I see the way she look at you." The old man shook his head and leaned forward. He spoke in Italian and explained that he wanted there to be no misunderstandings, so if Tom was happy he would stay in his native language.

Tom nodded.

He listened carefully and a great sense of relief overtook him. Brianna's grandfather told him about visiting Brianna the day Tom had left for Australia. He told him about the photographs and the letter he'd given Brianna, and why she'd gone to Scotland.

The old man sat back and stared at Tom, a frown wrinkling his forehead.

"I know why you married her. And it is all right. It was her mother's wish she be married and it has all worked out good." He explained he had kept his distance until he was sure it was the right thing for his granddaughter to be here. He didn't want to be selfish. He had seen the unsettled life Rosa had lived. When he described how he'd held his granddaughter in his arms and they had made their peace, Tom closed his eyes.

He missed her so much.

It was time for the last text. He explained what he was about to do and a wide smile took years of *Signore* Carranto's lined face.

"It's time," Tom said to the old man and pulled out his phone and pressed the letters firmly and confidently.

#8 *Marry me again?*

#9 *Love you*

#10 *Love you heaps*

#11 *Last message*

#12 *Over to you.*

Tom put the phone on the table and picked up his wine. *Signore* Carranto sat next to him and together they watched the phone and waited. It was seconds before it buzzed and Tom grabbed it from the table. He let out a great whoop and grabbed the old man in an embrace before giving him a smacking kiss on both cheeks.

"She's on the ferry!" he exclaimed and ran for the door. "Rain check on lunch."

Grabbing his bike, he jumped on it and pedalled furiously down the hill. The afternoon breeze from the harbour cooled his cheeks as he coasted down the bumpy road, excitement zinging through his veins.

It had to be good news. It had to be yes.

She wouldn't have come home if she didn't love him.

Tom was confident and wouldn't let the niggling doubts creep in. As soon as he saw her, he'd know.

The blast of the ferry's horn announced its arrival as it turned into the harbour. The pressure wave from the bow broke the surface of the calm water. Seagulls screeched and hovered above the ferry as it drew closer to the shore. Tom put the bike outside the marina and ran down the steps to the boarding area.

Brianna stood on the top deck, her hair braided and her thick fringe blowing in the stiff afternoon breeze. She was too far away for him to see her face, but she waved wildly as soon as she saw him and he waved back.

Tom stood patiently as the ferry docked and the tourist crowd shuffled off. Leaning against the wall in the shade of the terminal building, he waited.

A high-pitched squeal ahead of him caught his attention and he stepped forward, smiling as he remembered his first sight of those long bare legs sliding to a stop at the international airport in Sydney a few months ago. The girlish figure with a long dark braid flying behind her ran across the boardwalk in front of the ticket office and flung herself into his waiting arms. She rained kisses on his cheeks, her long legs wrapped around his hips. Tom smiled at her exuberance and dropped his head and captured her mouth with his. After a moment she pulled back and her dark gaze held his.

"I'm so happy you waited for me, Tom. I love you, love you, love you so much."

Arms looped around each other, Brianna chattered nonstop as they walked across to collect Tom's bike.

"I was wrong," she said.

"About a lot of things," said Tom.

She pretended to punch him on the arm and he stopped walking.

"I can do relationships. I just needed the right man."

"Come over here and kiss me again, woman. I missed you."

"Are you going to propose to me?"

"We're already married," he said between kisses.

"But I want to do it right."

Epilogue

As far as weddings went, well . . . it was different.

The setting was on a wild flowered-covered cliff top overlooking the azure blue sea. Mt. Stromboli put on a fine show for the guests. The bride wore a second-hand wedding dress because the groom had insisted she wore the same dress she had worn to their first wedding. The groom wore jeans and a black T-shirt, because the bride chose his outfit. The best man, Nick, held his wife's hand and their new baby gurgled as the vows were made.

The bride's grandfather held the hand of the groom's aunt. They had made their peace and the Italian cousins from the island suspected they may be attending another wedding in the not too distant future.

As the groom kissed his bride, a flurry of congratulations in Italian, and in Scottish and Australian accents surrounded them as their three families bestowed them with good wishes.

Tom had arrived holding Brianna's hand and he'd kept his arm around her for the whole ceremony. As the Italian cousins sprinkled them with confetti, he murmured against her lips.

"Have I told you what a beautiful bride you make, Mrs Richards?"

"Have I told you how much I love you, Mr Richards?" Brianna lifted her head and smiled at her husband.

One man, one woman, a second wedding…for a lifetime this time.

THE END

Outback Sunrise

ANNIE SEATON

Richards Brothers: Book 3

Dedication

This book is dedicated to all my grey nomie readers who travel this wonderful land of ours. I hope you enjoy the little glimpse of the Northern Territory.

Chapter One

Jessica Trent walked slowly between the rows of rental cars looking for the small red sedan described on the rental contract she clutched in her hand. The other hand had a firm grip on the handle of the leopard print suitcase that clattered along behind her. Her matching carry-on bag was perched precariously on top of the suitcase, and threatened to fall as it bumped against the laptop bag jammed underneath it.

"At last." She sighed with relief when she spotted the vehicle at the end of the row and stepped out briskly, relieved to finally deposit her luggage. The heat in the strong wind blowing across the tarmac was unbelievable, and the light silk of her skirt and long-sleeved jacket stuck uncomfortably to her damp skin. She unlocked the car, stowed her luggage in the trunk, slipped into the driver's seat, and turned the air conditioning up to top speed.

Pulling out her mobile, she switched it on, and an Australian service provider appeared almost instantly. She hit the speed dial for Monica's number, and then realised she had to put the international code prefix before the mobile number and she didn't have a clue what it was. All those details were stored in her laptop computer now buried in the trunk.

"Shit." Reaching down she searched for the lever to pop the trunk down and caught her fingernail beneath the hard plastic edge.

"Double shit." She examined her once perfectly manicured long red fingernails and glared at the broken nail of her index finger. Lack of sleep on the flight over had left her out of sorts. She took a deep breath before she opened the door. Heat blasted into the car, instantly dissipating the cool air from the air conditioning. She scurried around to the rear of the car and retrieved the laptop from behind the large suitcase. A strong gust of hot wind caught the door above her head and slammed it down onto her shoulders just as she straightened.

"Ouch." So far Australia wasn't doing much for her.

She backed out and slammed the door down. When she was back in the car, she reached up to her shoulder and groaned when her hand came away from her silk blouse that was now covered in grease. No way was she getting her suitcase out again to change. She would get to her destination first. And anyway, it was way too hot to get out of the car.

Firing up the laptop, she scrolled through her contacts and found the international prefix she had stored in her address book and entered the digits onto the touch screen of her phone.

"Come on, Mon. Pick up." The phone rang continuously and Jess could feel her temper rising when her best friend didn't pick up straight away. "Please," she muttered, drumming her fingers on the steering wheel. Finally, the call connected and she heaved a sigh of relief when Monica answered.

"Do you know what time it is, Jess?"

"Oh sorry, I forgot about the time difference."

"I suppose that means you've landed and you're down under safely."

"Yes, I've just arrived in Darwin. Has Gareth found a hotel for me?"

"He's working late tonight. There's a big campaign coming up and he has to go back to the UK for a photo shoot next week so he sent me an email from the office. I forwarded it to you before I went to bed. It's got the name of the closest town to the resort."

"Oh, thank goodness. I didn't know whether to book into a hotel here or drive straight to Cockatoo Springs."

"Have you looked at a map yet, Jess? I know what you're like. You'll drive off without even checking that you're even on the right freeway. Daly River is the closest town to the resort and there should be a couple of hotels there. I'll e-mail you some links before I go back to bed."

"I'll be fine, so stop worrying. Now that I know where to go, I can put it into the GPS and head off."

"Worrying?"

Jess held the phone away from her ear, prepared for Monica's rant as her friend's voice hit squeal pitch. Gazing through the window, she watched the palm trees across the tarmac bend in the strong wind. They had flown over a large bay just before the aircraft touched down and the screen on the back of the seat in front of her displayed the name Fannie Bay. It was a shame she couldn't spend more time here before she headed into the outback. The morning sunlight had glinted invitingly off the sapphire blue water and a line of resorts and sailboats had edged the coastline. Now it was late morning and high thunderclouds were building over the sea, and it looked like a tropical storm was on the way.

"Are you listening to me?" Monica's voice was getting louder with each word.

"Yes, I'm listening."

"Well, as soon as you get there safely, call me. Gareth said as long as you have the application in by the end of the month, you'll be fine. He heard through the grapevine that they aren't interviewing for the new position for a couple of weeks."

"How thoughtful of them. Just in time for Christmas." She glanced down at her watch. She did the quick time calculation and realised it was only eleven o'clock the night before in New York. "Go back to bed, hon. You've got the whole night ahead to sleep, and don't worry about me. I'm determined to get this job. And you know me, I never give up until I get what I want." She ended the call and leaned back on the seat, closing her eyes.

Two weeks. She had two weeks to track down the elusive wonder boy who'd created the innovative bush tucker chef school at Cockatoo Springs resort, and made it a worldwide phenomenon in less than a year. Then get an interview with him and write the best damned article she had ever written about this unique establishment that chefs from all over the world were clamouring to get into. Once the article was subbed, the interview for the fulltime job coming up at *Cuisine* magazine would be in the bag. The job would be hers; she just knew it. It had to be. Since she'd bought her apartment, she couldn't afford to just walk away from the PR job she hated. Working for media magnate, Larry Bartholomew was not what she wanted to do with her journalism degree. It was her off-the-cuff freelance interviews that always ended up as her most successful pieces, but it had been over a year since she had last produced the article that resulted in mega sales for the Christmas issue of *Cuisine* magazine. Once she got the permanent job at the magazine she would enjoy giving in her notice to sleaze ball, Larry. But no matter how bad things got there was no way she was going to run begging to her father for help, even if it meant losing the new little apartment she loved. She'd done her journalism degree, she'd written some fabulous freelance articles and now she was determined to prove to herself she could be a top food journalist.

And prove it to my him. She was already well on the way to proving to her father she could stand on her own two feet. There was no way she was going to run back to him to access her trust fund. He'd be lucky if she ever spoke to him again after the way he'd treated her last year.

Jess opened her eyes and looked down, surprised to see her hands clenched in her lap and she took in a deep breath as the cool air from the air conditioning unit fanned across her hot cheeks and restored a measure of her calm.

Food journalists had been trying to get a feature interview with this guy for the last six months, ever since the outback cuisine trend had hit the top restaurants of New York and Europe. No one had been successful getting an interview, and there wasn't even a photo of him anywhere but she had done her research.

Alessandro Gabrielle Ricardo. I am going to track you down and write the best damn article I can

Jess reached for her phone again, connecting it to her laptop so she could collect her email. Scrolling through, she quickly located Monica's message.

Daly River. The Banyan Tree caravan park.

She reached over and entered Daly River into the GPS.

Two hundred and nineteen kilometres south of the airport displayed on the screen. Doing a quick conversion to miles, she calculated she could do that in less than four hours and would be there well before dark. She slipped her sunglasses down, started the car, and turned right toward the boom gates at the exit. A horn blared in front of her and she quickly angled the car to the other side of the road when she remembered they drove on the left in Australia. She barely missed the silver Mercedes and smiled apologetically at the driver when he glared at her through his window. Turning onto the access road to the international airport, she followed the instructions of the robotic female voice of the GPS, concentrating on staying on the left-hand side of the road. She breathed a sigh of relief when she turned the small sedan onto the on-ramp of the Stuart Highway, set the cruise control, and relaxed into the drive. Thoughts scurried through her mind as she devised and discarded strategies for meeting the mysterious Mr Ricardo.

She'd overcome the first hurdle and was on her way down the highway to her destination…or close to it. She would book into the resort as a guest, but first would stay in the small town close by to the resort and then do an exploratory foray. Maybe they were hiring kitchen hands or waitresses and she could go in undercover and check him out. This could be exciting and a bit of fun…she thrived on a challenge and her investigative radar twitched.

Finding him and getting the interview would be her two biggest hurdles.

##

Three hours, and well over one hundred miles later, Jess approached a sign indicating the turn off to Daly River was two kilometres ahead. Even though it was only mid-afternoon, the sky was dark and huge thunderclouds were building in the sky as the storm had followed her down the freeway. The drive on the Stuart Highway had been slow, and she'd passed so many motor homes she'd lost count. She'd driven without a break, sipping on the bottled water she'd bought at the airport. Jet lag finally caught up with her and she turned off the freeway and followed the narrow, winding road to Daly River for another hour. The bitumen road ended, and just as she began to worry she'd taken the wrong turn, she crested a hill and a sign with Daly River, three kilometres, appeared.

Five minutes later, a small caravan park with a vacancy sign out front was the only sign of life amongst the short scrubby trees. She drove along the road until she came to a closed-up brick building with a police sign hanging crookedly out front, and then the road came to a dead end at a wide river. Turning the car around, Jess drove back to the caravan park to a timber building that had 'reception' written across the front window. She stepped out of the car just as the sky broke and large raindrops splattered on her silk suit. By the time she'd pushed open the door of the small office, it was pouring and rivulets of water were running across the driveway.

The woman at the desk looked up as the bell above the door rang. She reached under the counter, brought out a handful of paper towels and passed them to Jess. "Looks like you got a bit damp, darl."

"Thank you," Jess said, mopping at the sodden silk. "At least it's a bit cooler now."

"Bit of a worry when the heavy rains come this quick, though," said the older woman. "Early start to the wet season. Are you after a cabin or just shopping?" She smiled and looked Jess up and down, obviously taking in the suit and the Jimmy Choos.

"I was looking for Daly River. Have I taken the wrong turn?"

"Nope, you've found us, love. We are Daly River. Since the police station closed and the river cut the road to the other caravan park, we're it." She looked at Jess, curiosity filling her face. "So, why Daly River? You don't look like you're here for the fishing."

"I was hoping to get a room…or a cabin here for the one night. You do have vacancy?"

"I've only got one cabin left down the back near the river. The fishing season has started and the park is full."

"That will do nicely." Jess smiled and she scrabbled in her handbag for her wallet. The bell rang again as the glass door pushed open and a deep voice rumbled behind her.

"Are you the idiot driver who has blocked the loading bay?"

Jess jumped and dropped her wallet. Before she bent to pick it up, she drew herself to her full height, under six foot in her heels, and let the ice drip from her voice.

"Excuse me?"

"Ha…should have known it. A bloody Yank." The owner of the voice towered over her. "No idea about outback road courtesy."

Jess curled her nose as an unpleasant aroma pervaded her nostrils, and she put her hand over her mouth. She looked him up and down, not at all intimidated by the glowering look on the face of this…this person. Long legs encased in stained jeans, a tight black T-shirt moulding a broad chest, and a deeply tanned, unshaven face with shaggy black hair pulled back and tied at the nape of his neck with what looked like a dirty piece of string which trailed over one shoulder.

"What is that dreadful smell?" She bent to retrieve her wallet and kept one hand across her mouth.

"Live bait for crabs. Prawn, mullet and herring burley." He put his heads on his hips as she stood. "Look, love, I've got a load of barra to put into the cool room out here. It's sitting out in my truck in the heat and your bloody car is blocking the way, so if I ask nicely would you go out and move it?"

"Since you have been so polite, I will move it as soon as I check in." She hadn't understood a word he'd said about the smell and the accent didn't help either. Placing her keys and wallet on the counter, she turned to the woman who was watching the exchange with a broad grin on her face.

"May I have the check-in form, please?" She gasped as a large tanned hand whipped past her arm and grabbed her keys.

"What the hell do you think you're doing?" Jess tried to keep her voice level as he dangled the keys rudely in front of her face.

"I'll move the car for you. Janet here will get you all checked in," he said. "Which cabin, Janet?" He turned to the woman behind the counter. "I may as well park it for the sweet young lady."

Jess was at a loss for words. No way did she want this unkempt hulk knowing her room number.

"Last one on the left down by the boat ramp," Janet called after him as he strode to the door. "And watch out for the crocodile. There's been a biggie hanging around the ramp all day. The rain might get him wandering."

"Oh, and by the way." He paused in the doorway and looked back over one shoulder." Don't look at me as though I've just crawled out of the slime. The back of *your* pretty shirt is covered in grease." The door slammed shut behind him

Jess looked up at the woman behind the counter. "Are all Australian men so…so rude?"

"Nah, don't worry about Alex, he was in a rush. He'll be anxious to get home with the rain coming and he has a heap of fish to cool down. The season has just started."

Home? He looked like he belonged in a cabin in the wilds, and what's more he smelled like it.

Jess completed the check-in, picked up the door key, and stomped through the rain down to the back of the small park, and retrieved her keys from the rental car. She was relieved to see no sign of the smelly truck driver hanging about her room. Standing at the door of the cabin, she put the key in the lock of the flimsy door, pulling at her suit with her other hand. It was sodden, and sticking to her underwear. Water splashed as a black pick-up truck, loaded with blue crates, sped down the road past her cabin and slowed when it got to her car.

"And sweetheart, you can see right through the front of your suit. Nice view, though. Like the lace G-string." He laughed, gunned the engine, and took off. Mud splashed the front of her skirt and legs before she had a chance to reply.

Richards Brothers 1-3

Jess stepped out onto the road and gave him the finger.
Not the best reply, but satisfying.

Chapter Two

Alex Richards turned on to Cox's Road down past the conservation area. He'd probably been a bit tough on the woman, but she'd really annoyed him and he was in a tearing hurry.

If this rain didn't stop, the river would be up and he'd have to take the long route back to Cockatoo Springs and offload the fish before he left. He gunned the motor and the pickup fishtailed down the narrow road. The wet wasn't due for another fortnight and he'd misjudged the weather forecast and left his run too late. Even though he'd been in the Northern Territory for a couple of years, he still couldn't predict the weather with any accuracy. He'd missed the damn forecast this morning, and if the creek was up, he wouldn't be able to get the barramundi to the airstrip to be flown in to Cockatoo Springs in time, and it would have to go to Darwin instead. The new chef from London at the resort had specifically requested fresh barramundi as soon as he had his first catch.

The truck crested the hill and he cursed at the sight in front of him. Not only was the river up, it had already broken its banks and had spread into the scrubby trees in the conservation area.

Shit. He slammed his hands on to the steering wheel. It looked like it had been raining upriver for a while before it had hit downstream. The rain had only started here when he'd driven into town an hour ago. He picked up his mobile and made a quick call and organised for the courier truck leaving the next town for the local airstrip, to wait for him at the caravan park so he could transfer the load of fish across from the cool room.

He wasn't looking forward to driving back to the resort the long way. For a moment, he considered going back to Darwin and picking up the helicopter, but then decided if he got an early start in the morning, it would be almost as quick to take the shortcut through the gorge. In the meantime, he'd go back to Janet's and get a cabin for the night, after they'd transferred the barramundi to the truck.

Damn the early rain. It had stuffed up all his plans.

He drove back into Daly River, surprised to see it had already stopped raining. The afternoon sun was slanting through the trees and the sky had cleared from the west. Maybe the river would go down quickly…so long as there was no more rain. He might be able to take the short route yet. It all depended on whether the rains held off for a few more days.

After loading the refrigerated van and waving the driver off to the airstrip, he parked his pickup truck out the front of the park.

"Gotta room for me, Janet?" he called through to the kitchen as he waited at the counter. Janet came out wiping her hands on her apron and shook her head. "Sorry, Alex, all full up. The American girl got the last cabin. I think everyone on the road was a bit spooked by the early rain."

That'd be right. Miss America had already messed his day up, now she'd taken the last room.

"I guess I'll have to try the pub over at Douglas River."

Janet shook her head. "No go, I was just talking to Cliff on the phone. They're full over in Douglas too. Listen, the old trailer down the back is empty. If you are happy to shower up here, you can bunk down there. No charge."

Alex reached over and hugged the older woman. "You're a sweetheart. I'll unload and have that shower. That burley *was* extra ripe today."

Janet laughed. "I think poor Miss America was a bit overwhelmed."

"Bloody tourists. They come to the outback; they have to take us as they find us. What's she doing here anyway? She looks like she should be lounging by a pool somewhere.'

"Don't know." Janet shrugged. "She only booked in for the one night."

"Well, she's not my problem," Alex said. "I've got enough to worry about with this bloody rain coming early. You cooking tonight?"

When she nodded, he smiled. "I'll be up for dinner, then."

##

Two hours later, after a shower, a shave, and a quick nap in the trailer, Alex pulled on clean jeans and a fresh black T-shirt and made his way across to the small dining room behind the office. The backdrop of the sky was inky black, and the stars were brilliant white against the darkness. The croaking of frogs was overlaid by the thrum of insects stirred up by the rain. He took a deep breath and inhaled the dewy freshness of the night as he walked across the car park to the dining room.

There was no place like the outback.

The heavy rain had broken the heat and the night was quite pleasant, apart from the mosquitoes that buzzed around his head. Well, it was. Until he walked into the dining room. Miss America, as Janet called her, was the sole occupant of the restaurant, sitting at the bar sipping on a cocktail. Of course, he thought. A cocktail would go with the fancy duds. Obviously not a beer drinker. He nodded briefly to her and allowed a lazy smile to cross his face when recognition dawned.

"Nice evening," he said.

"Very pleasant," she said and turned her back to him to peruse the menu propped on the counter against an old bottle in a basket. Candle wax stuck in splotches to the side of the bottle, and Alex smothered a grin. Probably not the high-class décor this one was used to. He wondered what she was doing in a caravan park in an isolated outpost like Daly River. She looked as though she'd be much more comfortable in the club lounge at Cockatoo Springs.

Janet came through from the kitchen, order pad in hand. "Have you decided, Jess?"

Jess shook her head. "Still looking. Great menu…if you like fish."

So that was her name. She didn't look like a Jess. Even in the old rundown bar of Janet's establishment, she was dressed in something soft and silky that clung to her curves in all the right places, and hinted at a shadow of cleavage. He raised his gaze from her long bare legs, past her full breasts, and up to encounter a frosty stare. He stared back and she was the first to look away.

"What about you, Alex? A beer?"

He nodded and reached for the bottle Janet had pulled from the fridge underneath the bar, and then popped the twist top. The liquid slid down his throat and he started to regain his equilibrium. He sat at the far end of the bar and looked along the counter where Jess was perched on the stool.

"It's quiet in here tonight."

"All the fishos came in early, ate, and went to the recreation room. There's a football game on the big screen," Janet said. "Which way are you headed tomorrow, Alex?"

Janet wiped down the bar top in front of him while she waited for Miss America to review the menu.

"Back to Cockatoo Springs. If the river doesn't drop, I'll have to go the long way through Aboriginal land."

"Rain's stopped, anyway. Maybe it was just a storm?"

Miss America had put the menu down and was following their conversation with interest. Alex lifted his beer and toasted her.

"Hope the weather improves for your holiday here. Staying long?"

Jess picked up her drink and sipped it slowly, observing him without replying. Long dark lashes fanned around her almond-shaped green eyes.

Either the hair or the lashes were cosmetically enhanced.

Her lashes and brow were dark while her hair was honey gold. It tumbled onto her bare shoulders, the brightly patterned silky top held in place by thin straps. Her skin looked like it had never seen the sun. It was almost alabaster white. Tropical sun wouldn't agree with that.

Janet bustled around the bar carrying a tablecloth and flicked it across a small table near the window.

"You're the only two left to feed now. Alex, be a gentleman and apologise to the young lady here. Then you can give her a bit of background. She's headed for Cockatoo as well."

His head snapped up and he caught the slight grin on Janet's face as she picked up the tableware and napkins from the basket in front of him.

What was she up to?

She knew the road was out and she should have shared that fact with Miss America. And besides, all the guests at Cockatoo Springs flew in by helicopter from Darwin, there was no access from this far south unless you went bush. As soon as the tourists booked in, their travel arrangements were made for them. There was something wrong here. Janet winked at him and headed back into the kitchen. He had the distinct feeling he was being set up. Janet had been trying to pair him off with every female who came through Daly River since he had rolled into the park and bought her ex-husband's fishing boat after he'd signed the contract at Cockatoo Springs. She certainly needn't try it with his one.

No way. Not my type at all.

He turned and returned the stare of the American woman before he eased off the stool and walked the few steps to the other end of the bar where she was perched like a tropical bird, her elegant fingers with brightly painted red nails wrapped around her glass. Alex put his beer bottle down on the old chipped counter and held out his hand.

"I suppose an apology *is* in order," he said gruffly.

She put her drink on the counter and turned to face him, still not speaking.

He stood with his hand outstretched and waited. "I was out of line this afternoon. I was rude to you, and I apologise for the mud. I didn't mean to do that." He tried to keep his face serious, although the picture of her standing in the wet, clinging suit giving him the finger was one of the funniest things he had seen for a while. "Honestly."

She reached out and took his hand. Her long, slender fingers fit nicely into his.

"I'm Alex Richards, and you are Jess…?"

"Jessica Trent. And apology accepted." He held her hand a little bit longer before letting it go to reach for his beer. He could do dinner; it wasn't entirely her fault that his day had gone to shit.

His interest was piqued and Alex narrowed his eyes as he looked at her.

Or was she just like the others who turned up at the resort expecting to meet him and get fodder for their trashy magazines? He'd been sucked in too many times before. He knew he was a sucker for a pretty face and Emily wasn't the only one who'd conned him. But he'd hardened up a lot since those gullible days.

He was careful and there was no way any journalist could have tracked him down here to Daly River.

"Well, Jess Trent, seeing as we are the only two eating at this fine establishment tonight and—" He threw a glance at Janet "—our hostess only set one table, join me for dinner?" He waited, wondering whether she had a sense of humour.

"I'd be delighted." She wrinkled her nose delicately and smiled at him. "On one condition. Has that barley smell gone?"

"Barley?"

"The fish stuff."

"Oh, the burley." He laughed and assured her it was all gone as Janet came back from the kitchen and nodded with approval when she saw the two of them smiling.

"Okay folks, what'll be? The fish or the fish?"

Jess laughed. "I'll have the fish, I guess."

A ripple of interest flickered through him. He'd play the gentleman and find out what she was doing here. He was very interested in what a beautiful, elegantly-dressed woman was doing in a rundown caravan park in this backwater supposedly on her way to Cockatoo Springs.

If it turned out she was after Alessandro Ricardo, he'd send her on her way from here and make damn well sure she didn't get anywhere near the resort.

***

The soft light in the room hid the tired furnishings and the scuffed floor. Janet had lit the candle on their table and placed a small vase of wildflowers next to it. Jess looked up to meet an intent gaze focused on her face. Piercing blue eyes surrounded by deep lines looked steadily into hers. The smile lines around his mouth and eyes were white against the deep tan of his weathered face. Suddenly flustered, she reached for her glass and sipped. "So, tell me about this wet that you're talking about. What does that mean?"

"We have a wet season up here in the Top End from about November to March." The drawl in his Australian accent fascinated her. She'd barely spoken to any Aussies since she'd stepped off the plane this morning. Although after the long drive down here, she felt like she'd been here for days.

"The Top End?" It sounded like he knew the area pretty well and might be able tell her the best way to get to the resort tomorrow, especially if he was heading that way.

"The top end of the Territory. Top as in north. From Darwin and the islands, to about where we are now, down here at Daly River. I must have heard wrong. I thought Janet said you were going to Cockatoo Springs?"

His frown deepened and he looked at her while he waited for her to reply. It was hard to pick his age—the crinkly lines around his mouth and eyes maybe had more to do with the sun, than his age. The jet-black hair pulled back into a short ponytail at his nape seemed to be more for convenience than a fashion statement. He wore a faded pair of jeans and a plain black T-shirt, although they were cleaner than the set he'd worn this afternoon. Even though he'd shaved and looked groomed tonight, he still had a rugged, mountain man thing going on.

She tipped her head to the side, trying to decide how much to tell him. Sure, she wanted to get information from him, if he knew the area, but she didn't want to tell him too much. The roads around here seemed pretty isolated and she didn't know him or who he was. Mon had read her the riot act at JFK before her flight. But she'd never see this guy again, so there was no need to tell him the real reason for her sudden visit to the outback.

She leaned forward and lowered her voice despite them being the only customers in the restaurant. Janet was banging pans out in the kitchen.

"Can you keep a secret?"

He nodded slowly and held her gaze with those piercing blue eyes, and a small frisson of guilt ran up her spine.

"I'm an actress and I've come over here for a rest. I heard Cockatoo Springs was a private resort where you can get back to nature, and I want some time away from the … ah… artifice of Hollywood."

"Interesting." He seemed decidedly unimpressed. "Been in any movies I would have seen? You don't look familiar."

"Probably not. My…er…agent…is building my portfolio and we're very selective about what I take on."

"But you're already needing a total rest?" He put his head to one side and smiled, the smooth lines of his face softening.

"Yes, but I prefer not talk about it. So, what do you do?"

His eyes narrowed, and for a moment she had the distinct feeling they were both playing at the same game.

"I work out of Cockatoo Springs," he said. "I catch the fish and the crabs for the restaurant."

"Oh, how good is that?" she said enthusiastically. "You can tell me the best way to get there."

"The best way?" He leaned forward and propped his chin in his hand, and stared at her. "Didn't the booking agent make a travel plan for you when you booked in?"

"I haven't booked in yet. I decided to drive there myself. I'm used to driving. I …er… often drive from New York to LA for my work."

"So, you're on Broadway, too?" He looked at her and a huge smile crossed his face. He really was a looker, his white teeth contrasted with his tanned skin and blue eyes.

"What would be so funny about that?" She could feel the scowl crossing her face.

"Nothing," he said. "I'm just impressed. I haven't met any actresses before." He sat back and sipped his beer. "I'll have to make sure I get your autograph."

"Certainly."

The kitchen door pushed open with a clatter. Janet carried across two plates of food and placed them on the table in front of them. Jess drew in a startled breath as all thoughts of acting and Cockatoo Springs flew from her mind. She reached down, grabbed her phone from her bag, and leaned back in her chair framing the plate of food in the grid of the small screen of her iPhone camera.

She totally forgot about the man sitting across from her as she snapped six shots of the meal in front of her, from a variety of angles. She looked up at Alex, suddenly realising he was watching her with a suspicious expression on his face.

"Why are you taking a photo of your dinner?"

Get out of this one, Jess.

Monica had warned her about being careful. There'd been some pretty awful things happen in the outback; she'd seen the movies, read the news, and Monica had read her the riot act at JFK.

"First, Jess…don't tell everyone your life story in the first five minutes." Jess had rolled her eyes. "And second, don't be so trusting. There are scary people out there. Remember that movie we saw about the outback? 'Wolf Creek', I think it was called. "

. Okay, she'd done some theatre classes in college and a little bit of embroidering the truth wouldn't hurt. She'd had plenty of practice fudging her true identity at college and at the office, finding out the hard way that as soon as anyone found out she came from a wealthy, famous family, they looked at her differently. It was all about what they could get from her and not about true friendship. Monica had been the one exception and they'd stayed friends since high school.

After all, she'd never see this dude again. And if anything, she owed him one for the mud splatter this afternoon

"It's my first meal in Australia and I want to remember it," she said weakly.

So much for decent acting.

"An interesting habit," he said. "Although I agree, Janet's meals are spectacular. She's wasted in a place like this. It never gets very busy, and she does like to impress the guests."

Jess was barely listening to him. She had speared a piece of fish and raised it reverently to her mouth. She closed her eyes, savouring the taste, and trying to figure out the herbs that combined to give it the subtle flavour. She opened her eyes and that direct blue gaze was fixed on her lips as she chewed delicately. Pointing her fork at him, she pulled out her best imitation of her mother's voice.

"Has anyone never taught you manners? It is extremely rude to stare. Particularly when one is eating."

"You really are a case, aren't you?" Alex threw back his head and laughed. "When 'one' is eating? I think that 'rest' at Cockatoo Springs will do 'one' the world of good."

"Don't be smart. I'm just enjoying my meal. And I like to cook so I am figuring out what is in it."

"Unless you know your bush tucker you won't figure it out." Picking up his fork, he speared a piece of fish and chewed it without taking his gaze from hers. "Lemon myrtle and pepper berries."

"Bush tucker? What's that?" Although she well knew what it was from her research, she was curious to see if he knew much about the local food. And as well as the amazing article on Alessandro she could do another article using this guy; in fact she could do a whole series on the outback.

From the river to the resort. He was an interesting character and would certainly provide some eye candy on the glossy pages against the photographs of the bush tucker dishes. He could lean in front of that black truck of his and hold one of his big fish up for the camera…and flex his muscles. Maybe they could find a good patch of water for the background of the shot Her thoughts wandered away and she starting framing some words around the picture in her head. She looked up as his deep voice interrupted her thoughts.

"Any native flora or fauna used for cooking or medicinal purposes," he said. "It's a popular type of cooking up here in the Territory." She looked at him, her curiosity growing when he explained how the local bush tucker had become an international success.

"Cockatoo Springs has just made the papers. It took out first place in an international competition run by some flash magazine," he said with a hint of pride in his voice. "First out of the top fifty restaurants in the world this year."

Jess's head flew up when he mentioned the competition. It had been the catalyst for her trip—*Cuisine* had run it and that's where she'd first heard about the wealthy guy who'd made it an international success in less than two years. She took a deep breath and choked, trying not to spray him with food. A piece of wild rice lodged in her throat. She placed her hand over her mouth and coughed trying to dislodge it, until the tears ran down her face. She looked up gratefully when Alex handed her a glass of water.

"Thank you." She picked up the paper napkin and dabbed around her chin in case any food had escaped.

Alex leaned back in the chair and watched her wipe her eyes. Unease prickled down her back as guilt filled her. She hated lying, she'd seen enough of that from her father.

"Alex, I was not quite truthful before. I was being careful…because… you know…well…you never know who you meet in the outback."

"That's a wise way to be out here. It's rough country with some odd characters."

A wave of heat rose from her neck and she knew her face would be flaming red, thanks to her pale complexion. He was well spoken, and she decided to come clean. "I don't want you to think I'm taking advantage of you. I'm not really an actress. I'm actually here for my job or that is for a job I am trying to get."

He leaned forward to eat his meal and tipped his head to the side waiting for her to continue. Jess took a deep breath and waited until he had started to chew.

"I'm going out to Cockatoo Springs to do an article on the chef school and interview Alessandro Ricardo, the managing director. You seem to know a lot about bush cuisine, so it would be an interesting angle if I could use you in another article. You could tell me all about the fish, how you catch it, and where it goes." She spoke quickly, encouraged by the intense interest in his expression." I could even do a section on your business, all good publicity for you. Maybe take some photos?"

Now it was his turn to choke on his food. It must be those tiny pieces of rice…or the hot berries on the fish. Clearing his throat, he sat back and observed her for a moment without speaking, and frown lines creased his forehead.

"Hmm. That sounds interesting. No one has ever asked me about the barramundi fishing before. They've not really found it very interesting. Apart from the fishing tourists, that is, certainly not from a cooking angle." He nodded slowly. "I suppose it could help my business."

Jess was surprised to hear a snort from the bar, and she looked up as Janet hurried back into the kitchen.

"Now tell me, how do you intend to get to Cockatoo Springs?" he said with his arms folded across his chest.

"I'm going to drive there in the morning." A feeling of unease wound its way from her stomach to her chest, and it had nothing to do with the fish she had just eaten.

"You're going to drive three hundred kilometres across flooded creeks and billabongs? You must have a big four-wheel drive truck hidden away." His face was a picture. "And a truck driver?"

"Three hundred kilometres," she squawked. "What's that in miles?" She did the quick calculation in her head. "That can't be right. My directions said that Daly River is the closest town to Cockatoo Springs. That's why I drove down here from the airport."

"It is." He nodded sagely. "This is the outback."

Chapter Three

Alex almost felt sorry for the woman sitting across the table from him.

Almost.

He knew how hard food journalists from the top magazines had been trying to get an interview with his alter ego, managing director of Cockatoo Springs, Alessandro Ricardo, and it made hi angry . He'd only taken up the position at the request of his dead fiancée's family. They'd set the school up in her memory. He'd agreed and signed a two year contract on the strict condition he was a silent partner; it was a way he could get rid of the insurance payout from the accident. He didn't want the money, but he hadn't wanted to tarnish Emily's memory for her family. It was enough that he'd been hurt by what she'd done. Her family didn't need to know about it.

The promotional side of it drove him crazy. The stupid idea of him taking on an exotic sounding name as a figurehead for the school had been his assistant manager's idea. Mitch reckoned it was a way to keep away from the media, but it had backfired, and for some reason everyone wanted to know all about him. Christ, he was a lawyer and since he'd come to the Territory, he was happiest outdoors, messing about with his boats and crab traps once the school had been set up. He'd used his contacts to promote the place, and once they had Clay Bardi on board, a well-known indigenous chef who'd trained in London, chefs from all over the world had clamoured to get in.

The last thing Alex wanted to be was be some sort of celebrity figurehead and the subject of gossip magazines. But the media had latched onto the mysterious managing director of the Cockatoo Springs resort since they'd been named top restaurant in that blasted magazine, and the more he resisted, the harder they tried to get the scoop interview.

Things had gotten out of hand, from helping a family out to being trapped by his fake identity. He just wanted it over.

Gutter press. He despised them. His life was private and it was staying that way.

One reporter had even infiltrated his kitchen in the guise of a kitchen hand. Another one had registered as a guest in the resort and tried to get an interview with him via his bed. Sultry-eyed Catalina from *Hot Food* magazine had been bundled out unceremoniously clutching her shoes and bag to her chest when he had thrown her out of his private suite. She'd got the sex…but not the interview. Now here was another one after an exclusive. He'd been enjoying the conversation with Jess until she'd dropped the bit about being there to interview him. Lying women and the media. Two things that peed him off most.

No way, baby. You are in for a rude shock. But this one interested him.

What's the Top End? And this is the closest tow*n*, he mimicked to himself. She was green.

He still wasn't sure if she was being totally honest with him. If she was with a magazine like she said, they would have at least organised her travel. He ran his hand along his chin and thought quickly. He was not going to get caught out again. He could send her back to Darwin and tell her to get the helicopter in, but the best way to ensure she didn't get a back door entry to Cockatoo Springs was to keep her close. And she needed to be taught a lesson in honesty. He was sick and tired of the subterfuge of so-called professionals trying to get an interview with Ricardo under false pretences.

He looked across the table through the flickering flame of the candle. The wax had run down the bottle and was gathering in white waxy splotches on Janet's red tablecloth. Jess was chewing on her bottom lip. An ache settled in his chest as a memory of Emily flitted through his mind.

But for the car accident, she would have had to tell him how she'd been about to dump him for a new man. Instead, he'd found out about it after the funeral when the guy had requested a meeting with him. So, he'd dealt with grief, and dealt with lies. He'd never told a soul but he'd vowed never to get sucked in by a woman again.

Now, this one was looking at him wide-eyes as he tried to warn her off.

"The freeway looked fairly civilised to me as I drove down this afternoon," she said. "I think you're just trying to scare me."

Alex shrugged and turned his concentration to his meal and his thoughts. Damn woman had bought the past back with a vengeance.

"The Top End is rough…and dangerous. It's no place for a woman travelling alone," he said gruffly.

Especially one clad in designer clothes and stiletto shoes. But he kept that thought to himself.

Emily had chewed her lip when she was upset. He quickly buried that thought. The only time he allowed himself to think of that time in his life—pre Cockatoo Springs days—was when his loud and boisterous family came up to stay. Only then did he dwell on the past and what could have been. He'd found out after the funeral that she'd been ready to leave him. So, he'd dealt with grief, and dealt with lies. He'd never told a soul, but he'd vowed never to get sucked in by a woman again.

The transformation of a grief stricken and disillusioned lawyer into the barramundi fisherman and businessman he was now had been a long, hard road for him, and Alex guarded his privacy fiercely. Sex was for fun and pleasure. He kept his heart right out of it. There was no way he ever wanted to experience loss like he had when he'd lost Emily.

To death and deception.

If it hadn't been for the efforts of Nick and Tom, his two older brothers, he wondered if he would have ever picked up the pieces of his life. Now he intended to move on as soon as Clay, the new chef settled in. His contract was coming to an end in a few weeks. He'd achieved what he'd promised Emily's parents and more, and he wanted no publicity, no interviews, and magazine articles. He just wanted to fade into the background and let go of that stupid identity that seemed to fascinate everyone. Reality TV was responsible for most of this attitude. They thought they had an open door into anyone's life these days.

"Alex, are you listening to me?" Jess's voice intruded on his thoughts and he pushed his plate away.

"Sorry, what did you say?"

"I asked you which would be the best road to take to Cockatoo Springs tomorrow." Jess stared at him intently, and an unwelcome surge of desire hit him as he held her gaze. Her almond-shaped eyes were wide and her expression vulnerable as she worried at her bottom lip. A lush, full bottom lip.

Christ, she'd intended driving that little red box of a car across to the coast? He had to get the message across to her; if anything happened to her, he would feel bloody responsible.

"And I've told you already it is three hundred kilometres across flooded creeks and rough roads," he said.

Jess sat there with a frown wrinkling her brow. The bright red lipstick had disappeared between eating and choking fits, and he softened a little when despair clouded her face.

"Look, I'm sorry but there's no way you can drive in to Cockatoo Springs. The road from here is only for four-wheel drive vehicles. You'll have to drive back to Darwin and fly in."

A tear spilled onto her cheek, and she brushed it away impatiently. "Ignore me," she said brusquely. "I hardly ever cry. I'm just so disappointed and angry with myself." She plopped her elbows on the table and cradled her chin in her hands. "I'm always messing up. I do great work, but I'm not very good at organising myself." A rueful smile crossed her lips. "And this time, it means I've blown any chance of getting this interview…and my job.

Alex couldn't believe that any magazine would send a journalist this far without proper organisation and then sack them when they didn't deliver. If there was one thing he had kept from his law days, it was his sense of justice and fairness.

And integrity.

He hated lies and deception, and would be pleased when Alessandro Ricardo could disappear next month when the contract was up. Just because he kept to himself and didn't share his background with anyone, he still operated with honesty and integrity and truth… well, most of the time.

"Maybe I can help out." He was surprised when the words came from his mouth before his brain kicked in.

The look of hope that crossed her face tugged at his vulnerability. All three brothers were suckers for helpless females. Nick and Tom had both been lucky in life and love and were happily married and working on a tribe of kids to add to the Richards' clan. Tom and Brianna and their baby twins were in Italy, and Nick and Lissy lived in New Zealand with their toddler. Alex had no intention of going down the marriage path. It was not for him. Not now. Not ever.

"How are you going to help me?" she asked. "Find me a helicopter? I guess I'm going to have to drive back to Darwin and get myself organised."

He could arrange a helicopter for her with one phone call if he wanted, but after giving it some thought, he decided to offer her a lift out. *Keep the enemy close*. Once they got to Cockatoo Springs, he would decide how to handle her and he could always chopper her back to Darwin then. Whatever the outcome, there was no way she would ever find out who he was. And she needed a lesson in telling the truth.

He was Alex Richards, barramundi fisherman from the wild.

"I'm driving out there early tomorrow. If you trust me, I can give you a ride. Janet will vouch for me." He pointed to her meal. "Now enjoy your first foray into bush tucker before Janet brings out the spiced blood plum crumble I can smell cooking. I leave at five thirty in the morning."

***

After they'd eaten the dessert and finished with coffee, Alex stood and pushed his chair in. "If you decide to accept the lift be outside the office. On time."

Jess watched as he walked to the door. The tight jeans that hugged his butt outlined long muscular legs. She glanced back at Janet as she cleared the table.

"I can't believe the resort isn't close by." Jess shook her head.

"It's a decent enough drive in the dry," Janet said. "But with the wet starting early, the short road won't open up again till April. They've just opened a new bridge and that gives the tourists a better chance of getting up the river for the fishing."

"Thank you, and for the food. It was amazing."

The older woman's face lit up. "You think this is good, wait till you eat out at Cockatoo Springs." She put her head to the side. "You are going with him, aren't you? Alex Richards is a good man and I don't say that lightly. He's done it tough, but he's made a go of carting fish out of the river here for a couple of seasons. He's a gentleman and he'll get you to the resort in one piece."

Jess followed Janet across to the bar. "I'll settle my bill up now. Is there somewhere I can leave the rental car?"

"Leave the keys with me and I'll get my fella to put it in one of the sheds. How long are you going to stay out there?"

"Oh, not long. Just till I meet Alessandro Ricardo. I hope he's there." She sighed. "In my usual fashion I just tore over here. I didn't even think he might not be there. Anyway, if he's not there, I'll chase him down wherever he is."

Janet grinned. "Oh, don't worry, dear. He'll be there. I have no doubt about that."

##

It was still pitch dark when the alarm went off on Jess's phone the next morning. She ran the shower on cool water and tried to wake up—she was never at her best in the morning and certainly not before sunrise. She scrabbled through her suitcase looking for something suitable to wear in a fishing truck. Silky skirts, wraparound sarongs, and strappy sandals piled up on the bed as she searched for something more suitable.

Finally, she came across a pair of white knee-length Capri pants and teamed them with a loose silk top that knotted at the waist. The sandals would just have to do because she had packed no substantial footwear.

She'd been expecting a resort, not a fishing outpost, a two-star caravan park, and a smelly truck. She glanced down at her watch as she searched for a pair of dangly earrings. She had to look the part when they arrived. After all, it was one of the luxury resorts in Australia.

As soon as they hit the road, she would have to ring or email and make a booking. There had been no phone service last night, and she couldn't check her email or call Monica to report in. Probably because of the storm.

Oh, shit. It was twenty-five minutes past the hour and she only had five minutes to get out the front to meet him. Forgetting the earrings, she flung everything back into her suitcase, slung her handbag over her shoulder, and with one swipe of her hand dropped her array of cosmetics into the small carryon bag. She grabbed her laptop and opened the door, and was blinded by the bright headlights of a truck driving up slowly from the back of the hotel. It pulled up next to her, and by the smell of the fishing crates drifting from the back of the truck she knew her lift had arrived.

Alex opened his door and came around the front of the truck and looked at her bags.

"Sorry. They'll have to go in the back."

She held up her laptop and clutched it to her chest. "I'll hold this one."

"I have to pick up my dog and then we'll get going."

Jess looked at the back of the truck, loaded high with crates. He'd lifted the lid off a huge one and stowed her luggage into it. She'd never get the fish smell out of it.

"Where does the dog sit? In the back?"

"Up front," he said with a smile. "You're taking his seat. You'll have to nurse him."

Before she could reply, he flashed her a grin and walked around to the other side of the truck and swung himself up. She bit back a rude retort and heaved her laptop onto her other shoulder as he leaned across the cabin and opened the door for her.

She hated dogs. Ever since one of those little white fluffy toy things her mother always carted around bit her.

"Jump in."

She climbed into the truck and put her laptop and bag down where she could find a space amongst the assortment of nets and small, coloured, plastic fish covering the floor. Alex turned the truck out onto the main road. The dawn sky was a soft rosy apricot to the east. They travelled a few kilometres in silence before he took a turn across a high bridge and then onto a narrow dirt road that led down to the river. He pulled up outside a small shed surrounded by fishing nets and more of the huge blue crates that she was getting used to.

"No need for you to get out. I'll just unload the crates and pick up Bowser, hook up the boat, and then we'll be on the way." He looked at her steadily in the dimly lit cabin and his expression dared her not to comment on his dog's name.

"The boat? We have to take a boat to get there?" Jess tried to keep her voice calm, but it came out as an undignified squawk.

Alex climbed out of the truck and turned to her before he shut the door.

"No, I need the boat to check my crab traps in the rivers on the way to Cockatoo Springs." Jess let out a breath and sat for a few minutes wondering what the day ahead was going to bring. Once boredom set in, she pulled her phone out, pleased to see the service bars were strong again. Once her email downloaded, she checked messages and sent off a quick text to Mon.

Almost there. Will call when we arrive. Then she deleted *we* and replaced it with *I* before she pressed send. Her phone buzzed almost instantly as the reply came in.

Are u staying out of trouble?

No way was she going to tell Monica what she was doing. She

would hear the screech across the ocean.

Always. Call you tonight. Ciao.

She leaned back, yawned, and closed her eyes. The crashing and banging from the back of the truck overlaid the muffled conversation and the occasional laughter drifting through her window.

She would kill for a coffee.

A few minutes later, her wish was fulfilled when the aroma of coffee drifted through the cabin of the truck. She rubbed her eyes with the heels of her hands and reached out for the huge travel mug Alex passed through the open window.

"White, no sugar. Same as last night," he said passing her a coffee and a brown paper bag. "Muffins, not bush tucker, I'm afraid, but just as good. My mate, Wally's missus just made a batch and they're still warm. I called her last night and she's packed our tucker for the trip."

"I must have drifted off," Jess said sleepily. "Thank you." She sat up and peeked into the paper bag and the aroma made her mouth water even more. "Tucker? Do you mean bush tucker?"

"No. Tucker is food."

"This will do me till we get there," she said. "I'm still getting over that glorious meal last night."

"I doubt it will last you that long" Alex shook his head. "We'll probably get there late tomorrow, but if we strike any problems, we may have to camp out for two nights."

"What?" Jess's stomach plummeted and she stiffened in the seat. "Camp out? What do you mean camp out?"

"Do you ever listen?" Alex asked patiently. "I said last night the river is up and we're probably going to have to go the long way."

He opened the truck door and whistled. A quick scratching noise was the only warning Jess got before a brindle staffy jumped onto the seat and pushed his nose into her lap.

"Jess, meet Bowser." With a soft groan, she held her coffee high out of the dog's reach it as he sniffed around her arms and legs.

Oh, damn, I've really messed up this time.

Chapter Four

Finishing the last of her coffee, Jess placed the empty travel cup next to Alex's in the square console between the two seats. The dawn sky was light by the time Alex had jumped back into the pickup and swung it out on the main road. She turned around and peered through the back window to see what was rattling behind them, but a sheet of khaki-coloured canvas blocked her view. Moving closer to the window, she stared outside at the flat, boring landscape as the sun cleared the horizon, ignoring the little dog whose serious gaze was fixed unblinkingly on her face.

Not one word had passed between them since Alex placed the dog on her lap. Morning had broken and the sun began its climb into the vast outback sky. The landscape was monotonous and there was nothing to look at apart from high tussock grass and termite mounds that edged the road. The red dusty road stretched ahead in a straight line as far as she could see. In the far distance, plumes of white and dark brown smoke rose in the brilliant blue sky, and she glanced across at Alex who was intent on the road ahead. His long hair hung untidily over his collar and he'd rolled up his sleeves a few miles back. His tanned forearms arms were bare, and his right elbow rested casually on the open window frame.

"That's not a bushfire ahead, is it?" She pointed to the south…no… it would be the north; she was in a different hemisphere now and her sense of direction had gone completely AWOL.

"Ah, she speaks." The amused tone in his voice fired up Jess's temper, and she bit down the smart retort that sprang to her lips. After all, he was doing her a favour and it was his truck.

"I was drinking my coffee. It was very nice." She injected a sweetness into her voice she was not feeling. "Thank you."

"No, don't stress, it's not a bushfire. The savannah woodlands are burned off in the dry season every year," he said. "We're just coming into the wet now, so that should be the last of the fires once the rains come and stay."

She nodded and turned back to stare out the window, fighting the queasy feeling in her stomach. The truck bounced over the corrugations in the unpaved road, and the noise of the motor roared through the open window on his side of the truck. Diesel fumes wafted in, occasionally overlaid by the smell of fish.

"Are you travelling okay?" Alex asked as the truck hit a dip in the road and bounced hard.

She could have sworn he was getting amusement from her situation. His voice was full of mirth, but when she glanced across at him, his expression was serious and he was looking at the road ahead. Looking down, she tried to relax her hands, which were in a death grip in her lap, and straightened her legs out in the confined space on the floor.

"Yes, I'm fine, thank you," she said.

Hours and hours to go. She was blocking the thought of the journey ahead from her mind and focusing on each moment, and there were a lot of moments ahead if this was going to take a day, or God forbid more. *Plan the article in your head, store the description of the landscape, and think about the luxurious resort waiting for you at the end.*

Two days to go. How the hell did she get herself in this situation?

And a night camping in the outback? Maybe two?

There was no way she was going to tell anyone how badly she'd messed things up this time. No one besides the fisherman and Janet from the caravan park would ever know how irresponsible she'd been. Last time she'd forgotten to book a room, she'd been in Sri Lanka with Mon and her boyfriend, Gareth, and they'd shared their hotel room with her.

She grinned to herself. It sure had cramped their style having her on the sofa in their luxurious bedroom.

I can do it.

Why in hell did she decide to drive to this place? If she'd known there was a helicopter out there from Darwin, she would have caught that, and would be by now sitting around a pool, soaking up the sun and planning how to get her interview. It probably left from the same airport she'd flown into. And then there was the problem of getting back to Daly River to sort out the rental car. As soon as she was settled at Cockatoo Springs, she'd ring the rental company and arrange for a pick up. It might cost a fortune, but it would be less bother than trying to get back to Daly River to collect it. Next time, she'd listen to Monica and get herself organised.

The truck hit another rut in the road and her laptop case pressed into her legs. It was jammed between the backs of her knees and the floor, and she leaned forward to push it to the side.

"Put it behind the seat to give yourself some more leg room." The laconic drawl was followed quickly by a curse. "Oh shit, hang on."

A loud bang echoed through the truck just as Jess leaned down to reach for the laptop. The truck bounced hard and slewed to the right as Alex swung the wheel hard and hit the brakes at the same time. Her head banged against the window, and when the vehicle bounced over the rocks on the side of the road, the top of her head hit the back of the seat so hard it jarred her neck. Without thinking, she grabbed for the little dog that had landed on the floor at her feet, and held him tightly on her lap. The truck came to an abrupt halt. Red dust rose in a cloud around the cabin, and she waved her hand and coughed.

"Sorry about that. That hole was filled with bull dust, and I didn't see it coming." Alex opened his door and looked across at her with a frown. "Is your head okay? You hit the seat with a fair thump."

"I'm fine, thank you. It's the dust that's the worst."

Alex reached into the side of the door and passed her a bottle of water.

"Hang on to Bowser, will you? I don't want him taking off here."

"What are you doing?" The dog began to whimper when Alex got out of the car and tried to make a break for it. She held on to him tightly, terrified he would turn around and bite her. She so didn't do dogs.

"I'm going to check the truck. I want to make sure we didn't do any damage to the wheel when we hit that hole." He slammed the door and Jess put her head back and closed her eyes as the dog's whimpering turned into a full-blown howl. The truck swayed from side to side, and a few bangs and crashes spurred the dog onto even louder howls.

"Bowser, shut up!" The dog stopped howling and took up the high-pitched whimper again. At the same time, a stench wafted from his nether regions. Jess shoved the dog away and held it at arm's length, turning her head toward the window as the truck began to sway. She opened her eyes and craned forward as it rocked from side to side. Alex was gripping the big bar at the front of the pickup and as Jess watched he pushed at it again until the car rocked even harder. His T-shirt moulded to his chest and his muscles flexed as he strained against the weight of the car.

"Can I help?" she called out. For some reason her breath caught in her throat. It was the dust, not the eye candy at the front of the car causing the flutter in her chest.

"Nah, it's fine, thanks." With one final push, the car stopped rocking and he stepped back and looked down with a grin. "No major damage."

Alex reached in through the window across Jess. As he retrieved a dog leash from behind her seat, his forearm brushed across her breasts, and she jumped as a tingle shot through to her nipples. He called the dog over to the window. "Come on, little fella. Wee break." He clipped the leash onto the Bowser's collar and lifted the small dog through the open window.

"Do you need one yet?"

"One what?"

"A washroom break. Been a while since you finished that coffee."

"No, thank you," she said primly. "I'll wait for the next roadhouse."

Alex put his head back and laughed. The blasted dog joined in and barked until she put her hands over her ears.

His long-sleeved button-through shirt was open at the neck and the corded muscles of his tanned throat stood out as he clutched the dog to his chest. He stopped laughing and grinned at her.

"Sorry, sweetheart. None of them on this road."

"None of what?"

"Roadhouses."

"Well, how long till we get back to a main highway?" Jess folded her arms as uncertainty curled through her chest.

"This *is* the main road. We turn off onto the back road in about another hundred kilometres."

The sick feeling was firmly back in her stomach, and this time it had nothing to do with the odours in the truck.

***

Alex tried to keep the grin off his face. Teaching little Miss America a lesson in honesty was going to be so much easier than he'd thought. And she'd almost jumped a mile when he'd accidentally brushed against her before. He'd been peeved with himself when the blood kicked to his groin as her nipples had peaked through the silk shirt. Why not? A bit of fun wouldn't hurt?

He shook his head and put Bowser onto the ground, pointing to the other side of the vehicle.

"If you change your mind, there's a grove of melaleucas over there, just through the spear grass. The trees with the papery bark. And there's a roll of toilet tissue in the glove compartment."

She shook her head and leaned back on the seat, closing her eyes.

"Watch out for snakes, if you do change your mind."

He walked to the back of the truck and checked the boat was secure on the trailer before he headed off into the long grass with Bowser. He picked his way carefully through the cracked and dry ground between the termite mounds across to a clump of boulders. To his surprise, the ground was dry. The way the Daly River had come up last night he'd thought the rain had been more widespread. They'd only travelled forty kilometres to the west and it appeared there'd been no rain here at all. The weather was in their favour if that was the case. If the road stayed this dry all the way to Peppinmenarti, he'd be able to double back on the Port Keats road and save them some time. It all depended on how long the rains stayed away.

After waiting for the dog to lift his leg on every boulder in sight, Alex headed back to the truck.

Jess was leaning forward and looking into the distance.

"It's a long way, and the road's corrugated, but if it stays dry, we'll take the short cut." Alex opened the door and lifted Bowser into the truck. The dog scurried across the seat and jumped straight onto Jess's lap, trailing red dusty footprints across her pants. She scowled.

Miss America was in a fine mood this morning.

"There's a packet of dog snacks in the glove compartment." When Jess didn't move, Alex reached across in front of her, deliberately brushing his arm against her bare knees before he opened the compartment. Bowser's ears pricked up as the packet of liver treats rustled. A dollop of slobber hung from his jaw as he sniffed the air.

"Ew." Jess pushed him off her lap, but she wasn't quick enough. The slobber dropped onto her forearm and she wiped it on her white shorts.

"Oh, how disgusting." She crossed her arms and the silk strained across her generous breasts.

Alex laughed. "Sorry, he does have some bad habits. He's old enough to know better, but he's never learned."

The look she gave him showed she had begun to place him on a similar social scale as the dog. He was getting under her skin already and he hadn't even tried.

Good.

Jess didn't reply as she scrubbed her arm, smearing a wet patch onto the fabric of her pants. Finally, she heaved a big breath and turned to him.

"So how long will that take? Will we get there today if we go the short way?" She pushed the dog away and brushed at the marks on her legs.

"No, we'll still have one night under the stars."

She pursed her lips. "There's no need to make it sound like a holiday. I'll do that when we get to the resort. So, tell me about it. Why is it so far from everywhere?"

Alex looked across at her considering how much to tell her. He could tell her a little about the resort and she could do her article, if that was what she was really here for. But no interview with him. She wouldn't ever know who he was. When they stopped for lunch, he'd call Mitch on the satellite phone and see whether the first of the rains had hit Cockatoo Springs last night, and prime him about keeping the Alessandro Ricardo bit quiet when they arrived. One night should be enough to teach Miss America her lesson about survival in the outback and deceiving people to get what she wanted.

"It's on the edge of what they call the Kimberley region, one of the last remaining remote areas in Australia. It's a base for seeing lakes, diamond mines, and exploring the indigenous culture. The bush tucker school started up a couple of years ago."

"I heard they've snaffled one of the top London chefs to run the school."

"Yes, Clay Bardi is an indigenous guy who was raised in the Kimberley region, and he trained as a chef in Darwin before moving to Europe and taking the restaurant world by storm." He grinned at her. "Alessandro pulled a real coup getting him for the school."

"So, tell me about Alessandro. Is he as elusive as they say? And why when he's built up such a great school. Is he a chef, too or just the owner?"

"Look." Alex leaned across and pointed out her window. "Emus." He started the truck and diesel fumes entered through his window in a puff of black smoke.

"You might be used to this." She waved her arm and pointed a red manicured finger to the large birds running across the bare red dirt. "But it's a very different experience for me."

"Hmm, your trip from Broadway to LA wasn't quite as rough as this?"

"Oh, for goodness sake, I told you my real story last night. And I don't usually drive anywhere, I fly." Jess gagged and waved her hand in the air to clear the smoke. "Can you please close your window and put the air conditioning on? That smells disgusting."

Alex gunned the motor and the truck bounced sharply as it lurched over the rocks on the side of the road. Bowser finished chewing his snack and jumped back onto Jess's lap as the speed of the truck picked up.

"Sorry, love. Air con already on. It's a two by eighty system."

She turned to him with a frown. Beads of perspiration dotted her top lip, and she reached down the front of her top and pulled out a tissue, gently dabbing her face. His gaze lingered on the soft swell of her generous breasts beneath her shirt, and his blood heated as he took in the view.

"What's that?"

"Eighty kilometres per hour, two windows down." He lifted his gaze from the soft shadow between her breasts and nodded to her window. "If you're hot, wind it down. She's an old truck, and the air con died a couple of years back."

He reached over and grabbed his dog from her lap. "I'll hang on to him, though. He likes to stick his head out in the breeze." Jess leaned forward and grunted as she wound the window lever until the window stuck halfway down.

"Sorry, that's as far as it goes," he said. "Keep meaning to fix it, but I've been too busy with the fish and the crabs."

Bowser settled onto the seat between them and curled up to sleep. The road smoothed out and no more unexpected potholes appeared in front of the truck. They were getting close to the turn off to the shortcut. He glanced across at Jess as she pulled her phone from her pocket and stared at the screen.

"No point looking at that here. You might as well turn it off and save your battery. There's no mobile service all the way from here to the coast."

She shoved it into her bag on the floor. Her face lit up when she smiled up at him. She really was a looker. Shame she was less than honest.

"I'm not used to being disconnected. Might not be a bad thing. I spend too much time on social media these days."

Alex gestured down to her feet. "You've never been to the outback before?"

She shook her head. "I've never been to Australia before."

"I'll lend you a pair of socks when we stop. Those shoes aren't strong enough for out here. Be careful when you get out of the truck. The grass seeds of the black spear grass are very sharp, and if you step on one, it will go straight through those flimsy shoes." He looked at her, trying to figure out if she was as scatterbrained as her planning made her seem. "So, tell me about Jess Trent…really a former or wannabe actress, or always a journalist?"

"I'm just a wannabe journo out looking for a good story."

"Long way to come looking."

He glanced over when she didn't reply, and she looked away.

Definitely hiding something or not being quite truthful. Not what he needed or wanted.

The truck skittered across the potholes between the long ruts that had formed from the runoff from the heavy rains last wet season. The only sound for the next half hour was Bowser's snoring on the seat between them. Alex focused all his attention on the road. The corrugations were getting worse the further west they travelled.

"Ah, Alex."

"Yes? What's up?" He turned his attention to her for a moment. He hadn't noticed Bowser crawl back over to Jess. The small dog was curled up on her lap and her fingers were loosely threaded through his collar.

"Could we have that washroom stop soon?" Jess was looking at the window and her brow was wrinkled. "There are no trees?"

"Yup. You're right. There's no trees."

"So, what do I do?"

"I guess it depends how much you need a stop."

They'd been travelling for a while so he guessed it was as good a time as any to take another break. He pulled the truck to the side of the road, and the red dust billowed in through the passenger window. Jess waved her hand in front of her face as she coughed, and Bowser jumped off her lap.

Alex looped the leash through the dog's collar, and climbed out waiting for Bowser to follow him, but he turned in a circle and settled back on the seat. Jess stayed in her seat as well until he walked around and opened her door.

"I thought you needed a stop."

"I do." She swung her legs through the door and looked down at the bare dirt at the side of the road before lifting her gaze to meet his. "Are there any snakes here?"

"Sweetheart, there is nothing here." He spread his arms wide and followed her gaze as she leaned out and looked around. Deep blue sky, big sky, contrasted with the bare red dirt. The only thing breaking the flat, red vista was the narrow road heading west in a perfectly straight, unbroken line.

"No self-respecting creature would survive out here." Alex took pity on her as she looked hesitantly at the rough ground. She let out a soft gasp when he reached in and lifted her out, letting her slide down the front of him to the ground. A prickle of awareness shot through him as her soft breasts pressed against his chest, and he held her longer than necessary.

"I'll get back in the truck with Bowser, and close my eyes while you go around the back of the truck and use the…er…washroom." He shrugged. "Sorry, we don't have five-star facilities in the outback.

"Looks to me like you don't have any facilities." She stepped gingerly toward the back of the truck and waited for him to get back in.

Alex hoisted himself up into this seat. He lifted Bowser onto his lap and waited. "What do you reckon, little buddy? She's a looker, isn't she?" All he got was a snuffle in reply.

He leaned his head back on the seat and closed his eyes while he waited.

"Alex!" The shrill scream turned his blood to ice.

Chapter Five

Jess stood in the boat on the trailer behind the truck, her eyes fixed on the two strange looking creatures running across the dirt toward the road. Luckily, she'd been adjusting her clothing when she'd heard the sound, and without thinking she'd jumped up into the boat behind the truck.

Alex's laugh reached her as he appeared around the side.

"Jeez, don't panic. They won't come near us."

"What are they?" She kept her gaze fixed on the back of the creatures as their ungainly gait took them away from the road.

"Emus. I pointed them out to you before."

"They look different close up."

Alex held out his hand and Jess stepped up on the side of the boat. When she moved, her shoe caught in the coil of rope beneath her feet and she pitched headfirst over the side. Before she knew it, two strong arms were around her, and her face was buried in Alex's neck. Her heart was thudding and beat faster when she looked up and saw tanned skin almost against her lips. Strong corded muscles stood out in his neck, and a woodsy masculine smell she hadn't noticed before assailed her senses. She closed her eyes as embarrassment filled her, pushing away the temptation to slide her lips over that smooth skin.

"Sorry, I tripped." She pushed her arms against his chest, but he still held her tightly.

"Put me down, please. Can we just get back on the road and get as far as we can today?"

Alex carried her around the side of the truck and put her down before he opened the door. "You don't want a coffee break?" he said with a grin.

She looked around at the barren landscape surrounding them. The sooner they got going, the sooner she could get back to civilisation. And away from this guy who was unsettling her.

"No, just drive."

##

Jess leaned back into the seat and took a deep breath.

"Why don't you try and catch a nap?" Alex reached beneath the seat and threw her a small bottle of water.

"Thanks." She took a swig of the now warm water and recapped the bottle, and put it on the floor near her feet. Leaning her head back, she closed her eyes and tried to doze off, but the constant jarring of the hard road made it impossible, and Jess began to worry about the situation she'd got herself into.

Never again. When I get back to New York, I'll plan everything I do. No more rushing into situations without thinking them through first.

She'd messed up every part of her life over the past few years and now as a last resort she'd put all her effort getting this job to try and turn things around. She didn't need to work but she'd cut ties with her family. After the fiasco with Harrison, her ex-fiancé, she'd realised talking about her famous father and his wealth only brought trouble to her life. After she'd broken off the engagement she'd changed her surname from Van Lund to Trent, her mother's maiden name.

Overhearing Harrison's conversation with his best man at the rehearsal dinner the night before the wedding had opened her eyes. Not only was he after the money and prestige of joining the Van Lund family business by marrying her, he still had his girlfriend on the side. And his smarmy, preppy best man had the gall to congratulate him on his double accomplishment not realising Jess was standing right behind him. The look on Harrison's face had been priceless, and had told her all she needed to know.

The purpose of the rehearsal dinner had been for the relatives and friends of the bride and groom to meet and have a good time. Well, they'd met and no one had a good time, because Jess had fronted

Harrison in front of everyone, outed the girlfriend, and left town that night. She chuckled to herself. At least she could see the funny side of it now.

"Can't sleep?" Alex's deep voice interrupted her thoughts, and she grinned.

"Yes, I was just thinking about something funny that happened to me before I moved to New York."

And it had been funny. She realised she'd been pushed into the whole thing because all he'd been after was her family connection, and her father after had been in cahoots with them. She'd had no regrets, shed no tears, and it had been a lucky escape. But since she'd started work with Larry's company, she'd not touched a penny of her trust fund. Her father had said she would come crawling back to him for money, and she'd decided she would live on the street before she ever touched another cent of the family fortune again. If he could treat her like that, their relationship was toast.

"Tell me about life in the Big Apple." Alex glanced across at her.

"Okay. So, you want to know a little bit about me?" She turned in the seat and tucked her legs beneath her, facing him. He turned his attention back to the road, but with one arm resting on the window and the other lightly holding the steering wheel as the truck moved smoothly down the straight road.

"I live in New York and until recently I shared an apartment with my best friend, Monica. I work for a media company and I hate my job. I found out recently I only got it because my father pulled strings with one of his buddies." She bit off her words, she'd said more than she'd intended to. "Anyway, a great job has come up, and if I get this interview with Alessandro Ricardo it will give me a great chance of getting it."

"You want this job so bad you'll travel to the outback without booking a hotel, on the off chance of getting an interview with someone who doesn't give interviews?" He shook his head as he looked across at her curiously.

"Yes, I'll do anything to get it." She turned to him. "If you knew me better, you'd know I am determined. I'll try as hard as I can to pull this one off."

"Really?"

"I only have one shot at this. There is a full-time position open, and I know at least three journalists who are going after it."

"A city job? Or out in the field?" He turned his head briefly from the road and looked at her. "I'd hate being in an office. Give me my boat and a good catch of fish any day."

"You're lucky if you're happy that way, and you can run your business like that. I'm already having withdrawals because I can't check my phone out here."

"So, what will you do if you don't get this interview?"

"Oh, I'll get it. I have to. If I don't, it means I have to sell my apartment because I won't stay in the job I've got now."

He looked back to the road and she glanced up at him. A slight smile curled his lips and the crinkles deepened around his eyes. "I'm impressed with your determination. So, what are you going to do? Turn up and knock on Ricardo's door and demand an interview? You've got some balls."

"No." She laughed. This guy had no idea how the world of cutthroat business worked. She'd been brought up in the thick of it and knew all the tricks but she'd never lowered herself to that level before now. Maybe meeting Alex had been fortuitous. "You said you worked out of Cockatoo Springs?"

"Yup, I do."

"So." Jess grasped her hands together in front of her chest and stared at him. "Do you know him? Have you ever met Ricardo?"

Alex grinned at her, lifted his hand from the window, and gestured down to his work clothes.

"Who me? A simple fisherman?"

Disappointment surged through her. That would have been the

easiest way to get an introduction if Alex knew Ricardo.

"Have you made an appointment for the interview?" he asked.

"No, not exactly."

"Not exactly?" He flicked her a glance. "No hotel room booked, and no appointment? You like to live on the edge."

"He doesn't do interviews so that's why I can't book it, smarty-pants. I called from New York. I couldn't get past his secretary."

"Tell me, what are you doing here all the way from New York if he doesn't do interviews?"

"I am going to do my best to get one… somehow."

"An expensive trip for an interview you don't even have lined up."

"I'm in Australia, I'm on my way to the resort now, and the next step will be to get the interview." Jess dropped her hands to her lap and looked down. "This has turned out okay so far."

Alex threw his head back and laughed. "Turned out okay? That's how you ended up in my old truck heading across the outback with shoes and clothes fit for a night out? Oh yeah, you did that very well."

"Don't be rude, that was just one tiny, little mistake."

"You're telling me you've done worse?"

Jess tipped her head back on the headrest and cursed as her loose hair snagged on the chipped leather. She leaned forward and reached down into her bag for a clip.

"Oh yeah, a lot worse. But I got the interview." She turned and grinned at him as she held her up above her head with one hand.

"Tell me about it."

Jess gave up looking for a clip and her hair dropped down around her neck again. She leaned forward so it wouldn't snag on the headrest.

"Maybe later."

"There's some string in the glove compartment. You'll be cooler with your hair tied up." He reached over, dropped the door opened, and passed her a ball of blue twine.

"You've got a whole grocery store in there."

"It's the boy scout in me. Be prepared, I always say." He snapped the door shut and turned his gaze back to the road. "I use it to tie the crab traps together when I'm travelling."

Jess tried to break off a length of string with her fingers, but it was too strong. Alex stretched back in the seat and dug in the pocket of his jeans with his left hand.

"I've got a knife in here, but I can't reach it." He gripped the steering wheel and stretched further back. "See if you can get it."

Heat ran up Jess's neck. The last thing she wanted to do was poke about in his jeans pocket. She glanced over at him, and discomfort filled her as a small smile played about his lips. If that was how he wanted to get his thrills, no way was she going to play along. She sat up straight in the seat.

"It's okay. I'll wait till we stop." Opening the glove compartment, she shoved the ball of twine back in and a small box fell to the floor. She picked it up and pushed it back in and slammed the compartment shut. The heat from her neck ran up to her face and she was sure her skin was flaming red. She glanced over but his attention was on the road. A frisson of nerves jittered in her stomach as he turned and looked at her.

Talk about Mr Be Prepared Boy Scout. How many fishermen carried a box of condoms in their fishing trucks?

Her expression must have been easy to read.

"Like I said, Jess. Be prepared. You never know your luck in the big city or so they say."

"Well, you're in the outback now, and you're out of luck." She stared out the window as he roared with laughter.

***

Alex glanced across at Jess. The heat and the discomfort of the trip were starting to get to her. Her face was bright red and perspiration trickled down the side of her neck. He glanced at his watch and did a quick calculation of the mileage on the odometer on the control panel.

"Only about half hour to go before we hit the turn off. We'll take a break just after that. There's a nice little clearing on the river not far off the road. No red dirt and no emus there."

The look on Jess's face was priceless. By the end of this trip, she'd be able to write an article about keeping safe in the outback.

She had her head back on the headrest and her eyes were closed. His gaze travelled up the long line of her throat up to the unblemished skin of her face. Her softly parted lips were full and tempting. He still had to decide how far he'd go in teaching her a lesson in honesty, but it certainly wasn't going to be an unpleasant experience.

All was quiet as they covered the last twenty kilometres to the turnoff, the silence punctuated only by Bowser's soft snuffling as he slept. Thunderheads built to the north, and Alex slowed the truck as he peered out the window. There was only a little while to go until he had to make the decision of either taking the short cut across to the coast or going around the long way through the tiny settlement of Peppinmenarti.

Damn. His permit to travel through the private Aboriginal land was back in the office at Cockatoo. He hadn't given it a thought when he'd headed off last week. That pretty much made the decision for him. Without a permit to enter Aboriginal land, they'd *have* to take the short track and he'd have to hope the rain held off for one more night. The turnoff to the northeast appeared on the right, and he swung the wheel hard as the tyres spun in the fine red bull dust. Bowser barked, and Jess opened her eyes and blinked.

"Are we there?" She stretched her arms above her head and cursed as her hair snagged on the rough headrest again. Leaning back onto it, she untangled her hair and held it up in a knot on the top of her head.

Alex grinned as Bowser clambered back over to her lap. "Sorry, the old girl's a bit shabby. Not a lot of money in fishing."

"I'll pay you for driving me over, of course," she said.

"No need, I was coming this way anyway. And you've already spent enough, I'd say, if you're not going to have a job."

"We'll see." Jess pointed out the windscreen ahead. "It's a lot greener up this way?"

"Yeah, we're close to the Daly River again. It winds its way to the coast in loops."

She wiped the perspiration of her brow with the back of her free hand and held her hair above her head. "Anywhere to swim when we stop?"

He looked at her with a frown. "If you've got a death wish."

"What?"

"Crocs."

"Here?"

"Yes, here. You really didn't do your research, did you?"

"I thought only the saltwater crocodiles were dangerous. Aren't we a long way from the salt water?"

"Yes, we are. But they're here too, plus the freshwaters will attack if you provoke them, too."

Jess looked across at him and her green eyes were wide. "You're teasing me, right?"

He shook his head. "When I offered to bring you across to Cockatoo Springs, the main reason I offered, was to keep you safe."

Well, that was *one* of the reasons he'd offered. And she certainly had shown him she had no idea about keeping herself safe.

"The saltwater crocodile is a man-eater and they've invaded the river and creek systems of the Top End. They come as far as three hundred kilometres inland, and here we're only about a hundred kilometres from the coast. We wind in and out across the wetlands to get back up to Cockatoo Springs. As the crow flies, it's only about a third of the distance we spend on the road."

"You're just trying to frighten me."

A lazy swirl of desire kicked low in his groin. *Not now. Not yet.*

"Look, Jess, I might have teased you about other things, but this is deadly serious and you have to listen to everything I say and do it when I say to. Okay?"

"Oh…okay, as long as you promise you are being truthful with me. No sharing a tent because you say you have to protect me or stuff like that, okay?"

Alex laughed. He hadn't thought of that one. It would have been good ploy to upset her. In fact, he hadn't given much thought to the camping at the waterfall…yet.

"Not a problem. We'll stay well back from the water, and besides, I don't have a tent."

"What, we sleep out in the open? No way."

"No, I'll sleep in my swag in the boat and you and Bowser can have the back of the truck."

"What? With all that the smelly fish stuff?"

"I unloaded that when we stopped at Wally's and put the canvas canopy on the back of the truck. It might still smell a bit, but it'll keep the mozzies off you."

"The what?"

"The mosquitoes. Don't you have them in the States?"

"Of course we do, it was your accent that threw me."

"Anyway, make sure you cover up with Bushman's. There's some in—"

"The glove compartment," she finished off his sentence with a laugh.

At least she had a sense of humour.

He idled the truck to a stop about seventy-five meters from the water beneath a stand of melaleuca trees, their ghostly white bark bright in the mid-morning sunshine. The water was low and flowing slowly where a narrow U-shaped bay came off the main arm of the river. Fringed by white sand and overhanging trees, it was one of his favourite stops on the road to his resort. It would have been a good stop for the night, but he wanted to cover more of the road before he called it quits for the day in case it began to rain.

Reaching behind the seat, he passed a long-sleeved khaki shirt to Jess.

"Put that on, it will protect you from the sun and the insects."

While he kept digging behind the seat for a pair of socks, Jess took it off him and wrinkled her nose.

"Sorry, it's a spare fishing shirt," he said. "Pretty hard to get away from the smell of fish when you're around my truck." After a minute, he held up a pair of black work socks and grinned at her. "Success. Put these on under your sandals." He opened his door and pointed to Bowser. "Stay there, boy."

The dog stopped, and ran back across the seat to Jess.

"No way. I'm not putting your socks on." She threw them back over the seat and opened the door.

"Whatever, but don't come crying to get me to take the prickles out of your feet."

Walking around to the other side of the truck, he reached up to help her to climb down. She waved his hand away and jumped down onto the river sand, and stood there buttoning up the shirt while he cut a piece of string and passed it to her. She looked at it for a moment before she shrugged and tipped her head forward, gathering her hair in one hand and looping the string around it before tying it off.

"We'll stay here about half an hour. I've got some crab traps in the river I can check now, seeing we've come this way. Then we'll have a cuppa." He pointed to the stand of trees on the right. "There's a nice natural restroom over there. Just watch out for brown snakes."

"What about the crocodiles when you check the traps?"

"That's okay. When you come back from the 'restroom', I'll back the trailer down and drop the boat off. Do you want to come out in the boat and help me?"

"God, no. I'll wait in the truck."

Alex shrugged. "Offer's there if you change your mind."

***

Five minutes later, Jess stood and grinned as she adjusted her clothes. She tiptoed over to the area shield by the thick trees, and managed to avoid prickles and snakes. It was possible Alex might be exaggerating the dangers and trying to scare her. This restroom experience, out in the open under the trees, would be a story to tell in the office when she got home. For a New Yorker used to her creature comforts, she'd already learned a lot of new things in her experiences during the last twenty-four hours. Now that they were into the journey, her confidence had kicked back, despite being in the middle of nowhere with a total stranger with no company except for crocodiles, brown snakes, and mosquitoes.

And birds.

She looked up in appreciation as a flock of something black with bright red slashes in their tail feathers squawked overhead and settled in the trees above her.

"Red-Tailed Black Cockatoos." Alex sauntered over with Bowser on his leash trotting along beside him.

"They're beautiful."

"They're a protected species. Over at Cockatoo Springs, we—" He bit off his words and Jess looked at him.

"You what?

"Doesn't matter." He turned on his heel and dragged Bowser behind him. "Come on, I have to get this boat in the water, so we can't stand around yakking all day."

She shrugged and followed, watching where she placed her almost-bare feet. Her sandals were pretty but flimsy, and offered little protection against any of the hazards he'd described. She'd be spending as much time as she could in the truck, and she was not going to put on those socks. Wrinkling her nose, she looked down. The smelly shirt was bad enough.

Alex paused at the boat trailer and lifted three big wire mesh circles out of the boat and put them on the ground. Jess kept walking and stopped behind the truck. The tray on the back was covered with a square tent-like abode made of thick khaki canvas. It was zipped up tight all round and two large canvas flaps were held down with plastic pegs.

He glanced up at her. "That's your room. Unzip it and check it out if you want." His tanned face broke into a grin. "I've already had your bags delivered."

Jess reached up, and unzipped the zipper on one side, but she couldn't reach the top. It was too high. She climbed up onto the draw bar of the trailer, unzipped it to the top, and peered into the dim space. A foam mattress with chunky holes eaten out of it, by something she had no desire to know of, filled the small space. Her bags were thrown in a jumble at one end, and an old discoloured pillow and a dirty blanket lay in a heap on the middle of the mattress.

"Sorry it's not five-star accommodation."

Jess jumped when Alex's breath grazed over her ear. It was immediately followed by his warm body pressing up against her back. He leaned forward and pointed into the little space. Jess stiffened as he moved closer, and he casually looped one arm across her shoulders.

"Bowser chewed up some of the mattress last time he slept in there, and it might not be pretty, but it's still comfy." He stepped down from the draw bar of the trailer and held his hand out to her. She gripped it and hitched her breath. A jolt of heat ran up her arm. As her feet hit the ground, she dropped his hand and stepped away.

"What do you want me to do?"

"Stay in the truck with Bowser while I've got the boat in the water. It won't take me long to lift the crab traps. With a bit of luck, you might even get crab for dinner." He grinned at her. "Won't be as good as Janet's fish, but you can still take a photo if you like."

He moved in closer and looked down at her. "Crab on a campfire by a waterfall. Would that give you a good article and help you keep your job?"

"It would help but it's not quite up there with an interview with the famous Alessandro Ricardo and his chefs."

She moved back, feeling uncomfortable with his proximity. Alex was giving out mixed signals. Something wasn't right. He walked to the front of the truck and lifted Bowser back in before turning to her. "Can you back a trailer?"

"Can I what?"

"Just what I said. Drive the truck backward so the trailer goes straight in the water."

"Er…I don't know." And she certainly didn't want to try it.

"What say we give it a go? A lot safer for me if I can stay in the boat while you back the trailer in." Without waiting for her to answer, Alex opened the driver's side door and gestured for her to climb up

"Ah, I don't know how I'd do that. I'd prefer not to."

"Nah, come on, it's easy. If you can drive a car and follow instructions, you'll be fine. Just do what I say." He grabbed her hand and gently pushed her toward the vehicle. When she stepped up, his hand brushed her butt. She pulled away from him and slammed the door. Copying the way he'd placed his elbow on the windowsill, she looked down at him. "Now what?"

"I'll get in the boat and you slowly back the truck down to the edge of the river. When I yell out, hit the brakes and the boat will slide into the water. Much safer than me standing and pushing it in." He pointed across to the other side of the narrow river. "See?"

She followed the direction in which he was pointing and gasped. Three large brown shapes, which she'd thought were logs, were sliding slowly into the water.

"Oh, my God. Are they crocodiles?"

"Yup, sure are. Good size ones, too."

"You can't get in the water. What if they—" Jess bit her lip.

"Calm down. I'll be in the boat."

"But why do you have to go on the water?"

Alex leaned in through the window and put his hand on hers. The heat burned up her arm and she shook his hand off. It must be the outback heat that was causing this stupid reaction every time he came near her.

"I'm very touched by your concern for my well-being. I'm going in the boat because I need to pull up my crab traps. It's my livelihood." Alex looked at her, and his voice was patient. "You'd hate to see a poor fisherman go without, wouldn't you?" His face was way too close to hers and he'd put his hand back on her arm.

"Go without what?" she asked waspishly.

He held her gaze and a smile played about his lips. "Go without catching fish. What else did you think I meant?"

"Oh. Go and get in your boat and get your crabs," Jess snapped. "I don't care what you do. Just do it quickly so you can get me to Cockatoo Springs and I can get my interview and go home."

"Not enjoying the trip, then?"

Did nothing upset the man?

"No, I'm not. Between you and your smart comments, your lousy driving, the heat, the dust, your smelly dog, and the whole fish thing…" She waved her arm impatiently at the boat. "I just need to do what I have to do and then everything will be okay."

Chapter Six

Alex walked to the back of the truck, whistling happily, and climbed into the boat. The trip was beginning to wear on Jess and she was getting feisty. He'd seen the sassy side of her yesterday when she'd given him the finger, and he'd wondered how long it would be before her gumption resurfaced. Grinning, he unplugged the electric cable between the boat trailer and the car, and climbed onto the trailer.

After he'd unclipped the chain securing the boat to the trailer, he called out.

"Okay, take it slow and watch me in the side mirror." Jess watched him over her shoulder as she started the truck.

"Nice and slow." Reaching down, he grabbed both sides of the boat and braced himself so he wouldn't lose his balance when the small tinny hit the water. The truck backed slowly down the slope toward the water.

He'd been teasing her about the crocodiles, but the last thing he wanted was to end up in the water. That would be taking the rough fisherman act a tad too far. Despite his constant teasing and smart remarks, and his deliberate invasion of her personal space, she'd held her cool…until now.

"Now pick up the speed a little and when I yell stop, hit the brakes." The wheels of the trailer reached the edge of the water and she slowed the truck to a crawl.

"No, not yet, go faster! Pick up the speed. Now!"

The truck stopped.

"What in the bloody hell are you doing, woman?" Casting a quick eye out for any interested crocodiles, he jumped out of the boat and ran across the sand to the cabin of the truck.

Jess looked at him without speaking.

"What are you doing? I said go fast then hit the brakes."

"I couldn't hear you," she said calmly. "And that thing…" She flicked a red-painted nail to the back of the truck. "The little house camping thingy blocked my view."

Alex rubbed the back of his neck biting down on the words of frustration he was holding back. Drawing a deep breath and releasing it before he spoke, he forced a smile onto his face and spoke patiently.

"Sorry, I'll yell a bit louder this time." He stepped up onto the running board on the side of the truck and reached in.

"Now this is what I want you to do." He grabbed the wheel with one hand and turned it a quarter-turn to the left. "Drive back up the slope till you get to the top. You'll have to put your foot down a bit and then stop. Then we'll try again."

Jess looked at him and drove the truck back up the hill and he stayed on the running board beside her.

"Great. Stop here." He jumped down. "Now I'm going to get in the boat. What you have to remember is that the river drops off really quickly into deep water here, so when I yell stop, hit the brakes."

"Okay." Jess squared her shoulders and grasped the steering wheel with both hands. White knuckles contrasted with the red painted fingernails.

"Once the boat's in the water, drive back up to here and wait in the truck with Bowser. I've only got half a dozen traps in here, so it won't take me long to pull them out. Now that the wet is coming, I want to lift all the traps out for the season."

"Alex?" She looked at him and he couldn't decide if it was curiosity or suspicion in her expression. "How would you have done this if you'd been by yourself?"

"I would have risked the crocs. And moved bloody fast." He grinned at her. "Good money in crabs and they love them over at the chef school. Okay, all set?"

She nodded and he walked across and climbed back into the

boat.

"Okay, nice and steady." The trailer began to inch down the hill.

"Bit faster, Jess." She waved out the window and acknowledged his call, and the speed of the trailer down the riverbank increased.

"That's great, keep it going." He glanced back at the truck, caught her eye in the side mirror, and waved at her to keep going. The truck speed picked up and the wheels of the trailer hit the water.

"Okay, stop!" he yelled. "Now."

The truck stopped with a shudder and the boat slid off the trailer splashing into the river in one smooth movement. Alex reached down to start the motor as the truck roared back up the hill. A whoop came from the car. "I told you I could do anything I set my mind to."

Once the outboard had fired, he looked back up the hill Jess had parked the truck in the shade of a huge kapok tree. Her elbow was resting on the window and he gave her a thumbs up as she leaned out and grinned at him.

"That was fun. Can we do it again?"

Her cheeks were flushed and her hair was tied back with the piece of string he'd cut off for her when they'd stopped. *Didn't quite go with the designer clothes look.*

He smothered a grin. Shame she'd refused the socks. "Don't get out of the truck till I came back." His voice carried across the water and she acknowledged his words with a wave.

Alex turned the boat and headed it toward the mangroves up the river and tried to ignore the warm feeling in his chest. He'd started out to teach her a lesson, but was fast falling under her spell despite his best intentions. It would be interesting to watch when she got to Cockatoo Springs and see how long her determination held out.

Anything she set her mind to. Well, not this time.

It was good to be away from her for a while. If he wasn't careful, he was going to fall in the usual Richards' way. He'd learned the hard way with Emily and he wasn't going to be sucked in again. No matter how attractive she was.

***

Jess groaned and pushed the little dog away from her as yet another unpleasant smell wafted up to her. He snuffled in his sleep and curled up on the passenger seat. It was unbearably hot inside the truck. She tipped up her water bottle, draining the last few drops. Alex had been gone over half an hour and the temperature in the truck had risen as the sun climbed to its zenith.

"Little dog, I don't know what you've been eating, but it smells like rubber bands." It was a choice between the odour coming from the dog or the insects. A swarm of small black flies had arrived soon after Alex had disappeared around the bend, and she'd wound the window up except for a small crack at the top. They'd filled the cabin of the truck, but she'd managed to swat most of the stragglers with a rolled-up newspaper she'd found in the glove compartment. The heat was becoming unbearable and she was going to have to get out of the truck before she expired from the heat.

God, how the hell did I ever get myself into this situation?

When she'd found out she couldn't drive across to Cockatoo Springs she should have got straight back into the rental car and driven back up a real highway to the city. The date for her return flight back to New York was open, and the office was winding down for the Christmas break, so there'd been no urgency for her to get back to New York.

Reaching for Bowser's leash she picked it up and looked at the clip trying to figure out how to attach it to his collar. If they stayed well back from the water, it should be fine. She'd keep the dog close, stand near the truck, and keep her eyes open for all the other assorted venomous creatures that seemed to inhabit this country. No matter how small her apartment was at home, and how much traffic she had to battle every day to get into Manhattan, it was what she loved.

Despite what Alex had instructed, she couldn't stay in the truck a minute longer. Nor could the dog—he'd die of heat exhaustion as well. He said he wasn't going to be gone for long, and he'd been gone for ages. Jess clipped the leash onto the dog's collar and cursed as she lost another fingernail in the process.

"Shit," she muttered. "Please, somebody take me to a nice hotel room with a real bathroom, and air conditioning…and a manicurist."

Opening the door, she waved with one hand as the cloud of black flies descended before she'd even swung her legs out. Balancing carefully on the running board beneath the open door, she scanned the ground for snakes.

All clear.

Grabbing the dog under her arm, she stepped down to the fine white sand and groaned as a drop of slobber soaked through her silk top.

Look on the bright side. At least it's cool.

As soon as they were on the ground, she bent down and looked under the side of the truck, in case anything was sheltering from the hot sun. She didn't want any surprises jumping out and grabbing her leg. Walking around the front of the truck, she found a patch of deep shade close to the huge trunk of the tree and leaned against the smooth bark and closed her eyes for a moment. The air moved slightly, and she took a deep breath appreciating the cooler breeze as Bowser sat patiently at her feet. Her eyes flew open and she turned when something soft and feathery brushed against her cheek. She jumped back with a soft scream. A huge, pale-green praying mantis had a half-eaten brown moth between its pincers had landed on the tree trunk beside her face and was slowly devouring the moth's head. Jess shuddered and turned away just as the low hum of an outboard motor drifted across to her.

Thank God.

Before she could move, Bowser pulled on the leash and it dropped from her hand. With a screech, Jess ran after him. Forgetting all about snakes and prickles, and paying no regard to the ground beneath her flimsy sandals, she chased him toward the water and the oncoming boat.

"Bowser!" She screamed as the dog ran down the bank into the water and began yapping at the boat and his master.

"Shit. Bowser, get back." The more Alex yelled, the louder the dog yapped. "Jess, you stop right there. Don't you come any closer to the water."

There was no way she was going to be responsible for the little dog ending up in the jaws of a man-eating crocodile, no matter how bad he smelled or slobbered.

Kicking off her sandals, she ran down the sloping sand into the water and scooped the little dog up in her arms. A huge swirl in the water just out from the edge broke the surface and Jess froze, unable to move. Alex gunned the motor and the small aluminium boat whizzed across the river and over the spot where the water had swirled only seconds before. The boat roared onto the shore at full speed, scraped along the sandy bottom, and wedged on the sand beside them. He cut the motor and jumped out and grabbed her, pushing her and Bowser up the sandy bank.

"Jeez, Jess, are you okay?" He spoke quietly as if not to spook her any more than she'd already been. He wrapped his arms around her and held her tightly against his chest as she began to shake uncontrollably.

Burying her face into his chest, she nodded. "I'm sorry. I just couldn't bear the thought of him being eaten. I know I wasn't supposed to get out of the truck, but it was too hot in there." Her voice was muffled in his soft T-shirt, and she couldn't help but notice his chest was rock hard. His heart thudded against her cheek and she closed her eyes. "Thank you."

"You might be a city slicker pain in the ass, but I wasn't going to let you get eaten by a crocodile."

She didn't move for a minute, appreciating the strength of the arms holding her.

"Jess?"

Alex was looking down at her intently, his blue eyes narrowed. She held his gaze and her heart began to race as he lowered his head. She couldn't move, and she watched fascinated as his lips came closer.

They were a mere breath away, and Bowser yapped at her feet, interrupting them.

"I'm okay now, thanks." Pushing away, she walked to the top of the bank and picked up her sandals before going across to the truck.

She opened the door, climbed in, and slammed it behind her, taking deep breaths as she willed her thudding heart to slow down. Alex followed her and opened the other door and put Bowser on the seat next to her. The dog came across the seat and snuggled into her, obviously sensing her distress. A warm wet tongue scraped along the side of her face and she laughed shakily.

"That was a stupid thing to do, Bowser," she said. "You nearly got us both eaten."

Alex watched them through the open door. "You've made a buddy there. He doesn't usually take to other people."

Jess looked up from the dog to Alex. Perspiration ran down the side of his face and his shirt was damp. He held her gaze and her uncertainty was reflected in his eyes. She looked away as a shaft of warmth sent another shake through her body, but this time it wasn't fear making her legs weak.

***

Alex cursed himself as he headed back to the boat.

Christ, his stupid game of showing her up could have ended in tragedy. All she'd been doing was trying to look after his dog, and she could have ended up as crocodile bait. He'd seen some close calls over the past seven years, but that had been the worst.

What sort of idiot was he? Teaching her a lesson in honesty was one thing, but putting her in danger?

No more.

He'd put his head down and focus on getting them to Cockatoo Springs with no more incidents, and then he'd sort her out once they'd arrived safely. She could stay for a holiday, but he wasn't going to break and give in to an interview. He'd taken the job under sufferance, he'd built the school up faster than anyone had anticipated, but that was as far as it went. He was getting out soon, and Alessandro Ricardo was going to disappear for good. No matter how much Jess wanted to get a scoop and publicise it, his private life was private.

Not negotiable.

She could interview Mitch and get the information second hand if it meant she'd get a job out of it. He still didn't know whether she was being truthful, and once they got to Cockatoo Springs he wasn't going to stick around to find out.

Jess sat quietly next to him cradling Bowser on her lap while he backed the trailer to the water, and hooked the boat on. He drove back up the slope and parked beneath the stand of melaleucas, and then transferred the crabs into the iced cooler in the back of the truck.

"Just going to check the forecast, and then we'll have a cuppa and head off." He held up the satellite phone to Jess and she gave him a brief smile before he walked around the back of the boat and called Mitch, his assistant manager at Cockatoo Springs.

"Where are you, Alex?" Mitch's voice was muffled by the connection. "Clay's arrived."

"Just turned off the main road, I'm taking the shortcut across."

"Why? A bit risky with the rain coming."

"Long story, mate. I'll tell you when I get there. If I need help if the river comes up, I'll radio in and you can send the chopper out. Got a good haul of crabs for you, and the barramundi went to Darwin last night."

Mitch laughed. "It's already here. Clay checked and got it in fresh before they could freeze it. He's got the first class doing it today."

"Great stuff. I can't wait to meet him."

Alex ended the call and lifted the small cooler out of the boat, and walked over to the truck. Unzipping the canvas, he reached in and pulled the old blanket from the back.

Might as well give Jess somewhere to sit. She'd been very quiet since the episode on the water. He spread it on some soft grass well back from the river before going over and opening the door to the truck. Jess looked at him and anticipation filled her voice.

"Are we leaving now?

"Soon. Come and have something to eat and then we'll head off for the last leg. I hope." He was going to be honest about what was ahead. "I want to stop and get our camp set up before dark. It's raining up ahead.

"How do you know?"

"I was talking to my…to my mate at Cockatoo Springs. Rains started over on the coast last night so we're going to have to be careful."

Jess rolled her eyes at him as she stepped out of the truck. "Whatever. Can't get much worse, can it?"

Alex shook his head as she strode ahead of him to the blanket.

Oh yes, it can. If the rains start, we are going to get stranded on this back road and I don't know if I could handle being stranded in the outback with you for too long.

She had determination in bucket loads. He was enjoying her quick comebacks, and although she'd bitched about the heat and the dog amongst other things, she was giving it a go.

When he'd held her after she'd saved Bowser, a feeling, long-buried, had shimmied up into his chest, and he hadn't liked it one bit. Jess was playing havoc with his emotions, and he was angry at himself for putting himself into that situation. But the longer they travelled and the more he threw at her, the more respect he was developing for her toughness.

Even though she'd headed off in the wrong direction on her journey and ended up with him, she was coping despite everything he'd thrown at her. Even when he'd deliberately invaded her personal space and pressed up against her, she'd only looked at him and not commented. But that wasn't going to happen again, anyway, getting up close and personal with her was not an option. He was going to stay well clear. She was way too appealing and he wasn't going to go there.

##

Jess lifted the blanket carefully and looked around the edge of the

384

grassed area before she flopped down onto the ground next to him.

"Don't worry, I've already checked for snakes. Just watch out for those grass seeds I told you about." He held up the flask. "I'm sorry…no coffee. I've only got tea. Wally's missus puts the tea leaves in the flask and it's pretty strong, but it will quench your thirst."

"What do you do up here all year?" Jess looked at him over the mug of tea she'd accepted.

"In the off season, I do a bit of this and that around Cockatoo Springs. Sometimes I help with the tours." He looked at her. "There's a really good trip you should take if you stay there long enough. It's a trip out into the bush, gathering bush foods, and learning about bush tucker."

Her face lit up with interest and his stomach clenched. She was altogether too beautiful for his peace of mind. Even with her hair tied back with a piece of string and his old fishing shirt buttoned up to her throat.

"That sounds fabulous. I've never read about that. I could include it in my article." She tipped her head to the side and held his gaze. "Have you always fished up here? No other career?"

Alex looked up as the flock of red-tailed cockatoos squealed overhead. Something had disturbed them—he looked around to see what had set them off, but couldn't see anything around. He turned his attention back to Jess. Her mug was beside her and she'd sprawled out on the blanket on her stomach with her chin propped in her hands.

It wouldn't hurt to be truthful here.

"I came to the Territory two years ago."

"Where from?"

"A small town called Armidale in the middle of New South Wales."

"No fishing there?"

"No, not this sort of fishing. I grew up in the country, and I'd never held a fishing rod until I went out on a charter from Darwin and I was hooked. Pardon the pun.

"So, what did you do before that?"

"I studied to be an environmental lawyer and worked for the government in Brisbane for a while." Alex held her gaze in his and shrugged. "At least I ended up here, working in the environment."

"That's a big change. What made you leave law?"

He stared off into the distance and the raucous noise kicked up by the cockatoos stopped as suddenly as it had started.

"Life happened. I needed a change."

"Law wasn't for you?"

"Family circumstances."

He'd left Emily behind in the cemetery on that cold hill in Armidale and hadn't talked about her since he'd come to the Territory. Not only had he had to deal with her death, but her betrayal had screwed with his head and his emotions for the first year. He'd only started to move on these past few months.

"You're quiet." Jess rolled over and sat up, placing her hand on his arm. "And you have a sad look on your face. I hope I haven't upset you."

She chewed her lip looking across at him with concern

Feelings he hadn't let surface for years were filling his chest. He dropped his head and pulled Bowser over onto his lap.

"I have two brothers and three sisters. I'm the baby of the family. My two brothers, even though they are very different in personality, both disagree with how I handled a situation a couple of years back." Alex laughed shortly, but there was no amusement in it. "Nick and Tom both think I ran away from home, and they can't understand me giving up my law career." He looked up at the sky and lifted one hand.

"But hey, they were wrong. It's not all about money." He gestured around them. "Look what I have. The outback has looked after me, and I'm pretty damn happy. I haven't done too badly up here."

As soon as his contract finished in the next couple of weeks, he had to figure out what he was going to do with the rest of his life. But first, he had to sort out his passenger.

Chapter Seven

The raw pain in Alex's voice when he talked about the 'situation,' which had been the catalyst for him coming to the Top End, piqued Jess's interest. Even though she was a food journalist, she was always interested in people, and thoughts of using Alex's story as a second article played around in her mind.

He had offered that I interview him instead of Ricardo. I could do a series seeing I've come all this way.

She was curious about what had happened to spur him onto such a dramatic move in his life, but until he volunteered the information, she wasn't going to press him.

"Did you practise law for long?" She tipped her head to the side and looked at him thoughtfully. "How old are you, Alex?"

"I worked in the government department for a while, not in a law firm. I'll be twenty-eight in a few days."

His answer surprised her; she'd picked him as a bit older than her. The tanned skin and the shaggy hair had obviously contributed to her incorrect assumption.

She smiled. "So will I. What date?

"December tenth."

"You just beat me. And we're the same age..."

"This is where a gentleman would come straight back and say 'but I thought you were only twenty-one.'" He grinned at her. "Having a birthday bash?"

If her father had his way, there would be the full blown, ridiculous extravaganza at *Spago* in Los Angeles or one of the other restaurants where he and his latest bimbo could be photographed for some ritzy magazine. Although probably not— he wouldn't want anyone to know he had a grown-up daughter.

And her mother would be in a health spa somewhere in Europe, and wouldn't even remember it *was* her birthday. Jess had called her a few days before she'd left for Australia and her mother's personal secretary answered and told her she was in the Swiss mountains. Her mother had never gotten over her father's desertion, and even though she received a healthy settlement, she'd spent most of it to trying to recapture her lost youth.

"Jess?"

"Oh, sorry. No, no party. Maybe a dinner out with my friends, Monica and Gareth, in New York if she's still talking to me after this fiasco of a trip." She held her hands out in front of her and frowned at the state of her manicure. "Poor Monica tries to keep me organised. If she could see me now, she'd die… that is, after she'd killed me first. What about you? Do you have anything big planned? Or does the outdoor life not give you time for that sort of thing?"

Alex looked at her for a moment before he answered and she could almost see the wheels turning in his head.

"My family is coming for my birthday. They're not happy I don't make the effort to go home, so they all descend on the resort for a week or so every December."

"All of them?"

"Yes." He nodded and smiled.

She'd never had much of a family life and his family sounded fascinating. If they were staying there, someone obviously had money because it was a five-star resort, and she'd seen it featured in those coffee table books with photographs of the best resorts in the world.

Alex laughed and she gazed back at him. When he smiled, the ruggedness of his face softened. "Anyway, that's enough about me…you've got the potted Alex Richards' history now. I'll shout you a birthday drink before you go back to the States. How long are you planning to stay?"

"Until after the interview with Alessandro Ricardo."

He frowned at her and suddenly she wondered if any help he could give her would be worthwhile.

"It sounds like you know a few people at the resort," she said slowly. "Tell me what you know about Ricardo."

"He's a very private person. Look, Jess. I'll be honest. When you get there, you really should just have a break and forget the idea. He doesn't do interviews. Just forget about it and have a holiday."

"You say you don't know him, so how do you know that? Maybe the right person hasn't come along yet."

There was no way she was going to give up after all she'd done to get this far.

She was going to get that interview, and if Alex couldn't help her, she'd find someone else who could.

Without answering her, Alex stood and brushed the crumbs from his shirt. Bowser sniffed around the blanket and licked them up.

"Come on. We'd better hit the road." He held his hand out to Jess and she let him pull her up. Bowser wound between her legs and she lost her balance. Alex caught her and she came up hard against his chest. Laughing self-consciously to cover the heat surging through her, she pushed him away.

"Sorry, I seem to be making a habit of falling into your arms. Don't get the wrong idea."

Alex folded up the blanket and passed it to her before lifting the cooler onto his shoulder.

"Partner back in New York?"

"Nah. No way. Career woman to the core. Had one close call, but I found out just in time he was only after—"

"After?" Alex looked at her curiously.

"After an introduction to the boss," she said. "Um, he was after a job."

"Sounds like a low life. Using a woman to get what he wanted."

They were both quiet as they walked back to the truck. Alex seemed to be lost in his thoughts as much as she was lost in hers.

Five minutes later they were back on the red dirt road and heading west. The sun was blindingly bright through the insect-smeared windscreen. Jess reached down to her bag for her sunglasses.

"Could you pass me mine please?" Alex asked. "They're in—"

"The glove compartment..." Jess finished off for him. "The never-ending glove compartment."

Jess relaxed and leaned back into the seat. "Well, I'm going to start planning my strategy for pinning down the elusive Mr Ricardo. Oh no!"

She sat bolt upright in the seat before dropping her face in her hands and groaning. "Oh shit."

Alex hit the brakes and slowed the car looking across at her and his brow wrinkled. "What's wrong?"

"I meant to call Cockatoo Springs when I got to Daly River to make my reservation, but the rain and having to stay there for the night totally put it out of my head."

Alex started the truck again and pulled out onto the road. "No problem. You can stay at my cabin."

Why did he find that so amusing? She ignored the sexy smile on his face which made the laugh lines fan deep around his eyes.

"I can show you around."

Before Jess could answer there was a loud crack from behind them and the car slewed to the right. Alex hit the brakes and stuck his head out the window looking behind.

***

"Bloody hell." Frustration and anger warred in Alex's chest as he slammed his hands on the steering wheel. He took a deep breath and turned to Jess. "Sorry."

"What's wrong? Did we hit something?"

"There's something wrong with the boat trailer. The boat's hanging off it." He opened his door and walked back to the trailer. The two wheels were sitting at an angle, and the under frame of the boat trailer was sitting in the red dirt of the road.

"Shit." He kicked the tyre and walked around to Jess's window. "The axel of the trailer has snapped."

"How come?"

"All the corrugations on the road," he said. He should have taken it slower, but he'd been too interested in her conversation and hadn't paid enough attention to his driving. That could be deadly in the Top End. He was lucky it was only the trailer that had been damaged.

"What does that mean?"

"It means I'll have to leave the boat here."

"Won't someone steal it?" Jess pushed her door open and climbed down.

"Not in the condition it's in now. Come give me a hand and we'll be quicker."

Bowser jumped out of the truck and ran to the side of the road while Jess followed Alex around to the back of the truck. He pointed to the axel.

"We'll have to unload the boat and put as much of the gear in the back of the truck as we can. Especially the food and the crabs. Sorry, the crabs are going to have to go in the front with us. There's not enough air circulating in here, and if I unzip the windows your bed will be full of red dust for the night."

"In the cabin with the two by eighty air con?" Jess grinned up at him and his heart lurched. Last night in Janet's restaurant he'd thought how beautiful she was, but now, her clear almond-shaped eyes held his and his heart lurched.

No way, not going there.

He turned away from her and spoke gruffly. "I've just got to take the motor off the boat, and then I'll get you to help me pull the trailer off the road." Alex wiped his hands on his jeans before he lifted the side of the boat trailer.

"Will you have to come back and get it?"

"If I don't, it'll get swept away in the wet."

Her eyes were wide. "Do you mean this road will go under water?"

"Yes. For most of the summer."

Alex was looking forward to the camp ahead. It was going to be an interesting night. "You grab Bowser and get back in the truck, I'll zip this up. And then we'll get on the way. I don't want to get to our campsite too late." Huge thunderheads were spiralling up ahead, and he didn't like the look of the sky at all.

***

The first cloud covered the sun as they turned into the road to the camp. There were a couple of places they could have camped out, but Alex had chosen this one because it was on the highest ground. If there was a storm, they'd be dry up here.

He frowned as he slowed the truck. Jess was determined to go on with the interview and he'd seen her persistence over the past twenty-four hours. If she was that persistent at Cockatoo Springs, she'd figure how who he was in no time at all. He guarded his privacy fiercely and he was going to have to handle this very carefully. As soon as he got a chance, he was going to call Mitch and make sure there was no room for her at the resort when they arrived. She could stay in the spare room in the small cabin at the back of the resort where he stayed when he was hauling fish. That way he could keep her close and keep tabs on what she was doing. He wouldn't go anywhere near his beachfront villa this time—not until she was on her way back home.

Alex pulled the car to the side of the road, and looked across at Jess and Bowser. She was dozing with her head back on the seat, and her feet on top of the cooler holding the crabs. Bowser was curled up on her once-white pants, and Jess had the fingers of one hand tucked loosely into his collar, holding him secure. Her pants were streaked with red dirt and her silk top was dotted with water spots where perspiration had soaked in. Her hair was still tied back with the piece of string, but had loosened, and her topknot was hanging to one side. Her right hand was braced on the seat between them. He looked down and grinned.

Two long manicured red nails, and two snapped off with chipped nail polish, completed the picture of a dishevelled traveller. If she turned up at the reception desk of his five-star resort looking like that, eyebrows would be raised.

"Jess, wake up." He touched her hand lightly. She opened her eyes and stretched, and his mouth dried as the silk top pulled across her breasts. She was almost as tall as he was, and even though she was very slim, her breasts were full. The damp silk top strained across them tightly, and she crossed her arms across her chest and glared at him.

"I have to get out and turn the wheel hubs before I can put the truck into four-wheel drive. There's just a short distance to go to where we'll camp out tonight."

Jess unfolded her arms and looked out the window. "Rain's coming?"

"Not yet." He pointed up the hill. "There's a spring-fed freshwater pool where we can wash. It's away from the main river, and there are no crocodiles there.

"I'd kill for a wash now, and before we leave in the morning so I don't turn up looking like a hobo. I was thinking too… could I use your satellite phone to make a reservation? How long will you stay there?" Jess looked at him and Alex focused on manoeuvring the truck over the deep corrugation.

The driver's side dipped to the right, and Bowser rolled along the seat and landed in his lap. Jess gasped as the car tilted back the other way at the opposite angle, and she grabbed for Bowser as he rolled back toward her. It was likely he'd be at Cockatoo Springs for a couple of weeks. He had to make time to meet with Clay, the new chef, and to work out the program for the wet season. He also had a CEO from one of the big travel companies flying in for a two-day visit. He'd been difficult and insisted on dealing with Alessandro himself, and Mitch had talked Alex into the meeting with Larry Bartholomew before he left. Then the whole family was arriving in a few days for his birthday. Last year, they'd managed to keep his fake identity secret, and although they couldn't understand his motivation, he'd never confided Emily's deception to anyone else. He had this stupid idea it was gallant to keep her memory untarnished. If he'd known how hard it would be to run the place privately once the school had taken off, he would never have even taken the job on in the first place.

The next challenge was to keep it quiet for one more visit and then once his contract was done, Ricardo could disappear quietly.

"Ah… I'll stay a week or so and then I'll head to Darwin for the wet season.
You can still fish up there away from the rivers." He had to get Jess sorted and on her way home well before his family descended. And somehow, he had to convince her that an interview with Ricardo was out of the question. Then he had to get rid of this bloody fascination she was weaving over him.

It was safe here. No crocodiles. It was time to put another plan in place and turn back into the fishing hobo who pushed her buttons. He'd been way too accommodating and he wasn't happy with this connection that seemed to be springing up between them.

***

Jess gripped Bowser with one hand and held onto the bar on the dashboard with the other. The slope Alex was driving down was so steep; she was worried the pickup would tip over its front. Her legs were jammed between the large dark blue cooler on the floor on the passenger side, and the constant clicking coming from inside the cooler was unnerving.

"What *is* that noise?" She turned to Alex who was peering over the front of the dashboard at the drop below as he turned the wheel inch by inch.

"What noise?"

"That clicking noise."

"Oh, that's the crabs. As soon as we stop, I need to get them sorted. I didn't

394

have time to tie them up, and some had already thrown their nippers. They'll be our dinner tonight."

"Oh, okay." Jess turned away as an idea formed in her mind. "Alex?"

"Yes?" His voice was patient, but he didn't take his eyes off the terrain ahead as he reached down and changed down a gear. A loud grinding sound came from beneath the gear shift.

"Shit, that doesn't sound good." The speed of the truck picked up and he planted his boot on the brake pedal."

"What's wrong?" she asked.

"Sounds like we just did a gear." He cocked his head to the side and listened as he changed gears again. "Maybe not. I'll check when we stop." He gingerly lifted his foot off the brake pedal and changed down another gear, and the car still slowed. "Don't worry, it's okay. We're almost down to the clearing."

Jess turned and looked out the window. The road was narrow and the branches of the low shrubs were scraping against the glass.

"Oh, my God." She gulped, closing her eyes as a huge brown snake slid back into the bush beside the pickup.

"What did you say?"

"Nothing." Jess turned and scowled at him. "I cannot wait to get to the resort." She held out her hand and ticked off on her fingers. "I really don't know what's worse. Snakes? Flies? Crocodiles? Crabs? This old clunking pickup?" She put her head into her hands, and her temper fired as Alex looked down at Bowser and spoke in a conversational tone.

"At least you're off the list now, little man."

His tone got under her skin. "Please tell me this resort is really five stars and not one of those wilderness lodges where the guests are expected to rough it and enjoy themselves."

The smarter her mouth got, the more he smiled.

"No, everything Madame could possibly require is catered for at Cockatoo Springs." He pointed to her broken fingernails. "I believe there is a day spa where they do hair and nails…and massage. The rooms are luxurious, and of course the food in the restaurant is world class. But I forgot that's all you are interested in, isn't it?" He narrowed his eyes. "What will you do if you can't get a room? Will you catch the helicopter straight out, or will you stay at my cabin?"

Jess paused before she answered, sensing there was more to his question than just interest in her movements. "Of course I'm not going to leave. If can't get a room, I'll be very grateful for your offer, thank you. But I'm sure there'll be a room."

"I'll call my mate as soon as we're unpacked. Anyway, look." He pointed ahead. "We're finally here."

Chapter Eight

"Oh, my God. This is paradise." Jess opened the door, and the little dog jumped up beside her. "What about Bowser, does he need his leash?"

God, I can't believe I'm worried about a dog.

The heat in the Top End was turning her brains to mush, as well as her usually impeccable grooming. There was no word for how she looked…and felt. She reached up and pulled the string from her hair, shaking it all out, and regretted it immediately. Even though the sun was low in the sky, the heat was still unbearable.

"He's okay. There are no crocs here. I'll keep an eye on him. He won't wander far from me or the truck."

Jess slid out of the truck and stepped to the edge of the low bluff, looking nervously at the ground.

"Don't worry, as soon as the truck came in, any snakes would have taken off. If you leave them alone and don't provoke them, they'll leave you alone."

Jess forgot all about snakes as she looked over the edge of the drop. Water cascaded down the face of the rock in front of her to a deep green pool fringed with trees. The storm clouds had receded, and the late afternoon shade covered the western end of the pool. The water beneath the rock face below them sparkled invitingly as the cascading water hit the surface of the pool. Alex walked over and stood behind her.

"I love the Top End. There are hundreds more places like this, all off the tourist track and pristine."

"It sounds like the environmentalist is still in there."

"Nah, just someone who appreciates nature at its best. Now come on, let's get organised and then we can have a dip."

"Don't forget to use the phone and call about my booking."

"Right. I'll go and do that now."

Alex went around to the back of the truck and Jess waited at the edge of the bluff enjoying the view. All was quiet and when he reappeared, he held up the phone with a grim expression.

"Sorry, the battery's flat. I'll have to charge it up."

"How can you do that? I suppose there's a hidden power outlet in the glove compartment along with everything else." She tried to be flippant to cover the disappointment of not being able to contact the resort, and find out if her room had been held for her.

"Almost," Alex said. "There's an inverter in the back of the track."

Jess had no idea what he was talking about so she ignored him and looked out over the water. Perspiration trickled down her neck as they unpacked the truck, and she looked down ruefully at her ruined silk shirt. Alex carted the cooler from the cab of the truck and placed it in the shade beneath an overhanging rock. The heat was vicious, even hotter than last night. She'd thought the air conditioning in her room at the Daly River caravan park had malfunctioned because it had been so hot in there.

Maybe it was this hot in the outback all the time?

"Does it get any cooler through the night?" She swatted a fly away as Alex walked back to the truck for the next load.

"Not a lot." He frowned at her. "Jess, go and get the Bushman's out of the glove compartment. Not only are those black files annoying, but the midges will bite you. And the mosquitoes carry disease up here."

Jess shivered at the thought of something sucking her blood. She hurried over to the truck and pulled herself up on the passenger side. Alex had parked it awkwardly between two boulders, and backed it in as close as he could to the large cliff face behind it, leaving just enough room to get into the canvas tent on the back of the truck. The driver's side was lower, and she slid in through the narrow space between the door and the rock. She reached across to the seat before opening the glove compartment and poking around.

Of course. The first thing to fall into her hand was the box of condoms.

Well, he won't be needing them this trip. She shoved them to the back of the compartment and peered in. A small light green plastic bottle proclaiming Bushman's in red writing was jammed at the back of the space. She pulled it out and read the label:
Guaranteed fifteen hours of protection. That should just about see her out of this place and back into a civilised environment. Although, if she was honest, it was one of the most beautiful places she'd ever seen. She couldn't wait to get into that pool down on the rock platform.

After closing the compartment, Jess climbed out of the door and looked carefully down to the ground before walking around to the back of the truck. She'd find her swimsuit first, and then lather herself in this lotion.

Straining to reach the zipper to undo the back door, she cursed as she snapped another fingernail.

"Can't reach?" The amused voice came from behind her. "Step back. I'll climb in and pass some of the stuff out to you. I'll throw down the heavy stuff."

Alex reached up, unzipped the heavy metal zipper, and hoisted himself into the back of the truck. Jess peered in and got an eyeful of taut butt in snug fitting denim jeans. Heat ran up her neck and added to her already overheated state. She fanned herself, but it only moved the heavy hot air a little and didn't cool her at all. She blinked to remove the perspiration from her eyes; the back of the truck and Alex's butt blurred. Closing her eyes, she hoped desperately that a room would be ready and waiting for her tomorrow. A nice cool bath, clean clothes, and food were what she desperately needed. She'd had nothing to eat all day apart from the muffin when they'd headed off at dawn. No wonder she was hot and weak. She'd had no idea that driving on these treacherous outback roads would be so slow.

"Whoa, Jess. Are you okay? You're as white as a sheet." She opened her eyes. Alex turned around and was leaning out of the back of the truck, looking at her with concern.

"Just need something to eat. I'm okay."

He reached into the cooler, and passed her a bottle of water and a trail mix bar before he pointed to a small boulder beside the pickup.

"You sit there while I unpack."

Gratefully, she took the water and the snack, holding the cool bottle to her cheek. She wandered over to the rock and plonked herself down. Too late, she remembered she didn't even look for snakes...or scorpions...or crocodiles. Sipping on the water, she watched Alex unload the back of the truck. He pulled everything to the back of the canopy, and again she appreciated the view as he climbed backwards out of the pickup. He reached up and lifted her suitcase, and the muscles in his arm flexed as he lowered the bag to the ground beside the truck

"What have you got in the there? Rocks?"

"Ha ha, very funny. Just clothes. I have to look the part when I do the interview."

Alex turned to her and his gaze travelled up her dirty clothes and to her overheated face and tangled hair. "Ah, yes, mustn't forget the interview."

When everything was unpacked and on the ground beside the truck, he climbed down and made two trips across to the shaded area beneath an overhanging rock.

Jess finished the water, unwrapped the trail mix, and wandered over to where Alex was setting up their camp. "Can I help?" She looked curiously at a long canvas bag next to the cooler. "What's that?"

"That's my swag."

"Your what?"

"It's a combination of a bed, a tent, and a sleeping bag. All rolled up into one compact little bag. Haven't you ever been camping?"

Jess grinned at him and shook her head as she munched on the trail mix. "No… I didn't even go to summer camps when I was a kid. My father—"

He looked at her waiting for her to finish.

"Nothing," she said not wanting to talk about her father. It was too nice an afternoon to start thinking about him, and the way he'd treated her when she was growing up. Alex looked at her curiously as he gathered a pile of sticks and brush together. Jess wandered over and sat next to the circle of rocks he'd set up around the makeshift fireplace.

"My father thought camping was a bit ordinary. He preferred to give me what he called enriched experiences. So we went to art galleries, museums, and spent a lot of time in places where he could be seen." She sighed and wiped her forehead with the back of her arm.

"I know a lot about art, and old bones, but nothing about the outdoors." She laughed. "I also didn't know a lot about the Outback. I don't know if I would have come if I'd known what it was going to be like."

Alex stood beside her, his arms full of bits of wood. "Even for the chance of getting the scoop interview for your magazine?"

"Even for the interview." She shook her head and looked down at her clothes. "Look at me. I was totally unprepared for this."

"Well." He dropped the wood to the ground and squatted next to her. "As a fair dinkum Aussie, I'd better give you a better impression of the outback. What do you say about a swim?"

Despite the petulant expression on her grimy face, Alex was surprised by his need to keep looking at her. There was some sort of chemistry in action, and she fascinated him. He'd obviously been away from women too long, and he'd have to get out his little black book out when he got back to Darwin. He'd been missing out on that part of male-female relationships lately.

That's all it was. Nothing to do with finding her so bloody attractive.

"What are you thinking about?" she asked. "You've got a funny look on your face."

Caught out fantasizing about taking her to bed, or rather to his swag, Alex cleared his throat. He stood and held his hand out to her. She grabbed it and he pulled her up, ignoring the warmth of her hand in his. "Come on, we'll go for a swim and then I need to cook you a decent meal."

Alex looked down at her hand. Her fingers somehow had got entwined through his. Slowly he lifted his gaze up to her face. She'd pulled her hair back and retied it with the string and left her face unframed. Her clear green eyes were fixed on their joined hands and the blood rushed straight to his groin.

"Ready to swim?" he asked softly, ignoring the pulsing in his jeans.

Surprise flickered in her face when she glanced up at him. She didn't have to look up far; she was only a few of inches below his six three even in her flat sandals.

All rational thought had fled, and her lips beckoned his as she held his gaze steadily, her clear green eyes assessing him, and filled with the knowledge that she knew exactly what he was thinking.

Her lips parted a little and he dropped his head, capturing them beneath his. Her hands wound around his neck and he pulled her closer to him. Her mouth opened and he groaned, unable to help himself anymore, losing himself in the sweet depths. He lifted his hand and held her face gently while he deepened the kiss. Jess caught her breath on a soft gasp as his teeth scraped hers, and his tongue began a slow seductive dance with hers. His mind was just beginning to haze like the heat shimmering over the far horizon when she drew back and looked up at him

"And what was that all about it?" she asked.

"I needed to."

She reached down and held his hand up to her face, taking time to examine it, and he sensed she was avoiding his gaze. He tilted her chin up with the fingers that were resting against the side of her face.

"Was I out of line?" he asked, willing her to look up at him. When she held his gaze, lazy desire swirled in his chest. Although she didn't meet his gaze, he could see the smile playing about her lips.

"No, I'm a big girl now." Finally, she lifted her head and met his eyes, and the jolt that hit his chest almost took his breath away.

"I can take care of myself. But I don't know that I was quite expecting this."

Her face told him a different story. A soft flush sat on her high cheekbones and her lips were slightly open when she looked back at him, tempting him, but he dropped her hand. He turned away, trying to push away the need to take her in his arms and continue where they'd left off.

Too complicated. He didn't need any complications in his life.

Chapter Nine

Jess scrabbled around in her suitcase willing her heart to stop beating so fast.

It was the heat. She was dehydrated. She had a lot to worry about. It was her job.

It had nothing to do with this rough and hard fisherman, who had just taken her to heaven for a brief moment with his mouth. She glanced at him as he moved the coolers further into the shade of the overhanging rock. He was tough, and strong, and his face was rugged and unshaven, but his mouth had been soft and inviting, and he had taken her by surprise. Now all she could think about was getting up closer to him and trying it again.

No way. One night, and she'd be back in civilisation and doing the job she came here to do. She was *not* going to get side tracked. Imagine the text she could send Monica.

In the bush. Smelly fisherman. Great sex.

Because she knew it would be great sex. He had that lean whipcord, masculine body. His hands were strong and his hair was begging to be gripped while he—

"Jess?"

She jumped and smiled, drawn out of her fantasy. Pulling her swimsuit from her suitcase, she shoved everything back in, ignoring the red dust that was everywhere. She shook the dust from her swimsuit and looked around at him.

"Where can I change?"

He grinned back at her and then slowly turned around, putting his back to her. Jess let her gaze wander over his broad shoulders and the snug-fitting faded jeans encasing his butt.

"Right where you're standing." He stood waiting, and she figured he would be a gentleman. She undressed quickly, pulling on the sleek black swimsuit with the plunging neckline. Shivers ran down her back and turned into heat when they reached between her thighs and stopped.

"Okay, you can turn around now," she said.

Jess grinned as Bowser barked and ran over to her. She reached down to pat him, and knew she looked good. This swimsuit had cost her a fortune and it moulded her curves in all the right places, or so the saleswoman in the exclusive boutique had said.

"Thank you, Bowser. I'll take that as a compliment."

She glanced across at Alex. A pulse flicked in his cheek and he stood still for a moment while his gaze swept from her face to her feet. He took a step toward her, and her breath hitched, but he all he did was take her hand and lead her over to the edge of the bluff.

"Come on, you're in for a treat." His voice was rough.

Keeping hold of her hand, Alex helped her down the rocky slope, and Jess tried to ignore the warmth taking over her whole body.

It's only the heat. The hot air, nothing else.

Her sandals slipped on the loose rocks and she stumbled. Alex slid his arm around her back to hold her steady, and she fought the heat that began beneath his fingers, rippled down her stomach, and lower.

She needed to cool off in the water. As soon as possible.

When they got to the bottom of the hill, Jess stood silently and drank in the vista in front of her. From above she hadn't been able to appreciate the waterfall cascading down the rock just beneath where the truck was parked. From sixty feet above, water fell in a white froth over a series of stepped rocks down to the clear, deep pool edged by pure white sand. A tall tree with lacy foliage overhung the water at the far end, its lazy movement reflected in the still green depths. The gorge walls rose high, and she had to crane her head back to see the bright blue sky.

It was cooler down here next to the water. A slight breeze puffed and ruffled the surface of the pool. Jess turned to Alex who was staring across the water.

"This is magical," she said." I had no idea it could be so beautiful just a few hundred yards away from that dusty road." She leaned over the edge of the pool and peered into the water. "But are you sure there's no crocodiles?"

Alex laughed and dropped his head, reaching for the bottom of his T-shirt.

"No. No crocodiles. I can prove it. I can walk you back and show you that it feeds from a spring a few hundred metres back in the bush. There's not even any freshies up here."

Jess walked over and sat on the side of the pool and removed her sandals. "Okay, I'll take your word for it." She leaned over and trailed her fingers in the water and looked up with surprise. "Wow, it's hot!"

"Maybe not hot, but certainly warm." Alex squatted down beside her and pointed to the far end of the pool. Jess swallowed dryly as the muscles flexed in his arm.

And pecs, and a six-pack to die for.

"It's deep enough to dive down that end. It starts shallow here at the falls and the hot rock warms the water even though it comes from underground, and then it drops off pretty quickly. It'll be much cooler down that end."

"I should have brought my soap and shampoo down. I didn't think."

She caught Alex smiling at her.

"Go on, say how forgetful I am. I can see it on your face." Jess laughed as he shook his head.

"Never." He raised his hands in denial, and her gaze was drawn to the top of his unclipped jeans. A line of dark hair disappeared southward and her mouth was suddenly dry, again.

"I'll go up and get it. Where is it?"

"In the pink bag next to my suitcase. Just bring the bag down, thanks. It'll be luxury to have a wash in this warm water."

She turned and watched him climb back up the path. His jeans had slipped down a little, and a pair of black Calvin Klein briefs peeked over the top. The afternoon sun shone on the deeply tanned skin of his bare back.

Jess folded her arms across her breasts as she watched the taut muscles in his lean legs flex as he reached the top of the slope. When she'd climbed into his truck this morning, an interlude like this had been far from her thoughts. She'd fully expected to be checked and settled in her room at Cockatoo Springs by the end of the day.

If I have a room.

By the time he scrambled back down the path and placed her toiletries bag next to her, she had her desire under control. *Almost.* If he touched her, she was sure she'd ignite. To her relief, as soon as he'd dropped the bag beside her, Alex walked around to the far end of the pool and dropped his jeans. Jess busied herself in her bag, pulling out body wash and shampoo, and didn't look up again until she heard a splash at the far end. For a moment, there was no sign of him and then he surfaced and swam to the waterfall. Standing under the cascading water, he shook his head and tilted his head back beneath the streaming water. His hair was sleek and black, and plastered to his skull. She stared at his eyelashes, stuck together in spiky clumps around his deep blue eyes.

"Coming in? The water's beautiful."

Jess knew what would happen if she got in the water with him. It wasn't only the thought of the cool water lapping her skin that beckoned her. She swung her legs over the edge of the rock and slid in, sighing as the warm water caressed her skin. Bubbles ran up her legs as the water moved against her, and she pushed herself out to the middle to the deeper water and dived under. Opening her eyes beneath the water, she was amazed at how clear it was. She looked up and the blue sky rippled through the surface of the water above her. She surfaced and turned to face Alex as his strong hands grasped her waist.

He moved quickly, and in an instant his mouth was hot, hungry, and hard against hers. His hands held her tightly, pulling her closer, and she couldn't stop herself. She wound her legs around his hips and he groaned into her mouth. This kind of raw, primeval need was new to her. Sex was usually civilised and polite, and in a bed, after the required social preliminaries, but she responded in a way that was foreign to her. The low guttural moan that escaped her lips echoed the desire that coursed through her.

For the first time in her life, she surrendered without thought. He kissed her and she whimpered against his mouth and clutched at his shoulders.

"Okay?" He smiled down at her.

Jess nodded while she kept her gaze fixed on those dark blue eyes and wound her arms around his neck.

"It's a long walk to the glove compartment," he said roughly

"You should have thought of that box when you were getting my bag," she said playfully.

Alex dropped his forehead on hers and closed his eyes. "That would have been making a big assumption. I didn't intend for this to happen, you know."

"Neither did I." Jess pulled her head back and looked at him. "So, what are we going to do now?"

"If you keep looking at me like that, I won't think straight," he said. "How about I go back to the truck and it'll give you time to think if you really want to take up where we left—"

Jess ran her hands down the smooth tanned skin of his back as her lips cling to his. "Is that answer enough?"

"God, Jess."

She smiled and removed her arms from around him. "Okay, you go back up to the Boy Scout compartment…and I'll be waiting."

Alex dove under the water and swam across to the waterfall before he pulled himself up onto one of the rock steps beneath the cascading water. Even though her blood was zinging around her body with anticipation, she'd hadn't felt this relaxed or had as much fun since…since she couldn't remember when.

Closing her eyes, she tipped her head back and floated in the warm water, waiting for Alex to come back down the hill. The soft breeze picked up, cooling her damp cheeks and rustled the leaves of the branches overhanging the pool. The breeze dropped, but the rustling continued, and a soft grunt came from behind her. Jess opened her eyes and rolled over in the water as a frisson of fear rippled down her spine, replacing the anticipation of a moment ago. She stood, and turned slowly as the grunting got louder.

A huge black…thing…with slits for eyes and long yellowed tusks sticking from its bottom jaw stood at the edge of the pool, its dark beady eyes fixed on her. Black bristles poked through the red mud coating its massive shoulders. She watched as it strutted closer to the edge and scratched at the ground with its front feet. She gasped and moved slowly toward the other side of the pool, as far away from the massive thing as she could, while it snorted and folded its front legs under its huge bulk and dropped its snout into the water.

"Alex!" She screamed at the top of her voice and the pig lifted its head and stared at her. From the bush behind the huge boar, came a small sow and half a dozen piglets. The sow stood guard rigidly while the piglets joined their father at the edge of the shallow water.

Without removing her gaze from the creature, she reached down under the water with shaking hands, and pulled up her swimsuit as she backed into the deeper water.

Oh God. Can pigs swim?

Chapter Ten

Alex slid across the seat of the truck, the small box safely in his hand. Bowser was curled up on the floor of the pickup and opened one lazy eye before tucking his nose back under his paw.

Alex's blood ran cold when Jess screamed for him. He slammed the door of the pickup shut, and the box of condoms back through the open window. He took off at a fast run toward the rocky path until he reached the edge of the drop, looking over to see what had spooked her.

Shit.

A fat sow and seven piglets stood beside one of the biggest feral pigs he had ever seen.

"Stay in the water, Jess! Don't move. As long as you stay in the water it can't hurt you."

"Can it swim?" Her voice was shaking and she didn't take her eyes off the boar. It was huge.

Shit, just her luck to get bailed up by one. He scrambled down the rocky slope, small rocks skittering to the bottom beneath his bare feet. The boar turned and sniffed the ground. Picking up a fist-sized piece of rock, he flung it at the boar, but missed. Now at the bottom of the slope, the pig stiffened and turned toward him, snorted and dropped its head, charging for him.

Bloody hell.

Jess's scream followed him as he ran for the nearest tree. He grabbed the lowest branch and swung himself up. The tree shook as five hundred pounds of solid razorback crashed into the trunk two metres below. Just to be extra sure, Alex pulled himself up another branch before turning to the pool and checking on Jess.

She disappeared and he scanned around the pool, worried for a moment she'd climbed out the other side and was heading back up to the truck. Jess would have no idea how fast these suckers could move and how deadly they were. He let out a sigh of relief when the water rippled and Jess surfaced slowly over near the waterfall.

"Good girl, just stay over there. It can't hurt you."

"So what the hell do we do now? You're up a tree and I'm down here in the water." Her eyes were huge as she stared at the pig. "What happens next?"

"We'll have to wait it out."

"Are you serious?" Jess stood and folded her arms and flicked a glance up to him, only taking her eyes from the pig for a split second.

"Unless you want to climb out of the water and chase it away."

"No chance, buddy. You're the outback hero. That's your job."

Alex folded his arms and leaned back against the rough bark, and looked down as another snort floated up to him. But it hadn't come from the pig. Jess grinned up at him and when he looked at her she giggled again.

"Oh my God." The water splashed as she slapped her hands on top of it. "I so wish I had my camera. I could write the best article about the Aussie outback and its heroes…in their underwear."

Alex looked down at his black Calvin Kleins. "You won't find it so funny if the boar decides to settle his family in here for the night."

"Really?"

That quickly wiped the smile from her face. Alex slid down the trunk and settled in for a wait. He looked up and groaned as an avalanche of small rocks tumbled over the edge of the rock face, splashing into the water. Bowser was standing on top of the bluff, and if a dog could look happy, he would have beamed in anticipation of the fun to come. He took off into the bush, his ears flattened back and his neck muscles bunched.

"Oh, no. Make him stay up there. Send him back." Jess looked at Alex with wide eyes.

"No chance. He was bred for this—he'll be okay." Alex pulled himself up to watch the action below, hoping he was right. A little brindle bullet shot out of the bush, and before the pig could turn, Bowser had latched onto its ear. With a loud squeal, the pig shook its head, but the dog had a firm grip as his back legs stretched up.

"Look, Jess." Alex pointed to the sow and the piglets as they ran off into the bush. "Dad won't be far behind."

Bowser let go of the pig's ear and ran around in circles, yapping loudly. The pig pawed the ground half-heartedly before letting out one final snort and trotting off behind the others. Alex called Bowser over and he sat patiently beneath the tree waiting for him to come down.

"Some live outback action for you?" Alex jumped down and sauntered across to the pool. "Had enough entertainment for the afternoon?"

Jess rolled her eyes at him, before diving under the water and swimming over to the edge. Alex put his hand down and she glanced back over her shoulder before she reached up and took it.

"Are you sure they've gone?"

"Yep, they won't come back now they know our little pig hunter is here." He reached down and scratched Bowser's head.

"Great job, buddy."

Jess climbed out of the pool and let go of his hand. She reached up and squeezed the water out of her hair before walking over to collect her bag.

"What else have you got lined up for tonight?"

##

Even though she was showing a brave face and coming out with the sassy comments, Jess was unsettled. Her legs were shaking as she followed Alex and Browser up the hill, keeping an eye out behind her for the return of the pigs. He didn't put his hand out to help her, and she didn't look for it. If she was totally honest, it wasn't the pigs that had unsettled her. The interlude in the pool with Alex had touched her deeply. A level of need she had never before experienced had tugged deep within her and she was grateful to the wild pigs for bringing it to a halt. She wasn't ready for that, and she didn't want it in her life.

They reached the top of the hill, and Bowser scampered to the shade beneath the truck. Alex strode over and reached in, pulling his jeans from the truck and casually stepping into them before he turned to Jess. Her skin was already dry from the hot tropical sun, even though it was late afternoon, and her hair was drying in a huge tangle. Alex opened the back of the pickup and gestured inside.

"Do you want to climb in here? You can get dressed and sorted while I cook the crabs."

He seemed to sense she needed some privacy and time to herself, and she smiled at him gratefully.

"Thanks, I will. But how are you going to cook them? They're still alive."

"I'll drop them into the pot when the water boils."

"Ew, and you call yourself an environmentalist? That is so cruel."

"Yes, little Ms. Food Journalist, that's how you cook them." Alex shook his head and ran his hand down the side of her face. "Alive."

A jolt of heat ran from his fingers to his skin, and he held her gaze for a moment before he turned away and walked over to the other side of the low-burning fire to collect her suitcase. Jess unzipped the flap of the little camp house on the back of the pickup and put her cosmetics bag on the foam mattress.

"Make sure you put some of that Bushman's on and zip up the flap of the canopy. As soon as the sun sets, the mozzies will be bloody crook," he said.

She watched him tip the lotion into his hand and rub it onto his face, neck, and chest before passing the bottle to her. No matter how hard she tried, she couldn't stop her eyes following his hand as he rubbed brisk circles on his flat stomach. He was a good-looking man in prime condition, and her body reacted accordingly.

Get over it, Jess. If he chooses to walk around without a shirt, you can cope.

She clambered into the back of the pickup and wrinkled her nose. She closed up the flap. It was dim inside, and a combination of smells greeted her. The hot air was suffocating, and when she sat up straight to take a deep breath, her stomach protested, and she gagged. She pushed herself to her knees and opened her suitcase to find something clean and cool to wear. Several items of clothing were considered and discarded before she found a long silk skirt, which would protect her legs from the insects, and a spaghetti strap top with a light silk shawl to wrap around her shoulders. Dressing quickly in the small space, she ran her fingers through her curls and wound them up into a matching scarf to keep her hair away from her neck.

The memory of Alex's hands and fingers when he'd caressed her in the water shimmied through her mind, and she closed her eyes and swallowed.

One night.

One night sleeping in the back of the truck, and then some conversation tomorrow as they travelled. Then they would arrive at the resort and she'd get her room, say thank you, goodbye, and forget about him.

She could do it.

The unfamiliar feelings would be put aside and she would get on with the job and go home. She slipped on a pair of dangly earrings and a smudge of lipstick, followed by a light application of the famed Bushman's to prevent the mozzies…and the midges… and she was ready to go out and face the outback.

And Alex.

When she climbed out of the back of the pickup, the smell of garlic assailed her nostrils and she turned to the fireplace with a frown.

She must be so hungry she was imagining haute cuisine aromas.

There was no sign of Alex or Bowser, and Jess looked around nervously. The sun had set, and the lingering smoke from the grasslands fire drifted in on the light breeze. Wispy fingers of white smoke treaded thought the tops of the trees. All was quiet.

It was eerie, yet beautiful.

A flat rock next to the fire beckoned, and Jess retrieved the old blanket from the back of the truck and folded it, so it cushioned the hard rock. She sat and closed her eyes, listening to the quiet. The only sound was the occasional pop of the fire and a hiss as the water spat from the pot onto the coals. The faint sound of the waterfall sloshing in the distance added to the peace.

A few minutes later, slow footsteps and the snuffling of Bowser, announced their return.

"Sorry, Jess. I took him for a walk after I fed him, and he took off on me. Little bugger." Alex opened the door of the truck and lifted the dog into the cabin. "Are you ready to eat?"

"Yes, I'm hungry."

And not just for food.

"Wanna beer? It's all I have, sorry." Alex reached into the cooler. She held out her hand and he passed her a cold bottle before sitting across from her on the other side of the campfire. Placing the bottle against her cheek, she closed her eyes.

"What else are you cooking?"

Keep the conversation on food, you can do that without getting flustered.

"A sauce for the crab."

"And you just threw it together from what you have in the cooler? What's in it?"

"Secret ingredient. If I tell you, I'll have to kill you." Alex grinned at her and then his smile faded as he shook his head. "Oh, sorry, that was a crass thing to say. You've already had the razorback experience this afternoon. I didn't mean to be so flippant."

"You didn't scare me. Neither did the pig, really…once I knew I was safe in the water." Jess laughed and tipped her beer up appreciating the cool liquid in her dry mouth. "I enjoyed watching you climb up the tree in your—"

Whoa. Don't go there. She was trying to be nonchalant about the whole thing. If it hadn't been for the arrival of the pig, there would have been no holding either of them back. She couldn't figure him out. He said he'd been a lawyer and he was well spoken. And as much as he tried to push her buttons, she could tell that he was a good person and he'd looked out for her without hesitation when there'd been real danger Something about him being a wild fisherman in the outback just didn't make sense to her.

Alex didn't speak, but just looked at her over the fire. It was completely dark and there was no moon. The firelight flickered on his rugged face, highlighting the bluish black glints in his hair. He stood and Jess hitched a breath as heat ran through her. Alex walked over to pot and opened the cooler, placing the lid upside down on the ground. He put the cooked crabs on the lid and began to methodically shell them until a pile of steaming crabmeat filled the plate. He removed the smaller saucepan and set it next to Jess, before squatting in front of her.

"Now you are in for the treat of your life," he said softly.

Fascinated, she watched his fingers as he picked up a morsel of crab and dipped it into the sauce and held it in front of her lips.

His eyes held hers. "Hungry, Jess?"

***

A little nudge of shock ran through Alex as he held his fingers in front of Jess's mouth. Her mouth opened and the tip of her tongue ran over her lips. When he'd been walking in the scrub with Bowser, he'd been lost in his thoughts and hadn't noticed when the dog disappeared into the scrub. He was way too fascinated with this woman, and if it hadn't been for the pigs, he would have had sex with her in the pool this afternoon.

For the first time in two years, he'd lowered his defences and let his heart rule his head.

Jess was full of life, and despite being in an unfamiliar and hostile environment, she'd snapped back no matter what he'd thrown at her. Now it was time to put some distance between them Once they reached Cockatoo Springs, he had to make sure she didn't find out who he really was, and he also had to find some way to ease her disappointment at not getting the interview she'd come for.

Still, he couldn't understand it. She had the best of everything. Her clothes were top class, and she'd not given a second thought to leaving the hire car at Daly River. If she really needed a job that badly, she was throwing a lot of money around. Flying down under just on the chance of getting an interview.

She'd tried on the crazy story about being an actress last night, and maybe the food journalist story was a sham as well. Who knew what she was doing? Now he had to try to push away the heat that pulsed through him when she'd parted her soft, pink lips, ready to take the crab and the sauce off his fingers.

She leaned toward him and her lips touched his fingers, and he was lost. He was hungry for more than the crab. She'd lit a fire in him this afternoon and it roared back to life again as her lips circled his finger.

"Mmm." She pulled back and closed her eyes. "Garlic…and chili? What's that wonderful flavour? Crab?"

Alex turned away and reached for another plate. If she kept eating off his fingers, he wouldn't be responsible for his actions. He busied himself at the pot and tipped more sauce onto the crab before reaching into the cooler for the bread. Placing a large chunk on her plate, he passed it to her, and walked around to the other side of the fire.

"It is. Nothing beats the taste of fresh cooked crab."

Jess seemed to sense he was trying to put some distance between them and she lifted up her fork and ate quietly for a few minutes. Alex leaned back against the rock to get comfortable, grateful for the fire blocking her view. He definitely needed to go out in Darwin and get back into life. But to take care of his immediate and pressing need tonight, he was going to jump back into the cold end of the pool as soon as dinner had settled, and before he turned in for the night.

"Tell me about Cockatoo Springs." Jess put her plate down on the rock and lifted the bottle of beer to her lips. Loose curls fell from the scarf she'd tied around her hair, and she lifted her other hand to push it back. Alex shook his head as the firelight caught a huge ring on her middle finger.

How many women would put jewellery on around a campfire in the outback? They were poles apart. He had nothing to worry about. That feeling of wanting to get to get to know her a little better receded a little. *Just a little.* But the other need to keep her up close and personal still strained against his jeans.

"You must know something about the resort if you have a cabin nearby."

"Yeah, I wander around the kitchens a bit."

Jess leaned back and the shawl slipped off her shoulder. Her white skin glowed with an iridescent pearliness. It had been soft and silky beneath his lips and fingers in the pool this afternoon. He itched to reach out to her and pick up where they'd left off.

Alex stood up abruptly. If he didn't get away from her, he was going to lose control. "I have to check on the truck. I want to look at the gearbox. I didn't like that noise it made when we drove in."

He knew his voice was gruff.

"I'll see you in the morning. If there's anything you need through the night, just yell. Oh, and make sure you zip up the windows, because the mozzies will stay around all night."

If he was going to be hot and uncomfortable, she damned well could be too. He was getting more out of sorts by the minute. Why the hell did he ever offer to take her to Cockatoo Springs?

***

Blasted moody men.

They were all the same. As soon as things didn't go their way, they cracked it. One minute he was feeding her crab and gazing into her eyes like some love struck teenager, and the next minute he'd gone all rude and grumpy, and went crawling away to hide under his truck. Now she needed to find a bathroom, and the closest one was still fifty miles away at least.

418

I hate the outback…and camping. Give me five stars any day.

After she'd found a private spot behind the large boulders, Jess wandered over to the edge of the rock face overlooking the pool. Her feet made no sound on the sandy dirt, and she was sure Alex hadn't even noticed she was gone. The stars in the inky sky were brighter than anything she'd ever seen in the night sky, and they calmed her ill temper. She drew in a deep breath and sat on a flat rock gazing down at the water.

It was so beautiful out here. Despite the physical challenges, the vast space and the silence tugged at something deep inside her. The moon had risen while they'd sat around the fire, and now the moonlight was reflecting in the water. She really wouldn't mind spending more time in the outback and having a good look around.

She closed her eyes and imagined hiring Alex as her guide. She could find a decent vehicle—with air conditioning—and he could take her to all the beautiful places he'd talked about. If she didn't get the interview with Ricardo, the new job was toast anyway, and there was no point rushing home. The last thing she'd wanted to do was to touch her trust money, but what the hell? So what if her father thought she'd failed? She had no respect for him anyway, so she might as well make the most of it—he was loaded. She could still write her freelance articles if she didn't get the job at *Cuisine,* and travel the world.

She shook her head and pushed the thoughts away. That wasn't going to happen. She could daydream all she liked but she'd come here to get the interview and she was going to, and then the job would be hers. She was looking forward to getting to the resort and chasing him down. She'd survived the outback, how much harder was getting an appointment with the managing director.

Soft footsteps sounded behind her and her heart jumped in anticipation. She stared ahead waiting for Alex to speak to her…or touch her. Her skin prickled with anticipation and she closed her eyes. A wet nose pushed against her arm and she turned. Alex was nowhere to be seen. It was only Bowser who'd come to check on her. She lifted the little dog up into her lap and scratched at his head.

"Just you and me, then, hey little man?"

She had some thinking to do and she needed a good night's sleep before they headed off in the morning. Putting Bowser down onto the ground, Jess turned her back on the enticing pool and the moonlight, and headed for the most interesting accommodation she'd ever stayed in.

The fire was stoked high, and disappointment filled her when she saw the campsite was deserted. She climbed into the back of the truck, determined to get Alex out of her head.

##

Three hours later, she gave up trying to sleep. She'd heard Alex come back into camp a while back, and the zipper of his swag had sounded, and then all was quiet. As for her accommodation, she had never been so uncomfortable in her entire life. For the umpteenth time, she climbed back up to the high side of the small space and wedged the old, tatty pillow into the space near the back door. Alex had parked the truck on an angle and each time she'd dozed off, she'd rolled down to the other side of the truck, to finish hard up against the small outboard motor.

Perspiration trickled down between her shoulder blades and she sat up trying to find some movement of cooler air in the confined space. Her long skirt was tangled around her legs. She pulled it off impatiently and threw it on top of her suitcase. Her mouth was dry, and she was so very thirsty.

That's it. I've had enough.

Taking a deep breath, she quietly unzipped the canvas. She grabbed the blanket and pillow, and backed slowly out of the truck, sighing with relief as the cool air hit her bare legs. The fire had burned down to a pile of glowing embers. Alex's swag was zipped up and there was no sign of Bowser. Jess tiptoed around to the front of the truck, quietly opened the passenger side door, and slipped the pillow and blanket onto the front seat. She'd go and look at the water for a while until she cooled down, and then she'd try sleeping in there. It had to be better than the smelly canvas tent she was sharing with the outboard motor.

Her sandals were still in the back of the truck so she walked on her toes over to the edge of the bluff, using the bright moonlight to guide her steps on the sandy ground. Bowser gave a little short bark as she tiptoed past the swag, and Alex's quiet murmur sent a shiver down her back. Settling on the same rock as before, she pulled the light shawl around her shoulders and tipped her head back to let the breeze cool her face. She was wide awake now and the thought of trying to sleep in the front of the truck didn't appeal at all. A soon as they got to the resort, she could play catch up on her sleep...as well as hair treatments, showers, and manicures. Quiet footsteps sounded behind her and her skin tingled with anticipation.

Please.

"Are you okay?"

"Yes, just hot...and the accommodation is slightly smelly."

He cleared his throat and she looked up to a smile.

"I should have offered you the swag, but—"

"But what?"

"Nothing."

He turned away from her, ran his hand through his hair, and stared out across the water. His jeans were unbuttoned and hung low on his waist, his strong, bare shoulders outlined by the moonlight. He must have sensed her gaze and he turned slowly back to her. The blood pounded through Jess's veins and she waited, the electricity between them almost crackling in the air.

She jumped as a huge white flash lit up the sky. "Holy hell! What was that?"

"You're in for a treat. There's a dry storm brewing."

"How do you know it's a dry storm and it won't rain?" All she could think of was being stranded here for another night in that smelly space. She couldn't decide if that would be a good or a bad outcome.

"It will rain over on the coast. We'll just get to see the spectacular light show from up here."

Alex held his hand out to her and she looked up at him. "What?"

"Come on. We'll go down to the pool for a swim. It'll be cooler and the mozzies will stay away. We'll still get a good view of the storm from down there."

Jess took his hand and tucked the shawl around her shoulders, conscious of her bare legs. He led her down the rocky incline to the water. He gripped her hand without speaking, and tension hummed through her body. She let go of his hand when they reached the bottom of the waterfall and dropped her shawl to the ground. Slipping into the warm water, she floated on her back and watched the flashes in the sky that were becoming more frequent. A soft splash at the far end of the pool told her Alex was in the water with her. The water rippled around her and a sleek, black head broke the surface beside her. Alex turned to his back and floated next to her.

"Where's Bowser?" she asked.

"In the truck. I put him in there so he wouldn't chew my swag up."

Jess laughed.

"Yes, I've seen what he did to my bed."

They didn't speak for a few moments and floated together on top of the water watching the blue, pink, and dark green flashes filling the sky as the storm broke over on the coast.

"Amazing," Jess whispered. "Thank you so much for bringing me out here."

"To the pool?"

"No, out here." She lowered her feet to the sandy bottom and lifted her arm in a sweeping gesture. "Out here to all this. It is amazing. You've converted me to the outback, Alex."

"It is pretty special. I can't imagine being anywhere else."

"In fact, I've pretty much decided to stick around a while longer."

"What do you mean stick around?" Even in the moonlight, Jess could see his eyes narrow.

"After I get the interview, I've might extend my holiday. If there's room, I'll stay at Cockatoo Springs and take some of the tours."

She looked at him and an unfamiliar shyness filled her. "Ah…how would you feel about showing me around a bit more if I did stay for a bit longer?"

"Do you know how expensive it is out here?" Alex put his hands on her shoulders, and her heart took off as the blood zinged around her body. "I thought you needed to keep your job. That's why you had to get this interview."

She shot him a glance and his brow was wrinkled in a frown. "Look if it bothers you that much to spend any more time with me, I'll just do my own thing. Forget I ever mentioned it."

"It doesn't bother me." His fingers pressed into her shoulders. "Well, it does in one way."

"What way?"

Alex groaned and pulled her close, and heat rushed through her.

"This way." He grabbed her hair in his hands and tipped her head back, his mouth crushing hers. Jess lifted her legs and wrapped them around his waist, the slickness of his bare skin burning hers even in the cool water. She stroked his back, her fingers sliding over his wet skin, and his muscles bunched beneath her hands. He raised his head and looked at her, the moonlight shadowing his rugged face. Jess leaned forward and nibbled at his bottom lip, running her fingers through the long wet hair that clung to his neck

"Your place or mine?" she murmured against his mouth.

"Mine" he said with a quiet laugh. "I thing Bowser's in yours now."

***

Alex followed Jess up the hill, unable to keep his hands away from her. He bent and put his arms beneath her knees, sweeping her into his arms and strode the short distance to the swag. The heat between them pushed all thoughts of anything but the feel of her from his mind.

"Boy scout?" she whispered against his lips and sanity returned for

423

a brief moment. Alex stood her gently on the ground and reached down to unzip the swag.

"Get in there and wait for me, woman." His heart rate picked up even more as she ran a finger down his chest and reached up to kiss him.

"Don't be long." Even her voice was temptation.

Jess bent and climbed into the swag, and the sight of her long legs disappearing into the small tent was enough to make Alex pick up the pace as he strode across to his truck.

"Stay." Bowser turned his back and curled back up on the floor as Alex scrabbled on the floor until he found the small box he'd thrown through the window earlier. A moment later, he dropped down and crawled into the swag where Jess was waiting for him. Alex caught his breath—she was every bit as beautiful as he'd imagined.

Jess drew a breath as he kneeled beside her. He placed his hands on each side of her face and took her mouth in a slow gentle kiss, and then lay down beside her. She lifted her head, feathering kisses along his jaw.

"Alex?" Her voice was soft and wanting.

"What's the matter?"

"Not fair," she whispered against his lips.

"What's not fair?" He lifted his head and looked down at her.

"You've got the five star room."

"Okay, caught out," he said. "I admit it. I was trying to teach you a lesson."

"What sort of lesson?"

"A lesson about the danger of taking lifts with strangers in the outback." He laughed. "But it sort of backfired on me, didn't it?"

She shot a grin up at him. "I think it turned out pretty well…for both of us. I can only see one problem."

"What's that?" He dropped another kiss on her nose. "It's a long way to the en suite."

She held out her arms and he took up where he left off when she'd interrupted him.

Chapter Eleven

Jess squeezed the water from her hair and let it run down her neck. The temperature of the pool was cooler this morning because the sun hadn't reached its peak yet. Alex wanted to get an early start.

They'd had little sleep through the night, and he was keen to get on the road before it rained. The sky was dark and heavy, very different from the starry clear sky that had been above them when they went down for another swim in the middle of the night. They'd dived and frolicked, unable to keep their hands off each other. Their play was interrupted by trailing fingers and lingering kisses at regular intervals.

When they dried off and returned to the swag, Jess dropped into a deep sleep until Alex woke her at sunrise, pointing to the ominous sky, and she'd hurried down the hill for a quick wash. If she was turning up at a luxury world-class resort, she wanted to look the part. Or at least somewhat clean.

She climbed the rocky slope and Alex's deep voice reached her. He beckoned her over as he spoke on the phone.

"Thanks, mate. Yeah, it's a shame. I'll tell her and get back to you to book the helicopter seat."

He reached over and put the phone back inside the truck, a frown on his face. "Sorry, Jess. Bad news."

"For me or you?"

"I suppose it depends which way you look at it." Alex put his arms loosely around her waist and held her gaze. "No room at the inn, as they say."

"Oh no, it's full?"

"Yes. My mate, Mitch, checked for me. So, what now?"

"Do you want me to get them to book the helicopter to Darwin for you?"

Disappointment pierced Jess's chest. Until a minute ago, Alex had been friendly and playful, even after he took the call. Something had changed his mood instantly, and she had no idea what she'd done.

"I still want to try and get my interview." She folded her arms across her chest and stuck her chin out. "I'm not going to spend two days crossing the outback and then just hop into a helicopter and go home. It would have all been for nothing."

Alex grabbed her shoulders and stared down at her. "All of it, Jess? All for nothing?" He dropped his head and took her mouth in a hard kiss. She stepped back and touched her fingers to her lips.

"No, some of it was good. Wonderful, in fact." When he turned away without commenting, she followed him, wanting to lash out. She was sick of men and their ability to hurt her. At least with Harrison she'd known he was after her money. Alex knew nothing—or very little—about the real Jess and still he turned away from her. Tears stung the backs of her eyes and she couldn't help the feeling that it was all coming to an end. "Yes, the scenery was magnificent and the swimming hole was fun. Yesterday, you offered me a room at your place. Does that offer still stand, or now that you've had your fun with the easy Yank, have you changed your mind?"

"Jess, don't talk like that." He strode over to the fire and began to pack up, and she knew he didn't want to be near her. "Don't put yourself down."

"Well, does the room offer still stand?" Her voice sounded as though she was begging and she hated it. "I'd love to stay with you while I chase up Ricardo. And my great organisational skills have kicked in yet again and now there's no room at the resort, so can I stay with you or not?"

Alex ran his hand through his hair and absentmindedly dug in his pocket for a piece of string. He held her gaze while he tied his hair back. His cheeks were covered with dark stubble and his expression was grim. If she hadn't known better, she would have found him intimidating, but she knew he was a good person. He'd looked out for her throughout the trip, and it was only this morning that he'd changed back into the gruff fisherman.

Something was bothering him.

"Did you get some bad news on the telephone? Oh well, it's none of my business." She turned away and gathered up her things and looked down at her dirty clothes. "Besides, they probably wouldn't have given me a room anyway looking like a stray from the outback."

Warm hands descended on her shoulders, and she held his gaze.

"I offered a room to you and I am a man of my word." Alex tugged gently on her arm, and Jess turned around to face him. "If you want to stay, my offer still stands."

He held her gaze and she tried not to react as she looked up into his deep blue eyes, wanting to ignore the warm shivers that were igniting a fire low in her belly.

"I don't want to see you disappointed when you don't get your interview," he said. "I like you, Jess. I like you a little too much for my own peace of mind, and I'd hate to see you hurt."

"That's a strange term to use, Alex. Disappointed maybe, but not hurt."

He leaned down and brushed a much gentler kiss across her lips. "Come on, I want to beat this rain."

Quietly she helped him pack up the truck and throw sand on the glowing embers of the fire. As Jess walked to the truck and opened the door, she looked around. She would always hold this campsite in the middle of the outback close to her heart.

***

When Jess had chewed her lip and looked up at him with those wide green eyes, remorse had spiked Alex's chest. Unfamiliar warmth that had nothing to do with sex stole over him, and he knew he didn't want to hurt this woman. There was only one way this could end if she found out who he was. She'd assume he'd been lying to her about everything and slaked his sexual need with the 'easy Yank' as she'd called herself. Someone had obviously done a number on her. Underneath her confidence, he could see how sensitive she was, and easy to hurt.

Shit. He was going to be so bloody careful when they reached Cockatoo Springs. As well as not wanting to reveal who he was to a freelance journalist, he didn't want to hurt her either.

He turned the truck onto the road and glanced across at Jess. Bowser was curled up on her lap, and she was staring thoughtfully out the window.

Easy Yank. Nothing could be further from the truth, and he felt guilty that she thought that. He wanted her on that helicopter and out of here before she could mess up his life and get herself hurt in the process. He'd been more than content, happy with the way things were, before she'd arrived on the scene.

Mitch had been taken aback when he'd told him he was bringing in a guest, and more so when he'd asked him to say there were no rooms available. In reality, the resort was half-empty, but he didn't want her anywhere near it, snooping around without him nearby. It would get busier in a couple of days when Clay ran his first course and the international chefs arrived on the helicopter from Darwin If she still insisted on staying with him, he would have to keep her close by. And that was going to be hard because the CEO of the luxury travel company was there for their meeting. Mitch said he'd flown in early, and if he didn't see him straight away, the deal was at risk. It was the last big deal he had to finalise before his contract came to an end, so he'd have to book Jess on a tour tomorrow if she stayed, while he got himself cleaned up and into a business meeting.

And my family is about to hit the resort too. Alex ran his hand through his hair.

"Worried?"

"Huh?"

"You look worried," she said. "Are you worried about the rain coming?"

"No, we'll be fine. Mitch said it's clear over on the coast." He straightened his shoulders and smiled at her. "It's only about a two-hour drive from here. I'll bet you're wishing you took the helicopter in? The flight from Darwin only takes twenty minutes."

"I've seen the true outback." She lifted her hands and her brow wrinkled in a frown. "But a manicure will be nice."

"So you're going to stay for a day or so?"

She glanced across at him from beneath her lashes. "More if the mood takes me. It all depends on what happens when we get there."

Shit. He would have to put a plan in place fast. He wasn't used to this sort of double dealing. Using Alessandro Ricardo for the business promotion had never been a problem before. Mitch handled the staff and he'd always had the business meetings with clients in Darwin. Because of the isolation of the resort the mostly backpacker staff changed over frequently, and they rarely stayed more than a few months. Those who knew him, knew him as simply, Alex the fisherman. But he had a feeling his life was about to get very complicated.

Chapter Twelve

Alex held the door open and gestured for her to enter the small cabin. Jess had been expecting a fishing cabin like the one at Daly River where he'd picked up the boat, but this cabin beside the resort was quite luxurious.

"Is this yours?" She turned to him curiously as he followed her inside.

"Ah…sort of." He bent down and picked up Bowser, carried him across to the sink in the small utility room, and turned the tap on to fill the tub. "I…er… rent it from the resort and use it as a base most if the time I'm up here." Alex looked away and busied himself with Bowser, lifting him into the tub, and sponging the red dust of his coat. "Let me clean up this little guy and then I'll show you around."

Jess wandered across to the window past a white leather sofa. Soft *flokati* rugs were scattered across the polished timber floor. The whole place screamed money, and she could see why Bowser was having a wash before he was allowed inside.

A water sprinkler spun lazily in the early afternoon sun throwing rainbows across the lush grass at the front of the cabin. Across the road, a gleaming expanse of white sand shimmered in the midday sun, and in the far distance a couple strolled along the beach hand in hand.

Alex walked across to the window, towelling the dog with a large white cloth.

"So, we're close to the resort?" she asked.

"Yes." He put the dog down and Bowser's claws tapped on the timber floor as he ran across to Jess and put his paws up on her knees.

Alex stood close, and she could feel the heat the heat of his body. She closed her eyes, fighting the need to lean into him.

"Yes, it's just through that high hedge over there. See that wall? There's a gate a short way along." He moved away and Jess opened her eyes as he opened a door leading out to the small front balcony. She followed him and he pointed to the north when she heard a helicopter.

"There's the early afternoon helicopter. It comes in twice a day. Few people come here by road. The boat comes in twice a week and brings a lot of the supplies in." He leaned back on the timber railing and stared at her intently. "Do you want me to see if I can get you onto the helicopter tomorrow morning?"

Jess clenched her jaw and gripped the railing. "Alex, just come straight to the point." She didn't look at him and kept her eyes on the dark blue helicopter that was swooping low over the beach. "I appreciate that you got me here, but if you don't want me to stay here, just come out and say it. I told you I didn't come all this way to get here and give up."

Alex didn't speak until the helicopter disappeared, and the only sound was the wind rustling the palm trees on the sandy beach in front of them. He put his hand over hers on the railing, and she held her breath waiting for his reply.

"I just don't want you disappointed." He gazed out to the water. "It's going to be boring for you. You won't be able to go to the resort. They…I mean… Mitch...is really strict about that. The facilities are only for guests." He slapped his free hand on his hip and turned to her. "I know what I can try for you. I will ask Mitch if you can go on one of the tours while you are here. There's probably a bush tucker tour tomorrow. What do you reckon?"

"What do I reckon?" She grinned at him, mimicking his Australian drawl. "I reckon that sounds just the sort of thing that would help me find out a bit more about Ricardo's chef school."

Hope filled her. Maybe she could go on the bush tucker tour, get to spend more time with Alex, and get material for her article at the same time.

"As long as I have a bed." Heat filled her cheeks as she thought of sharing a real bed with him. "I'll do the tour and stay a couple of days." She looked at him as determination filled her. "I'm not sure about what to do yet. I might check out the restaurant before I go looking for Ricardo. If you've any friends in the kitchen, perhaps you could ask if there are any kitchen hands needed? I could do some hands-on research."

"Okay." He lifted his hand from hers. "Come on. I'll show you your room and get your bags out of the truck. While you get yourself settled, I'll see Mitch about…the fish. So, I'll ask around for you."

Alex showed her a small bedroom off the living room and pointed out the adjacent bathroom before he went to the truck and brought her bags to the back porch. He set them down and went into the utility room, and came back out with a handful of cloths.

"Sorry. It's got a bit dusty, and I think the oil from the outboard has leaked into one of your bags. There's a washing machine in the cupboard if you want to wash anything while I'm gone."

"Thanks." Jess took the cloths from him and began to wipe the red dust from her large suitcase.

"Make yourself at home." Alex reached around the doorway and flicked a switch.
"That'll cool the place down a bit for you." He walked over to the truck and opened the door. "There's coffee in here, but no food. I'll be gone a while, but I'll sort dinner out. I'll leave the cooler here in case you get hungry, and Jess, be careful. Don't go wandering around. The resort is fenced in, but this cabin is out in the open, and there could be salties around."

"Great," she muttered to herself as the truck drove off. "Don't worry. I won't be going anywhere."

She'd been stuck with him in a pickup for the last forty-eight hours. What was one more day stuck in his cabin?

##

Jess unpacked and rinsed the red dirt from her clothes, putting anything that wasn't made of silk in the small clothes drier. Alex had her so spooked about crocodiles slithering through the garden she wasn't brave enough to go to the small clothesline outside on the grass, so she draped her silk shirts and wraps over the living room furniture. She took a quick shower in the bathroom, surprised at the luxury of Italian tiles in a worker's cabin.

Wandering into the bedroom where Alex had put her other bags, Jess hitched up the towel tied around her chest. It was a large white bath towel monogrammed with the letters 'CS'—the resort obviously looked after this cabin. Alex said he'd be a while, and she was waiting for her things to dry. Jess reached up and twirled her wet hair into a knot and dug into her bag for a clip, and her fingers brushed against her phone.

"Shit, Monica."

Grabbing it, she turned it on and sighed with relief when five high bars indicated full service. She hadn't given Monica a thought all day, and her friend was probably panicking wondering what the hell had happened to her.

Yep, eight missed calls.

Every hour, on the hour, until a couple of hours ago.

Jess pressed the return call button, and held her wet hair back with one hand waiting for the greeting she knew would come.

"Jessica Trent!"

She held the phone away from her ear as the usual high-pitched squeal was amplified through the phone. She let Monica speak for a full minute before she interrupted.

"Calm down, Mon. I'm okay."

"Where the hell have you been? Is there no phone service in the outback? That had better be the case, Jessica, because I am fit to kill you. Even Gareth was worried when you didn't call."

"I'm okay. I've just arrived at the Cockatoo Springs…sort of."

"Where have you been? Did you get the interview yet? What do you mean sort of?"

"No, no interview yet. I had a bit of a detour. I'll tell you all about it when I get home."

"So what's the deal with Ricardo? Can you get an appointment with him?"

Jess sighed. "I'll tell you all about it when I come home. I'm back in civilisation now. I'll email if I have any news and let you know when I'm flying out. I don't even know if Ricardo is here, he is such a recluse."

"He *is* there," Monica said.

Jess dropped her wet hair and sat forward on the edge of the bed. It fell to her shoulder and cool water trickled down between her breasts and she took a quick breath as Monica continued.

"There's a big deal going down. Gareth was reading the *Wall Street Journal* to me this morning and commented on how great your timing was."

"What sort of deal?"

"Larry Bartholomew, *your* boss, is over there with one of his other companies, Worldwide Luxury Tours. Apparently, he's at Cockatoo Springs negotiating with Ricardo as we speak."

Jess jumped up and did a happy dance, punching the air as Monica continued. "All you have to do is wander around the resort until you bump into him, and voila, one look at Jess Trent, the beautiful journalist and you will have no trouble getting Ricardo to talk to you."

Ricardo was here. First problem solved. But getting him to talk to her was going to be a bit harder than what Monica thought. She was going to have to approach this very carefully, especially with Larry in the picture.

"It's going to be a little bit tougher than that, I think. I can't believe Larry's over here. And I can't just wander around, I'm not even—" Jess cut off her words so she didn't have to explain it all to Monica and flopped back down on the bed. She dropped her head into one hand.

Wander around the resort? How the hell was she going to do that?

"Mon, do me a favour?"

"What?" Monica's voice was suspicious. "I know your favours."

"Oh, for goodness' sake. All I want is the phone number for Cockatoo Springs."

"Why? Just look at the stuff in your room. They always have it all over the pens and books next to the bed."

Jessica took a deep breath. "Sweets, just look up the number for me and I'll explain when I get back."

"Okay, give me one minute. I'll Google it."

Opening the sliding glass door to the small veranda off her room, Jess stood looking across at the high brick wall covered with tropical vines as Monica looked for the number. So close…

"Here it is."

She hurried back inside and grabbed a pen and wrote the number on the back of her business card.

"You're a lifesaver. I'll email you as soon as I get my computer hooked up to the Wi Fi."

"Jess, what's happening over there? I know when you're up to something. Just keep safe, okay?"

"Don't stress. I'm having a fabulous break, and I've got lots to tell you." She ended the call and threw her phone onto the bed before hurrying into the bathroom to dry her hair and put some make-up on. If all went to plan, she was going to brave the crocodiles, get over to the resort, and get her interview after all.

Chapter Thirteen

"Bloody hell, Alex." Mitch, his assistant manager and long-time friend slapped a hand to his forehead and shook his head. "Look at you. The most important business meeting you've had all year and you look like the wild man of Borneo."

"Yeah, I know, I know. I have to get a haircut and clean up."

"Have a shower, find a suit, and I'll send one of the girls from the beauty salon over to the villa to give you a haircut."

"No. I'm over in the cabin…and you can't send anyone over there."

"Has this got something to do with that phone call about not having any empty rooms?"

"Yeah, we have—or I have— a problem. I have a journalist over there determined to interview Ricardo."

"And you found her in the middle of the outback?" Mitch shook his head and held his hands up, an incredulous expression on his face. "No, don't explain, we haven't got time. Bartholomew was furious when you weren't here this morning."

"Stuff him, that's his problem." Alex walked around the desk and sat in the chair. "I'll see him when I'm ready. He needs us more than we need him, from what I've been reading. He can wait."

"Sometimes I think I worry more about the success of this place more than you do. You're never really happy unless you are out in the wilds." Mitch sat on the chair opposite Alex and ran his hand through his short-cropped hair.

"I've only got to worry about it till next week. Contract's up and I'm out of here."

"So you've paid your dues?" Mitch said quietly. He was the only one Alex had confided in, and it had helped Mitch respect his request to stay private.

"Yes, the Emily Young School of Bush Tucker has made its mark in the food world and I can move on."

"So, tell me about this journalist? How did you hook up with her?"

"She's beautiful, brave, and I think…no, I know, I'm in trouble here, mate." He stared past Mitch and didn't speak for a moment. When he looked back at his manager, he was the subject of a very intense gaze. "I can't get her out of my head. For the first time in a long time, I've let a woman get under my skin."

"So, what's the problem? Tell her who you are, make her sign a confidentiality agreement, and a no-reveal clause of your identity in her newspaper. Move her into the villa, have a fling, and send her on her way."

"She doesn't work for a newspaper. She works for Larry Bartholomew's media company."

"That's a bit suss. Do you think he sent her? Was she scoping you out?"

"No, she doesn't know I'm Alessandro."

"Are you sure? It seems a bit coincidental she's over here the same time as her boss. Does it really matter to you that she doesn't find out who you are?"

Alex shrugged. "When I came up here after Emily died, I promised her family I'd get the place started. You saw how messed up I was. It suited me then, and it suits me now to finish up when the contracted time is up. I don't want my photos plastered over a magazine and all my life laid out for public consumption. Alessandro Ricardo can disappear gracefully." He stood and wandered over to the wall and looked at the awards of recognition they'd received over the years. "You've done a great job as the front man, Mitch, and I've appreciated being able to stay behind the scenes. It was such a stupid idea, the idea of having a mysterious owner, although it did get us a lot of international press. I'm ready to move on."

Mitch followed him over and clapped him on the shoulder. "Maybe it's time to say it is Alex Richards running the show?"

Alex looked out across the resort, past the high brick fence in the direction of the cabin. "No, there's no need now. I'll get Jess in the kitchen. She can get some information for her article, and then we'll go our separate ways. I don't need any more complications in my life. I'm keeping it simple."

##

Before he went back to the kitchens to meet the new chef, Alex made a quick detour to his own large villa at the beach side of the resort. He pulled out his suit and hung it in on the door to air for his meeting tomorrow. Glancing around the walls at the photographs of his family, he smiled. They'd all descend on Cockatoo Springs for his birthday next weekend, and he was looking forward to seeing them. Which reminded him, he'd forgotten to organise to keep her busy tomorrow. He picked up the phone and dialled Mitch's extension.

"I forgot to ask you. Is there a bush tucker tour tomorrow?"

"Yeah, leaves at seven thirty."

"Can you book Jessica Trent on it for me?"

"Will do. How do you want to handle it? Will you take her to the bus or get her collected at the cabin?"

"Yes, at the cabin. Tell Terence to collect her there. I don't want her wandering around just yet."

Next stop was the kitchens, and Alex pulled up and went around to the back of the truck and unzipped the canvas at the back of the pickup. He took a step back as the combined smells of fish, gas, and dog hit him full on. Stepping forward, he reached back in to lift out the cooler full of mud crabs and he grinned.

No wonder Jess had ended up in my swag. Maybe it hadn't been my rugged sex appeal after all

He pushed open the door to the air-conditioned kitchen and placed the cooler on the stainless-steel bench.

"Anyone around?" He wandered into the restaurant, pausing when he saw the chefs, the sous-chefs, and the kitchen hands sitting at the tables taking notes. An unfamiliar man in chef trousers and a patterned bandanna tying his black, curly hair back, stepped over with his hand outstretched.

"You must be Alessandro. Mitch said you'd be bringing the crabs."

He ushered the new chef back out to the kitchen, away from the curious looks of the staff, before he held his hand out to him "Clay, great to meet you."

"Likewise. Thanks for the barramundi. It arrived last night and we're already planning a feast tonight. Quite a few guests flew in today, and we've got some food journalists in too."

Alex groaned.

"Jeez, they must be stalking me," he muttered, wondering how to handle it. His life had become way too complicated over the past two days.

Take me back to the scrub and the fish.

Clay tipped his head to the side with a frown. "Problem? How do you want me to handle them? Interviews or not?"

"No. Just feed them and if they ask any questions, tell them he will be putting out a press release in a day or so."

"Alessandro? Sorry, I thought you were Alessandro."

Alex gave a wry laugh. "Long story, mate. I'll fill you in over a welcoming beer later. Anyway—" He reached out and shook Clay's hand again. "Great to have you on board." He went to the large cool room and opened the door. Reaching in, he pulled out a bottle of chilled white wine before turning back to the chef.

"A favour, mate? I've got a friend staying who'd like to see how the place works. Could you do with another kitchen hand for a few days?"

"If she's got no food handling certificate, she'll be on wash up duty. That okay?"

"That's fine. Her name's Jess and I'm just Alex when you talk about me, if you do, Okay? No mention of Alessandro."

Clay grinned at him. "Whatever you say, you're the boss."

Alex headed for the door, picking the empty cooler up on the way. "Can you get one of the staff to bring two meals over to my cabin? Make sure you tell them I'm in the cabin, not the villa."

Clay gave him a wave. "No problem."

Chapter Fourteen

Jess put her mobile back into her bag and stared out the window, confusion filling her mind. She'd dialled the number Monica gave her for Cockatoo Springs, the same resort Alex had told her only today was full. The reservations clerk had just informed her rooms were available now.

Now, as in today. Right now.

Of course she hadn't told him she was right next door. Why would Alex have said there were no rooms? A warm feeling filled her chest, but it was quickly followed by uncertainty.

If he'd been so keen to have her stay, he could have just asked her, there was no need for game playing. Anyway, he'd seemed more enthusiastic about her getting on the helicopter, and going home than anything else. Maybe he had a girlfriend…or a wife, God forbid, here on the resort. But she shook her head. If that were true he wouldn't have installed her into his cabin.

Would he?

Jess's heart gave a crazy leap when Bowser yapped and jumped up. His ears pricked and his little head cocked to the side. The now familiar sound of Alex's pickup truck roared in through the screened door where the dog stood whimpering. She stood and smoothed her hand over her hair as she walked across to greet him, her silk skirt swishing softly against her bare legs, her bracelets jangling on her wrist. A shower, clean clothes, and access to the world via her telephone had restored her equilibrium, and now she was going to put on the performance of her life to hide the confusion filling her. Closing her eyes, she waited for the door to open to see how he would greet her. Was he hoping she might have gone, or would he be pleased to see her?

The door squeaked and then all was quiet until a low wolf

whistle came from across the room. Her heart thudding, she turned and met Alex's gaze. His eyes were hooded and he looked at her for a long moment before speaking.

"What have you done with my Jess?"

"Your Jess?" Her own low throaty voice surprised her.

"Yeah, my Jess of the Outback." His face lit up in a wide grin. "You know, the one with the string in her hair and the dirty clothes?"

"Sorry, can't help you there. Haven't seen her." She smoothed down her brightly patterned silk skirt with a shaking hand. Alex walked over to her, his bare feet quiet on the timber floor, and took her hand in his. He picked it up and examined the short-clipped fingernails, free of red nail polish.

"They're her hands," he said softly as he lifted her hand to his lips, turned it, and kissed her open palm.

She swayed toward him, but he gently grasped her wrist and held her away before he dipped his head and lightly brushed her mouth with his lips.

"Let me take a quick shower and then I'll tell you my news."

"News? Have you talked to Ricardo?"

"Patience, my dear." He dropped her arm and went back outside, returning with a bottle of wine. "Pour the wine. I'll be quick and then I'll tell you."

Jess muttered to herself as she opened the wine and searched through the cupboards for some glasses. The kitchen was bare, and the room was more like a hotel room, with only essentials.

Opening the last door, she cheered to herself as she found the glasses. She tried to block the picture of the water droplets on Alex's muscled chest. She poured her wine, and put the bottle and the other glass in the refrigerator, next to the jug of water, which was the only other thing in there.

Maybe he'll take me over to the restaurant for dinner? Maybe I'll get to see Cockatoo Springs tonight?

Moving across to the window, she looked out at the ocean, flat and silver in the soft moonlight. The sun had set just before Alex had come back and the night in the outback seemed to descend with no dusk. She leaned her forehead on the cool glass and tried to focus. Hopefully, he'd heard Ricardo was there too and spoken to him already, singing the praises of the journalist who wanted to interview him.

Ha, and pigs might fly too.

The bathroom door closed and the smell of fresh soap drifted across to her. The fridge door opened and the clink of the wine bottle clicking on the glass filled the quiet room. Outside, it was silent, and the bright lights of the resort next door lit up the night. Alex came out of the kitchen holding his wine glass, pausing in the doorway where he leaned on the frame and sipped his wine, looking at her.

A loose white shirt hung over a pair of knee length chinos. Jess turned slowly, and desire shot straight through her.

"Welcome to Cockatoo Springs."

"Thank you." She walked over and clinked her glass against his. He reached up and held her hand.

"You look beautiful, Jess. I should have taken you out tonight."

"To the resort?" she asked hopefully. "Maybe we could we go there for dinner? My treat to thank you for the ride here."

Alex led her over to the leather sofa and sat down, pulling her next to him. She looked at his tanned legs brushing against her pale calves. He followed her gaze and lifted her legs up across his lap, and a shiver ran along her back when he trailed his fingers along her toes.

"No need to thank me. Dinner is being delivered to the cabin. We have the whole night to ourselves."

A curl of anticipation wound its way through her body.

"I can think of better ways to spend the night than sitting at some restaurant." His voice was low, and he didn't take his eyes from hers. "Not a mosquito or a crocodile to disturb us."

"Or a pig?" She laughed, and it dispelled the sexual tension gripping her.

His laugh was deep and sexy. "You really did cope with the

outback very well for a first timer."

"I will never forget the sight of you up that tree in your underwear."

"Aw, come on, Jess, you're supposed to remember me saving you. I'm the outback hero, remember?"

"That is how I'll remember you when I go back to New York. A real Crocodile Dundee," she said softly. "Now tell me what's happening. Did you find out if there is a tour tomorrow?"

"Yep. After I dropped the crabs off, I went over to the office. You're booked on the tour that leaves at seven thirty in the morning. They'll pick you up here at the cabin, and they'll take you out to the grasslands in a small four-wheel drive bus and show you how to collect all sorts of bush tucker. One of the chefs goes on the trip and they cook damper for morning tea and flavour it with the bush tucker you collect."

"Damper?"

"A loaf of bread baked in the fire."

"Sounds great." She lifted her wine glass to her lips. "And did you find out about Ricardo?"

Alex shook his head slowly and frowned. "Sorry, Jess. He's not there at the moment."

"Oh." Disappointment shot through her. Damn him. If Monica was right, Alex was lying to her. She'd said Ricardo was here for a meeting with Larry. And that was another problem.

Even though she would try to meet Ricardo and get that interview, she'd keep a low profile if Larry were around. As well as being her boss, he was one of her father's *nouvelle riche* buddies. She was going to have to play it very carefully if he *was* here with Ricardo. She didn't want him to know she was after the interview until the article was in the bag, and the less her father knew about her whereabouts, and what she was doing, suited her just fine. But why was Alex so damned determined she had to forget about this interview?

She looked up and his gaze was fixed on her, and she could have sworn there was a flush on his cheeks. "Well, I guess I'll just have to use the bush tucker trip for information and then see if I can chase him up at his conference."

"I've got more good news for you."

She tipped her head to the side. Alex reached up and lifted her hand to his mouth.

"The day after your bush tucker tour, you've got a start as a kitchen hand washing dishes in the school kitchen. That should give you an insight into how the school works. You can stay here in my cabin for a few days. I'll take you over to meet the chef tomorrow."

Jess squealed and launched herself at him. "That is wonderful. Thank you so much."

"Clay, the chef, has got you on wash up duty. You'll soon get sick of that." He slid his hand around the back of her neck, and anticipation curled in her stomach. "More wine?"

She nodded, and Alex lifted his hand away. Jess put her head back on the soft leather of the sofa as he went to refill her glass. Three stairs led up to a low mezzanine level where the master bedroom was located. A wide timber railing ran along the edge of the room and small glass candleholders with tea candles inside were placed at small intervals. It really was a romantic little cabin. Things were looking up— a bush tucker tour, and an in into the kitchen, and a night in Alex's cabin. She might get this article written yet.

Alex came back out with the wine bottle, and she held her glass up for a refill.

"I have to go out really early tomorrow. I have some things to organise before I return to Daly River late next week." He put the bottle on the floor next to the sofa, reached over, and brought her legs back up onto his lap.

"So, you spend a bit of time in this cabin?"

"On and off."

"Would you call it home or do you live somewhere else?"

"What's with the twenty questions, Jess? I'm a pretty boring bloke."

"Oh, I don't know. I was thinking about writing that other article with you as the outback hero. If I can't have Ricardo, I can write about you. You could take your shirt off and lean across the front of your pickup or wrestle a crocodile or something." She reached over and ran her hand down his chest.

Alex choked on his wine and coughed. He put his glass on the floor next to the bottle and put his hand over his mouth. Jess patted him on the back as his face went red and his eyes watered as he shook his head.

"I don't think that would sell many magazines or help you keep your job. I thought this was a do or die interview to save your job?"

Jess trailed her fingers up his cheek and wiped the dampness beneath his eye with her thumb. "If it doesn't work out, I'll keep writing till I get a job at another magazine." She tipped her head to the side. "Outback dude chases pig on a hunting magazine cover maybe. Oh, how I wish I'd taken a photo."

He pursed his lips and frowned, and she couldn't hold her laughter back.

"Oh Alex, for such a tough guy, you are so easy to tease."

With a low growl, he grabbed her hand and tugged her so her bottom slid up into his lap. "I'll show you how to tease, woman."

Before she could reply, his lips descended on hers in a hard kiss and Jess forgot all about pigs, magazine articles, and jobs.

Jess closed her eyes as his lips caressed hers

"You confuse me, Alex," she whispered. He kept his gaze on her and smiled a slow lazy smile as he held her close. She pushed all of her worries out of her mind.

Just them. She could worry later.

"I love touching you. Your skin is like silk." His fingers lingered on her shoulders.

She slid off him and soon she was lying beneath him, smoothing her hands over his back beneath his shirt. Impatiently he shrugged it off but stilled as there was a loud knock at the door.

"Alex? Are you in there?"

"Alex?" There was a loud knock on the door. "Are you there?"

Alex pulled his shirt back on "You might like to sit up. Our dinner has arrived," he whispered. "Coming!" he shouted to the person at the door.

Jess sat up on the sofa hastily rearranging her clothing. She ran her hands through her hair, which she knew would be in a cloud of disarray.

"Come in, Mitch." Alex's voice was strained, and Jess looked across to the door curious to see who it was.

"I was in the kitchen when they asked one of the kitchen hands to bring your dinner over." The tall blond-haired man placed a tray on the dining room table and glanced across at Jess with a quick smile. "I was walking over here so I said I'd take it over."

He sauntered across the room and smiled at her.

"Hi, I'm Mitch... a mate of this big lug here. I hope he's been looking after you. Shame we couldn't give you a room."

"Yes, it was a shame," she said watching them. "I was so looking forward to staying at Cockatoo Springs, but silly me, I forgot to book and then you were all full up!"

Satisfaction filled her as she intercepted a look between the two men. There were rooms available. The lie had been deliberate and they both knew it, but she wasn't going to let on that she'd woken up to whatever it was they were doing.

"Did you say you walked over?"

"Yes," Mitch said and Alex frowned. "It's a lovely night."

"What about the crocodiles?"

"Crocodiles?" He almost gulped as he shot a look at Alex. "What about them?"

"I thought it was unsafe to roam around because of the salties."

"Oh yes. I just know where to walk," Mitch said hurriedly backing away toward the door.

She narrowed her eyes as he smiled at her.

"Anyway, nice to meet you, Jess." He turned to Alex who was standing by the door tight-lipped.

"Alex, have you got a minute? I want to talk about the…fish." Mitch walked to the door, and after he and Alex had gone outside Jess moved across to the table. Delicious aromas were coming from beneath the covered tray and she lifted the lid as her temper built.

* * *

Alex got rid of Mitch as quickly as he could.

"Watch out for the salties on your way back," he called out. Mitch turned and gave him a thumbs up.

He closed the door behind him and walked in.

Whoa.

She was looking at him, and it wasn't pretty. Walking up to him with a damn you-look on her face, she poked a finger in his chest, and he took a step back. "So, what was that all about?"

"What?" He widened his eyes and tried to look innocent.

"He came to see you about the fish and braved the crocodiles, did he? What brave friends you have. You're *all* outback heroes. You tell me, why are you so determined to keep me here in your cabin and away from the resort? So much that you lied about it and cooked up some scheme with your friend."

Before he could answer, Jess pulled a chair out and sat down and put her elbows on the table, her fingers clenched in front of her chin. "Don't bother answering. I'll figure it out. Now I'm going to eat and then I'm going to bed. Alone."

The meal was silent. Alex dug deep for conversation to break the ice, but every time he opened his mouth to speak, Jess stared him down. After they'd finished the crab soup, he pushed his plate away. "What's really eating you, Jess?"

"I know what you're up to, Alex."

His mouth dried and he stared back at her, waiting for her to say she had somehow found out who he really was. He wasn't ready to tell her yet.

448

Tomorrow maybe, after he saw Bartholomew.

"Caught me out, how?"

"Why did you lie about there being no rooms? If you wanted to get in my pants, you didn't have to go to anywhere near the trouble you did. I'm the easy Yank, remember?"

He reached across the table to take her hand, but she snatched it away.

"Don't say that about yourself, Jess."

"In the afternoon, when I come back from the tour, I'm getting a room. One of the *many* vacant rooms tonight," she said.

"Jess, I can explain."

"Pah." She pushed her chair back. "No more lies. Thanks for the lift, Alex. Have a nice life."

Her skirt swirled around her calves as she walked to her room, her back ramrod straight, and then she slammed the door.

Alex dropped his head into his hands and groaned. Maybe it was for the best, but he hated the thought that he'd hurt her. The look in her eyes when she'd called herself the easy Yank tore at his heart. He had to make this right.

Chapter Fifteen

Jess slept poorly with one ear open to listen for Alex leaving, her mind churning, full of her plans for the day. Rolling over, she thumped the pillow and lay still for a minute before giving up on getting back to sleep.

Dawn was about to break. The first glimmers of pink light were tingeing the edges of the dark sky through the window. The back door closed and she heard Alex call to Bowser, and a couple of minutes later the pickup roared to life. The headlights shone on her window as the truck headed past the back of the cabin. Fighting the tears that clogged her throat, she squeezed her eyes shut. It was time she took control.

Crawling out of bed, she dug through her clothes looking for something suitable to wear back out into the outback. This time, she knew what to expect. The only thing she didn't have was a decent pair of boots.

By seven o'clock, she was showered and dressed, and her packed bags were lined up against the back door. She still hadn't decided how long she was going to stay at Cockatoo Springs. It all depended on what today brought. She sipped the coffee she'd brewed. For all she knew, Ricardo could be there already, or if he wasn't there yet, he would be here soon. You couldn't believe one word that came out of Alex's mouth, and besides Monica had said Ricardo *was* here having a meeting with Larry Bartholomew of all people.

Jess stepped out onto the back porch to wait for the tour bus. The sun was already burning hot, so she stepped back into the shade. The heat shimmered over the red sandstone cliffs in the distance. All was still and quiet, and Jess smiled as she glanced across at the lush lawn.

Talk about gullible. She'd believed every word Alex had said and had expected to see saltwater crocodiles roaming around. You'd think a journalist would be savvier. *Sucked in by bedroom eyes and a sexy smile.*

Well, today was a new day and as soon as she finished the bush tucker tour, and got some information for her article, she'd check into the resort and enjoy a few days there before flying home to the North American winter. If Ricardo was here and she did manage to snag some time with him—well, that would be a bonus.

The sound of an engine reached her, and for a moment her heart picked up a beat. She stepped to the front of the porch and grasped the low railing, peering up the road. But it wasn't the pick-up. A high vehicle emblazoned with Cockatoo Springs Tours on the side trundled up the narrow roadway and pulled on to the lawn across from the cabin. Jess turned and lifted her bags out. Hopefully, Alex would still be off fishing, or crabbing or wrestling crocodiles for a while yet.

"Morning, love." The wide smile of the Aboriginal bus driver greeted her. "You're the last one on."

"Is it okay if you drop me back to the resort after the tour? Do you have room for my bags?"

"Not a problem."

First hurdle overcome.

The bus had one empty seat at the very front. Jess tucked her small bag under the seat and sat down, and reached for her seatbelt.

"Whoa, love. Do you have closed in shoes in your suitcase?"

Jess looked down at her leather sandals. They were the most substantial footwear she had with her, apart from the closed in stilettos she'd worn with her suit on the trip over.

"No, this is all I have."

"You can't get off the bus at the gathering site unless you've got closed in shoes." The bus driver shrugged. "Sorry, safety regulations."

Jess leaned over and spoke in a low voice. "I don't *have* any other shoes with me."

He shook his head. "You're welcome to come along for the drive and see the sites, but you won't be able to get off the bus when we gather, and I'll have to give you your morning tea on the bus."

Jess chewed her lip. "I'm sorry, I didn't realise. My…er…friend here booked the trip for me."

What to do? She reached over and leaned on the driver's seat.

"I'll change my trip to another day, then." She put on the best persuasive smile she could muster. "Would you have time to give me a ride to reception before you leave?"

"Not a problem." He turned the motor off and picked up his microphone. "Just a slight detour back to the resort, folks, for this beautiful young lady. Have a read of the brochures in your seat pocket. There is a map of our trip up the coast."

"I really appreciate this." She looked out the window in amazement. She'd read up briefly on Cockatoo Springs after the restaurant had won the award in *Cuisine* and she was trying to find more information about Alessandro Ricardo and the unique concept of the bush tucker chef school. But this luxury was beyond her expectations. The bus passed through the gates and around a high rectangular fountain with sandstone edges, which reflected the colours of the cliffs she had noticed in the distance earlier. *Welcome to Cockatoo Springs* was written in large gold letters on the side of the sandstone edge. A water spout cascaded in the centre of the pool, and the flowing water glistened in the morning sun. It reminded her of the pool and the waterfall at the campsite, except this one had cute ducks paddling on the water.

Don't go there. Move on.

It was early and workers swept the leaves up around the water feature. Jess looked on curiously as a man in a white jacket followed a waddling duck and bent down.

"What's he doing?" she asked as she pointed to the man following the ducks.

The driver laughed. "He's got a great job. Duck pooper-scooper." He changed up a gear and the bus climbed a slight incline. The sparkling ocean opened out in front of her.

Low-level villas on the low slope were almost hidden amongst a profusion of palm trees and brightly coloured tropical plants. A series of paths led down to one of the biggest swimming pools she had ever seen. It was hexagonal shaped with wide walkways through the pool.

"How beautiful is that?" she whispered to herself.

The driver pulled up outside a building marked *Reception* and opened the door.

"You haven't been over yet?" he asked.

"Er, no, I stayed at my friend's cabin last night. I'm checking in today."

Once her bags were unloaded and the concierge had loaded them onto a trolley, the driver climbed back onto the bus and Jess waved.

The automatic doors to the building opened, and she welcomed the blast of cold air from the air-conditioned reception area. Small palm trees filled the interior in large colourful pots on the shining marble floor, and she crossed the room to the desk.

"Good morning," the male receptionist said. "Checking in? I didn't hear the helicopter."

"No, I came by road." Jess reached down into her bag and removed her credit card. "I don't have a booking, but I rang earlier and I was told there were rooms available."

The clerk tapped on the computer and looked up with a smile. "Yes, I can give you a pool room. Your name?"

"Jessica van Lund." She hated using her father's name, but all her bank accounts were in her legal name.

He ran her card through the terminal and handed her a plastic card. "You're in room two over near the beach side of the pool. Would you like to walk over or shall I order you a cart?"

"Oh, I'll walk. I'll explore on the way." It was too soon to do any digging about Ricardo. She'd get settled before she started work. Once she logged onto her computer, she knew there would be a mountain of email to clear, but that could wait.

"I'll send your luggage over. Enjoy your stay with us, Ms. Van

Lund."

A burst of noise and activity came from behind her as she turned around. Two toddlers with black ringlets and wide brown eyes ran across the marble floor, chased by a tall man in black jeans and T-shirt.

"Allegra! Luca! Come back here." The toddlers hid behind one of the sofas and giggled.

"Tomas, they're okay. Chill out."

Jess looked with curiosity at the woman with the Scottish accent who walked over to the reception counter. She was tall with a long dark braid, dressed casually in khaki shorts and a T-shirt.

"They've been cooped up in a helicopter and a bus for two hours." The woman turned to Jess with an apologetic smile. "Just watch you don't get ambushed on your way out. They think they are Dora and Diego in the jungle."

The man shrugged and walked over to join his wife. Jess smiled as she watched the children. The father had an Aussie drawl, the mother, a strong Scottish burr and if she wasn't mistaken the children were chattering away in Italian.

The receptionist held his hand out to the man standing next to her and shook it vigorously. Jess reached down to collect her handbag from the counter.

"Tom, great to see you! Can't believe it's been a year since you were here for Alex's birthday last year."

Jess froze and snuck a look at the man beside her.

Yep, she could see the resemblance. Alex's family had arrived.

##

After Jess got to her room, she stood at the window looking down at the large swimming pool in the centre of the resort. She'd enquired about meeting the chef, but the guy at the reception desk said he wouldn't be in the restaurant until this afternoon. She'd go over and see this Clay guy as soon as he was over there. If she couldn't work there, maybe he'd do an interview and show her around...or at least set up an appointment for one.

Jess bit her lip, trying to ignore the heavy feeling in her chest. Once she'd realised Alex had been lying to her, and she'd lost her temper, things changed. She had to accept he'd been playing with her all along, and as usual she'd been sucked in. For a couple of nights, there'd been a connection between them. It wasn't just sex…or that's what she'd thought.

When will I ever learn?

She brushed the tears away angrily before they could fall. Now that she was here, she'd make the most of it. On the desk beneath the window a glossy covered compendium listed the services provided by the hotel. First stop, the beauty salon to restore her confidence. Second stop, the pool.

Alex could go take a flying leap.

Chapter Sixteen

The hairdresser lifted the black cape off Alex's shoulders with a flourish. *"Voila, a new man."* She ran her fingers along his hairline. "Alex, you have a white mark on your neck where your hair was so long."

Alex stood and brushed the remaining hair from his suit trousers and tucked his shirt in as he looked in the mirror.

Christ, he hated this part of the job.

All dressed up and looking like a businessman did not sit comfortably with him, but it was a necessary evil. This deal was important and it was the last meeting he'd be having as the managing director. As soon as he signed the contract with Bartholomew, he'd go back to the cabin, get changed, and wait for Jess to come back from the tour. By the time his family descended, he would have made his peace with her, and hopefully she'd be happy to move into the villa with him until she went home. There was no reason they couldn't spend some time together before she went back to the States once he explained why he'd not told her the truth. And he'd give her his first ever interview about Cockatoo Springs and the award-winning chef school. But not about him—he wasn't prepared to go that far.

"Thanks, Wendy. I did leave it a bit long this time." He strolled across the salon and looked across at the doorway to the day spa. "Busy day ahead here? I have a friend staying here who'd like a manicure."

"Send her over. We'll fit her in." Wendy raised her eyebrows. "Friend or family? Having friends at your party this year for a change?"

He grinned. "Friend. Family doesn't arrive till the weekend."

Wendy shook her head. "How long have you been out fishing in the outback? It *is* the weekend."

"Shit. What day is it?"

"Friday. Your party is tomorrow night. The staff is looking forward to it." She gave him another smile and nudged his ribs. "Your sister-in-law is booked in for a treatment this afternoon. You do know your secret is out, don't you?"

Alex narrowed his eyes. "What secret?"

"Clay let it slip in the kitchen last night and it went around like wildfire." Her grin got wider. "You have no idea, do you…Alessandro?"

"Oh, shit."

"We've all suspected for ages. Wondered why a simple barramundi fisherman had the luxury villa on the beachfront kept vacant for him."

Okay he's known this would happen one day, but now Jess being on the scene complicated matters. He'd have to get to Jess the instant she got off the tour. He hoped like hell his name wouldn't come up in discussions. Surprisingly, it just didn't seem to matter that much anymore; the only thing that worried him was Jess being upset. His secret was out, the contract was almost over and he needed to get to Jess before she found out through someone else. She was really angry with him, so he didn't think she'd ask about him. But she might try to ask around about Alessandro.

He reached into his pocket and passed Wendy a tip. "Look after my sister-in-law. Which one is booked in today?"

"Lissy."

Alex stepped out onto the covered walkway that crossed the pool. It was the quickest way to the executive suite where Bartholomew was waiting for him. As soon as the contract was signed he'd seek out whoever of his family had arrived and then he'd wait for Jess. If it all worked out to plan, it would be a great weekend.

Larry Bartholomew was dressed casually in white jeans, and a bright yellow T-shirt stretched tightly across his huge paunch. He took Alex's hand in his large beefy grasp and spoke in a booming voice.

"Good to meet you, son." Alex stiffened, taking an instant

dislike to the gregarious American.

"Now before we look at the paperwork, I want to see all around this place. Your man showed me the contract and it looks all fine and dandy, but I want to see what you think makes this place so special. Maybe I could meet the new chef from London? What do you say, boy?"

"Good." Alex headed for the door. The quicker he did the tour, the sooner the paperwork was signed and he could get away from business and find his family before Jess got back. "Come this way. We'll do the kitchens first and then I'll show you the grounds."

Alex strode out, and the big man hurried along behind him, and was huffing by the time they reached the kitchen. A couple of the sous-chefs were filleting barramundi at the big sink under the window.

"Another fresh shipment in?"

"Yes, they came in on the helicopter about an hour ago."

"The helicopter's in already?"

"Yes, they put on three extra trips this morning. Remember, your family are all arriving today for the party tomorrow night."

"Yes." All the more reason to get this tour over and done with. "Clay's not around?"

"No, he went back to Darwin on the chopper to collect some Asian spices he couldn't order through the supplier. He's coming back in the last helicopter after lunch."

Alex turned to Bartholomew. "Clay's not here. You'll have to meet him later. We'll take a quick tour. One of the vehicles should be there so you can see the level of comfort we'll offer your clients."

"Great!" His loud voice echoed through the large kitchen. "Then we'll get this signed and we can have a drink, boy." Larry slapped him on the back, and Alex clenched his jaw, counting to ten silently before he lost his temper and blew the deal. If it hadn't been for Mitch telling him what a great opportunity it was to break into the overseas luxury market, he would have put the skids under this obnoxious guy straight up.

Alex led him across to the pool area, pointing out the unusual bar located in the middle of the water.

"How about a drink, now?" Some sunbathers lying on the pool lounges near the bar looked across as Larry's voice carried loudly across the water. Alex shook his head.

"There's a bar in the executive suite. We'll get the contract signed first."

He turned and stepped onto the path toward the eastern side of the pool. Bartholomew didn't follow, and Alex turned around waiting for the portly guy to catch him up.

"Gotta love hanging around these places, don't ya reckon? Some nice bikinis around."

Alex nodded with a tight smile. "I have another appointment, Larry. If we don't hurry, I'll have to get my assistant to sort the contract signing out."

Larry followed him with a grunt and they walked across the small bridge dividing the pool from the bar. Alex flicked a glance across to the sun lounges and his breath caught in his throat. On the other side of the bar, Jess was lying on a sun lounge on her stomach. Her head was turned away from them on the pillow, and her arms were crossed beneath her head. A tiny red bikini showed way too much skin. Alex grabbed Larry's arm and motioned him to the opposite direction.

"What the hell is she doing there?" he muttered to himself.

Why wasn't she on the bush tucker tour? The last thing he wanted was for her to see him in his suit doing a deal.

Christ, the day was getting more complicated by the minute.

"Sorry? What did you say?" Larry said.

"I just thought you might like to see the gardens and where the day tours go out."

Larry followed him slowly as Alex strode from the pool area to the bottom floor of the building. "I'd rather have that drink."

"You can come back to the pool later," he said tightly. "If you want your tours to come here, we'll do it my way."

"No need to snap my head off. You want this deal or not?" Larry frowned at him and Alex tried to placate him with a smile.

"Sorry, Larry. I've got a lot of meetings ahead of me today. Look, there's a bottle of fifteen-year-old single malt whisky in my office to seal the deal. As soon as we sign on the dotted line, we'll have that drink."

When they reached the end of the corridor, he shoved the office door open and strode across to his desk and picked up the phone.

"Mitch, I need you. Bring the contract in, please. We're ready to sign." He hung the phone up and turned to Larry, gesturing to an armchair.

"Sit down. I'll pour the drinks." Alex crossed to the small bar by the window and reached for the whisky. He leaned forward as a flash of red caught his eye. Jess was standing beside the sun lounger knotting a red sarong beneath her breasts. As he watched, she turned and headed along the path and disappeared between the trees.

As soon as Mitch arrived and the contract was signed, he was going to track her down and find out what she was doing here. She should be safely up in the gorge collecting bush tucker by now.

He glanced up as Mitch opened the door, and Larry held his hand out.

"I'll have mine neat," Larry said.

"One for me too, please boss," Mitch said. He raised his eyebrows when Alex shoved a glass toward him slopping the whisky on his fingers.

"Mitch." Alex tried to focus on the business at hand, but all he could think of was Jess and wondering if she was heading back to the cabin. "When we finish here, I have another meeting. Can you show Larry around, please?"

"No problem." He shot Alex a curious glance as he held his hand out for the contract. Pulling a pen from his pocket, Alex signed with a flourish and put the contract on the table in front of Larry.

"I may see you around later today, Larry. A pleasure doing

business with you." He shook the man's hand briefly and headed for the door.

"Mitch, I'll be out for a while."

He dashed over to his beachfront villa, keeping an eye out for Jess in case she'd come back to the pool, but there was no sign of her. He threw his suit jacket on the sofa. After pulling his tie loose, he unbuttoned his shirt with one hand and dialled reception with the other.

"It's Alex. Have we got a guest by the name of Trent booked in yet?"

He tucked the phone beneath his chin and stepped out of his suit trousers while he waited for the receptionist to check.

"No guest checked in or booked ahead by the name of Trent. Are you expecting a guest, sir?"

"No, that's fine. Thanks." Alex hung up and let out his breath slowly, relieved Jess was still over at the cabin. She must have wandered over for a swim. Maybe she'd calmed down and they could talk. He'd head straight over there now. It looked like he was going to have to own up to his deception. If the word had gone around about him being Alessandro, he wanted her to hear it from him and no one else.

"Shit," he muttered beneath his breath as he pulled his jeans on. "How did everything get so complicated so quickly? Why does how she feels bother me so much?" Next week couldn't come soon enough. Handing over the management to Mitch and spending the summer fishing was looking very appealing. And then when the season was over, he had some big decisions to make. Was he going to stick around the Territory, or go back south and find a law firm? Or he could travel to the States and look up Jess, if she was still talking to him.

Alex headed to the resort through the pool area in case Jess had come back, but there was no sign of her. It was almost lunchtime and the sun loungers were empty. He nodded to the barman who was filling ice buckets in preparation for the usual after lunch rush to the pool.

"Alex!" For a moment he thought it was Jess and he turned around slowly, but grinned when he saw the woman with a riot of curls running across the pool bridge toward him.

"Lissy!" He lifted her up when she reached him and twirled her around. When he set her down, she hugged him close.

"Alex, it's so good to see you."

He held her hands and looked at her. "So do you, Lissy. Where's my big brother and that nephew of mine?"

"We're up in the lagoon wing next to your parents. They've arrived too. And Tom and Brianna and the twins are on the other side of us." Lissy raised her hand and held his chin and scrutinised him. "Look at you, all tanned and fit. This place has certainly agreed with you. You look a lot better than you did last year."

Alex leaned forward and dropped a light kiss on her forehead. "It's been a good year, Lis. I'm ready to move on."

He looped his arm around her shoulder and turned her in the direction of the bridge. "I'll take you back to your room and say a quick hello to the family."

He looked around, keeping an eye out for Jess. "I've just got something I have to do before I can settle in and catch up on all the family news."

"I thought you'd handed most of the work over to Mitch."

"Yes, I have. It's something personal. I'll fill you all in later if it works out.

"If it doesn't, I might crack the whisky open."

Alex smiled wryly as they stopped in the middle of the small bridge and exchanged a glance as they both remembered the last time the Richards' brothers had shared a bottle of whisky. It had been the day of Emily's funeral. Lissy looked up at him and her hers filled with tears.

"So you're really okay?"

Alex used his thumb to wipe away the tear that rolled down Lissy's cheek. His sister-in-law was a rock when Emily was killed, and he'd gotten to know her well. He'd never let on to any of his family that Emily had deceived him.

"Yes, I'm really okay. I've moved on, Lis."

Chapter Seventeen

"Damn you," Jess said under her breath. "Damn you, Alex."

She stood at the side of the large window overlooking the pool. She bit the side of her cheek to force away the tears that were threatening to fall. When she saw Alex head toward the pool her heartbeat kicked up, and she'd stood watching him stride across past the pool bar. She decided to act maturely and tell him she was in the resort and was about to turn to head to the door. And let him explain what he'd been up to, because she had known there was something.

When the woman ran across to the bridge to him and Alex took her in his arms and kissed her, Jess's world shattered and she realised what he was hiding. A searing shaft of jealousy engulfed her, and she slid down on to the sofa in front of the window.

She'd been right all along. He'd wanted her in the cabin because he already had someone here at the resort. She would bunker down in her room until she could get the first flight out of here. Stuff the interview and stuff the job.

An ache began in the middle of her chest and moved up to her throat. For a few minutes she allowed herself to wallow in self-pity and then the anger kicked in. Why should she give up the entire reason for being here just because a man wooed her into his bed?

***

"I'll be back in a half hour or so, I just have to go to the cabin and see someone." Alex hugged his mother for the second time and grinned over the top of her loose black curls at his two older brothers. Having his family here made him all the more determined to make his peace with Jess.

He'd make her see reason. It would be fun to have her at his birthday dinner and he was looking forward to introducing her to his family. He just had to convince her she could trust him.

Nick slapped him on the shoulder as he walked to the door.

"Good to see you looking fit and well, mate. Lissy says you're moving on next week?"

"Yes, contract's up and the school is established and going really well. I've made a few enquiries down in Brisbane, but I was thinking about taking a trip to the States first. I'll tell you about it later over a drink."

He closed the door and left his family, grinning at the noise that came through the door. It was just like the noise that always filled his parent's home when everyone was visiting. Once his sisters arrived with their families, the resort wouldn't know what had hit it.

The door to the cabin was closed and he pushed it open slowly.

"Jess? Jess, are you there?" He checked each room, but there was no sign of her or her belongings.

"Where is she, little buddy?" Alex reached down and scratched the little dog's back. "I wonder where she went." Picking up the phone, he dialled reception. "Has a Ms. Trent registered yet?"

When the clerk said no, Alex began to worry. He called the helicopter office.

"Bill, it's Alex. Have you taken any passengers out this morning?"

"No, mate, I'm just about to fly to Darwin to pick Clay up. I've got an empty bird. Had no one go out so far today. Just incoming guests."

Worry pinched at his gut. Surely, she wouldn't have tried to get out another way.

Where was she?

He picked the phone up again and dialled reception again. "Bill, have you checked in a tall blonde woman this morning?"

"I only just came on duty."

Shit. He ran his hand through his newly cropped hair, surprised to feel the stubble beneath his fingers.

"Can you have a look and tell me if any female guests have registered this morning by themselves and get me their room numbers."

He stood at the door looking at the sofa, remembering the feel of Jess's smooth skin beneath his hands last night.

"Three, Alex."

"O'Reilly, Van Lund, and Petersen. Rooms 114, 115, and 231." Bill laughed. "Not sure if their blondes or brunettes. Does she have to be a blonde?"

"Very funny."

Giving Bowser a quick pat, he headed back to the resort where he headed to the gift shop. He bought three small gift baskets and made his way up to room 114. He knocked on the door, waited, but there was no reply. He knocked again and waited for a few moments before knocking on 115.

"Just a moment," an unfamiliar voice with a British accent called out.

A petite dark-haired girl opened the door and a taller redhead peered over her shoulder. Alex cleared his throat and handed them one of the baskets. "Good morning. A welcome gift from management. Is one of you in 114?" He presumed the pair of them may be travelling together and have side-by-side rooms.

The redhead piped up. "Yes, I'm in 114."

Alec handed over the second basket of chocolate and flowers, before crossing to the lift and going to the second floor. He tapped lightly on the door of room 231, one of the larger rooms that overlooked the pool.

"Who is it?"

Alex sagged with relief when Jess's voice came through the door.

"A delivery."

"I'm not expecting a delivery."

"Open the door, Jess."

"Why?"

"Because I want to talk to you."

"We have nothing to talk about."

"Please, Jess." Alex put the basket on the floor, prepared to wait her out.

The door opened slowly and Jess peered around the edge. His stomach dropped when he saw her face.

"What do you want?" Her eyes were red, and he was sure she'd been crying.

"I want to talk to you. He reached down for the basket and held it out to her. "Peace offering?"

"Thank you, now go away and leave me alone." She took the basket and began to shut the door. Alex jammed his foot in the space and received an icy glare in return.

"While you're here, you can answer me one question?" she said.

"Yes?"

"Does the job in the kitchen still stand? I might as well get something out of this awful trip."

"Do you want to?"

"Of course I do."

"Can I come in? Please? We can talk about it."

"No."

Alex sensed he wasn't going to get anywhere by persisting. "Grab me a pen and a piece of paper."

Jess closed the door and for a moment he wondered if she would come back. Then the door opened again and she passed him a hotel notepad and pen without saying a word. He wrote down Clay's name and the phone extension of the kitchen and handed it back to her. She closed the door in his face and the hollow feeling in his stomach was almost as bad as the loss he'd experienced two years earlier when Emily died.

****

Jess frowned at the mirror when she washed her face. Her eyes were swollen, her face was blotchy, and it really bugged her that Alex had seen her like that.

What was he playing at?

She'd seen him with that woman and had nothing more to say to him. No matter if he wanted to apologise for whatever he'd done, or give her flowers and chocolates. She gritted her teeth. She was immovable and she would not give in and listen to him. Picking up the phone, she dialled the extension he'd given her.

"Clay."

"Hello, Clay, my name is Jess. Alex said I might be able to talk to you about a kitchenhand job?"

"Sure, come on down and see me. I'm in the restaurant now."

"I'm on my way."

##

"Jess, wait!" She took a step back when a firm hand grabbed her elbow. Larry Bartholomew leaned in to hug her.

"Hello, Larry. I heard you were here."

"Just signed a million-dollar deal with Alessandro Ricardo," he said smugly.

So it's true. Ricardo is here.

Jess felt the first glimmer of excitement as her spirits lifted a tiny bit.

"Your father said I might see you here." Larry kept his hand on her arm and she pulled it out of his grasp.

"My father doesn't know I'm here."

Larry leaned in close to her and tapped his nose. "Yes, he does, and what's more he told me you are after an interview with Ricardo." His alcohol-infused breath wafted in front of her. "But there's no need. Don't waste your time. I know all about it and I've already decided to give the job to one of the other freelance journalists. Seeing you're here, we could have some fun together, and who knows what might happen when the next job comes up."

He reached over and ran his fat hand down her arm. The knowledge that her father was tracking her life and career made her feel sicker than

Larry already was, and Jess's vision blurred. She leaned in close to tell him exactly what she thought, lowering her voice as there were several people close by on sun lounges.

"Take your hands off me."

Before she could finish, Larry looked away from her and his voice slurred.

"Ricardo, can I buy you another drink."

Alex held her gaze steadily as her world came crashing down around her.

Alex Richards. Alessandro Ricardo.

The penny dropped. Just one more thing he'd lied about and the biggest betrayal when he knew all along she'd been looking for Ricardo. The whole time, from the very first night they had dinner, he'd lied and pretended to be someone else.

I will never trust another man as long as I live.

Gritting her teeth, she forced herself to relax and turned to Larry with a bright smile.

"It was nice to see you, Larry. Say hello to my father for me." She turned away, ignoring Alex who was speaking quietly to her boss. She stood straight and held Alex's gaze as she walked toward the building. A movement next to her caught her attention and she looked up at a woman with a tumble of black curly hair. She looked familiar, but she didn't know who she was. Jess flicked a tight smile in her direction and turned toward her room. A hand grabbed her shoulder; she stopped and lifted her chin high.

"Take your hand off me." She kept her voice low as the woman watched them.

"Jess, we need to talk. I can explain. I had my reasons."

"No, Alex…Alessandro. There is nothing you could say to explain your lies." The woman behind Alex sat up on her sun lounge, following the exchange with great interest. "I am not a bit interested in what you have to say to me. You are a scheming liar, through and through."

He grabbed her arm again. "Jess, there's a lot of stuff I need to tell you. I am not going to let you go while you are so upset.

"Upset." Her voice rose. "You think this is upset. Buddy, you ain't seen nothing yet." She clenched her jaw and glared at him. "Now take your fingers off my arm before I *show* you how upset I can get."

She shook his hand off and strode down the path straight to the reception building. Find the first helicopter out of here and she was on it. There was no way she could look at that man—Alex, Alessandro whatever he decided to call himself—without choking him.
He'd played her for a fool and this easy Yank had fallen right into his arms more than once. Hooked and reeled in like one of his smelly fish and she'd fallen for it, wide-eyed and believing.

She threw her room card onto the counter and the clerk looked up at her.

"Sorry, ma'am. I didn't hear you come in.

"I need a seat on the first helicopter out of here." She looked at the young man as he stared at her. "Please."

"I'm sorry, ma'am, they're fully booked today, even with the extra flights. We've had a lot of guests changing over."

Sweat broke out on her forehead despite the air conditioning, and Jess mopped at her brow with shaking fingers.

The clerk clicked the keyboard and looked at the screen. "The first flight out to Darwin is tomorrow afternoon."

"Book me on it, please. Room 231."

***

Alex stood by the pool and watched Jess stride off. She held her head high and almost swaggered along the path, but he'd seen her eyes. Deep, deep hurt filled them and he was filled with remorse. She turned the corner of the building and disappeared from his sight.

How the hell was he going to explain and apologise and convince her he'd been going to come clean this afternoon?

A gentle hand tugged on his arm. "Do you want to tell me how you made that beautiful girl so sad?"

He looked up and shook his head slowly. "Mama, did you see all that?" He held out his arms and his mother hugged him back.

"Yes, I did. Your sisters have arrived and I decided to have some quiet time around the pool. Brianna and Lissy, and your three sisters, are in the day spa and Nick and Tom are over at the playground with the children."

Warmth filled Alex's chest and some of the distress eased. He dropped his chin into Tessa's hair. "Where's Dad?"

"Where do you think?"

"In your room reading some academic tome?"

"You always were clever." Tessa nodded and smiled up at him. "Now tell me about your lady friend. Can I help?"

"Walk with me. I have to get rid of that horrid man." Alex tucked his mother's hand into the crook of his elbow. "I much prefer fishing to business. Next week, I'm out of here. Come to my villa and I'll tell you the whole sad story."

***

Jess sat cross-legged on her bed, peering at her laptop screen, searching for a flight from Darwin to New York. She'd called Monica to tell her she was on the way home, and called the rental car company arranging for the car to be picked up in Daly River. She'd almost had to mortgage her apartment to pay for it. The earliest she could fly out was tomorrow night via Sydney and Los Angeles.

Thirty-four hours.

Which made it a long, long time until she could lock herself in her apartment, get right away from the world, and lick her wounds. She was tempted to write the damn article anyway and expose Alessandro Ricardo as sexy barramundi fisherman Alex Richards, but her ethics wouldn't let her do that, no matter what a lowlife liar he was.

And what was the point anyway? Larry had already given the job to someone else.

The mouse hovered over the booking and she hesitated.

What was she waiting for? Did she really expect him to come

470

knocking on the door and declare his undying love for her? When would she ever learn? All men were users. The whole damn lot of them. *Her father, her ex-fiancé, Larry Bartholomew, and most of all Alex or Alessandro.*

God, she didn't even know who he really was, or what his real name was.

She almost fell off the bed as a light tap sounded through the door. It was so soft, she wasn't even sure it was at her door. Jumping off the bed, she smoothed down her short dress with shaking hands and wound her hair up, clipping it back. She'd wait. If it was her door, they'd knock again.

Tap, tap.

Then an unfamiliar female voice called her name "'Jess? Are you there?"

Slowly, she opened the door and peered around. The woman who'd smiled at her beside the pool and watched the exchange between her and Alex stood there.

"I know you don't know me." She tipped her head to the side and smiled. "I'm Tessa. Tessa Richards. Can I come in?"

"Tessa Richards?" Jess opened the door and stepped back.

Deep brown eyes lit up in a smile. "I'm Alex's mother."

"Oh." Jess swallowed and wondered why she was here. "So, he is Alex Richards, then."

"I saw how upset you were when you left my son and I wanted to check on you."

It was a long time since anyone apart from Monica had cared about how she was. Her eyes pricked with tears and she couldn't hold back the single tear that rolled down her cheek.

"I'm fine."

Tessa held her arms out. "Oh, sweetheart, you're not."

Jess crumpled and burst into tears. "Why does it always happen to me?"

Tessa smoothed her hair as she sobbed into the shoulder of the mother of the man who had broken her heart. It was surreal—a strange woman comforting her in a way her own mother had never done.

After a couple of minutes, she pulled back. "I'm sorry," she said between hiccoughs. "How embarrassing. You don't even know me."

Tessa went over to the small kitchenette and pointed to the kettle. "May I?"

Jess nodded and sat on the side of the bed while Tessa filled the kettle.

"Tea or coffee?"

"Coffee, please." Jess sat up straight and wiped her eyes, mortified by her show of emotion.

Tessa carried the cups over to the small table by the window, with a jug of milk and sugar bowl. Jess shook her head.

"Just black for me, thanks."

Tessa sat and gestured for her to join her. "I need to tell you a story."

Jess looked at Alex's mother. Jet-black hair without a single strand of grey was held back with a bright red ribbon. Soft wrinkles around her eyes spoke of years of laughter. She stirred her coffee and set the spoon on the saucer.

"I saw the way my son looked at you and I knew straight away you were special to him." Tessa picked up her cup and blew softly on the hot liquid. "Two years ago, I worried if he would ever smile again. Now I have seen him smile, and I know he has found his happiness again."

Jess frowned remembering their conversation about something personal that had been the catalyst for Alex giving up law and moving to the Top End.

"Whatever you have given him, you have broken down the wall he erected around himself. He thought he could protect himself and prevent himself from suffering again."

"What happened?"

"He was engaged to a sweet, sweet girl. He and Emily bought a house in Brisbane where Alex was about to move from his government job and start with a top law firm. She was killed in a mindless accident by a drugged-out truck driver and the grief took control of him. I know there is more, but Alex has never shared it, but I suspect it is why he signed the contract to manage this place for two years."

Jess closed her eyes. She couldn't imagine what Alex had gone through.

"We're a very close family despite being scattered over the world. But we lost Alex for two years. The only way to stay with him was for us to come up here, and we have a family pledge that we will share his birthday each year, no matter what we are doing."

Jess blinked away the tears that were blurring her vision.

"Jess, this year, my Alex is back. He is alive and full of life for the first time since Emily was killed. I saw the way he looked at you." Tess squeezed her hands. "I beg you to give him a chance."

Jess pulled her hands back and dropped her head. "I can't say I have been through the grief Alex has, but I saw him with another woman." She lifted her gaze to meet Tessa's and her voice caught. "I can't take the risk of trusting my heart again."

"Oh, my dear. Look in the mirror. Look at the expression in your eyes when you talk of him."

Jess covered her face with her hands, shaking her head. "I don't know."

They were quiet for a moment and then the phone rang, breaking the silence. Jess crossed the room and picked it up, her hands shaking.

"Yes?" She listened, disappointment settling deep within her as the voice of the receptionist came over the phone. She listened and nodded, turning away from Tessa's curious gaze.

"Yes, please. I'll be ready. I'll have my bags ready to collect."

She turned to Alex's mother and couldn't stop the tears spilling from her eyes.

"I'm sorry, Tessa. I need time to think this through. I'm getting picked up in half an hour. There's a spare seat on the last helicopter to Darwin this afternoon."

Tessa stood. "Well, I'd better let you get packed up then." She walked to the door. "I understand you have to do what is right for you. And trust me, he has no other woman. It may have been one of his sisters or sisters-in-law you saw him with."

Jess's vision blurred as the door closed quietly behind the mother of the first man who had truly captured her heart.

Chapter Eighteen

Jess adjusted the headphones over her ears and listened to the bright and breezy voice of the helicopter pilot.

"Welcome, folks, and I hope you've enjoyed your stay at Cockatoo Springs." She leaned her head on the glass and closed her eyes, blocking out the view of the opalescent water below.

The call had come too quickly. She'd made the instant decision to take the ride out and she was regretting it. Now she knew she'd been too harsh when she judged Alex. His reason for keeping his privacy had been his decision to make and he was entitled to put up those barriers. If she was honest, she had done the very same thing, changing her name informally back to Trent. The circumstances that had thrown them together had not been entirely of his doing, and she couldn't blame him for anything that happened since.

In one fleeting moment she knew she could be persuaded. Perhaps she should have listened to what he had to say. Static sounded in her headphones and the pilot spoke.

"The territory is a big place, folks, and if you look below, you can see one of the magnificent sandstone escarpments that are a feature of this landscape. Take a good look, you won't ever see that one from the ground. The land was formed by…"

Jess switched her attention from the commentary to her problem at hand.

She wouldn't ever see any more of this rugged landscape from the ground or air. Once she was back in New York, she was going to quit her job with Larry and chase all of the freelance articles she could find. Screw Larry Bartholomew and his fixing of jobs. She'd make sure her father couldn't find out every detail of her life. She was going to have that one out with him as soon as she got back to New York.

The helicopter banked sharply to the right and she blanked out his voice. Until the helicopter began to lose height and she paid attention.

"…apologise again for the delay. We have to make a quick trip back to Cockatoo Springs. Nothing to worry about. Just a message from management that has to be dealt with." He turned and grinned at Jess and gave her a thumbs up.

No, it couldn't be.

She fought the tingle of anticipation curling in her stomach.

No, he wouldn't.

The helicopter descended to the helipad, and she kept her eyes tightly shut. She wasn't going to allow herself to be disappointed. She gripped her hands in her lap and took a deep breath. A light touch on her leg caught her attention and she slowly opened her eyes.

The pilot pointed to her seat belt as the other three passengers looked on curiously. "The boss wants to see you."

Jess looked out the window and the pilot slid the door open.

A tall man with short black hair in a pair of faded denim jeans and a white T-shirt leaned back against a dusty pickup truck. A little brindle dog sat patiently at his feet. Tears pricked her eyes. The pilot took her hand and helped her down the step to the skid. Jess walked slowly over to the truck, her hair blowing across her face in the afternoon breeze.

"Hello, Jess."

"Hello, Alex." She reached up and pushed the strands from her face. "Is that what I call you?"

"That's who I am," he said looking down. "I called the helicopter back because there was a sad dog here that missed you. He was upset because you didn't say goodbye."

Jess looked down at the dog sitting at Alex's feet. "Hey, Bowser."

When she said his name, he jumped up and put his front paws on her knees and she scratched the top of his head. The little staffy stretched his head back and looked at her with adoration in his warm brown eyes. She looked up and warmth filled her from her head to her toes.

"Mine's not the only heart you've captured, Jess," he said softly.

Lifting her hand, she brushed her fingers against his bare neck. "I like you better with long hair and your piece of string."

Alex reached up and placed his hand over hers and held it against his neck. He lowered his forehead to touch hers. "We have a lot of talking to do. I never meant to hurt you."

"I know." His lips hovered over hers while he waited for her to finish speaking. "And I was less than truthful with you."

His breath whispered over her lips and she closed her eyes. The warmth of his mouth took hers in a gentle kiss full of unspoken promise.

They both ignored the cold, wet nose that pushed between their legs. Eventually Bowser gave up and ran across to join the rest of the Richards family who stood outside the gate to Cockatoo Springs.

And there wasn't a crocodile in sight.

Epilogue

Twelve months later

Jess's computer dinged and a message came up on the screen. *Meeting in my office… now.*

She logged off and picked up her cardigan from the back of the chair. She was surprised how cold these executive offices could get. And if she knew the boss, it could be a long meeting. He didn't spend much time in his office, but when he did, the meetings went on forever. She opened her office door and smiled at the name plate on the door.

Jess Trent. Senior Executive. Publicity.

It hadn't taken quite the years she'd thought it would, but she'd made it.

An office with her name on the door.

Granted, it was a bit of a detour from where she'd been heading, but the last year had been a stepping stone to bigger things than food journalism. She tapped lightly on the door of the office and was called in. Her boss was sitting in the large leather chair looking out the window at the busy scene below.

"Come in, Jess." He swung the chair around and looked at her. "I have a problem I hope you can help me with."

She looked at him without speaking. He rose from the chair and came around to stand beside her.

"I'm getting the offices refurbished and I don't know what to put on your door."

She frowned and shook her head looking up at him. "What do you mean?"

"Well, the name plate could be Jessica Trent or Jessica Van

Lund."
Alex dropped to one knee and pulled a small silver box from his pocket. "Or I'd be much happier if it was Jessica Richards."

Jess gasped and kneeled down beside the man who had given her so much happiness since she had moved to Cockatoo Springs one year ago.

"I think Jessica Richards sounds wonderful.

"

THE END

Visit Annie's website to subscribe to her newsletter to stay up to date with release dates: annieseaton.net

Other Books by Annie Seaton

Daughters of the Darling
From Across the Sea
Over the River (2024)

Porter Sisters Series
Kakadu Sunset
Daintree
Diamond Sky
Hidden Valley
Larapinta
Kakadu Dawn

Pentecost Island Series
Pippa
Eliza
Nell
Tamsin
Evie
Cherry
Odessa
Sienna
Tess
Isla

The Augathella Girls Series
Outback Roads
Outback Sky
Outback Escape
Outback Wind

Annie Seaton

Outback Dawn
Outback Moonlight
Outback Dust
Outback Hope

An Augathella Surprise
An Augathella Baby
An Augathella Spring
An Augathella Christmas
An Augathella Wedding

Sunshine Coast Series
Waiting for Ana
The Trouble with Jack
Healing His Heart
Sunshine Coast Boxed Set

The Richards Brothers Series
The Trouble with Paradise
Marry in Haste
Outback Sunrise
Richards Brothers Boxed Set

Bondi Beach Love Series
Beach House
Beach Music
Beach Walk
Beach Dreams
The House on the Hill

Second Chance Bay Series
Her Outback Playboy
Her Outback Protector
Her Outback Haven
Her Outback Paradise

Richards Brothers 1-3

The McDougalls of Second Chance Bay Boxed Set

Love Across Time Series
Come Back to Me
Follow Me
Finding Home
The Threads that Bind
Love Across Time 1-4 Boxed Set

Bindarra Creek
Worth the Wait
Full Circle
Secrets of River Cottage
A Clever Christmas
A Place to Belong

Others
Whitsunday Dawn
Undara
Osprey Reef
East of Alice
Four Seasons Short and Sweet
Follow the Sun
Ten Days in Paradise
Deadly Secrets
Adventures in Time
Silver Valley Witch
The Emerald Necklace
A Clever Christmas
Christmas with the Boss
Her Christmas Star

About the Author

Annie lives in Australia, on the beautiful north coast of New South Wales. She sits in her writing chair and looks out over the tranquil Pacific Ocean.

She writes contemporary romance and loves telling the stories that always have a happily ever after. She lives with her very own hero of many years and they share their home with Toby, the naughtiest dog in the universe, and Barney, the rag doll kitten, who hides when the four grandchildren come to visit.

Stay up to date with her latest releases at her website: http://www.annieseaton.net

If you would like to stay up to date with Annie's releases, subscribe to her newsletter here: http://www.annieseaton.net

Awards

2023: Winner of the long contemporary RUBY award for Larapinta

Finalist for the NZ KORU Award 2018 and 2020.

Winner ...Best Established Author of the Year 2017 AUSROM

Longlisted for the Sisters in Crime Davitt Awards 2016, 2017, 2018, 2019

Finalist in Book of the Year, Long Romance, RWA Ruby Awards 2016 Kakadu Sunset

Winner ...Best Established Author of the Year 2015 AUSROM

Winner ...Author of the Year 2014 AUSROM Best Established Author, Ausrom Readers' Choice 2017 Book of the Year